Home at Last

Home *at* Last

BROADMAN
&HOLMAN
PUBLISHERS

NASHVILLE, TENNESSEE

BONNIE LEON

0-8054-2155-6

Published by Broadman & Holman Publishers,
Nashville, Tennessee

Dewey Decimal Classification: 813
Subject Heading: Fiction—Alaska

1 2 3 4 5 6 7 8 9 10   06 05 04 03 02

Dedication

In memory of my father, who knew how to live every moment.

~

Acknowledgments

Life happens, even while writing a book. I would like to thank my prayer partners who helped me make it through these pages while life happened. Thanks to Carol, Gail, Judie, Julia, Myrn, and Wendy. I love you.

Chapter 1

Luke dropped onto his bunk, glad to be alone. Leaning against the bulkhead, he ripped open a letter from home.

"Dear Luke," his mother began. "I hope you're well. Ray, the children, and I pray for you every evening, but I still worry. Is the navy feeding you enough? Next time you make it home I'll fix you a blueberry pie; hopefully that will help persuade you to take leave."

Luke's eyes rested on Ray's name. *If he weren't there, I'd be more than happy to go home.*

"I miss you terribly. We all do. Brian and Susie say hello. Susie says to tell you she's making a card for you and that she picked a bouquet of wildflowers just for you. They're a bit ragged, being they're the last of the season, but if not for the Indian summer we're having, there wouldn't be any left. She also sends you a hug and a kiss. Brian wants you to know he caught a huge trout in the creek yesterday, 'bigger than any you ever caught'—those are his exact words. He also says he wishes you were here to fish with him. He often tells us that when he grows up he's going to join the navy just like his big brother and be a damage-control man on the USS *Nevada* just like you. He's very proud of you."

Luke smiled, envisioning seven-year-old Susie picking wildflowers in the field alongside the farmhouse and twelve-year-old Brian snagging his fish, blue eyes sparkling as he proudly held up his prize. It had been nearly two years since he'd left home and more than ten months since his last leave. He missed his family. Letters and photographs just weren't enough. It was time for another visit.

I'll have to see about putting in for holiday leave, he thought, then remembered Ray Townsend, and his anticipation evaporated. The thought of that man living in *his* house was more than he could stand. *He has no right to be there. I'll never accept the marriage. Not ever.*

Hatred embraced for years had become bloated. Luke envisioned the man he believed had killed his father, then married his mother, and the rage swelled. Time had not healed the hurt. Each visit home only fed his resentment and bitterness. Seeing the curly-headed mountain man rule in his father's home gouged his heart and worked to graft his resentment even more firmly to his soul.

Ray should be the one who's dead, he thought, envisioning his father and feeling the hurt of his death. "Enough," he told himself. This line of thinking would only lead to more pain. He forced his eyes back to the letter.

"Laurel and Adam often come for supper on Sundays. Little William is no longer so little. He'll be four this Christmas, and it looks like he's going to be tall like his Grandpa Hasper and Uncle Luke. He has your father's easy-going way." Luke smiled, remembering how the last time he'd been home his nephew had reminded him of his father.

"He's a regular little boy these days," his mother's letter continued. "Always searching for bugs and special rocks, and even doing a little fishing. Adam's still writing for the *Tribune.* His stories are very popular in Chicago. I'm afraid he's getting itchy to do something for the war effort in Europe, however. I pray he doesn't do something foolish like travel overseas to write about the war. I don't know if I could stand having both of you in harm's way."

Luke didn't consider himself to be in any real danger, not unless the Japanese attacked the United States, which everyone said was unlikely. He wasn't so sure he agreed with the consensus, wondering if people might be underestimating the Japanese.

Things seemed peaceful in the Pacific, and Luke wouldn't have minded being sent to the Atlantic to do some bona fide fighting. *This is a good ship. We'd do some real damage against those Kraut U-boats,* he thought, believing that sitting in port in Oahu was a foolish waste of gun power. He returned to the letter.

"Celeste came by yesterday and told me she and Robert are 'very serious.' Ray wonders if Celeste is too independent for marriage. I guess only time will tell."

Luke's eyes wandered to the photograph of Mattie he'd taped on the bottom of the bunk above his. *We should be married and having children,* he thought, angry with himself for not having had the courage to tell Mattie how he felt about her. They'd written, but the letters had remained chatty and sociable. They never talked about anything serious, and she seemed happy to keep it that way. *She's probably seeing someone else.*

"What we had was nothing more than a childhood romance," he told the photograph. He gazed at the beautiful native Alaskan woman and couldn't keep from wishing that someday they might be more than friends. With her brother Alex gone, Luke and Mattie didn't really have anything to bind them together. Alex had always been the one to make them a threesome.

Luke's mind returned to the day his best friend had died. He would forever live with the memory of Alex being swept away by the crushing ice flow. Even now it was hard to believe the spirited young man was dead. Alex had loved life. Everything Luke knew about native ways Alex had taught him. He missed his friend. *If only I hadn't gone out on the ice that day.*

For a few moments Luke's mind remained with Alex, then his eyes focused on the pages in his hand. His mother talked about their dog Spot and what a good watchdog he'd turned out to be, and about the fall harvest, which had been below expectations. Pests had waged a war of their own against the farmers. "We hope for better next year," she said.

"Ray and I both brought down mountain sheep this fall. Now that Brian is old enough, Ray is teaching him to hunt. For a twelve-year-old, Brian does well. He's set on dropping his first moose this year. He's very determined, and I believe he'll do it."

Luke clenched his jaw. *I should be the one teaching him how to hunt, not Ray.*

"Hey, you want a Coke?" Barry Randal asked.

"Sure," Luke said, looking up at his best friend. Barry tossed him a pop, and Luke barely caught it before it fell to the floor. "Hey, watch it!"

Barry laughed and handed him a bottle opener. "You look awfully serious. That a 'Dear John' letter?"

"No. There's no one to send me one." Luke pried the lid off his drink. "This is from my mother."

"Must be bad news. You look like a storm cloud." Barry leaned against the bulkhead and took a swig of his pop.

"Nah. Just wish I was there, is all." Luke folded the letter, returned it to its envelope, and slid it into his shirt pocket.

"I thought you liked the navy."

"A fella can like what he's doing and still miss his family. My brother Brian's learning to hunt. I wanted to be the one to teach him. We used to go fishing a lot before I signed up. I never really thought about missing out on the time with him." Luke swiped black hair off his forehead and sipped his Coke. "It's hot in here," he said, sitting up and swinging his legs over the edge of the bunk.

"Yeah. Well, that's Hawaii for you," Barry said with a grin. "Balmy weather's hard to take," he teased.

Luke heaved his pillow at his friend.

Barry grabbed it easily and fired the weapon back.

Luke ducked and left the pillow where it landed.

"How about heading into town tonight and seeing what's cooking?" Barry smiled broadly, displaying big teeth beneath an overly large nose. "I hate to think about all the young women in town who will be missing me if I don't show up."

Luke looked at his buddy. His big, friendly face certainly wasn't handsome. "I'm sure they'll mourn your absence," he said sarcastically.

"Not if I'm there," Barry said confidently.

"I'd like to get off this tin can, but I've got duty tonight." Luke walked to a table standing against the wall between two sets of bunks. He checked a roster on the wall above it. "I've got duty the next four nights. Don't like the night shift; it fouls up my sleep." He glanced at Barry. "I'm not sleeping good anyway."

"What's up?"

"Nothin' really. Just a bad feeling."

"About what?"

Luke hesitated. He didn't want to be an alarmist. "I'm not so sure the Japs are as stupid as everyone thinks. They could be up to something. I got a feeling they're going to heat things up."

"Nah. Security hasn't been tightened, and the officers are out playing golf every day."

"Yeah."

"The Japs know better than to start a war with us. They're no match for our navy or military. And if they're stupid enough to try something, we'll flatten them." Barry took another gulp of his Coke. "They might be stupid, but not that stupid."

"They've been gaining ground against the Chinese. And I heard their navy is tough and prepared."

"The Chinese aren't us. Besides, they're still negotiating with Washington. Nothing's going to happen as long as they've got ambassadors on American soil."

Luke finished his drink and tossed the bottle into a trashcan. "Maybe." A siren sounded and he jumped.

"What a time for a drill," Barry said, ducking through the small door and stepping into the passageway.

"If the Japs aren't up to something, why all the drills?" Luke asked. "Someone's nervous."

Luke wolfed down the last of his mashed potatoes, then finished off a glass of milk.

Barry shook his head. "You eat like there's no tomorrow, but you never put on a pound." He patted his own stomach. "I've gained ten pounds since joining."

Luke forked apple cobbler. "It's a curse," he said with a grin, shoving the dessert into his mouth. He chewed. It wasn't as good as homemade, but it wasn't bad either. "I sure miss my mother's cooking. She puts on a real spread for Thanksgiving."

"Yeah, there'll be more food than even I can eat at my house," Barry said. "Sure would like to get home for the holidays. I put in for leave." He leaned on the table. "You going home?"

"Nah. I figure I'll stay put. I like the weather better here."

"You hate the heat. So, what's holding you here?"

Luke poked his cobbler, then looked at Barry and said simply, "Ray Townsend."

"What about him? You gonna' let him keep you from seeing your family?"

"It's just easier to stay away." Luke pushed his plate aside. "He'll sit at the head of the table, slicing up turkey or some other wild carcass he's shot—as if he owns the place."

"Well, he does kind of . . . own the place, I mean. Since he married your mother and he's taken on the work. What's hers is his, right?"

Luke glared at the table. Finally he growled, "He lives there and he works there, but me and my father are the ones who proved up that place. He stole it out from under us."

Barry glanced at Luke's half-eaten cobbler. "You gonna' eat that?"

Luke shook his head no.

Barry slid the plate in front of him and scooped up a large bite. "Seems from what you've told me, your mother loves him, and they decided to move in there 'cause it would be easier on your brother and sister. Sounds reasonable to me."

Luke's anger swelled. Barry's practicality wasn't helping. He glowered at his friend. "Just because something's reasonable doesn't make it right."

"What do you think would have been better?"

"It would have been better if that bear had killed Ray Townsend and not my father."

Barry finished the last of the cobbler.

"Doesn't anything ever get you steamed?" Luke asked. "Don't you hate anybody?"

Barry thought and chewed. "I get mad when I have reason to. And no, I don't think I hate anyone. Oh, a few folks who get my dander up, but I figure getting into a sweat over someone else's stupidity ain't worth the trouble. I like to live peaceably with the world." He picked up a metal cup in his big hand and drained his coffee. "I have an uncle who's kind of irritating. He's always snorting." Barry did an imitation of his uncle's snort, and Luke couldn't keep from laughing. "I think he has a sinus condition," Barry said with a grin.

Luke's laughter died, and he turned serious. "That's not the same. Your uncle didn't kill your father."

Barry was quiet a long moment, then leaned on the table. "Isn't it time you let go of that? It's been how many years since your father died?"

"Four. And he was murdered."

"Maybe you should think about your mother instead of yourself. Your hating her husband can't be easy on her."

Luke stared at the table.

"Maybe you ought to talk to her. Obviously she doesn't blame this guy, or she wouldn't have married him."

Luke didn't have to talk to his mother. He knew how she felt and that his resentment hurt her. He remembered the relief he'd seen in her eyes when he'd shown up at their wedding . . . and the disappointment later when he'd made it clear nothing had really changed. But even the thought of forgiving Ray Townsend made him angry. The man didn't deserve it. He was taking advantage of his mother's tolerant, forgiving nature. Luke looked at Barry. "You don't know this guy. He's sleazy, and he's a murderer. How can I just let loose of the fact that he killed my father? If not for Ray Townsend, my father would be alive right now. My dad would be taking my little brother fishing and hunting, not that phony."

Barry leaned back in his seat and folded his arms over his chest. "From what you told me, your father's the one who decided to stand up to that bear. Ray didn't make him do it."

"Yeah, but it was Ray's fault that my father was in that position to begin with. I can't forgive him." He pushed away from the table, picked up his tray, and plodded toward the kitchen where he unceremoniously dumped his utensils and tray. Without looking at Barry, he left the crowded mess hall and headed for his berthing compartment.

Grabbing his mother's letter out of his pocket, he plopped down on his bunk to reread it. He could see the farm with the forests and mountains bordering it; he could smell the pungent fragrance of rich loam; he could feel the fight of a fish at the end of his line. A longing for home settled over him.

Shortly after his mother's wedding, he'd decided to leave and never return, but he had moments when he craved the northern wilderness despite its brutality, even though it was a place that stole lives. He'd lost his brother, his father, and his closest friend. He could still see his brother Justin weak and dying, his father's closed casket, and hear Alex's calls for help as he was carried away amid ice and frigid water. Luke squeezed his eyes closed, trying to shut out the images.

When he opened them, his gaze settled on Mattie's face. Her brown eyes drew him in. She was living in Anchorage, but that wasn't far from Palmer. He needed to see her. He had to tell her how he felt. Ray Townsend could be ignored.

He rolled out of his bunk. He'd put in for leave.

Chapter 2

LUKE CARRIED A CHAIR FROM THE FRONT ROOM INTO THE KITCHEN AND SET it at the table. "Sure smells good in here. You're sure there's enough? I'm plenty hungry." He grinned.

"I've made enough, even for you," Jean said, closing the oven door. Her face flushed from heat, she straightened and looked at her son. "It's so good to have you home. I've really missed you."

"I've missed you too," Luke said, inhaling the aroma of roasting turkey. "And I've missed your cooking."

Jean gave him a once-over. "You could use some fattening up."

"I'll do my best. An early Thanksgiving should help."

Jean stirred the gravy. "I wish you could be here for Christmas."

"Yeah, me too. But the navy's not letting loose of many guys, not even for the holidays."

Brian ambled into the kitchen. "I wish you could stay for the real Thanksgiving. Celeste and Robert will be here then."

"I'm sorry I missed them," Luke said. "Why did they decide to take a trip now?"

"You know how hard farmers work all through the summer. Robert figured this would be a good time—before the weather turns real cold."

Luke headed for the front room to get another chair. "Robert's been a good friend." He stopped at the doorway. "I wonder what would've happened if he and Laurel *had* gotten married."

"Oh, they'd have been happy enough, but not really content, not *in* love," Jean said. "It wasn't meant to be." Her eyes twinkled. "I remember Laurel telling me how Celeste had a thing for that young man right off the bat. Those two are a good pair."

"Too bad they're out of town. Make sure to tell them hello for me," Luke said, disappearing into the living room and reappearing a moment later with another chair.

"I'll tell them."

Brian walked to the stove. "Hey, Mom, we get to have two Thanksgivings, right?"

"Maybe. We'll have to see how Ray feels about it."

Ray's the one with the final word now, Luke thought, hating the idea. He set the chair down.

"We could invite Jessie, plus Robert and Celeste will be back," Brian said.

"We'll see." Jean glanced at Luke.

Luke crossed to the stove and dipped his index finger into a corn casserole sitting on the warming shelf, then stuck the finger in his mouth. "How's Jessie these days? Are she and Laurel still working on that book?" He reached for another taste of casserole.

"Keep your fingers out." Jean shooed him away from the stove. "Yes, they're still working on it. But Jessie's getting on in years, and it's hard for her to work the long hours. Plus, your sister's busy being a wife and mother. So the book's taking a lot longer to finish than they figured."

Luke sneaked another taste of casserole and smacked his lips. "Good stuff. Barry would love this."

"Now, get out of that." Jean frowned at Luke. "You've mentioned Barry before. He a friend?"

"Yeah—a buddy on the ship. He's from Salem, Oregon. He sleeps on the bunk above mine, and we work together. He's a good guy."

Jean opened the oven door and poked the turkey with a silver tine. "Looks done. Could you lift it out for me?" She glanced at the window. "I wonder where Laurel and Adam are? They ought to be here."

"You know Adam. He's probably lost in his latest story," Brian said, leaning his elbow on the table and cradling his cheek in his hand. "So, Luke, what do you do on the ship?"

"I'm damage control."

"What's that?"

"I help keep the ship running."

"So, what do you do exactly?"

"I keep up the fire-fighting equipment. A hose that doesn't work ain't much good. And I fix hatches."

"What's a hatch?"

"They're doors on the ship, only they're the ones below the water-line. I have to make sure they're in good shape, you know, keep the gas-kets and hinges working. Basically I fix whatever needs fixing."

"Have you had any fires on your boat?" Brian asked.

"Nope." Luke hefted the bird to the counter, then transferred it to a platter his mother had set out. "Want this on the table?"

"Yes, please."

"So, where's Ray sitting?" he asked, resentment needling him. "Ray shouldn't be the one to slice the family turkey." Luke carried the bird to the table.

"I was thinking that maybe you would like to carve the turkey this year," Jean said. "You're the guest of honor, after all. You sit at one end and Ray at the other. Put the bird wherever you want."

Brian walked to the end farthest from the back door. "Ray usually sits here," he said.

Do I care? Luke thought angrily, but said, "All right. Then I'll sit here." He placed the turkey at the opposite end of the table. "Where is Ray, anyway?"

"Doing chores. Susie's helping him." Jean glanced at Brian. "Could you go out to the barn and tell them it's time to wash up?"

Just as Jean finished speaking, Ray opened the back door. His large frame filled the doorway. He stroked his trim beard and sniffed the air. "Mmm, something smells good."

"Luke fixes stuff on his ship and fights fires," Brian said.

"That's what I hear." Ray's uncertain eyes settled on Luke. "I figure you're good at it too."

Determined to be civil, Luke said, "I do OK."

William marched in from outside. "Hi," he said, wearing a broad smile. "Grandma, these are for you," he said, holding up a jar of pickled beets.

"Why, thank you." Jean took the jar and hugged the little boy.

Laurel and Adam hung their coats on the back porch and walked into the kitchen, each carrying a pie. "Afternoon, Mama," Laurel said, planting a kiss on her mother's cheek and setting the pie in the warmer. "This is rhubarb. Adam has the blueberry. Luke's favorite, or so I hear."

"You got that right." Luke hugged his sister, then shook Adam's hand. "Good to see you, brother-in-law."

Susie skipped in, her feet muddy.

"Stop right there, young lady," Jean said. "Take off those filthy boots."

Wearing a pout, Susie returned to the porch. Sitting on the bench, she slipped off the wayward boots and walked to the table.

"You kids get washed up," Jean said.

Brian, Susie, and William raced for the kitchen sink, jostling for first place at the faucet. Brian, being the oldest and largest, won.

Laurel stepped around the table and hugged Ray. "Good to see you. The last couple of times I was here, you were off hunting or working on your trapline."

Luke cringed inwardly. *How can she be so friendly toward him?*

"Just getting ready for winter is all." Ray's cheery gaze settled on Jean. "Looks like the best cook in Palmer's been busy."

Jean smiled. A flush colored her cheeks.

The display of affection sickened Luke, and he wished he could leave.

"Everything's ready." Jean set a bowl of mashed potatoes on the table, then returned to the stove for gravy and carrots. Laurel and Adam set out the rest of the food.

Everyone sat down. Ray clasped Jean's hand and bowed his head. The rest of the family closed their eyes. "Father, we thank you for your bounty," Ray began. "We thank you for keeping Luke safe while he serves his country. We ask, Father, that you continue to protect him, especially when he heads back to sea." He paused. "I thank you for this fine family. You have been good to us. We praise you for all your gifts. Amen."

Instead of listening to Ray's heart, Luke only heard his own indignation—his only thought was of his father, who *wasn't* sitting at the head of the table. And because of his bitterness, the celebration seemed a counterfeit. He fought the pull to leave, loving his mother too much to hurt her that way. Luke accepted a dish of sweet potatoes from Brian.

Spooning out a helping, he passed it on. Staring at the orange vegetables languishing on his plate, his only thought was of Ray's unlawful claim on his home.

"Luke?"

A hand moved across his line of vision. "You there?" Adam asked.

"Oh, yeah. Sorry."

"You're supposed to slice that turkey. And I'm starved."

"I guess my mind was somewhere else." With as much bravado as he could muster, Luke picked up the carving set, stabbed the bird and cut into it, then distributed portions of roasted meat.

For several minutes everyone ate in relative silence, except for occasional compliments to the cook and questions about food preparation. Finally, their hunger partially satiated, they slowed their eating and Adam asked, "So, Luke, what do you expect in the Pacific?"

"Expect?" Luke set his knife on the edge of his plate. "I don't know. I'm just a damage-controlman. I take orders. The big brass don't let me in on military plans."

"Well, what's the scuttlebutt?" Ray asked.

Luke took a bite of turkey. "There are lots of rumors. I can't say what's real and what's not."

"Are the Japs going to attack us?" Brian asked, shoving a forkful of potatoes in his mouth.

"Nah. I don't think so. They'd be fools to try. We're too powerful," he added, hoping he sounded convincing.

"Every night our local militia holds drills at the community hall," Laurel said. "And we practice blackouts."

Ray leaned his forearms on the table. "Not a bad idea. Siberia's only fifty miles or so from Alaska, and Japan's just over six hundred. We're within striking distance."

Luke looked hard at Ray. "They're not going to attack. In fact, we're sending ships to San Pedro. We wouldn't do that if we were expecting a Japanese strike."

Although Luke spoke with authority, he felt none. Ray was probably right. Still, he wasn't about to agree with him. "You're wrong," he said matter-of-factly and took a bite of cranberry relish. Looking at his mother, he said, "This is good."

"It's Jessie's recipe," Jean said, her voice tight.

Luke turned his attention to Laurel. "You two ever going to finish that book on Alaska?"

"As a matter of fact, we're doing the final edit and plan to send it to the university before spring."

"Good for you. Do you think I could get a copy?"

"Sure. 'Course, it's not one of those trashy spy novels you read. It's mostly natural history plus stories about Alaska and its people. You might not like it."

"I read more than just spy novels."

"OK, then. I'll send you a copy."

Susie rested her elbows on the table and looked at Luke. "I wish you weren't going back to that ship. Can't you stay home?"

"I'd love to, but I've got a job to do."

"If there wasn't a war, could you?"

"We aren't in a war. The war is in Europe. But I'm still needed."

"Oh." Susie looked puzzled.

"I've been thinking about doing some reporting for the *Chicago Tribune* on what's happening in Europe," Adam said. "Things are hot over there."

Worry lines creased Jean's brow. "I thought you'd decided to stay put."

"He has," Laurel said decisively. "Other men can write about the war." She gave Adam a defiant look. "We need you here."

Adam folded his arms over his chest and leaned back in his chair. "It would just be a short stint. I believe that as a newspaperman I ought to do my part in recording history. If everyone left it to someone else, there'd be no record of what's happening."

"Adam, please." Laurel's tone had turned to pleading. She didn't say more. Instead she looked at William and said sharply, "Keep your elbows off the table, and sit up straight." Wearing a wounded expression, the young boy did as he was told.

Susie looked from Adam to Luke. "Will you get hurt?"

Luke reached out and rested his hand on the little girl's arm. "I'll be fine, and so will Adam. You don't need to worry about us. The war will be over soon."

Jean set her napkin on the table. "Couldn't we talk about something else, please?"

"Hurry up. We're going to be late," Brian said, peering in the mirror and straightening his tie.

"You have a date or something?" Luke teased.

"Maybe."

Luke ruffled Brian's neatly combed hair. "I don't believe it."

"Hey. Cut that out!" Brian smoothed his hair, then ran a hand over his cheek. "You think I need to shave?"

Playing along with Brian's adolescent fantasy, Luke examined his brother's face. "Soon maybe. A little stubble is starting to grow."

"Where?" Brian asked, looking in the bureau mirror.

"Hey, you two, it's time to go," Jean said, peeking in the bedroom door.

"OK." Brian took another quick glance at his face.

Brian and Luke followed Jean and Ray out of the house. Susie was already sitting on the porch.

"I'm taking the truck," Luke said.

"We'll meet you there." Jean headed for Ray's car.

"Can I ride with Luke?" Brian asked.

"Me too." Susie ran for the truck.

"Fine by me," Ray said.

"Come on, you two." Luke strode to the pickup. While his brother and sister settled on the worn front seat, he turned the key and pumped the gas. The old truck groaned, then fired. Luke's mind filled with memories of earlier days when his father had been the one who'd driven this pickup and he'd sat beside him. Fighting melancholy and no longer feeling like attending a dance, he followed Ray and his mother down the driveway.

When they arrived at the community hall, light and music radiated from inside. Susie and Brian ran ahead, hurrying up the stairs and disappearing through the front double doors. Luke stood at the bottom of the steps and waited for his mother.

He hoped Mattie would be here. Although she lived in Anchorage, maybe she'd be home visiting for the weekend. *Does she ever think of me?*

he wondered, smoothing the jacket of his dress blues and closing his pea coat. He was considered quite a catch by some of the ladies on Oahu.

He scanned the parking lot, hoping he might see Mattie. His heart hurried when he spotted her walking toward the building.

She caught his eyes and waved. When she reached her old friend, Mattie took his hands in hers. "Why, Luke Hasper. What are you doing here? It's wonderful to see you!"

Luke smiled. "It's been too long," he said, enveloped in Mattie's affection.

"I didn't know you were in town. Why didn't you tell me you were coming?"

"Didn't know you were interested," Luke teased.

"Of course I am."

Ray and Jean stopped at the bottom of the steps. "How good to see you," Jean said, hugging the young native woman.

"It's good to see you."

"How are your mother and grandmother?"

"Fine. Although Grandma's slowing down. She's not quite herself these days." Mattie's brown eyes were momentarily touched by sadness.

"We better get inside and check on the children," Ray said, guiding Jean up the steps. "Nice to see you, Mattie."

"So, how've you been?" Luke asked as they moved up the stairway.

"Good. I'm living in Anchorage now—working at a photography store."

"That sounds great."

"I'm still in Alaska," she said dryly.

"And . . . that's bad?"

"Yes. I don't want to live here," she said, stepping inside. The song "Ferryboat Serenade" swirled around them. "I want to see the world." She gazed across the room of twirling, swaying couples. "Lively crowd."

Luke nodded, thinking about how good it would feel to hold Mattie in his arms. He studied her. She was more beautiful than he remembered. She'd gathered her black hair up on her head, exposing a slender neck, and left soft bangs to frame dark eyes.

"Hello there, Luke. I heard you were going to be here," Jessie said, approaching the couple. She stood directly in front of Luke and rested her hands on his arms. Her body was slightly stooped and her face lined, but her eyes were still bright. "You've grown up." She winked at Mattie. "He's a fine-looking man, don't you think?"

Mattie blushed.

Undaunted, Jessie continued, "I'd say he probably has to carry a bat to keep the women away."

Luke ran a hand through his dark hair. "Never had that kind of trouble, Mrs. Harrison."

"It's just plain Jessie to you."

"Sorry. Jessie, then."

"It's good to have you back in town. You staying long?"

"No, ma'am. I have to be back on the ship in three days."

Her voice serious, Jessie said, "I've been praying for you, and I'll continue."

"Thanks. I could sure use it."

The song ended, and "Fools Rush In" began. Luke turned to Mattie, hoping to have a dance, but she was already heading for the dance floor with someone else. Feeling discarded, Luke stood and watched. *I knew it was no use believing we had a chance,* he thought, his mood wilting further when she laughed at something her partner said.

When the music ended, he hurried to Mattie and tapped her on the shoulder, determined not to miss another opportunity. "You want to dance?" he asked as another tune began.

It was a fast song, and he struggled to keep from looking like a fool as he tried to swing dance. He'd hoped for something slower. However, it didn't take him long to find the rhythm, and he laughed as he twirled Mattie away from him, then spun her back into his arms. When the song ended, the two crossed the room to a punch bowl and quenched their thirst.

When the song "Trade Winds" began, Luke asked, "You want to try again?" Mattie nodded, and they joined the other couples on the dance floor. This time Luke held her in his arms, and they moved easily and comfortably together.

After that, Luke and Mattie danced only with each other, except for a quick turn with his sisters Laurel and Susie, and finally his mother. Jean seemed serene and content, but believing it to be a façade, Luke couldn't keep from asking, "Are you happy, Mom?"

Looking directly into her son's eyes, she answered, "Yes, I am. I have a good life."

Luke nodded. He'd hoped for a different answer. "Don't you miss Dad?"

"Yes. Of course I do—every day. I'll never stop missing him."

"How can you be married to someone else then?"

"I'm not sure just how it works, but God makes us able to love lots of people. I still love your father, but I also love Ray. He's a fine man and takes good care of me and the children."

Luke could only nod.

"I wish you would be happy for me."

"I understand. I . . ." He didn't know what to say. Just thinking about his mother being with that man infuriated him. "I just can't. I wish Dad were here."

"Luke, we can't change how things are. Life is what it is. I'm grateful for all I have."

The song ended, and Ray recaptured his wife. "Mind if I take back my bride?" He smiled, but Luke glowered as the two danced away.

"What's up? You look awfully glum," Mattie said as she joined him.

Glaring at Ray, Luke straightened his shoulders. "Him. That's what's wrong."

"They seem happy."

"They are," he said sullenly.

"You should be glad your mother has someone to share her life with."

"Yeah. I know." Forcing a smile, Luke asked, "You want to get some air?"

"Sure, but it's pretty cold. Feels like snow."

"That's all right by me. I could use a little cold after months in Hawaii."

They walked down the steps, and Luke took Mattie's arm. Their breath hung in the air. Glancing up at the sky, Luke said, "Looks like the clouds are moving out."

"I love the winter sky." Mattie tilted her head back and stared at the black ceiling speckled with brilliant stars. "That's one of the things I'm going to miss."

"Miss?"

"I thought you knew. I'm moving."

"Where you going?"

"Seattle, at least for now. I figured I could get a job in the shipyards. They're looking for workers."

"Why Seattle?"

"I don't know. It's a place to live that's not here." Mattie looped her arm through Luke's. "Let's walk." They left the sound of revelry behind and moved down the dark, quiet street. "You know, when I was a kid I had the biggest crush on you." A smile touched her lips. "I thought you were so handsome."

"You did, huh?" Luke grinned. "And what about now?"

"Well, you're still handsome. I've always been partial to dark hair and blue eyes. 'Course, you're looking very intense these days." She gently brushed her fingers across his forehead and pushed back a lock of hair.

Luke felt as if he'd been touched by fire. He caught Mattie's hand and stared into her dark eyes. "I used to have a crush on you too," he said, his voice hushed. "I still do."

Silently Mattie met his gaze.

"Would you be my girl?"

Mattie stepped back. "You know I care for you, a lot. I might even love you, but I'm just now starting to live my life—away from here, away from my past. I need to make a new start, and I can't wait for you to come home to begin."

"You don't have to stay here to wait. But I thought you loved Alaska. Why leave?"

"Living here is like carrying around a curse. Everyone knows I'm a native. I just want to be like everyone else, and if I live somewhere else, I can just be a woman with dark hair and eyes, nothing more and nothing less."

"I don't care where you live if you'll just wait for me."

Mattie was quiet for a long moment. "I can't. I have to begin fresh—with a clean slate. That means I can't have a past—no history, no attachments."

"How can you do that?" Luke was afraid. He was about to lose her. "You know I don't care whether you're native or not."

"That doesn't matter. You're part of my past. If I'm going to be someone new, I can't be who I was."

"You can be whoever you want to be." Luke hated that he was begging and clamped his mouth shut. He felt sick. He'd thought they might have a chance. "Please don't say no."

Mattie pulled away. "I . . . I can't." She turned and took a step, then looked back. "Please stay safe, Luke," she said and hurried away.

Chapter 3

LUKE FELT A SHARP NUDGE IN HIS SIDE.

"You gonna sleep all day?"

With a groan, he pried open his lids and looked at someone's foot.

"Get up, lazy bones."

Recognizing Barry's voice, Luke pulled his pillow out from under his head and covered his face. "Leave me alone. I worked all night."

"I did too. Remember?" Using the toe of his shoe, Barry prodded Luke again. "It's 1400 hours. And we've got better things to do than sleep."

Luke lifted the pillow and peered up at his friend. "Like what?"

"Like get off this can. Me and some of the guys are taking liberty. It's Saturday. The clubs'll be jumping tonight."

Luke let his eyes shut, then yawned. "Give me a few minutes."

"I'll be back in thirty." Barry headed for the door. "Be ready."

Luke nodded, but Barry had already gone. He rubbed his eyes, glanced at his watch, then looked up at Mattie's picture and remembered the reason for his heavy mood. She'd never be his. He should have told Barry to go without him. He was in no mood to whoop it up.

He traced the edge of the picture with his finger. "Why can't you wait? We could have a life together," he whispered. Frustration replaced melancholy. "What's so bad about our past? Everyone has a past. I'd be good for you."

Luke's mind roved over his own painful history. Sometimes the only thing a person could do was leave the memories behind—pretend they never happened. He smirked. "'Course, that doesn't work either." *Maybe by the time I'm discharged she'll feel different. She just needs time to have her independence and live her own life. Yeah, and maybe she'll meet someone else,* the cynic in him said.

He rolled onto his side and off the bunk, careful not to hit his head as he climbed free. He yawned again and stretched. *It'll be good to go out with some of the guys,* he decided. *I could use some fun. I can't spend my life mooning over a girl I'll never have.* He grabbed a towel from his locker and headed for the showers.

By the time Barry returned, Luke was in his dress whites and tying his shoes. Barry leaned against the door. "Looks like it's just the two of us, buddy. Scott and Jake got duty. They've put on an extra watch." He leaned out the door and looked down the corridor. "And they're not sending us down to San Pedro. No ships are going."

"None? I wonder what's up."

Barry shrugged. "Don't know. Maybe you were right. Maybe the Japs are up to something."

Luke straightened, adrenaline shooting through him. "Yeah. Maybe. But it would make more sense for them to attack the Philippines instead of Hawaii."

"I hope you're right." Barry stepped into the corridor. "We better get out of here before they cancel all liberty."

"Where do you want to go?"

Barry threw an arm over Luke's shoulders. "I met a real pretty barmaid the other night. Maybe she's working."

"Barhopping? I don't know. That gets old after a while. Right now my stomach's hollow. I need to eat."

"All right. We'll eat. And then go to the bar." Barry grinned.

"OK, but I don't want to go from bar to bar. We'll just end up finding trouble."

"That's fine by me. I know just the place. Like I said, there's a luscious lady there." He chuckled. "And if she don't work out, there are lots of other babes to go around."

"Is that all you think about?"

Barry acted as if he were considering the question, then said matter-of-factly, "Yep. You don't?"

"No, I don't. There are other things in life."

"Oh, yeah. Like what?" Before Luke could reply, Barry continued, "Mooning over that dark-haired beauty from home isn't any different from me searching out a dish."

Luke couldn't hide his surprise. He thought he'd managed to conceal his infatuation.

"You think I don't know about the picture?" Wearing a grin, Barry turned and darted back into the sleeping compartment. He rolled onto Luke's bunk and, resting his head in his hands, stared at Mattie's photograph. "She is beautiful," he said with a broad smile. "Guess I can't blame you for missing her."

"All right. All right." Luke reached in and grabbed the photograph and shoved it in his locker. "She's part of my past. I just forgot to get rid of the picture. Now, let's get out of here." He headed for the door.

After putting away a couple of steaks, Luke and Barry stepped out of the diner and into an early evening breeze. Ambling down a sidewalk, Luke breathed deeply of ocean air mingled with the sweet fragrance of tropical flowers.

"So, where do you want to go?" Barry asked.

Luke stopped and stared at the beach, watching palms sway. "Here is fine," he said. As if fixed in place simply to display God's handiwork, the sun rested on the horizon, touching the bay and bordering mountains with a golden blush.

The two men stood for a long while, watching the fiery ball slide into the sea. Finally Barry said, "That's enough sightseeing. So, where ya' wanna go?"

Luke shoved his hands into his pockets. "Do we have to go anywhere?"

"Well, that was the plan. I mean, I like a sunset as much as the next guy, but it's time to shove in the clutch and get moving."

Still staring at the bay, Luke said, "It's hard to believe the Japs might bomb here. It's just about one of the most beautiful places I've ever seen."

"Yeah." Barry folded his arms over his chest. "Don't figure the Japs care much about how pretty it is."

Luke glanced at Barry. "You think we're in for it?"

"Maybe. But from what I've been hearing, they're making their move to the southeast. I don't think we really have much to worry about." He took a step. "Now, can we go?"

Luke nodded.

"No more talk about the Japs or about war for the rest of the night. Let's have some fun."

Barry shouldered his way through a crowded club. Luke followed in his wake. Cigarette smoke lay like cloud cover, and the smell of liquor emanated from every corner. Barry stopped at the bar and scanned the room. A band tripped through "Jeepers Creepers" while couples jitterbugged. Wearing a broad smile, Barry said, "We should land a couple of dames—no trouble." He slapped Luke's back. "Maybe you'll forget that little native girl back home."

"I already have," Luke said dryly.

"Yeah, sure. Let's get us a table." Barry headed for one just as it was vacated.

Luke followed. Almost immediately after they sat down, a waitress wearing a tight skirt and blouse with the top two buttons undone approached their table. She smiled at Barry and smacked her gum. Luke thought she would be a lot prettier if she'd wipe off the red lipstick and rouge.

"What can I get you two handsome sailors?"

"A couple of beers," Barry said.

"You sure that's all you want?" she asked.

"You got something else?" Barry asked suggestively.

Luke wished he hadn't agreed to come along. Barry was a good friend and a nice fella, but tonight he was mostly annoying. Navy or not, Luke hadn't been able to liberate himself from his moral upbringing. When he thought about it, he didn't really want to.

"That's for you to find out," the barmaid bantered. "I'll be right back with your drinks." She sauntered away, rolling her hips.

"Mm . . . mmm," Barry said, watching her go and leaning on the table. "This is just what I needed." His head bobbed to the music.

Luke glanced about the room. It was crowded with servicemen looking for a good time. Most of them were collected into groups, but some had found women to share their evening. All the men and some of the women had hungry eyes.

Shaking his head, Luke wondered why he had come with Barry. This wasn't what he wanted. His gaze took in a petite, dark-haired woman, then moved past her. Then his eyes returned. She looked Hawaiian. Standing with her hands behind her back, she looked as if she were trying to disappear into the wall. She reminded Luke of Mattie.

Barry leaned toward his friend. "She's a real knockout. Go over and talk to her."

Luke straightened. "Nah. She wouldn't be interested in me."

The waitress returned with their beers. Barry paid for the drinks and waved a bill in the air. "I've got a tip. What do you have?"

With a saucy smile the barmaid snatched the bill and walked away.

Barry guzzled his beer. "I got my eye on a gal." He nodded toward the bar. "See that blonde over there?"

Luke turned and looked. A tall blonde in a filmy rayon dress sat on a barstool. Legs crossed decorously, she tossed her hair off her shoulder and dropped Barry a seductive look. "She's not exactly the kind of girl you want to take home to your mother. What do you want with someone like her?"

"You're kidding, right?"

Luke looked at Barry. "What's gotten into you? For crying out loud, you're acting like a goof."

Barry took a swig of his beer. "I figure if we're going into battle, I ought to have a little fun before I die."

"Who says we're going into battle, and even if we are, you're not dying."

Barry looked straight at Luke. "How do you know that? We could both be dead by this time tomorrow. You never know when your time's coming."

"So, you want to live like you're dying by throwing away your principles?"

"I'm not throwing them away. I'm just misplacing them for a night." He emptied the bottle. "You know, I've spent my whole life bein' a *good* boy. I went to church on Sundays, didn't drink, didn't smoke . . .

never been with a woman. I haven't lived enough to die. I figure it's time."

"So, let's say you *live*, then you die. How you gonna' feel standing before God? You'll have to face him, you know."

"I didn't know you were such a drip."

"I guess I am if that means I care about what happens in the hereafter."

"Well, you know what I'm here after," Barry laughed.

Luke didn't smile.

"Come off it," Barry said, leaning back in his chair. "Don't be so serious. I just want to have a little fun." His eyes lit up and settled on something beyond Luke. "Hey, she's heading our way."

Luke turned and watched the blonde stroll toward their table. She stopped in front of Barry, glanced at Luke, then settled her eyes on his friend. "You want to dance, or something?" she asked in a voice that reminded Luke of wind chimes.

Barry stood. "What else?" With a triumphant glance at Luke, he took the woman's arm and guided her toward the crowded dance floor.

Luke settled back in his chair and sipped his beer. He felt jumpy and ill-tempered. *There's nothing wrong with a little fun*, he told himself. *Barry's just dancing. What's wrong with me?* But the seemingly happy couples around him only deepened his sour mood. Now that Barry was hooked up he felt like a third wheel. It was time to go back to the ship. He stood intending to leave but instead bumped into someone.

"I'm sorry," he said, regaining his balance and steadying the person. He looked into a pair of eyes the color of rich, brown garnets. It was the woman he'd noticed earlier, standing against the wall. He quickly stepped back.

She smiled. "It was my fault," she said, straightening her skirt. "I wasn't paying attention to where I was going. I guess I was in too big a hurry to get out of here."

"You're leaving?" Luke asked disappointed. "Why?" *What a stupid question*, he thought. *She doesn't owe me an explanation.*

"I guess I'm just not the party type. I really don't belong here. I only came because a friend convinced me to. She promised it would be fun. But if you don't know anyone . . ."

Luke held out his hand. "Well, I'm Luke Hasper. And it's nice to meet you."

"Kekili." She smiled shyly. "I'm glad to meet you too."

"What a beautiful name. You're Hawaiian?"

"Yes. I was born on the Big Island. In fact, I just moved here a couple of weeks ago."

"Would you like to sit down?" Luke pulled out a chair, and when she didn't immediately sit, he asked, "Or maybe you'd like to dance?"

"No. I'm not much of a dancer. I'll stay, but just for a few minutes." She sat and folded her hands in front of her.

Luke settled back into his seat, forgetting that only minutes before he'd been feeling lonely and had wanted to leave. Leaning on the table, he asked, "So, you live here in Oahu?"

"Yes, but I grew up on a pineapple plantation on Hawaii."

"I can't imagine giving that up for this."

"I didn't really have a choice." Kekili's voice softened. "My father died, and we lost the plantation. I'm living with my sister now."

"I'm sorry."

"Things happen. We just have to go on."

"You know, years ago my family lost our farm in Wisconsin—the drought. Anyway, we moved to Alaska and started over. I know how hard it can be."

"There are farms in Alaska?"

"Oh, yeah. There's good farmland in the Matanuska Valley. We just have a small place. Well, actually my mother lives there with my little brother and sister. My father died and she remarried."

"I'm so sorry."

Gloom settled over Luke. "Yeah, he was killed by a bear a few years ago."

Kekili blanched. "How awful." She rested her hand on the table beside Luke's. "Do you want to farm like your father did?"

"I don't know. I left Alaska and joined the navy, hoping I'd find out what I wanted, but I still don't know."

A soft smile touched Kekili's lips.

"So, what do you do here in Oahu?"

"I work for the U.S. Naval Station—in the typing pool." She

grimaced. "I don't like it much, but it's a job. I'd rather be growing pineapples."

The waitress came to the table. "Can I get you something to drink?"

Kekili looked at her. "I am thirsty. A Coke?"

The woman looked at Luke. "You?"

"I'll have the same."

She lifted an eyebrow. "Two Cokes it is."

Kekili was easy to talk to, and the time passed quickly. She laughed at Luke's jokes, smiled at the appropriate times, and told him a lot of the islands' history. She was fun, and Luke liked being with her.

His arm draped over the blonde's shoulders, Barry lurched toward Luke. "Hey, buddy, we're leaving," he said, slurring his words together so badly Luke could barely make out what he'd said. Barry grinned. "Looks like you're all set. I'll see you back at the ship."

"Yeah. See you at the ship." Luke watched his friend stumble out of the club.

Kekili looked at her watch. "It's late. I better go. I've got church in the morning. I promised my sister I'd help with the children. They're singing."

"Do you live far from here?"

"No. Close enough to walk."

"Do you mind if I tag along?"

"I wouldn't mind the company." She picked up a light blue sweater at the coat check.

"So, do you like children, or did your sister con you into helping?"

Kekili chuckled. "Well, I wasn't conned, and I do like children. But I'm helping mostly because my sister's nervous about the whole thing. She's never done anything like this before. She's been reminding me for weeks. 'Now don't forget, Sunday the seventh,'" Kekili mimicked her sister, using a high nasal tone.

"Does she really talk like that?"

"No. Well . . . sometimes." They both laughed.

After leaving Kekili at her front porch, Luke headed for the ship. He didn't feel much like sleeping, so he walked slowly, enjoying the evening air. He liked Kekili, but she wasn't Mattie. A familiar ache settled over him. No one was Mattie.

"She doesn't want me." He picked up his pace. "Well, there are other fish in the sea. I can have a life without her," he said but figured if someone as sweet and beautiful as Kekili couldn't distract him for more than a few minutes, he'd probably never get over his childhood sweetheart.

He pushed his hands into his pockets and looked up at a round December moon resting in a black sky. Its light splashed the bay, but the waters looked dark and dangerous. Luke suddenly felt cold. He gazed beyond the harbor toward the Pacific and its shadows. Apprehension enveloped him. He started jogging, hoping to shake off his anxiety. Although breathless when he arrived at the ship, the feeling remained, and he knew it would be a long night.

Chapter 4

A JAPANESE TASK FORCE PUSHED SOUTH. IN FANLIKE FORMATION, CRUISERS and destroyers plowed through heavy seas, acting as a shield for six carriers. The large, imposing flattops pitched in angry swells, nosing through huge waves that washed across their flight decks. In spite of the severe weather there would be no deferment of their mission—bombers, torpedo planes, and Zeros would be launched despite the peril.

In the dark hours of early morning, planes were moved to flight decks, their airmen eager and tense. Some prayed, others boasted of forthcoming kills, but many were thoughtful, their minds on family and country. As the time to embark approached, bravado grew. Today would be the beginning of a new era—Japanese supremacy.

Flyers entered their cockpits, parachutes strapped to their backs and white scarves around their necks with the word *hissho*, meaning "certain victory," imprinted on them. Engines were fired, and the air pulsated with a deep rumble. Airmen adjusted goggles and maneuvered for takeoff.

A Zero moved into position, rolled down a perilously short runway, and lifted off. For a few moments it disappeared below the bow, skimming the rough seas, then lifted upward, its lights blinking in the dark sky.

One plane after another followed, and the men of the First Air Fleet circled and waited for their comrades. Burnt orange colored the morning sky as the First Air Fleet turned southward.

Pearl Harbor slept.

~

Preparing to rendezvous with a tug that would guide it into Pearl Harbor, the USS *Antares* moved through the quiet Pacific waters off Oahu. An officer lifted binoculars to his eyes and scanned the waves. All looked clear; then he spotted a peculiar object cutting through the sea, leaving a small wake. "What do you make of that?" he asked another officer. "There off the stern of the tug."

The helmsman saw what he thought looked like a conning tower and sent for the captain.

"Out there," the officer said, pointing.

Turning binoculars seaward, the captain searched, then stopped. He studied the object. "It's a sub all right. But whose?" he asked, then answered his own question. "It's got to be a Japanese sub. Sound general quarters."

The alarm went out, the guns were loaded, and the ship moved in on the enemy. The *Antares* fired. The first round missed; the second hit the sub just below the waterline. For a moment it appeared the enemy ship would heel over and sink, but instead it submerged and moved toward the *Antares*, sliding beneath the destroyer.

"Roll depth charges!" the captain shouted.

At 0653, the submarine sank, and the encounter was reported to the Fourteenth Naval District's officer on watch. The official who noted the incident sent the information to the duty officer who sent it to his supervisor who handed it on to his superior. In the end, it was decided no action should be taken until the report could be verified.

And still Pearl Harbor slept.

～

On the north tip of Oahu, 230 feet above sea level, a Mobile Radar Station stood, watchful. On the morning of December 7, 1941, two privates were on duty. Just before shutting down at the end of their shift, an unusual image appeared. A large target moved toward their shores.

Something big was happening! His hands shaking, one of the men called in the reading to the Information Center. "We've got something on the oscilloscope—about 120 miles out! It's one of the biggest sightings I've ever seen!" he shouted into a portable phone.

The officer on the other end of the line remained calm. He knew a squadron of B-17s were flying in from California. That's all it was. "Don't worry about it," he said.

The privates continued taking readings. Their last report recorded the approaching planes' location at twenty miles from the base.

And still Pearl Harbor slept.

$\sim$

After a restless night Luke finally climbed out of his bunk at 0730, exhausted and irritable. He tripped over a pair of shoes that had been left in the middle of the room and grabbed hold of a chair for balance. The chair tipped, and Luke followed it to the floor.

"Hey, keep it quiet!" one of his bunkmates grumbled. "Can't a guy get any sleep around here?"

"Sorry," Luke muttered, standing and righting the chair. After dressing in a pair of blue dungarees and a pale blue work shirt, he set his cap on his head. Quietly he opened the door, stepped into the corridor, and headed for an upper deck. *Fresh air will feel good,* he thought.

Once on deck, he leaned on the railing and stared at nearby mountains bordering the east end of the harbor. Plump clouds rested on their peaks and dappled the sky. The air was still, the world serene. Luke breathed in deeply, hoping to capture the peace and quiet his restlessness.

A small boat motored across the bay, accompanied by the echo of church bells drifting across the water. Luke wondered which church Kekili attended. *I ought to be at church,* he thought. *Focusing on God might settle my edginess.*

He scanned the skies. What was he expecting? Why the unease? There was nothing out of the ordinary; life was tranquil.

He sniffed and caught the aroma of coffee. "That'll help," he said and headed for the mess hall. There were only a handful of men ahead of him. It was still early. Pouring a cup of black brew, he sipped. It was strong, as usual, and no one had bothered to set out sugar.

Luke headed for the galley in search of sweetener. While the chief cook barked orders and checked food for doneness and quality, sailors flipped eggs and pancakes, others stirred hot cereal or watched over sizzling bacon, and some filled warming trays. A cluster of men worked at the sink, washing and drying pots, pans, and dishes. No one paid attention to the young petty officer searching for something to sweeten his coffee.

When Luke didn't find any sugar, he decided it was time he learned to enjoy his coffee black. Cup in hand, he returned to the deck. Other than those on duty, only a smattering of men were up and about.

The color guard and twenty-three-member band, wearing dress-whites, assembled. It was time to raise the colors. Eight bells signaled 0800 hours, a whistle blew, and the flags climbed. The band played the "National Anthem." Careful not to spill his coffee, Luke straightened and saluted.

A buzzing sound cut into his consciousness. Unwilling to be disrespectful, he kept his gaze on the flag. The buzzing became droning. The band played. Finally Luke looked to find the source.

Planes? Where did they come from? He squinted, trying to distinguish the markings on the approaching aircraft.

Must be ours on maneuvers, he decided, then spotted a red circle on the wing of a plane heading directly for the *Nevada*. His mind didn't comprehend immediately, then he realized the planes were coming in at an attack angle. A torpedo was released. Adrenaline shot through him. His heart thumped. "Japs! Japs!"

machine-gun fire clattered against the fantail, and the first bombs exploded. Absurdly, while bullets shredded the American flag, the band continued playing, hurrying to reach the end of the "National Anthem." A siren called men to battle stations. Sailors, like ants scurrying from a burning mound, spilled out of doorways from lower decks. Some were half dressed. Others, running for their posts, pulled on clothing.

Ducking machine-gun fire, Luke sprinted for cover. Antiaircraft blasts answered, echoing in his ears. The pings of flying bullets and shrapnel were all around. He crouched behind a gun mount to catch his breath and get his bearings. With a sense of triumph, he watched a smoking Zero plummet toward the bay like a dying hawk. *We'll beat 'em,* he thought.

"Fish in the water!" someone shouted.

Luke gazed at the tracing in the water as a torpedo rushed at the *Nevada*. He braced for an explosion. The ship shuddered and listed to port. Smoke boiled up from below. His eyes and throat burning, Luke yelled, "We need men on the hoses!"

Moving toward the nearest hose, he tripped over a fallen sailor. "You all right?" he asked, kneeling beside the seaman. There was no answer. He grabbed the man's shoulders and lifted him slightly. The stranger's head dropped back, and blood flowed from his mouth. Dark fluid soaked the front of his blue shirt.

"There's nothing you can do for him!" someone shouted from behind Luke.

Realizing the truth, Luke lowered his shipmate to the deck. Suddenly panicked, he glanced all around. Men moved like shadows in the heavy smoke. There was yelling and screaming, and sailors were falling all around him. A sharp pain seared his thigh. Luke looked down to see a dark stain soak into his pants.

"Come on! Get on the hoses!" the man shouted and yanked Luke to his feet.

Dazed, Luke stumbled after him. "The hoses. Right," he said, staring at another Zero trailing smoke as it dropped toward the bay.

"Get with it!" The sailor ducked through a door and disappeared.

A thunderous explosion and roaring ball of fire erupted from the *Arizona,* which was anchored alongside the *Nevada*. The power of the blast catapulted men on the nearby ship into the air and over the side. Screaming sailors floundered in the bay where a burning oil slick spread across the top of the water.

The *Nevada*'s list worsened. *We're going down!* Luke thought, watching as more explosions ripped the *Arizona* apart. It burned fiercely, and Luke could feel its heat and hear the crackle of flames from where he stood. How could this be happening? He felt firm hands on his shoulders.

"Come on, we've got fires to fight," Barry shouted, then glanced at Luke's leg. "You all right?"

"Yeah. It's nothing. I'm fine." Luke clapped his buddy on the back. "Let's keep this ship afloat."

"I'm with you," Barry shouted over the din of machine-gun fire, booming guns, and explosions from nearby ships. Wailing sirens echoed over the bay.

The two men headed for the bow where the ship had taken a heavy hit. Grabbing a hose and directing it at blistering flames, Luke waited for the water. When it didn't come, he shouted, "Turn it on!"

"I did!" Barry turned the nozzle again—no water. He threw the hose down and ran for another, getting the same response.

"How're we gonna' fight a fire with no water?" Luke asked.

"They can't all be busted."

The fires burned and spread, and the smoke thickened as men searched for undamaged hoses.

Ducking as bullets strafed the deck, Luke glanced at the widening oil slick. Another bomb shook the ship, and the jolt hurled Luke over the railing. Gripping the metal handrail, he dangled above the bay. Glancing at the oil-laden water below, he scrambled to climb aboard.

Barry grabbed his arm and hoisted him back on deck. The ship's engines fired, and with a groan it moved out of its berth and headed into the channel. "We're making a run for it!" Barry shouted.

Men struggling to stay afloat in the oil and water swam toward the moving ship. A line was tossed, and two men grabbed hold. Luke and Barry got on the other end and helped haul sailors aboard. Hanging out over the water, Luke reached for a man's hand. Their eyes met. Gasping for air, the stranger's eyes were fiery red, his face and body black with oil. Luke managed to grasp his hand, but his skin completely separated from his body, and the sailor dropped back into the water. Stunned and powerless, Luke watched the man disappear into the burning sea. He knew the image would be forever etched in his mind.

They moved past the *Arizona*. Heat from the blazing ship radiated so intensely it threatened the shells on the *Nevada*. Using their bodies as shields, men stepped in front of the bombs. Choking on smoke, Luke prayed they would have sufficient protection and forced his mind to turn from the horrifying possibilities. Instead, he concentrated on hope. If they could make it to open sea, they'd have a chance. *Almighty God, we need your help. Protect us. You are more powerful than any Japs. Help us now.*

They steamed past the *West Virginia*. She'd taken several hits and had settled in the bay mud. The *Oklahoma* had heeled over, leaving her underside exposed. Screams of the drowning resonated through Luke. Although the *Tennessee* and *Maryland* smoked, they seemed intact. The last ship at the end of Battleship Row was the *California;* it was engulfed in flames and sinking.

"I can't believe this is happening," Luke said. "We've no navy left."

"It's happening all right." A crewman, his hand clapped over a shoulder wound, leaned against the railing beside Luke. The injury was bleeding profusely, and even through soot, his face looked pasty white.

"You better get to sick bay," Luke said, shifting a shoulder under the man's good arm.

"I'm not going anywhere—not as long as I can stand."

Two consecutive blasts rocked the ship, knocking both men to the deck. Luke looked around for Barry. He didn't see him. *There's no time to worry about him now,* he thought, pushing to his feet. *He'll be all right.*

He turned his attention to the injured sailor. "You're no good to anyone dead. You're bleeding real bad. Come on. I'm taking you to sick bay." He shifted his shoulder under the man's good arm and moved toward the door.

It was blocked by a sailor whose lifeless body was crumpled and bent between the casings. "What's your name?" Luke asked, focusing his eyes on the sailor he'd been helping.

"Steve."

"My name's Luke." He leaned Steve against the bulkhead and dragged the dead man out of the doorway, fighting back rising bile. Again, bracing his shoulder under Steve's arm, he said, "Let's go," and steered him toward the stairway.

Steve was pale, and his skin felt cold and clammy. "You doing all right?" Luke studied the man. His blackened face dripped with sweat, but he gritted his teeth and nodded.

Peering through heavy smoke and struggling to breathe, Luke ducked through hatches and staggered down one corridor after another. He'd never thought much about where sick bay was located, but now he wished it weren't so deep in the ship, and he'd begun to wonder if it was such a good idea to take the wounded there. What happened if the ship sank?

Another blast shook the *Nevada.*

"This looks bad. Real bad," Steve said, his voice trembling. "Maybe we ought to go back up. I want to go back." He pulled free and stumbled down the corridor the way they'd come.

"Wait!" Luke called, but the sailor ignored him and staggered away. Luke followed him.

Luke stepped onto the deck, hoping for fresh air. Instead, he sucked in gaseous fumes and lost sight of Steve. Coughing and staggering toward the rail, he tried to see through billowing smoke. He heard the spray of bullets and felt the barrage of bombs. The Japanese were trying to keep them from escaping the harbor! Metal fragments hurtled through the air, and Luke felt a knifing pain in his upper arm. Blood oozed from a fresh wound.

Bullets strafed the deck, and Luke ducked back inside a doorway, dropping to his knees. The *Nevada*'s antiaircraft guns clattered as they returned fire. "Give it to 'em!" Luke yelled. "Get those dirty Japs!"

He felt the ship shift and change course. The smoke cleared for a moment, and he caught a glimpse of Hospital Point. The anchor clanked as it was let out. *We're going down,* Luke thought, looking about at the dead and wounded. The smoke closed in again and thickened. He pushed to his feet. "I've got to get on those fires."

More Zeros buzzed the *Nevada.* Explosions shook the ship.

The vessel shuddered to a stop, knocking Luke off his feet.

A soot-blackened sailor offered him a hand. "Come on! The ammo's gonna blow if we don't get water on it!"

Believing this would be his day to stand before God, Luke followed.

Chapter 5

SNOW BLASTED THE WINDSHIELD OF MATTIE'S CAR, AND HER WIPERS FOUGHT unsuccessfully to clear the glass. Forced to peer through a small clean spot on the pane, she periodically scraped away ice creeping from the inside edges of the window. The car slid as she rounded a curve, and she wrestled the steering wheel. Her course finally corrected, she relaxed slightly. She had to see Luke's mother. She would know. She must have heard something.

I can't believe this is happening. War? Just the word made her tremble. What would become of Palmer and the rest of the country? Would the Japanese bomb in the United States? And what about Luke? He was in the middle of it all. "Lord, please let him be all right," she prayed. "Please."

Nearly passing the driveway in the white gale, Mattie made a quick turn and almost sent the car into the ditch. Gaining control of the vehicle, she bumped toward the house. Adam and Laurel's truck was parked alongside the porch. *Of course the family would be here,* she thought.

She pushed the gearshift into first, turned off the engine, and stepped into the numbing cold. Huddling in her parka, she sprinted toward the steps. Laurel opened the door and waited, her hand on the knob. Her usually warm hazel eyes were mournful, and her lips were drawn into a grim line.

The knot of trepidation in Mattie's stomach tightened. Gripping the porch railing with her gloved hand, she carefully took the steps. The two women faced each other, neither speaking; then seeking comfort, they clung to one another.

Finally they stepped apart, and Laurel said, "Come on in out of the cold."

Following her friend inside, Mattie asked, "Have you heard any-thing?" Steeling herself against the answer, she paid extra attention to making sure the door was closed securely.

"We haven't heard." Laurel pursed her lips, then added, "We're still waiting."

Disappointed and thankful all at once, Mattie said, "At least it's not bad news."

Clutching a homemade doll, Susie walked into the kitchen. "Hi, Mattie," she said somberly. "Did *you* hear from Luke?"

"No, sweetie. I haven't." Mattie cupped the seven-year-old's chin. "We'll hear soon, I'm sure. But Hawaii is far away, and it'll take time."

Adam walked into the kitchen. "Hi. How you holding up?"

"All right . . . I guess."

"Can I get you some coffee?" Laurel asked. "It's pretty strong. We've been up most of the night."

"No. I don't think my stomach could take it." Mattie dragged off her gloves, stuffed them into her coat pockets, then with Adam's help slipped off the parka. He hung it from a hook on the back porch.

Mattie followed Laurel and Susie into the front room. It felt tomb-like. No one had bothered to open the curtains, and the outside cold had settled inside. Jean and Ray sat on the sofa, hands clasped. Jean didn't seem to notice Mattie at first. She stared at the radio, which crackled and buzzed quietly. The skin beneath her eyes was stained blue, and she looked as if she hadn't slept.

Young William rummaged through a toy box, oblivious to the upheaval.

Brian sat on an overstuffed chair in the corner, his eyes red-rimmed. He looked at Mattie but didn't smile. "Hi."

"Hi there," Mattie said, her voice extra gentle.

"Oh. Mattie," Jean said, as if just noticing her. "How good to see you." Her eyes pooled.

Unexpected feelings of love and concern swept over Mattie. She crossed to Jean and kneeled in front of her. "I'm so sorry," she said and wrapped her arms around the woman. Mattie had come hoping to find solace, but giving comfort proved to be of greater help.

After a few moments Jean straightened and wiped the tears from her face. "I'm sure he's fine. I know it."

"We're waiting for President Roosevelt to speak," Ray said and stood. "Could I get you some coffee? It's a cold day." He nodded toward the window as if to prove his point, then said, "Hmm. It's about time we opened the curtains, don't you think?"

Mattie nodded and smiled. "I don't feel like any coffee, but thank you."

Before settling into a taupe-and-rose-colored parlor chair, Adam pulled back the window coverings. "It's still coming down."

Laurel sat on the arm of the chair.

Adam patted her hand. "We heard the news late yesterday. How about you, Mattie?"

"I didn't find out until I went to the post office this morning. I couldn't believe . . ." She stopped, knowing this line of thinking wouldn't help. She sat on the sofa beside Jean. What could be said? She was certain everyone was as shocked as she was. The world had changed so rapidly. Life had seemed comparatively calm, even with her plans to move. Now she didn't know what she would do.

"Luke told me there wasn't going to be a war," Brian stated. "How come those Japs attacked us?"

"I guess they had their own plans," Adam said. "No one knew."

Mattie stared at a volley of ice crystals pelting the window. How could Luke have been so wrong? He'd seemed certain everything would be fine. Now he might be dead. Her mind reeled at the thought. The news reports had said hundreds, maybe even thousands had died.

The radio came to life, and a man's voice greeted listeners.

Immediately Ray crossed to the radio and turned up the volume. The receiver crackled, and the voice announced, "And now, President Roosevelt."

Silence followed, then more static. Finally a solemn voice broke through. "Yesterday, December 7, 1941—a date which will live in infamy—the United States of America was suddenly and deliberately attacked by naval and air forces of the Empire of Japan.

"The United States was at peace with that nation . . ."

Mattie's nerves bristled, and she thought of the last time she'd seen Luke. He'd been so handsome, so sure of himself. Now ... now he might be lying dead on a burning ship or at the bottom of Pearl Harbor. What if he were lying injured in a hospital? The thought wrenched her heart, and she fought tears. There must be something they could do. She had to know if he was still alive or if he was ... *No! He's fine,* she told herself. She squeezed her eyes closed, hoping to shut out the image of his battered, injured body, his cries of pain.

Luke had been her friend since he'd first arrived, five years before. She'd often tagged along with him and her brother, Alex, on their excursions. They'd fished together, set traps, and she'd even been included on a few of their mushing jaunts.

Alex and Luke had been superior to her at everything they did, except ice-skating. She remembered racing across the frozen river with the boys chasing. They'd been faster, but she'd usually outmaneuver them.

The years passed, and they were forced to grow up. Now that Alex was gone and she and Luke were adults, things were different. There'd been a time when she thought that one day she and Luke would get married. Of course, that didn't happen. After Alex's death the threesome didn't exist anymore, and Luke left the valley.

She'd missed him. He'd been a good friend. Luke was one of the few who never seemed to notice her nativeness. She'd simply been a comrade. *I shouldn't have turned him down at the dance. I should've told him I'd wait. What if he's dead? If only I had another chance.*

President Roosevelt's voice penetrated her thoughts. "Yesterday the Japanese government also launched an attack against Malaya. Last night Japanese forces attacked Hong Kong." Gasps sounded around the room. "Last night Japanese forces attacked Guam. Last night Japanese forces attacked the Philippine Islands. Last night the Japanese attacked Wake Island. This morning the Japanese attacked Midway Island."

Laurel pressed a hand to her mouth. "Dear Lord."

Jean's eyes filled and she shook her head.

"The world's gone mad," Ray said in disbelief.

"It's only the beginning," Adam said. "The Germans and Italians will follow. Just wait and see."

Her hands shaking, Laurel smoothed her collar. "The whole world will be at war. What happens then?"

Susie's chin quivered, and tears filled her eyes. "Will there be a war here?"

"Oh, no," Ray said. "Not here." He held out his arms, and Susie crossed to him and stepped into a hug.

Needing a distraction, Mattie escaped to the kitchen. She grabbed a cup from the cupboard and filled it with coffee. She didn't bother with milk or sugar. *The stronger the better,* she thought. Was it possible for a war to destroy the world? What would happen to her and the people she loved? Would they face an invasion? Cradling the hot cup between her hands, she stared out the window at the white rage thrashing the valley. As fierce as this storm was, it certainly wasn't anything compared to bombs and mortar. She sipped the hot brew, not even noticing its bitterness.

The president's voice penetrated her determination not to hear. "Hostilities exist," he said. "There is no blinking at the fact that our people, our territory, and our interests are in grave danger." The strength and tension in his voice fell over the listeners, and the room seemed to vibrate with the coming calamity. Mattie knew where he was heading. *No. Please no.*

"With confidence in our armed forces—with the unbounded determination of our people—we *will* gain the inevitable triumph—so help us God.

"I ask that the Congress declare that since the unprovoked and dastardly attack by Japan on Sunday, December 7, a state of war has existed between the United States and the Japanese Empire."

War. Mattie hurried back to the front room. Maybe she hadn't heard correctly.

"So, that's it then," Adam said. "We're at war."

"Can I fight?" Brian asked.

"Of course not," Jean said harshly.

Brian's bravado drooped and he sat down. "Why not? I'm almost big enough to shave."

"You're twelve years old, and kids don't fight wars," Laurel said. "Now that's enough."

Susie leaned against her mother. "Is Luke dead?" she asked, her voice small.

Jean placed her arm around the little girl and pulled her close. "No. Of course not. We'll hear from him soon."

"I'm enlisting." Adam stood.

"But you said . . ." Laurel's voice trembled. "You said you would stay."

"That was before. Now everything's different. I have a duty—to my country."

"What about your duty to your family?" Laurel took his hand. "Please, Adam. No."

"You're thirty-two," Jean interjected. "That might be too old."

"I don't think so. I'm strong and healthy."

"What about your son and your wife?"

Adam looked at William. Then his eyes settled on Laurel and he let out a heavy breath. "I have to do something. Maybe I could be a war correspondent. That wouldn't be as dangerous."

"Why do you have to go at all?" Laurel asked.

"We have to stand up to the tyrants of the world. There are some things worth fighting for—like freedom."

Looking defeated, Laurel stood, draped her arms around Adam's neck, and rested her cheek against his chest.

He held her gently. "I just want to do my part."

Laurel's tears relayed her concession. Adam would go.

"Someone has to record history. I'll be careful."

Jean pushed to her feet and headed for the kitchen. A kettle banged as she shoved it under running water and then set it down hard on the stove. She reappeared and stood in the doorway. Her lips pressed tightly together, she said nothing for a long moment. "I won't have my family and loved ones getting killed one at a time for some ideal. There must be another way."

"Jean, honey, it's out of our hands," Ray said. "Come and sit down. I'll get you a cup of coffee."

"I don't want coffee. I've had enough coffee."

Ray walked to her and gently pulled her to him.

Her shoulders drooped, and she pressed her forehead against his wool shirt and cried. "What if he's dead? What if he's gone?"

"He's not dead. He'll be home," Ray reassured her.

Mattie's anger boiled to the surface. "Men! What's wrong with you? Always fighting, always having to do the *honorable* thing!" She turned on Adam and glared at him. "Why? Why do you fight?"

Adam stared at her blankly.

Mattie continued, "It's always men! In Europe, Hitler's been pushing his weight around, now the Emperor of Japan has to have his piece of the world, and you," she said pointedly to Adam. "And . . . and Luke. He just had to go off to the navy! You can't wait to go and fight! Women aren't like that. Why are you?" She pointed at Jean. "Look what it's doing to your mother-in-law and to your wife. Don't you care?"

"I never said I wanted a war. No one wants war. But sometimes there's no other choice." Adam was yelling. "If no one stands up to the bullies, they'll rule. Is that what you want?"

Mattie didn't have an answer. She understood the logic of what he was saying, but she couldn't accept war as a choice. More quietly she said, "Maybe freedom isn't worth peoples' lives." Grief spread through her as she thought of all those who had already died. "Those men in Hawaii—they had families—mothers, brothers, sisters. Those sailors and soldiers aren't coming back. What happened to their freedom?" she asked, her voice shrill.

She pushed past Jean and slammed her half-full cup of coffee down on the counter, then returned to the front room. Standing in front of the window, she watched the snow hurl itself at the house. "I had a teacher once who told me that each snowflake is special, different. There are none the same. But they still melt and disappear." She whirled around and faced Adam. "They die, just like us." She bit down on her lip to hold back tears. "Peoples' lives matter. My brother's dead, and my grandmother will be soon. I don't want anyone else I love to die." Tears came and she swiped them away.

"No one's saying people should die," Ray said, stepping in. "Sometimes there's nothing to be done about it—the world can be an evil place. And we've all got to do our part to stop the wicked."

Mattie could feel the fight leave her. "I don't want to help," she said softly. "I just want to get away. I've been planning on leaving Alaska.

Now seems a good time to go. I'm not waiting around to see who comes home, who lives and who dies."

"Mattie," Laurel said softly. "It's going to be all right. Luke will be all right."

"How do you know? He's probably dead right now! Lying in that stinking bay!"

Susie whimpered and Jean pulled her close. "That's enough."

Realizing what she'd said, Mattie was horrified. "I'm sorry. I didn't mean that." She looked at the stunned faces. "I didn't mean it." She turned and headed for the back door. "I've got to go."

"Are you really leaving the valley?" Laurel asked.

Mattie didn't turn around. "Yes. I'm taking the first ship to Seattle. I'm not going to have anything to do with this war."

"You can't run away from it," Ray said quietly.

She turned and looked at him. "I'm going to try." She pulled on her coat and gloves and opened the door. "Please don't write. I . . . I don't want to hear from any of you."

Chapter 6

RAY WALKED INTO THE FRONT ROOM, A COFFEE MUG IN EACH HAND. "IT'S A little strong," he said, handing a cup to Jean.

She looked at the black brew, enjoying its heavy aroma. "That's all right. I need it strong," she said, her voice somber. Standing at the window, she absentmindedly fingered a button on her bathrobe. The white world outside felt bleak to Jean. Wind gusts sifted ice particles into the air. A sudden draft caught at a bush growing alongside the house, and with a faint screech it clawed the window.

Cradling her mug, Jean said, "You'd think we would have heard by now. We should have heard something."

Ray rested a hand on her shoulder. "We'll hear. Soon." He massaged her shoulder with his big hand. "Try not to worry."

Jean turned red-rimmed eyes on her husband. "You don't know how it feels. He's not your son."

Her words felt like a slap, but knowing her retort came from anguish, Ray said gently, "I know." Setting his cup on an end table, he steered her toward a comfortable chair. "Sit." He gently pushed her onto the cushions and slid an ottoman under her feet. Resting his hands on the arms of the chair, he leaned over and planted a kiss on her forehead. "He's not my son. But I care about him. And even more than that I care about you. I . . ." He could feel his emotions rise but suppressed them. "I hate to see you like this. Have faith. God hasn't forgotten you or your son."

"I do have faith. But I also know that God doesn't always give us what we want." Her eyes teared. "I've lived through the death of a son and my husband. I know God has *his* plans . . . that's what frightens me."

Taking a handkerchief out of her pocket, she blew her nose and dabbed at tears. "I pray for God's mercy. I don't think I can bear any more . . ." She couldn't finish and yielded to weeping.

"There's a lot in life we can't explain and maybe won't ever understand—my wife and son's death, Will's dying and Justin . . . I don't know what God's plans are. But we can trust him.

"The Bible says the Lord is the same yesterday, today, and forever. He doesn't change. He *is* trustworthy and merciful. There's a big picture out there that you and I can't see. We just have to believe God's in control." He smoothed Jean's hair. "He wants us to see beyond our fears and to rest in him."

Jean captured Ray's hand and pressed it to her cheek. She took a deep breath. "I've always been able to grab hold of him, but this time . . . I don't know—it's just harder."

"I love you. I hate to see you like this. You haven't slept in three nights."

"I'm sorry. I guess my faith is weak."

"Don't apologize. You have more faith than anyone I know."

"I wish that were true." Jean managed a small smile and patted the front of Ray's wool shirt. "I don't mean to worry you." Gazing into his compassionate eyes, she added, "And I'm sorry about the comment about Luke. I know you care and that you understand suffering all too well. I'm just scared. The thought of Luke never coming home . . ."

Ray pulled her into his arms and held her tight. "I'm sure there's a reason we haven't heard. It must be a real mess over there in Hawaii. Everyone must be trying to get messages home. It's probably chaos. I'll bet Luke's worried about you. He knows you're waiting to hear from him, and I'm sure he's doing everything he can to get word to you." He kissed the top of her head and straightened.

"I hope you're right."

Silence fell over the room. A clock hanging on the wall ticked . . . ticked . . . ticked.

Finally Ray said, "I'm glad the kids went out to play. Good for them to get some fresh air."

"It's awfully cold, don't you think?"

"It's not so bad. And they're bundled up good. You know Laurel. Soon as they get to her place she'll get some hot cocoa into them. Plus, she'll probably have them bake up a batch of cookies. Maybe they'll bring some home. I wouldn't mind."

"I ought to be doing some baking myself," Jean said, pushing out of her chair. "We're nearly out of bread."

"I'll give you a hand."

"Well, thank you, sir," Jean said, taking a stab at cheeriness. She glanced down at her bathrobe and seemed surprised to find herself still in night garb. "Oh dear. It's nearly eleven o'clock and I'm still not dressed." She headed for the stairs but stopped when she heard the sound of a vehicle in the driveway. Glancing out the window, she paled and clutched the neckline of her gown. "It's a telegram messenger," she whispered.

"With good news, I'm sure," Ray said boldly.

Jean started for the back door.

Ray followed, keeping a hand on her back.

Jean pulled open the door and rushed to the porch. She stood stiffly, waiting for a young man who methodically put the car in gear and turned off the engine, then too slowly climbed from the vehicle and walked toward her.

"Morning," he said, then dug into his pack and retrieved a message. "Telegram, ma'am." He held out an envelope.

Her hand shaking, Jean took it.

With a nod, he said, "Good day," then turned and headed back to his car.

Staring at the envelope, Jean returned to the kitchen. She stood in the middle of the room, turning the telegram over and over in her shaking hands. Finally she held it out to Ray. "I . . . I can't."

Ray took the envelope and ripped it open. He quickly scanned the page, then eyes shimmering, he looked at Jean.

"Oh no! Please, no!"

Ray grabbed her by the shoulders. "Jean! It's good news! He's all right!" He laughed and pulled her into his arms. "He's all right."

∽

His leg stiff and aching from the shrapnel he'd taken, Luke limped down Kekili's street. He hadn't heard from her and wondered if she'd made it through the bombing all right. Aside from an occasional toppled palm tree, a few cracked windows, and holes chewed in the street from Japanese bullets, the neighborhood looked untouched.

She was probably on her way to church when they hit, he thought. Looking down the street, then allowing his eyes to roam over an open field, he imagined civilians being gunned down. *Please, not her.*

He stopped in front of Kekili's house. It seemed intact. The front walk was clear. Greenery hugged the front porch. He walked to the door and knocked. No one answered. He tried turning the knob, but it was locked. *Please be here,* he thought and moved around to the side of the house. He peered through a cracked window, but it was dark inside, and he couldn't see anything but his own reflection. He walked around to the back of the house and tried the door. It was unlocked. He stepped inside.

"Hello," he called. No answer. "Hello."

Closing the door, he stepped into the kitchen. It was tidy with yellow checked curtains at the window and a matching tablecloth neatly draped over a small table. Bowls with crusted milk, along with spoons, sat in the sink. Beside them were two partially filled coffee cups. Luke's apprehension grew. "Kekili," he called. Where was she? And where were her sister and the children?

The silence of the house shouted. The floor creaked as he made his way into the front room. It was dark and cool. The soft tick of a clock whispered. Luke stood in the middle of the room, not knowing what to do. Where should he look?

He checked the coat closet. It contained a wool coat, children's jackets and sweaters, and a car coat. A pair of boots sat in a corner of the closet. The blue sweater Kekili had worn the night they'd met wasn't there. Was it usually?

As if he might offend the stillness of the house, he moved slowly and quietly to a bedroom. The bed was made, its white spread unruffled. A bathrobe hung from a hook on the inside of the bedroom door. A book lay on the bed stand. Luke picked it up and glanced at the title. "Hmm, *Of Mice and Men* by John Steinbeck." He thumbed through the pages and stopped at a bookmark, which had been placed between pages 220 and 221. He returned the book to the bed stand and took a peek into another bedroom, which was crowded with two beds and a mishmash of children's and adult belongings. Finally, with more questions than answers, he headed toward the back door. After taking a final look around the kitchen, he stepped outside and walked down the street.

Something was wrong. Kekili hadn't been to work. He'd already checked there. Remembering Kekili's gentle eyes, her steadiness, her beauty, Luke couldn't imagine her dead. "Not her, Lord," he said. "Someone like her shouldn't die."

His mood heavy, Luke forced his feet to move. Maybe she was at a friend's or in the hospital. He decided to check the local shelters and the hospital. She might be a patient, or maybe she was helping care for the injured. With little hope, he limped toward the nearest emergency clinic.

Walking into the sunshine and leaving the last of several shelters, Luke wondered what to do next. There was no place else to search. She was gone. *I barely knew her. She was just someone to make me less lonely for an evening,* he told himself. He thought his feelings callous and wondered if already the war had changed him. Had he seen too much violence, too much viciousness, too much suffering? Only one battle had taken place. What would happen after a campaign of battles?

He headed for the base hospital to see Barry, thinking he'd check again to see if a civilian named Kekili was a patient. His thoughts moved to Mattie. What was she doing now that the country was at war? She must be frightened. He needed to see her.

Guilt touched him. What would she think if she knew he'd spent the day searching for a beautiful Hawaiian girl? He felt as if he'd been unfaithful. *How can I be disloyal to someone who doesn't want me?* he chided himself, deep sorrow knifing him. Mattie was the only one for him. *Maybe with what's happened she'll change her mind and wait for me. Nothing's the way it was.*

Even now, as the truth of the world's circumstances hit him, fear and disbelief spiked through Luke. Germany and Italy had declared war on the United States, and the *world* was truly at war.

Nothing would ever be the same.

Walking into the base hospital, he inwardly recoiled at the smell of antiseptics, medications, and what he guessed to be the odor of decaying wounds and blood. He strode down the hallway, doing his best to ignore the moans emerging from bandaged bodies in the rooms he passed.

I hope Barry's better, he thought. The last time he'd seen him, his friend was barely recognizable. His face had been badly bruised and swollen, and Barry hadn't even known Luke was there. Drugs had been doing their job of blotting out pain and the world.

Luke stopped just outside his friend's door, took a steadying breath, then walked in. Barry slept in a nearly upright position in the third bed from the door. He still looked as if he'd been beaten, but the swelling had decreased. Luke glanced at the other beds as he passed. One man slept, another stared, his head swathed in bandages.

Luke didn't want to see more and kept his eyes on Barry. He stood over his friend, the screams of the dying and injured echoing in his mind. So many had died.

Breathing deeply and evenly, Barry didn't move. *He'll probably sleep for hours,* Luke decided. *I'll come back later.* He turned to go.

"So, you're gonna' walk out on me, huh?" Barry croaked.

Luke stopped and turned back. "I thought you were asleep."

Peering through a blackened eye, Barry pushed himself up slightly with his good arm and good leg. "Who can sleep?" He glanced at his injured limbs.

"You feeling better?"

"Yeah. A little. I could use some company. It's pretty boring here in zombie land." He glanced at the other patients. "I think I'm in the best shape here." Barry nodded at a chair beside his bed. "Have a seat."

Luke obeyed. "You look better."

"Yeah? Better than what? Those Japs shot me up pretty good." Barry's usual jovial expression was absent. Instead his mouth was set and his eyes hard. "I can't wait to show them Nips just how I feel."

"We'll get our chance," Luke said. "There's already talk of repairing the *Nevada.*"

"When do you think that'll be? I thought she'd been run aground and was pretty much a scrap heap."

"She's bad, but they figure she'll sail again. I don't know how long it'll take. The word is she'll be dry-docked in Bremerton for a while."

"I'm not waiting around. Once I'm out of this hospital I'm back on duty. I've got a score to settle."

"I already put in for a transfer. No word yet though." Luke gave Barry a once-over. "I'd say you've got a ways to go before you're ready to ship out."

"Doc says I'll heal up in no time." He glanced at Luke's leg. "So, how are you feeling?"

"Better than you." He rested his hand on his wounded arm. "Nothing but flesh wounds. I'm nearly good as new. Leg's a little sore, but it's healing. My injuries aren't bad enough to keep me from returning to duty. We'll show those Japs who we are," he said through gritted teeth. He glanced at the windows. "They shot up everything. A lot of guys died, and not just military personnel." He looked at his hands. "I went by Kekili's place. She's not there. I searched everywhere."

Neither man spoke for a moment, then Barry asked, "Is a list of casualties posted?"

"Yeah, but I don't know if civilians are on it. There's probably a separate list for them."

"It'll be in the paper," Barry said, his voice weary.

"Hard to believe someone as first-rate as her could be dead."

Barry nodded.

"We've got friends dead too," Luke added bitterly, the screams of bombs and dying men echoing through his mind. "One minute a person's here—alive and breathing, and the next . . ." He shook his head. "I'll never understand it."

"Maybe she'll turn up," Barry said. "Maybe she went back to her home. Didn't you say she grew up on one of the other islands?"

"Yeah. I hope you're right."

A nurse walked in and approached Barry. "Time for your medication." She smiled at Luke, her blue eyes sparkling. She seemed too cheerful. Handing Barry a small glass and two pills, she said, "These will make you feel much better."

"Just in time," Barry said, taking the pills.

The nurse checked his pulse. "I've got work to do here. You might want to leave."

Luke was tempted but said, "Nah. Go ahead." He kept his eyes averted from what she was doing and kept talking to Barry.

She unwrapped his bandages, then cleaned the wounds and reban-
daged them. "You're healing nicely," she said in a professional tone. "But
you need rest. See that your guest doesn't stay too long."

"No, ma'am," Barry said.

"We need you well. We could use the bed," she quipped before moving on to the next patient.

Barry leaned back against his pillows and tucked his good arm
under his head. His eyes closed and wearing a satisfied grin, he said
sleepily, "The food ain't so great, the therapy ain't much fun, but the
nurses aren't half bad. I wouldn't mind seeing her when I get out of
here."

Luke shook his head. "You'll never change—dames, dames, dames."
He chuckled, but his mind returned to Kekili. In his gut he knew she was
dead, and he hated the Japanese for what they did to her and to all the
others. He couldn't wait to get back at them.

This new resentment mingled with the bitterness he'd been carrying
for Ray. It consumed him. But Luke felt entitled—if anyone was allowed
to hate it was him.

"So, do you know when the ship will get under way?" Barry asked.

"No. But like I said, I'm not waiting. I've already put in for another
ship. I want to get into this war before it's over. We're going after those
Japs."

"With what? There's not much of the fleet left, and a whole airfield
of planes was blown to smithereens."

"There'll be more planes and more ships built. We'll be ready."

"Like we were Sunday?"

Luke didn't answer. He walked to a window and stared out at the
harbor. Smoke still drifted skyward, and a huge oil slick spread across
the bay. He could see the underside of the *Oklahoma*. Men still worked
to free those trapped. Using torches, they cut through the hull, searching for survivors. How many men lay dead or dying right there in the
harbor?

His bitterness billowed like a towering thunderhead. "We'll get 'em.
They'll be sorry."

Chapter 7

HOPING THE SNOW WOULD HOLD OFF, MATTIE PEERED THROUGH THE CAR window at a gray sky. The heater rattled as it labored to warm the old Pontiac. Despite its efforts, the interior of the car was barely above freezing. If the clouds let loose, the snow would freeze to the window.

Keeping a tight grip on the steering wheel, she bumped over the frozen track leading north to Palmer. A few flakes fell and stuck. "I should have gotten the heater fixed," she said, her breath fogging the air.

It hadn't seemed necessary. She rarely made the trip from Anchorage to Palmer unless she took the train. This time, however, she had possessions that needed to be packed for her trip to Seattle.

The idea of facing her mother and grandmother about the move made her stomach roll. Since booking passage, she'd dreaded this trip home. She'd actually considered writing a farewell letter with a request that her things be shipped, but she couldn't bring herself to do it. She and they deserved a better goodbye than that.

Her family had adjusted to her living in Anchorage, but they'd been unable to accept her moving to the outside. She knew that they would see this trip home as a last opportunity to make her see reason, and she steeled herself against the arguments she knew were coming. The idea of spending two days under their barrage was almost more than she could imagine.

More snow fell. "Drat!" Mattie kept moving and switched on the wipers. One frozen crystal at a time stuck to the window, and the windshield wipers only served to compress the snow into ice. Soon Mattie could barely see.

"I'll be glad to be rid of this weather," she bristled, pulling to the side of the road. Drawing her hood tightly closed, she pushed open the car door and climbed out, huddling against the cold. First she pried the wipers free, then using the edge of a dull ulu, she scraped away the buildup of snow and ice. She glanced at the ancient native tool. "Well, you're good for something," she said, dropping back into the driver's seat and returning the ulu to its place in the glove compartment.

Continuing on to Palmer, her mind wandered to the upcoming reunion. *I wish they understood. It makes absolute sense to leave.*

It was time for her to move on, and Seattle offered Mattie opportunities she'd never have in the backwoods of Alaska. Plus, there she would face less prejudice—in fact, Mattie figured most people probably wouldn't even know she had Indian blood. If only her mother and grandmother would give their blessing to her life's new direction. She wished they'd join her—make a new start themselves. The corner of her mouth turned up. "That will be the day."

"I couldn't pry them out, and I can't stay," Mattie said, noting the stark differences between her feelings and those of her family. They had an overabundance of pride about their heritage, and she couldn't wait to put it behind her.

By the time Mattie reached Palmer, the snow had stopped. Passing through the small town, she was careful to keep her eyes forward, unwilling to look at the familiar landmarks—the post office, mercantile, train depot, and other businesses. Unprepared to say good-byes, she didn't make eye contact with pedestrians. She'd already placed the town and its people in her past. It and they were best forgotten.

She stopped in front of the cabin she'd known as home. It looked neglected and disheveled. The log house huddled among thickets of snow-sheathed alder and birch. Smoke drifting from a chimney billowed over the roof, then caught the wind and traveled upward.

Mattie remembered herself as a young teen who'd been too embarrassed of her home and family to bring friends there to visit. She felt a flush of shame, especially at the realization that she hadn't really changed her view. When she was a girl, the tiny cabin had represented security and warmth, but one day she'd seen the reality of it. The house was more hovel than home—it was nothing more than a native hut.

Alex had never seemed to mind. She should have been more like him. He didn't hesitate to bring home friends. Luke visited more than the others, and in time he'd seemed like family. Even she hadn't been embarrassed at his visits. 'Course, Luke was different; he'd never judged.

She smiled, remembering his dark handsome looks, his boyish outlook on life. He would nearly jump with excitement over a fish on the line or a moose in his rifle sights. When her brother Alex taught Luke how to mush and trap, he'd always listen with fascination, ready to try a new skill, up for any adventure. He'd been special.

Anxiety swallowed the memories. Now there was a war, and Luke was in the middle of it. She didn't want to think about it. She wouldn't think about it.

Her mind refused to obey and returned to their first meeting, his immediate love of Alaska, his fearless embrace of the culture, and his daring personality. It had sometimes frightened her. She wished he were less gutsy, especially now. He'd most likely live longer.

He'll probably be heroic and die in battle somewhere, she thought sullenly. Mattie hit the steering wheel and told herself, "Stop it. He'll be fine. One day he'll get married and settle down here in the valley and raise a houseful of kids."

Even as she said the words, she wasn't convinced. There was no guarantee he'd make it through the war—no one knew who was coming home. The only certainty was that nothing was certain. What was Luke doing now? Had he been transferred to another ship? Was he in a battle somewhere in the Pacific?

With a sigh Mattie opened the car door. "Well, I know one thing—he's not fighting ice and snow." Stepping into cruel wind that pulled at her hood and stung her face, she wished she were in Hawaii with its sunshine and warm breezes.

Curtains at the front window moved, and Mattie saw a face peek out, then quickly disappear. Dread of the impending farewell intensified as she headed toward the house. Her boots broke through the fresh layer of snow, squeaking with each step.

When she reached the porch she stood for a moment; then taking a steadying breath, she put on a smile. "I'm as ready as I'm going to be," she said and opened the door and stepped inside, shutting out the wind's howl.

Expecting to be greeted by her mother or grandmother, she was surprised to find an empty room. "I'm home," she called, closing the door. "Hello." It felt overly warm. "Mama? Grandma?"

The shuffle of her grandmother's slippers came from a back room. The old woman hobbled to the doorway. She didn't offer her usual toothless smile. Instead she simply nodded and moved toward the kitchen, her shoulders more hunched than usual. Barely picking up her feet, she toddled to the kitchen stove and lifted a kettle. "Would you like some chia?"

"Yes. Tea sounds good," Mattie said, setting her small traveling bag on the family's worn sofa. "Where's Mama?"

"Chopping wood," the old woman said, wearing a resolute expression. She was unable to disguise the sorrow in her dark eyes.

Mattie heard the thump of boots on the front porch, and the door opened. Her arms loaded with wood, her mother, Affia, walked in. She smiled. "I thought I heard someone drive up." She pushed the door closed with a hip, walked to the stove, and dumped the firewood into a box. Brushing her palms clean, the small native woman pulled her daughter into her arms. "I'm glad you are here."

"I had to come," Mattie said, suddenly sad.

"Well, that is good." She smiled. "It's a cold day." She retrieved three mugs from the cupboard and set them on the counter.

Mattie lifted a heavy-coated, gray cat off the sofa. Stroking him, she sat and settled the animal on her lap.

"Have you heard from Luke?" her mother asked.

"Yes. He's fine, just waiting to be assigned to another ship. He might already be on board and sailing."

"He should come home," Mattie's grandmother said.

Affia grabbed a spoon from a drawer and set it in a sugar bowl. "He would if he could. But nowadays men and boys must fight."

Shaking her head, Mattie's grandmother poured tea into the cups. "I do not understand this fighting. In my day the Shamans would pray, and then we would talk. And then we sang and danced. There was no need for fighting."

"Things aren't like they used to be." Mattie set the cat on the floor. "Everything's different now." She gazed out the tiny front window. "I'm tired of snow. It will be good to live in a place where the winters are warmer." As soon as the words were out, she wished she could reclaim them. She hadn't intended on bringing up her move so early in the weekend.

Mother and grandmother glanced at each other. "I hear it rains a lot in Seattle," Affia said, handing her daughter a cup of tea.

"I'll get used to it." Mattie sipped.

"I do not think it will be so easy," her grandmother said, limping toward a straight-backed chair. Cradling her cup of tea, she sat.

Mattie's mother took a chair opposite the old woman. Silence anchored itself in the room.

The cat jumped back onto Mattie's lap, his motor humming. She gratefully accepted his company and caressed his long fur. Staring at her feet, she wished she could think of something to say. Finally she asked, "How are you feeling, Grandmother? It looks like your lumbago is bothering you."

"Oh yes, a little. But I'll get along," the old woman said. She compressed her lips, and her cheeks sank in.

Mattie nodded.

Again silence.

Think, Mattie. There must be something to talk about. I'm leaving in two days.

Sounding nonchalant, her mother asked, "So, when does your ship sail?"

"Monday morning."

"This time of year it might be rough. You would be wise to wait until summer."

Mattie knew what was coming. She couldn't give in—she needed to stand firm. "I can't wait," she said with more confidence than she felt. "It's time for me to move."

"What is a few months?" her grandmother asked. "You have your job . . ."

"I'll get another."

Affia frowned. "I understand, but—"

"I've made up my mind. There's no changing it."

Her mother set her cup on its saucer. She didn't look at her daughter. "Yes . . . I know that, but . . ." She turned her eyes to Mattie. "Where will you live?"

"There's a YWCA in Seattle. I can stay there until I find an apartment." To soften her earlier decree, Mattie crossed to her mother and dropped a kiss on her cheek. "I'll be fine. Please don't worry about me."

"We worry," her grandmother said matter-of-factly. "And there is good reason. The world is not a kind place. And I am afraid you will find out in a not so good way. And now the war has brought a great evil to the world."

"Grandmother, you're overreacting."

The old woman settled dark eyes on Mattie. "A world war is big trouble. It cannot be taken lightly."

"There is no war in Seattle."

"The war is everywhere," she said firmly. "You are better off here with your family, with your ancestors."

Mattie chewed the inside of her lip. She needed to be straightforward but hated the hurt she knew her ideas would inflict. "That's just it, Grandmother. I don't want to be with my ancestors. I don't want to be Alaskan." Mattie walked to the kitchen stove and refilled her cup. She had to make them understand. She looked at her mother and grandmother, then said solemnly, "If I could change my ancestry, I would."

Neither woman expressed shock. Their faces remained fixed. "You do not have to be ashamed," her grandmother said. Her eyes glistened. "Do not be ashamed."

"I am," Mattie said, her voice barely more than a whisper.

"You are wrong," Atuska said. "One day you will know."

"Maybe, but right now I can't change how I feel. I can't live here anymore. I have to leave. I hate this place."

Nothing was said for a long moment. Mattie's grandmother set her cup and saucer on a table beside her chair. "Here is not so bad. And you should not leave unless you can go . . . walking. If it is more than that— it is too far. You should not move to the outside. It is a dangerous place. Here you have the land, the fish, and the birds. There is plenty to eat. You have friends, family. What will you do in a city?"

"I'll be fine." Mattie knew her next words would cut at her mother and grandmother's hearts, but they needed to be said. "I hate who I am. I'm tired of people degrading me—us, just because we happen to be native. The injustice, the mocking is too much. And I'm not going to suffer it anymore. Why do you?"

"Mattie," her mother said gently. "Most people aren't like that. We have good friends here."

"Yes, we have friends," Mattie conceded, "but we also have enemies who aren't afraid to let us know how they feel."

"They are ignorant people, not enemies." Affia met her daughter's eyes. "You can run away, but you cannot escape who you are. Everywhere you go, you will be there."

Mattie was scared—scared that what her mother said was true and scared she would be trapped here. "No!" she burst out, then continued in a softer tone. "You're wrong. I can change my life. If I live somewhere else, it will be better. I know it will be." She gazed out the kitchen window at the close forest. Frost sealed a cottonwood, and Mattie could feel the suffocation of the tree. She'd felt like that most of her life.

She whirled around and stared at her mother and grandmother. "You can't change my mind. I'm going. And I don't want to talk about it anymore." She picked up her small suitcase. "I'll put this in your room, Mama."

The weekend was more difficult than even Mattie had expected. Under an onslaught of convincing arguments, she'd nearly changed her mind more than once. Now she was on her way, moving toward freedom. She felt almost giddy, enjoying the sense of liberation.

She turned the car into what she still considered the Hasper farm. Although Jean Hasper was married to Ray Townsend, Mattie couldn't help but think of it as the Hasper place. She held no animosity toward Ray Townsend. He'd been good to Jean and the children, and he'd actually done a respectable job of farming. Still, in Mattie's mind it was the Hasper farm.

She stopped the car, turned off the engine, and climbed out. Jean stepped onto the back porch. "Mattie. How good to see you. I was hoping you'd stop by before you left." Jean met the young woman at the bottom of the steps. Taking her hands, she said, "Come on in. Laurel's here, and I just took an apple cake out of the oven." The two women walked into the house.

"I was so glad to see it was you." Laurel hugged her friend. "I didn't recognize the car."

"I bought that a couple of months ago. It's not much, but it gets me to and from work."

Laurel stepped back and planted her hands on her hips. "I can't believe you're moving away. We'll never see you."

"You will. I'll be home from time to time." Mattie knew her visits would be few. Travel was far too expensive.

Brian walked in. "Seattle's a long ways away. I remember when we took the boat from there."

"It is far away," Mattie had to admit.

Laurel wrapped an arm around her friend's shoulders and escorted her to the front room. "Maybe I'll travel south and see you."

They sat side by side on the sofa. "That would be wonderful. To be perfectly honest, I won't be able to come home often."

Susie skipped into the room. "Hi, Mattie." She crossed to the young woman and laid an arm over her shoulders. "How are you doing?"

"Good."

Susie seemed satisfied with that answer and sat beside Mattie.

"How are your mother and grandmother taking the move?" Jean asked, handing her guest a plate with a piece of apple cake buried in whipped cream.

"Not so good. This morning was hard. Mama cried. Grandma was real quiet. You know how she can be."

"We'll miss you," Jean said.

The room fell silent, and Jean returned to the kitchen for more cake. Once everyone was served, she sat in the overstuffed chair.

"Where's Ray?" Mattie asked.

"Out checking traps. It's been a good season. He's figuring on doing well at the Winter Carnival."

"I'll miss it this year." A flicker of regret touched her.

Everyone settled down to eating. The only sound was the clinking of silver on glass plates.

Susie scraped the last crumb from her dish, then set it on the coffee table. "Why do you have to leave?"

"There's a new life waiting for me in Seattle. I've got to go and live it."

"It might not be what you expect," Laurel said softly. "Problems follow us no matter where we go."

"I understand I'm not going to be a different person, but hopefully people will see me differently."

"What's wrong with the way you are?" Susie asked indignantly. "I like you."

Mattie smiled. "Well, thank you. But not everybody does."

"How come?"

"There are lots of reasons." She didn't want to get into a discussion about race.

"I don't get it."

"Susie, that's enough," Jean said.

"Well, I don't understand," Susie persisted.

"It's mostly because I'm native." Mattie took a bite of cake.

"I'll bet not very many people really care that you're native."

"Maybe." Mattie set her half-eaten cake on the table and stood. "I better be going. I've still got a stop to make before I head back."

"Please write," Jean said. She crossed to the young woman and pulled her into her arms.

"I will. I promise." Mattie looked at her friends. "I'm sorry about what happened last time I was here. I just lost my temper. I want you to write, and I'll write back."

"We understand," Jean said. "Do you mind if I send Luke your new address? He's been asking after you."

"No, I don't mind. Luke and I will always be friends."

Laurel walked Mattie to the car. Mattie opened the door and leaned on it. "Well, I'll see you someday."

Covering Mattie's hand with hers, Laurel said, "There's nothing wrong with being native. God knew what he was doing when he made you."

"You don't understand what it's like."

"That's true, but I wish you didn't feel so bad about yourself."

Mattie threw back her shoulders. "I'll feel a lot better once I'm out of here." She ducked into the car.

"You can't run away from who you are—no matter how far you go."

Resentment filled Mattie, and she wished she hadn't stopped at the Hasper farm. Why couldn't they leave well enough alone? "Bye, Laurel," she said and closed the door.

Mattie had one last good-bye to make before leaving town. She drove to the bridge where her brother, Alex, had drowned. She stopped and walked to the riverbank, where she stood staring at the frozen waterway. Like a hot blaze, sorrow burned through her. She missed him—his confidence and the way he enjoyed life. He'd never been ashamed of who he was; he'd always been able to dismiss the contempt of others. Mattie wished she were more like him.

She straightened her shoulders. "Alex, please forgive me for leaving. I can't help it. I'll see you someday." She turned and headed for the car.

Chapter 8

Cold air seeped around the edges of Mattie's hood and scarf and chilled her neck. Staring at the dark waves of the Pacific, she pulled her parka close and leaned against the ship's railing. *I hope the weather doesn't turn bad.*

So far the trip south had been uneventful. The weather, although cold, had been quiet, and the sea relatively smooth. A sharp breeze cut across the deck and caught at Mattie's skirt, making her thankful for wool stockings. Retying her scarf, she gazed at gray puffs of clouds hanging just above the choppy sea.

A tendril of mist drifted down from the billows and swelled. It moved across the water toward the ship, enveloping the vessel in a moist vapor that wet the deck and railing, along with Mattie's clothing. Ignoring the dampness, she continued to stare, hoping for a break in the fog. For a brief moment it swirled away, and she thought she spotted a shoreline. A blast from the ship's stacks startled her.

"Oh, how I wish they wouldn't do that," a voice said from behind Mattie. "I swear I'm never ready for it, and then I'm frightened half out of my wits."

Surprised that someone was standing so near, Mattie whirled around. A young woman with shoulder-length curls spilling from beneath a fur cap stood against a bulkhead. She wore a magnificent, knee-length fur coat and loose slacks and puffed dramatically on a cigarette.

"I nearly jump out of my skin every time they blow that thing," the woman said. "What could they possibly be blasting at? Who or what is out there?" She peered into the mists.

Mattie felt her confidence waver. Clearly this woman was part of the "upper crust," and Mattie wasn't used to talking with such people. She tried to come up with a reply. "I think I saw something off the bow a moment ago. I don't know what it was." Cringing inwardly, she thought, *Of course you didn't know what it was. What a stupid thing to say.*

"Really?" The stranger gazed toward the front of the steamer. "Do you think it was another ship?"

"No. It wasn't moving. Maybe it was land."

"I thought we were a long way from shore."

"An island perhaps?" An icy blast of wind lifted Mattie's skirt, and despite her wool hose, gooseflesh raised on her legs.

"Oh dear, it's absolutely freezing," the woman said, glancing at Mattie's stockings. "I should have been sensible and worn wool instead of rayon." She settled hazel eyes on Mattie and smiled, which emphasized the high cheekbones in her heart-shaped face. Painted red lips framed white teeth. "Meryl Raison, and you are?"

"Mattie Lawson," Mattie said apprehensively, certain this must be a young socialite who was only momentarily out from under her mother's watchful eye. Mingling with the lower class would certainly not be allowed.

"Mattie. What a darling name. I love it!" Meryl flicked ashes over the railing, then took a long drag on her cigarette. "I've always thought Meryl was so plain—boring, boring, boring. I swear my name has no life to it at all."

"I like it. I think it's very . . . uh, romantic."

"You think so?"

"Yes."

"Well, thank you." Meryl pulled her coat closed under her chin. "It's so cold. I was so glad to leave Alaska behind, and I'll be even happier to get off this ship. I'm counting on the weather being warmer in Seattle."

"They say it rains a lot."

"It does, but in between the rain it's really fabulous and not dreary at all. I think the city has an unfair reputation for dreariness. Don't you?"

"I've never been there."

"Well, take it from someone who's spent many pleasant hours walking the city's streets and lakesides. It's really a lovely place." Mischief touched Meryl's eyes. "More than that, it's fun—Seattle has terrific clubs and there's always something to do. In fact, I like it so much I'm thinking of staying on a while."

Another passenger stepped through a door behind them, and warm air whooshed out.

"Oh my, that feels good. Would you like to go inside and get something hot to drink? I could certainly use some warming up."

"I'd like that," Mattie said, puzzling over why this high-born would want to spend time with her. Following Meryl inside, she expected someone to step up and put an end to the association. They walked into the dining hall, and Mattie took a seat across from her new "friend."

Meryl sucked the last of the life out of her cigarette, then crushed it out in an ashtray. Drumming red nails on the table, she said, "I'm sure that even at this hour we don't have to get our own drinks. You'd think they'd have—"

Before she could finish the sentence, a waiter appeared. "May I get you something, madame?" he asked with a quick bow. He smiled slightly, which tipped his small mustache sideways.

Mattie stifled a giggle. She felt giddy and had to admit to liking the special attention. Since boarding, she'd felt invisible. Meryl's presence made all the difference, which reminded her she really had no idea who this woman was.

"I'd like a cup of very black, very hot coffee, please," Meryl said. She looked at Mattie. "How about you? It's my treat."

"Coffee's fine."

With a small bob, the waiter hurried away.

Meryl leaned back in her chair and crossed her legs. "That bed of mine is so hard I'm feeling absolutely stiff. After this I'm ordering a bubble bath."

"You can do that?"

"Why certainly. All you have to do is ask. Where have you been? On these ships the staff is here to take care of our every need."

Really? Mattie thought. *Not my needs. Maybe I ought to try it though. A bubble bath would feel wonderful.* Even as she considered the possibility, she pictured the likely response to a native's request, and her courage wilted.

"I noticed you a few days ago," Meryl said. "There aren't many young passengers. I've been meaning to introduce myself, but I just never seemed to have time. Bridge and shuffleboard are always demanding my attention." She chuckled.

Her voice reminded Mattie of the ring of Jessie's fine china. She and Alex had been invited for lunch many times, and when Jessie left the room Alex would tap his plate with his silverware. She smiled at the memory, then said, "I've never played bridge or shuffleboard." She glanced out the window and admitted, "I've been keeping to myself."

"For heaven's sake, why? Life is short. Especially these days, we need to live every moment. Never waste precious time, I always say." Meryl leaned forward. "I'll teach you bridge and shuffleboard."

The waiter returned with their coffee. Meryl tipped him generously. "Please keep that coming, will you?"

"Certainly, madame," the man said and left.

Meryl leveled intelligent eyes on Mattie. "So, what is it you're up to?"

"Up to?"

"Why are you on this ship? It's not exactly the best time to be sailing in the Pacific."

Reminded of the Japanese threat, Mattie's gaze traveled back to the windows and the waves beyond. "I'm moving to Seattle."

"And what do you plan to do there?"

"I'm not sure. I figured I'd get a job—maybe at the shipyards. I hear they're hiring."

"Recruiting, I'd say. You can't turn on a radio or read a magazine or newspaper without seeing ads about our 'duty' to our country."

"I don't care about the war effort. I just need a job."

Meryl leaned her elbows on the table and raised penciled eyebrows. "Is this your first time away from home?"

"Yes," Mattie said, embarrassed to admit her lack of world experience to this obviously well-traveled, knowledgeable woman.

"Don't let it bother you. You'll get into the swing of things. Actually, I only left home a little over a year ago. I've been wandering about exploring the world. Eventually I'll get married and settle down, but until then I want to see absolutely everything!"

"All by yourself?"

"Oh, yes. I wouldn't have it any other way. Family would only intrude on my plans."

"Where are you from?"

"San Francisco. My younger brother, who's absolutely annoying, still lives there with my mother and father, who are very unhappy with me at the moment."

"Why?" Mattie asked.

"They're insistent that everyone live the life that's expected. They had mine mapped out—they'd even chosen just the right man for me." She dipped a silver spoon into sugar, sifted it into her coffee, and stirred. "Well, I wasn't having any of that. So I set out to make my own way. And I've had a lot of fun."

"Where have you been traveling?"

She set her spoon down demurely on the saucer. "I'm just returning from Alaska. My family has friends there, in Anchorage. Before that I was in Fiji. What a glorious place, although a bit primitive." She sipped her coffee. "I've been to Montana, where I stayed on a ranch. In Wyoming I watched a geyser shoot straight up into the air—very exhilarating." She lifted heavy curls off her shoulder and resettled them.

"What is your favorite place?" Mattie asked, certain Meryl must be the most exciting person she'd ever met.

She reached into a small handbag and fished out a silver cigarette case and matching lighter, then offered a cigarette to Mattie.

"No, thank you. I don't smoke."

With a shrug Meryl took the cigarette, tapped it several times against the case, then lit it. After inhaling deeply, she blew smoke toward the ceiling—dramatically, like Bette Davis might in one of her movies. "The most exciting . . . is probably New York City. It's a fabulous place, huge and very glamorous. I saw several plays while I was there. I loved *Panama Hattie* with Ethel Merman. Oh my, what a voice!"

"It sounds exciting."

Meryl sipped her coffee. "Maybe we can go sometime. I'll show you all the sites—especially the Empire State Building. It's the most unbelievable place! You're a hundred stories above the city, and you can see for miles."

Mattie couldn't believe she was sitting here having coffee with someone like Meryl. This kind of thing never would have happened in Alaska.

"Tell me about yourself," Meryl said.

Mattie didn't know how to answer. She'd never done anything really exciting. "There's not much to say. My life has been pretty uninteresting. I've lived in Alaska since I was bo—"

"Let me guess," Meryl cut in. "You're the child of a gold miner." Mattie shook her head no. "A hunting guide?"

Mattie smiled. "No."

"Hmm. I have it—"

"Wait," Mattie said, uncertain she liked Meryl's game. "My father was a fisherman. He didn't do anything exciting; he just fished. And he was killed in a bore tide several years ago."

"Oh, I'm so sorry," Meryl said, laying a hand over Mattie's. "I'm truly sorry."

Meryl's tenderness was touching. Any rancor Mattie felt dissipated. "It was a long time ago."

"I always thought that living in a vast wilderness must be very romantic."

"It's not," Mattie said dryly.

"Weren't you frightened? I mean, there are bears and wolves and all kinds of wild creatures; plus you have blizzards and deadly cold."

"It's not really dangerous. You just have to know the risks and think before you do some things. I'm glad to be leaving." Mattie sat up straight and smoothed the front of her skirt.

Meryl studied her. "I like you, Mattie. We should have an adventure together in Seattle."

"I don't have much money. First thing I need to do is get a job and an apartment."

Meryl leaned toward Mattie and said softly, "To tell you the truth, I barely have a penny to my name. When my parents ordered me to return home, I refused, and well . . . they cut me off." She pressed her lips together. "So now I'm just a poor little rich girl."

Mattie couldn't keep from staring. "I never would have known."

"Well, you're not supposed to. You've got to act like you have money, and people will treat you like you do."

When the waiter returned, the new friends gave each other a conspiratorial look as the man worked to please them. Again and again he returned to refill their cups and see to any needs.

"Where are you staying in Seattle?" Meryl asked.

"Until I can find a job, at the YWCA."

"Do you mind if I tag along? I've never stayed at a YWCA before."

"No, I don't mind. But I'm sure it's not what you're used to."

"Maybe not. I really don't care. As far as I'm concerned, I can be poor the rest of my life—if that's what it takes to keep my parents off my back."

Mattie studied Meryl. She liked her. A wild mane of curls framed wide hazel eyes filled with mischief. Meryl had no pretenses. She was just who she was. Of course, she hadn't been completely honest about her financial circumstances, but Mattie understood and excused the lie.

"We ought to be roomies," Meryl said. "We'll stay at the YWCA until we can find an apartment together. What do you say?"

"I say yes." The two shook hands.

"OK, then. Friends and roommates." Meryl smiled. "Seattle, here we come." She held up her cup, and the two toasted.

Fog swirled around the bow as the ship approached the Seattle docks. Lofty buildings poked up into heavy mists. Mattie leaned on the railing, hoping to get a better view. "I'm so excited—and scared," she confessed.

"For heaven's sake, why? You have nothing to be frightened of. This is a grand city. It's not too big and not too small. And the surrounding countryside is really lovely. You'll like it. We'll have lots of excursions. The people are friendly too."

"Even to someone like me?"

"What do you mean, like you?"

"You know . . ."

"You mean because you're an Indian?" Meryl asked incredulously. Mattie nodded.

"You're very pretty and quite nice. Why would anyone not like you? I'd trade my curls and hazel eyes any day for your straight, black hair and brown eyes."

"My being native doesn't bother you?"

"For heaven's sake, no."

Mattie smiled, momentarily happy with the world. Maybe it *was* true. Maybe all she'd needed to do was leave Alaska.

"You don't have to worry about that sort of thing. Down here people don't pay much attention. You'll fit in just fine." Meryl studied her nails. "Course, if I was native I'd be proud of it. I'd want everyone to know."

"No you wouldn't. You don't know what it's like. People look down on you; they think you're lazy, a thief, unclean."

"Really? Seems barbaric to me." Meryl buffed her nails on the front of her coat.

Mattie studied the dock. A smattering of people waited. The horn blasted, and dockworkers prepared to secure the ship.

"We better get our bags," Meryl said. Her step light, she headed for her room. Glancing over her shoulder, she called, "I'll meet you at the bottom of the gangplank."

"All right," Mattie said, thankful she had a friend in this new world. Now that she'd arrived, the idea of challenging a city this size was intimidating. She'd hate to do it alone. Quickly taking the stairs, she hurried down a dimly lit corridor and burst into her room. Grabbing the two small bags she'd packed earlier, she headed back to the upper deck. Crossing the catwalk, she watched the wash below, her heart hammering. This was it, a new beginning!

Twenty minutes passed before Meryl appeared. Her silk skirt swirled away from her legs as she nearly skipped across the footbridge. A man followed, pushing a cart piled with bags.

"I was beginning to worry you'd gotten lost," Mattie teased.

"Isn't it exciting?" Meryl took in the activity around them, her eyes finally settling on a longshoreman. He was tall and broad chested, with thick arms and wavy blond hair. "There are so many good-looking men here," she whispered, her eyes continuing to take in the scenery.

Mattie hadn't really noticed. Her mind was on finding the YWCA and getting around the city.

"Let's take a cab," Meryl said. "There's one there." She nodded at a taxi parked on the street.

"I thought you didn't have any money."

"Oh, I have a little. At least enough for a ride." She fairly pranced to the car and looked in the window at the cabby. "We need a ride to the YWCA. My bags are over there," she said, nodding toward the pile of luggage and climbing into the car. Scowling, the driver retrieved the bags and dropped them in the trunk.

Mattie added hers. "Can you take us to the YWCA, please?"

"Yeah. The YWCA." He closed the trunk and climbed in behind the wheel while Mattie slid onto the seat beside Meryl. "You got money?" the cabby asked, glancing in the rearview mirror.

"Of course we've got money," Meryl said.

"All right." The driver flipped on the meter and pulled into traffic.

Meryl and Mattie settled back and gazed at buildings stacked alongside the streets. Pedestrians jostled for space on the sidewalks and swarmed across intersections. As they moved away from the docks, automobile traffic became more congested. Cars, trucks, and buses crowded the road.

Mattie tried to relax, but the honking and revving engines set her on edge. She didn't like the smell either. It was a peculiar combination of the harbor, exhaust, and baked goods. Suddenly feeling misplaced, Mattie wished she were home and wondered if this was all a big mistake.

The cab stopped in front of a simple brick building. "This is it," the driver said and stepped out. He unloaded the bags and set them on the sidewalk, then held out his hand for his fare. "That'll be four bits."

Meryl dug in her purse, came up with the coins, and dropped them into his hand. "Have a good day," she said brightly, then turned to Mattie and took her arm, steering her toward the building.

Mattie glanced at the luggage still sitting where the driver had left it. "What about our suitcases?"

"Don't worry about that. Someone will get them."

Mattie doubted the YWCA had bellboys, but she didn't want to argue.

"We need to get settled, change our clothes, and go and see some of this city. There are great clubs with good music and good-looking men."

Mattie was tired and would have preferred making an early night of it, but she didn't want to disappoint Meryl, so she simply smiled and said, "OK. Sounds like fun."

Meryl was shocked that they had to retrieve their own bags, but in good humor she helped haul them up the stairs to their room. It was simple—two bunks, a plain wooden table with an ancient-looking lamp, and a closet. Meryl asked, "So, where do you want to go?"

Feeling slightly more adventurous, Mattie said, "Anywhere is fine with me."

Meryl guided her out the door and down the stairs. "It's time for some fun." She laughed. "I can't wait to show you what life is really like."

Chapter 9

A MIX OF RAIN AND SNOW GREETED LUKE AS HE STEPPED OFF A NAVY TRANSPORT and walked across the tarmac at Boeing Field. Huddling inside his pea coat, his duffel bag slung over his shoulder, he headed toward the terminal. *This is a far cry from Oahu,* he thought, glancing at a gray ceiling.

Luke didn't really care about the weather; all that mattered was Mattie. She was in Seattle, and he was here to see her. He had only three days before he had to report to the USS *Wasp. I hope she'll talk to me,* he thought, pushing through a door. Almost immediately his eyes landed on a telephone booth. Working out a plan for the day, he headed toward it. He'd call a taxi to take him to Mattie's, then get settled in a hotel. Luke had managed to get her address from her mother. Although Mrs. Lawson had warned him that Mattie didn't want to see him, he was determined to make it happen. *I can't go into this war without talking to her.*

Luke thumbed through a telephone directory, stopping at the ad for a local taxi service. After talking to a dispatcher, he walked outside to wait for his ride. The wet snow mixed with rain was still falling, so he pressed his back against the building, sheltering himself beneath a narrow wedge of roof.

He hadn't been waiting long when a cab pulled up, splashing through a puddle and spattering his dress blues. He heaved the bag into the back of the taxi, climbed in, and wiped at his wool pants.

The driver glanced over his shoulder. "Where to?"

"Broadway." He handed the cabby a slip of paper with the address. "You know where that is?"

"Sure do." The man returned the slip, and with barely a glance over his shoulder, pulled away from the terminal.

Luke sank back and took a deep breath. *Not long now,* he thought, willing away his anxiety. The city looked dreary in the fading daylight, and apprehension enveloped him as they headed toward it.

Open fields and woodland groves were interspersed with warehouses and homes—*an odd mix,* Luke thought. They neared Seattle, and department stores, eateries, theaters, clubs, and office buildings replaced open ground. Streets, like dark rivers, cut through the city, flowing up and down steep hills. Gazing at passing buildings, Luke wondered where Mattie lived.

The cab driver dove in and out of traffic, occasionally muttering at a reckless driver or pedestrian. More than once a horn blasted as the cabby cut off traffic while maneuvering.

"I'm in no hurry," Luke finally said, gripping an armrest.

"No? Well, I am. It's been a long day, and I've got a sweet wife waiting for me at home." The stout driver grinned at Luke in the rearview mirror.

Luke smiled but wished the man would keep his eyes on the road.

"So, you got friends here?" the cabby asked, his eyes turning forward just in time to see a car cut in front of them. He swerved, and without even touching his brakes, glided into the next lane.

Luke's foot pressed hard against the floor of the taxi. "Yeah. A friend."

"Any family?"

"Nope." Luke stared at the road, and each time he thought the driver ought to brake, punched the floor with his foot.

"You got a girl? You look like you're home on leave."

Wishing the man would pay more attention to his driving and less time meddling, Luke answered curtly, "I'm here to see a friend."

"Where you from?" the driver asked, seemingly unaware of Luke's irritation.

"Alaska, originally. But I was at Pearl Harbor when it was bombed."

The driver swung his head around. "Man! You're lucky to be alive! I'm proud to meet you." He reached over the seat and offered Luke his hand.

Still keeping his eyes on the road, Luke shook the man's hand and thought he'd be lucky to live through this ride. "Hey! Watch out!" he hollered, then tumbled sideways as the driver veered to keep from rear-ending a line of congested traffic.

"Sorry," he apologized. "But it's not every day I meet a real war hero."

"I'm not a hero," Luke said, resettling himself on the seat. "Just a sailor."

"Well, I'm rooting for you guys, and so is the rest of the country. God bless you."

"Thank you," Luke said, feeling remorse at his earlier displeasure and display of annoyance.

When they finally pulled to the curb, Luke climbed out, relieved to be free of the car. He dug into his pocket for the fare. "How much?"

"For you? Nothin'. Just take care of yourself." The driver saluted and drove away.

Gripping his bag, Luke turned and stared at a five-story brick building. Rows of small windows looked down on the street. He retrieved Mattie's address and glanced at it. "Number 403," he said, tucking the paper back into his pocket and heading for the front steps. He opened a single door and stepped into a small entry with a narrow hallway stretching out straight in front of him. A staircase leading up was on his left, and rows of metal mailboxes crowded the wall to his right. He started up the steps.

By the time he reached the fourth floor, he was slightly out of breath. *Tenants here must be in good shape,* he mused and walked down the hall a short distance, stopping in front of room 403. He stared at the door. What if she wouldn't see him? He almost wished he hadn't come. At least that way he wouldn't have to face rejection.

Taking a steadying breath, he rapped on the door. His spine straight and shoulders back, he waited. No one answered. He knocked again. Still, no answer.

"Now what?" he asked, glancing up and down the corridor. "I wait," he answered himself, returning to the staircase. He set down his duffel bag and sat on the top step.

Luke waited a long while. Residents moved past. Some acted as if he didn't exist; others eyed him suspiciously. An old woman gasping for air shuffled by. She smiled at him as she stepped onto the landing and rounded the staircase, then plodded up the last flight of stairs. A little while later, she tottered down, this time gazing at him. Three steps later she stopped, turned, and stared at him. White wisps of hair splayed out from her head like a halo, and watery blue eyes met his. She pursed her lips and pressed a hand to her chest. "My, oh my. All these steps are almost too much for an old woman like me."

"Can't you move to a different apartment?" Luke asked as he stood up.

"Heavens sakes, no. They're just never available." She smiled and her eyes crinkled. "I like to think that I'm a few steps closer to heaven." She chuckled. "I probably am—I'm sure I'll keel over one of these days just from the exertion."

"Of course you won't," Luke said, uncertain of an appropriate response.

She peered at Luke. "You waiting for someone?"

"A friend."

A hint of suspicion touched her eyes. "And who might that be?"

"Mattie Lawson. You know her?"

"Oh, yes. She's such a dear thing." She frowned slightly. "I'm not so sure about her roommate, Meryl. I'm afraid that girl has a lot to learn about life."

"Meryl?"

"Meryl Raison. Don't get me wrong. She's a fine person, just a bit spoiled and full of vinegar."

Luke nodded. "You don't happen to know where Mattie is, do you?"

"Not for sure, but it's Friday, so my best bet would be that those two are out at the club. They love to dance, you know. Now, in my day young women stayed closer to home." She sighed.

Disappointment hit Luke. He didn't have much time, and if he couldn't talk to Mattie tonight . . . "I guess I could come back tomorrow. You think she'll be here?"

"Probably. If you want to see her right away, she's probably at the Trianon. That's their favorite place—they have good music, and lots of young folks are always there."

"What's the Trianon?"

"It's a dance club." She patted down an untamed tuft of hair. "From what I hear, those two really kick up their heels." She smiled softly and seemed to be somewhere else. "I was once quite a dancer myself . . . in my heyday. I know I don't look like much now, but the boys used to come calling. I only had eyes for James though." Sadness touched her eyes. "Dear James, if he hadn't died back in '32 we would have been married sixty-two years this summer."

Luke knew he ought to feel bad for the old woman, but he couldn't squelch excitement at the thought of seeing Mattie. It took all his control not to bolt down the stairs in search of her. He managed to smile and nod. "Sixty-two years. That's a long time."

"It certainly is. He died of cancer. I've been alone since. But I have my family right here—all these young folks. They need someone to watch out for them." Her eyes sparkled, and she focused her attention on Luke. "Sorry, but I don't even know your name, young man."

"Luke Hasper, ma'am."

"I'm Roseline Talbot. It's nice to meet you."

"Nice to meet you, ma'am. Could you tell me how to find the Trianon?"

"Let me think."

Luke wished he could hurry up her thought processes.

"Seems to me it's down on Third and Wall. You'll have to catch a bus. It's a ways out."

Luke started down the steps. "Thank you, ma'am. Maybe I'll see you again some time."

"If you're here abouts, I'm sure we'll run into each other."

"Well, thanks again," he said, hefting his bag and starting down. He stopped. "Oh. Could you tell me where the bus stop is?"

"Just at the corner as you leave the building. Turn to your right. One will come along soon."

Luke nodded and quickly moved down the stairs. By the time he reached the last floor, he was taking the steps two at a time despite his duffel bag. When he pushed through the outside door, he had to force himself to keep a moderate pace.

More snow than rain was falling now, and darkness had captured the city. Streetlights shimmered in the moist air. Luke strode to the street corner and waited, hoping a bus would show up soon. As if answering his wish, a bus appeared almost immediately and rumbled down the street, stopping in front of him. The doors whooshed open and Luke stepped inside. "I'm going to Third and Wall."

"This'll take you there," the driver said. "And there's no charge for military." He smiled.

"Thank you," Luke said, taking the final step and walking down the aisle. He dropped into a seat midway back and scooted to the window, dragging his bag out of the aisle. He gazed at storefronts and pedestrians. Some people ambled, seemingly unaffected by the weather; others hurried, hiding beneath umbrellas, newspapers, or shopping bags. Store windows displayed shoes, hats, dresses, and a myriad of other items. Lights inside the stores glowed against the night's shadows.

Careful to keep an eye out for the Trianon, Luke leaned back and folded his arms over his chest. In spite of his country upbringing, he liked the city. Something always seemed to be happening. Seattle on this snowy night, with its lights glowing and residents bustling, felt friendly.

Luke had already decided not to return to Palmer after he was discharged; maybe this would be a good place to settle. People seemed friendly. 'Course, he'd have to go home sooner or later. If it weren't for Ray Townsend, the idea would be inviting; but just the thought of that man living in his home needled Luke. It would be a while before he was ready to visit. Then thinking of his mother, Luke knew he couldn't put off the trip too long.

After making several stops, the bus finally pulled to the curb in front of a building with a brightly-lit sign that read Trianon. "This is it," he said and exited the bus.

Stepping onto the sidewalk and into wet snow, he watched the bus drive away, its exhaust fogging the air with its foul smell. He turned and faced the club. A couple, their arms linked, walked out accompanied by the pulse of drums and saxophones. Luke gathered his courage—what would he say to Mattie? What if she wasn't here? What if he didn't get to see her before shipping out? He felt the misery of uncertainty.

His mind didn't quiet but carried him to an even worse possibility. What if she *was* here but wouldn't speak to him? The misery swelled. "Don't go borrowing trouble," he told himself and walked toward the entrance.

Removing his navy cap and stuffing it into his back pocket, he stepped into a dimly lit room. A band blasted "The Hut Sut Song" and couples crowded the dance floor. Luke walked to a railing along the upper level that overlooked the bopping pairs. Leaning on it, he watched laughing couples boogie, jig-walk, and twist to the catchy rhythm. He searched for Mattie. After a few moments he caught sight of a woman with long, black hair bopping across the room. Luke's pulse picked up. He strained to get a better view but couldn't see her face. She had Mattie's build and height. *It must be her,* he thought. The woman's partner twirled her away from him. She turned—it wasn't Mattie. Luke pushed down disappointment.

He continued to scan the room. Bouncing, finger-snapping soldiers and sailors crowded the edge of the dance floor, waiting a turn with one of the ladies. People stood along the wall or sat in sofas and chairs placed around the room. Smoke, like a filmy cloud, drifted on a breeze created by skirts and flailing arms and legs.

Luke couldn't find Mattie.

All of a sudden he saw her. Light touched her face. He stared at the beautiful woman. A tall man with blond hair moved across the floor with Mattie in his arms. He expertly twirled her away from him, then back into his embrace. She looked up at his handsome face, clearly enamored. Luke's mood drooped, and he considered leaving.

She'd found someone else.

No. You didn't come here just to turn around and walk away. He rested his duffel bag against the balustrade, shrugged out of his pea coat, and hung it over the railing, then retucked and smoothed his shirt. Walking stiffly, he made his way down the steps and onto the dance floor, staying close to the wall. When he was near Mattie, Luke stopped.

He waited, hoping she'd see him. She didn't. Her dark eyes alight, her black hair shimmering under the lights, she moved with rhythmic grace. An aching pride and adoration filled Luke. She wasn't *just* another beautiful woman; she was Mattie, his comrade and—his love. What had happened to them?

When the song ended Mattie clapped, then resting her hands on her partner's chest, she leaned in close to him. He placed a possessive arm around her. Luke felt like an intruder and decided retreat was his best option. It was then that Mattie spotted him.

Their eyes met and held. Mattie's widened. As if sleepwalking, she moved toward Luke, stopping directly in front of him. She said nothing, but her eyes were sad and penetrating.

"Hello, Mattie," Luke managed. "I was in town . . ."

"I can't believe it's you," Mattie cut in, her voice a whisper. "What are you doing here?" Her eyes teared. "I heard you'd been hurt."

"I'm fine. Got a little shrapnel in my leg and arm, but I healed up."

"What are you doing here?"

"I'm on leave, but I'm shipping out in a few days. I'm assigned to the USS *Wasp.*"

A shadow touched Mattie's eyes. "Oh." Her partner joined her and slipped an arm around her shoulders. She turned to him. "Uh, Steve, this is my old friend, Luke Hasper. Luke, this is Steve Carpenter."

The men shook hands. "Good to meet you," Steve said, his voice deep and booming.

Luke felt small and wished he could disappear.

"Navy man, huh?"

"Yep. Navy." Luke didn't know what else to say. He had no interest in Mattie's date.

Silence fixed itself between the two men.

"Well, well, well, who's this beautiful boy?" a striking woman with a mane of curls asked as she joined the threesome.

"Oh, Meryl, this is my friend, Luke," Mattie said. "He's from Alaska."

"Very nice to meet you," Meryl said with an open smile. "Mattie never told me how handsome you Palmer boys are."

Luke could feel his face heat up. "Not all the boys. Just me," he managed to quip, surprising himself.

Meryl laughed. "And funny too. I like that." She glanced at Mattie and lifted an eyebrow, then turned back to Luke. "So, what are you doing in town?"

"I'm on leave, but I'll be shipping out in a few days. Thought I'd come by and see how Mattie's doing."

"Oh. I see." Meryl's hazel eyes sparkled with mischief.

Luke remembered the old woman on the stairs and her description of Meryl as being full of vinegar. *I'd say she's right,* he thought.

The music "Starlight" drifted across the room, and couples headed for the dance floor.

When Luke didn't ask Mattie to dance right away, Meryl grabbed her friend's arm and dragged her toward him. "I think you ought to share a dance with your old friend."

Embarrassed, Luke said, "You don't have . . ."

"You want to?" Mattie asked.

"Sure."

Meryl turned to Steve. "How about it? You want to take a twirl? I'm feeling absolutely lonely tonight."

"I'd love to," Steve said, seemingly eager. He took Meryl's arm, and the two disappeared into the crowd.

Mattie and Luke stared at each other. Finally Luke broke the silence. "So, you gonna help out a poor lonely sailor?" He held out his hand.

"I wouldn't want to let down a military man," she said and allowed him to lead her into the throng of dancers.

Luke swung her into his arms, and the two swayed amidst the crowd. He gazed down at her, and unable to restrain his admiration, he said, "I swear you're more beautiful than the last time I saw you."

"Must be city life," Mattie said, relaxing her body a little.

"Well, it sure agrees with you."

"I'm happy here. I like it, even the crowds and the noise. And I've met lots of different kinds of people. In fact, one of my friends is a Negro."

"Your friend Meryl seems real nice."

"She is. I've learned a lot from her. She's a good friend."

Luke twirled Mattie, but not so expertly as Steve. "So, you working?"

"Yes, at the Port of Embarkation. The pay is good, and it's steady work."

"Must be interesting, seeing the ships come and go. And I suppose it helps with the war effort."

"I really don't care about the war effort," she said acidly. "It's just a job." Mattie pulled away from Luke and walked off the dance floor.

Confused, Luke watched her go, then followed. "Mattie. What did I say?" he asked when he caught up to her.

"Nothing. I'm just tired. And I came with Steve. I don't think it's polite to dump a date. Do you?"

"No. But can I see you tomorrow? Before I go?"

Mattie wouldn't look at him. Instead she studied the dancers, her arms folded over her chest and her expression glum. "No, I don't think that would be a good idea." She dropped onto a sofa and crossed her legs. "I have a new life here, and I like it. I don't need or want anything or anyone from my past."

Luke stood over her. "If that's how you want it, I guess I can't change your mind. I . . . I just wish—"

"No. My answer is no." Mattie stood and walked away.

Bent slightly under the weight of his duffel bag, Luke walked through the darkness toward downtown. "I should've known." He didn't bother to avoid puddles. The snow had stopped, but the night air was cold, and a sharp breeze carried the chill off the waters of Puget Sound.

He passed a hotel. The interior was lit up and looked warm. Luke stopped. "I suppose this is as good as any." Opening the door, he stepped into a small, carpeted lobby and walked to a reception desk.

"May I help you?" a tall, thin man with a mustache asked as he emerged from a back room.

"I need a place to stay."

"Yes, sir." He turned a ledger so it faced Luke. "Sign here." He pointed at a line about midway down the page. Luke signed. "How many nights will that be?"

"Just one." Luke had decided to leave the next morning. Nothing was holding him here. Maybe he could get a flight to Anchorage. It would be good to see his family. If only Ray Townsend wasn't there.

Taking an offered key, he walked down the hallway and up one flight of stairs. *Why doesn't she care about me anymore? She did, once.*

By the time Luke reached his room, he'd decided he had to know. He pushed the key into the lock and turned it. Stepping into a tiny room, he flipped on a light and closed the door. He wouldn't leave without trying just once more.

He dropped backward onto the bed and lay staring at the ceiling. *I'll go to her place first thing in the morning. If she still feels the same, at least I can say I tried.*

Chapter 10

His heart heavy, Luke threw back his blankets, then sat up and swung his legs over the side of the bed. He stared at the floor a moment, then stood and walked to the window. The first faint light of morning dropped a touch of gray on the surrounding buildings. Snow, illuminated in streetlights, still fell, and a couple of inches of powder smothered the street. The outside world looked dull, befitting Luke's mood.

After showering and dressing, Luke headed for the lobby. Treading softly, he walked down a dimly lit corridor, the flowered carpet muffling his steps. The foyer was empty except for a clerk sitting behind the counter, a cup of cold coffee waiting on a table beside him. His eyes were closed, and his chin rested on his chest. Luke waited for him to open his eyes, but he didn't stir, and his breathing remained deep and rhythmic. Luke cleared his throat. The clerk slept. Finally Luke punched a bell sitting on the counter.

With a snort, the man lifted his head and opened his eyes. He blinked and tried to focus on Luke. A crooked smile broke out on his long, narrow face and he swayed to his feet. "Guess you caught me. Sorry." He hitched up his pants. "Worked the late shift all week and I'm not used to it." He leaned on the counter. "What can I do you for?"

"I was wondering if you would tell me where I could get some breakfast."

The clerk glanced at the clock—6:05. He scratched his head. "It's kind of early, but I think Irene's Café opens with the birds. It's only two blocks down. They serve biscuits as good as my mother's. Only don't tell my mother that." He grinned.

"Thanks." Luke headed for the door and stepped into the chilly morning air. Huddling inside his pea coat, he trudged down the street, white flakes collecting on his coat and hat. The street was mostly empty except for a rare taxi or bus sloshing through the snow.

Lights from inside the café emanated warmth and invited him inside. The cozy-looking diner felt like a friendly beacon. He stepped inside, and the aroma of perked coffee and freshly baked donuts made his mouth water in spite of his wretched disposition. He considered sitting at the bar, but that might mean he'd have to converse with the waitress. Instead he chose a table sitting against the back wall of the empty restaurant.

Immediately a stocky woman in her forties carrying a coffeepot approached. "You're up and about early." She smiled. "How about some coffee? It's fresh and it's the real thing, none of that imitation stuff."

"Sounds good. Thanks."

After filling his cup with dark brew, she asked, "So what'll you have?"

"I heard you make good biscuits."

"The best."

"I'll take a couple of them and some eggs and bacon."

"Comin' right up." The waitress turned and sauntered toward the kitchen.

When Luke finished eating, it was still too early to go to Mattie's. He grabbed yesterday's newspaper, which had been left on the table beside him, ordered another cup of coffee, and settled down to read.

The United States wins and losses in recent battles were listed, along with a picture of a Japanese Zero spiraling into the sea, plus another one of a burning U.S. ship. There was also an editorial about Japanese Americans, which raised the question of whether they could be trusted or not. The writer had suggestions about what he thought ought to be done with them. Luke read on, stunned when he read that Japanese American citizens might be placed in relocation camps. He considered the idea but wasn't sure just how he felt. He guessed it was possible that some of them *could* be spies.

He folded the paper, and his mind shifted to Mattie. What was he going to say to her? What might change her mind? He thought through possible scenarios, but each one brought him back to the same unacceptable conclusion—him going his way and not looking back.

"Can I top that off for you?" the waitress asked.

Luke glanced at his nearly empty cup, then back at the woman. She looked as if she'd climbed out of bed late and had forgotten to comb her hair. "No thanks. I'm fine."

She gazed at the war headlines in the paper. "Hard to believe, ain't it?" She shook her head, then leveled teary eyes on Luke. "I pray for you boys every day."

"We need all the prayers we can get. Thanks."

Wearing a sad smile, she moved on to a new customer.

Leaving a nickel on the table, Luke pulled on his coat and headed for the door. He needed to see Mattie. Hopefully she was up by now.

He intended to go straight to Mattie's place, but instead walked the streets, stopping to stare at window displays. At the Bon Marche he studied a too-thin mannequin draped in a silky lavender gown, then glanced at his watch. It was only 8:30. If Mattie got in late she was probably still sleeping.

He moved on. At 'I' Magnum, he stopped to gaze at a sterling silver set glistening beneath display lights. A set of china with a delicate floral pattern sat beside the flatware. They reminded him of the ones his grandmother had given to his mother. She'd had to leave them when they'd left Wisconsin. Before that they'd been set out on the table for every Sunday dinner. Maybe one day he'd buy her another set. Or maybe if things worked out with Mattie, he could get her some nice china.

Unable to wait longer to see Mattie, he headed for her place. Once at the apartments, he took the front steps two at a time, swung open the door, and quickly climbed the stairs. He half expected to meet Roseline Talbot. He figured she probably got around to visiting folks in the building regularly.

Finally he stood in front of Mattie's door. He stared at it a long while, unable to generate enough courage to knock. What if she told him to leave and never come back? What if she was angry with him for being here at all? He almost turned and left, but his longing for her was more powerful than his fears.

He knocked.

No one answered. He knocked again.

Finally a voice from inside mumbled something. Whoever it was sounded half asleep. "I'm too early," Luke said with a groan. Disturbing Mattie's sleep couldn't be helpful. Someone from inside unbolted a lock, and Luke readied an apology.

Meryl peeked around the edge of the door. "Oh, it's you. I had no idea Mattie was expecting you . . . not at this hour."

"She isn't. I'm sorry for waking you up. I can come back later."

Meryl swung open the door. "You're here. You might as well come in."

Meryl barely resembled the exotic and exciting woman he'd met the previous night. Curls, like springs gone awry, spiraled straight out from her head. Oversized pajamas dragged on the floor, sleeves hung below her hands, and a baggy bathrobe was draped half on and half off her slim frame.

"Well, are you coming in or not? I realize I'm not a lovely sight first thing in the morning, but that's no excuse for bad manners." She wore a half smile.

Realizing he'd been staring, Luke stepped inside. "Is Mattie up?"

"She's in the shower. That's why I'm here. Otherwise, I'd still be getting my beauty sleep." She peered at a mirror hanging on the wall and screwed up her face. "I could certainly use some."

Trying to tame her curls, she ran a hand through her hair, then giving up, she grabbed a cigarette case off the kitchen counter and dropped onto a straight-backed chair. Removing her silver lighter and a cigarette from a matching silver case, she tapped the cigarette several times on the case, then lit up, taking a deep breath. She coughed. Pressing a hand against her chest, she said, "The first drag of the morning can be a rough one." She smiled, her hazel eyes beginning to look more awake. "You smoke?" she asked, offering the case.

"No, never took it up."

"I suppose growing up in the backwoods the way you did protected you from the sins of the world." Mischief lit her face.

"No, there was plenty of sin. Smoking is just one I passed up."

She took another puff, this time without coughing. Looking at a door on the far side of the room, she pulled herself out of the chair and crossed to it. Knocking, she said, "Mattie, you've got company."

"What? What did you say?" a voice asked from behind the door.

"You've got company."

The door opened, and Mattie stuck out a towel-covered head. "What?" Her eyes stopped on Luke. "Oh. Luke." She dropped back, disappearing from sight. "What are you doing here?"

"Now that's a cordial welcome," Meryl teased, returning to her seat and tapping her cigarette against the edge of an ornate ashtray.

"I didn't mean it that way. I'm not dressed. I wasn't expecting anyone." She peeked out again. "I'll be right out." The door closed.

"Have a seat," Meryl said, draping one leg over the other and swinging a slippered foot back and forth. She closed her eyes. "Oh, I could have used another five hours at least." She peered at Luke. "Did you get up with the birds?"

"Earlier." He smiled.

"About the time our feathered friends got up, I went to bed."

Luke's hopes of a premature ending to Mattie's date withered. Although he knew he had no say in her life, he hated the idea of her being out at all hours dancing and having fun—with Steve. "I was afraid you two had gotten in late. I'm sorry for coming by so early."

"Actually *I* got in late. Mattie was a wet blanket and headed home just after you left." Meryl's eyes held mischief.

"Oh." Luke's spirits lifted. Maybe she hadn't had much fun.

"'Course, I didn't really mind." Meryl grinned seductively. "That meant I got Steve to myself. He wasn't happy with Mattie for leaving him stranded." She tossed her hair. "I didn't mind being a substitute though. I think he likes me."

"You didn't have a date?" His mind still on Mattie and Steve, Luke didn't consider the rudeness of the question.

"No. I didn't have a date. Neither of us did, really. We went on our own, but I think Steve expected to spend the evening with Mattie." Meryl yawned. "'Course, now he knows what a party pooper she is." She smiled playfully and stretched her arms over her head.

"So, has she been talking your ear off?" Mattie asked, stepping out of the bathroom. She'd dressed in a casual yellow sweater and tan skirt and had braided her black hair into a single plait that hung over one shoulder. The yellow sweater enhanced the golden hue of her skin, and Luke thought she looked even more beautiful than she had the night before. She crossed to the kitchenette and poured herself a cup of coffee. "You want some?"

"I'm dying for coffee," Meryl said dramatically.

"You couldn't get it yourself?" Mattie asked.

Meryl's mouth dropped into a pout.

"I can get my own," Luke said, walking toward Mattie. "You always did make good coffee."

"I still do. But these days we're stingy with it. Seems there are shortages on everything." Mattie filled three cups. "Good thing I started perking this before I climbed in the shower," she said, handing a cup to Meryl. She looked at Luke. "You want cream or sugar?"

"Black's fine."

Mattie gave Luke his coffee, then took her own and sat on the sofa.

Cradling the hot cup between his hands, Luke sat on the opposite end.

"So, what are you doing out and about so early?" Mattie asked.

"Woke up. Couldn't sleep. So I had some breakfast, then started walking and ended up here." Luke looked at Meryl who was watching him intensely. He wished she'd go back to bed. He wanted to talk to Mattie . . . alone.

"So, why do you think you ended up here?" Meryl asked pointedly.

"Why?" The question surprised Luke. "I . . . I just did. I guess I wanted to see Mattie." He glanced at her. "We're friends."

"Good friends are hard to find," Meryl said with a crooked smile. She sipped her coffee, then cast a knowing look at Mattie. "I think we ought to cherish the ones we have." Again she rocked her foot back and forth. "Please don't let me stop you from getting reacquainted."

Luke thought she might leave them alone, but she didn't move. Gathering his courage, he said, "I was kind of hoping we, Mattie and I, could talk alone." He glanced at Meryl but couldn't hold her bold gaze.

"Oh, I never repeat private conversations," she said.

Mattie shot her a look of exasperation. "I know a place we can go. It's down a few blocks. Close enough to walk."

"You mean Mannings?" Meryl asked. "I would just love one of their donuts. They make the best in the entire world. Could you bring one back for me?"

"Sure," Mattie said, standing and finishing her coffee before setting the cup in the sink. She walked to a coat closet just inside the door. "Do you mind going to a coffee shop?"

"No. Not at all." Luke stood and set his cup beside Mattie's, then quickly crossed to her and helped her with her coat, then opened the door.

"See you later," Mattie said, stepping into the hallway.

"Bye." Meryl waved. "Have a wonderful time."

"Nice seeing you again." Luke followed Mattie out. As soon as the door was closed, he said, "That Meryl's something else."

"She's a good friend," Mattie said defensively.

"Don't get mad. I didn't say she's not. She's . . . well, she's just different."

"Yes, she is," Mattie conceded. "Maybe that's because she was raised in San Francisco's upper class. Growing up, Meryl could do pretty much whatever she wanted whenever she wanted. She's still like that sometimes, but I like her. She has a good heart, and she's one of the most honest people I've ever known."

Mrs. Talbot reached the landing just as Luke and Mattie took the bottom step. She smiled at them. "Oh, there you are, sweetie. How are you today?" She took Mattie's face in her knotted hands and kissed her cheek.

"I'm fine. You?"

"Oh, not so bad. This cold weather plays havoc with my rheumatism, but other than that, I'm feeling pretty spry." Her eyes sparkled. "I see you and your young man met up."

"Hello, ma'am. Good to see you again."

"He's not *my young man*," Mattie corrected. "He's just a friend, from Alaska."

"Alaska, huh? I've always wanted to go there. Don't suppose it will happen now though, not at my age."

"You're not missing much."

"I don't believe that," the old woman said. "Now, what are you two about today?"

"We're just going for coffee," Mattie said.

Mrs. Talbot nodded. "Enjoy. I'd better get on up to Jasmine's. She's feeling a bit poorly."

"What's wrong?"

A guarded looked passed over Mrs. Talbot's face. "She told me not to say anything." After glancing up the stairs, she whispered, "Someone beat her."

"What? Who?"

"I don't know. Guess it happened at work."

"Why would anyone do such a thing?" Mattie turned, ready to ascend the stairs. "I'd better go up."

"No. She doesn't want to see anyone right now. I just happened to check on her and found out she was in a bad way."

"Is this a friend of yours?" Luke asked.

"Uh-huh."

"Why would someone beat her up?"

Mrs. Talbot was silent for a long moment, then said, "Jasmine is a Negro. And you know how some folks can be." She compressed her lips. "The way people around here are behaving is out-and-out shameful."

"Please tell her I'll be by to see her later," Mattie said.

"I'll tell her, dear, but I don't know if she'll see you."

"Ooh, that makes me so mad!" Mattie stormed as she and Luke stepped into the frigid morning air. "I can't believe people!"

Ignoring the ice, Mattie's feet pounded the stairway as she descended the front steps. Her hands in fists, she continued, "Jasmine told me some people at work were angry because she'd been promoted."

"Can't she go to the police?"

"She did once before . . . when there was some trouble. They didn't do anything. I guess they talked to some people, but nothing came of it."

"I want you to stay out of this, Mattie. I don't want you hurt."

She stopped and whirled around to face Luke. "Stay out of it? She's my friend! How can you ask me to do such a thing?"

"I . . . I didn't mean—"

"Never mind. Just forget it." She strode ahead.

Luke followed, knowing his chances of building something more than a friendship with Mattie were dwindling. At this rate, by the time he left town she might not even be speaking to him.

They stepped into the coffee shop, and a bell hanging from the door announced their arrival. "Booth?" Mattie asked.

"Sure." Luke followed her to a booth and they sat across from each other. Silence lodged itself between them. Luke picked up a salt shaker, loosened the lid, then tightened it, then loosened it again. His mind was blank.

It was Mattie who finally brought up their relationship, but not in the way Luke had hoped.

She reached out and captured his hand and the salt shaker. "Could you put that down, please?"

Securing the lid for the umpteenth time, he set it on the table.

"Luke, I'm glad you stopped by this morning. I value your friendship, but please don't bring up anything about us being a couple. OK?"

Luke's enthusiasm and hopes for the day evaporated. "It's just that . . . well, I can't help how I feel."

"It's friends or nothing," Mattie said. "That's all I want. It's all I can manage right now."

Luke had no choice. "All right. Friends." He held out his hand, and they shook.

He ordered coffee and donuts, and gradually the tension between them fell away. They reminisced about their days in the valley—how they'd met and how Luke, an eager teenager, had dragged Mattie and Alex home to meet his family. Mattie admitted to being intimidated by the encounter. She hadn't known how the outsiders would feel about having Indians in their home.

"When I think about it now, it seems silly. Your family's so nice." Mattie pinched off a small bite of a sugar donut and popped it in her mouth. "That Brian, he was so curious, especially about my being native." She chuckled. "I think I fell in love with him right off the bat."

Luke couldn't resist. "How about me?"

Mattie winced. "I thought we agreed."

"I know. I know." He gave her a boyish smile and ran his hand through his short-cropped hair. "You can't blame me for trying."

"It must be hard on Brian . . . on all your family to have you gone. Especially with the war on." Her voice had turned somber. "What's it like? Being on a ship . . . and knowing you could be attacked at any moment?"

"Before the bombing we didn't figure on an attack. Now . . . I can't wait to face off with 'em. They're gonna pay for what they did."

Mattie was taken aback at Luke's vehement tone.

"I'm gonna kill as many as I can," he said, then rolled back tightened shoulders. "Let's talk about something else. Seems all anyone talks about these days is the war."

"All right," Mattie agreed.

They sat talking and laughing until after one o'clock in the afternoon. Before saying good-bye, Luke convinced Mattie to see him the following day, and they planned a trip to Woodland Park.

The next morning, driving rain hurled itself upon the city. By the time Luke arrived at Mattie's apartment, he was soaked. He stood in the hallway, a puddle forming at his feet.

Answering his knock, Mattie opened the door. "Come in. You poor thing."

"Doesn't look like a good day for a trip to the park."

"We can have an inside day then. How about a game of cards?" Mattie stripped off his soaking coat and hung it in the bathroom.

"Sounds like fun." Luke glanced about. "Uh, where's Meryl?"

"She had to work."

Luke nearly said good, then decided against it. He didn't want to take a chance of getting Mattie angry.

"I'll make popcorn," she said, hurrying into the kitchenette.

Luke followed. "Anything I can do to help?"

"You can clear the table."

He moved a cup and saucer to the sink. "So, how's your friend Jasmine?"

"I guess she's going to be all right." Mattie shook her head. "If I were her . . . well, I don't know what I'd do, but I'd do something."

Luke nodded. "There's probably not much to be done if what you say is true. It's a shame, though." He pulled off a tablecloth covering the table and folded it.

"So, you still like rummy?"

"I do," Mattie said, sitting across the table from him.

The two friends played Hearts, Rummy, and Black Jack. The strain between them had vanished, and the old friendship they'd always shared had returned. Now they laughed at each other's antics and spurred the competitiveness of the other.

It was a perfect afternoon. Then, while playing a game of Rummy the light mood was lost when they each saw a card that should have been played. Simultaneously they called out, "Rummy!" and slapped the card.

Luke's hand fell over Mattie's. Instead of letting loose, he left it there. Mattie didn't pull her hand free. Her dark eyes held his. Unable to suppress his ardor, Luke leaned across the table and kissed her.

It was brief and tender. Neither spoke. Their hands remained clasped.

"You do love me, too, don't you?" Luke asked.

Mattie didn't answer.

"Please, Mattie, marry me. We belong together. We always have."

Mattie's eyes pooled with tears. She shook her head. "I can't." She slipped her hand out from under his. "I'm sorry, Luke. Maybe I do love you, but I can't marry you. I just can't. If we get married, we're ... united, joined. I ... I just can't think about you being in the war. I'd be afraid all the time. Living like that would be misery. And I won't go back to Alaska."

Luke didn't hear her. All he knew was that there was hope and she loved him. "Mattie, it'll be all right. No Japs or Krauts will touch me. And we don't have to move to Alaska. We can live somewhere else. Here is fine."

"If we get married, we're not just good friends anymore—we're one. Everything will be different, and I know I couldn't bear the thought of you out there ... somewhere in the Pacific ..." She straightened. "With things the way they are now, I'm not yours and you're not mine. If something happens ... nothing really changes." She stood and walked to the sink. "And you might not think you have to live in Alaska, but you do. I know you. You're part of it. Plus, you have the farm."

"No. Ray has the farm," Luke said, unable to keep the old bitterness out of his voice.

"One day it will be yours." She filled a glass with water and took a drink, then turned to look at him. "I like it here. I'm my own person. I don't worry about what I look like—the color of my skin and my eyes and hair. I don't expect to hear the word *Siewash* thrown at me. Here I'm just part of the crowd."

"There must be some way to work this out."

"There isn't. I've thought about it." She set the glass in the sink. Without looking at him, she continued, "We're friends forever, but only friends. Let me love you that way. Please."

Luke couldn't give up. He crossed to her, took hold of Mattie's shoulders, and turned her so she faced him. "No matter where you live, you'll be native. You can't change that."

"No. You're wrong. Here it's different. People don't see an Aleut Indian. They see me."

"What about Jasmine? They care that she's a Negro."

Confusion momentarily touched Mattie's face. "That's different."

"Why?"

Mattie didn't answer, but her expression was one of resolve.

Luke knew he could not convince her, not today anyway. He took a deep breath and let it out. "OK. But I'm not giving up. One day you'll be mine."

"No. I won't. I can't." Mattie strode toward her room. She stopped and turned to look at him. "I'm sorry," she said, then disappeared through the door, closing it decisively.

Chapter 11

LAUREL TUCKED THE BED COVERS AROUND WILLIAM'S SHOULDERS. "GOOD night, sweetheart," she said and kissed his forehead.

The little boy reached up and wrapped his arms around his mother's neck. "I love you, and I love Daddy. When is Daddy coming home?"

Laurel hated having William ask about his father. She didn't know when Adam would return. All she knew was that he was somewhere in Europe. Her heart ached at the thought of his being so far away and most certainly in danger. She forced a smile. "God is watching out for Daddy. I'm sure he'll be home before too much longer."

"What's too much longer?"

"I don't know for sure when he'll be back, sweetie."

"He has to be here before summer," William said.

"Summer it is then." Laurel caressed his cheek. "Maybe winter will pass quickly." She straightened. "It's time for you to sleep. Sweet dreams." Quietly she walked out, leaving the door ajar so heat from the stove would warm his room.

She crossed to the firebox and banked the fire for the night. Wind whistled under the eaves and snatched at wooden shingles on the roof. Laurel peered through an ice-encrusted window at the outside darkness. She couldn't see any lights from nearby farms. She felt alone.

Laurel's mind wandered to Adam. He was in another world—a dangerous world. She'd received only two letters since he'd left in January. He'd been assigned to a squadron of fighter pilots and bombers stationed in England but was uncertain if they'd remain at the base outside London or be relocated. He'd complained that there'd been too little action. He was seeking a transfer. *Too little action? London is right in the middle of it. Why do men want to fight, to see "action?"*

"I don't understand," she said, crossing to her chair and picking up the sewing she'd left in a basket. She'd been crocheting a doily for her bed stand. Holding it up to the light, she studied her work. The pattern was intricate, and she'd done a fine job, but she took little pleasure in it. Laurel sat. "I just wish Adam would come home." Resting her head against the back of the chair, she closed her eyes and imagined he was with her. His presence made her feel safe.

A sharp clang and the sound of squawking chickens reverberated from outside. Laurel straightened, alert. "Something's at the chickens!" Pushing out of the chair, she snatched the rifle from its shelf on the wall and rested it against the back door, then threw on a coat and pushed her feet into fur-lined boots. After pulling on gloves, she grabbed the rifle, opened the door, and peered into the darkness. Since the moon wasn't out, she'd need a light.

Returning to the kitchen, Laurel lifted the lantern from a shelf and lit it. Holding it high, she stepped onto the porch and into a frigid wind. It was clear and moonless. The cold cut through her as she headed for the chicken house. Scuffling and squawking emanated from the coop. "Lord, please don't let it be a wolf," Laurel prayed. "Or a wolverine," she added as an afterthought, deciding the aggressive animal might be just as formidable as a wolf.

Her feet broke through a layer of ice covering the snow. Each step produced a loud crunching sound, and she was certain whatever was in the chicken house would hear her, but the ruckus continued.

Darkness pressed in, making the light of her lantern seem weak. She gazed into the blackness, wishing the lamp's glow could penetrate the shadows. *If one wolf is in the coop, there might be others,* she thought. "You're being silly," she told herself. "It's probably nothing more than an irksome varmint." Although she knew bears were supposed to be hibernating, she couldn't help but wonder if one might have wandered out. *I wish Adam was here,* she thought as a fresh uproar erupted from inside the chicken house. She considered retreating, but the chickens were too important. She couldn't lose them.

Laurel moved close to the coop door and stopped to make sure her gun was cocked and ready. She set the lantern in the snow beside the building and noiselessly lifted the latch, then eased open the door.

Quickly grabbing the lantern while struggling to keep her gun at the ready, she looked inside. Glistening eyes stared from the far side of the coop. An animal crouched in the corner. It darted across the floor. Laurel leaped backward, adrenaline shooting through her. She raised the gun! The creature ran at her, then a flash of gray flew past. It was a wolf! No—a fox. Laurel's tensed muscles loosened slightly, and she fired. The animal yipped and fell.

Letting out a breath of relief, Laurel lifted the fox. "You should have stayed away from my chickens." She scanned the room. Most of the flock was still perched on roosts, looking a little ruffled but uninjured. A few huddled on the hay-strewn floor, pressing their quivering bodies against the wall. The room looked as if it had been showered with feathers. Two hens were dead, and one rooster was nearly lifeless. They'd have to go in the pot.

Laurel put the injured rooster out of his misery and carried the three chickens to the house. She'd have to pluck and butcher them if they were going to be of any use. Weary, she set to work.

After finishing with the chickens, she dragged the fox into the barn. *Adam should be here,* she thought, momentarily angry. *This was too much for a woman to handle all alone. He should have stayed.* Almost immediately she recanted the idea. She was being selfish. Adam was serving his country. What could be more important than that?

She gazed at the black sky where brilliant lights flickered. *Aren't William and I important too?*

A soft voice whispered, "Yes. And you have not been forgotten."

The flush of guilt returned, and Laurel chastised herself for her lack of faith. Adam would return, and she and William would be fine while they waited. They had plenty of food, wood for heat, a snug home, and good friends and family. Her time would be better spent praying for Adam and the others fighting for freedom. "Forgive me," she said and headed back to the house.

The following morning Laurel skinned out the fox while William watched. He stroked the fur and talked about the day when he would grow up and be able to hunt.

After stretching the pelt across a board, Laurel rested it against the barn wall. She would flesh it later; now she needed company. The fur would wait a few hours while she visited Jessie and worked on the book. She returned to the house to cook breakfast.

William finished up the last of his mush while Laurel did the dishes. She looked at her son. "You want to go to Grandma's?"

He smiled. "Yes. Is Grandpa going to be there?"

"Uh-huh. You can help him with chores."

"Can I milk the cow?"

"Maybe. You'll have to ask Grandpa."

After breakfast was finished, Laurel and William bundled up and set out. Laurel was certain her mother would be more than happy to watch William while she was at Jessie's. She looked forward to spending time with her old friend. After the previous evening's excitement, she needed Jessie's unruffled company.

"Thanks, Mama," Laurel said, giving William a kiss good-bye. "I'll be back before supper."

"Why don't you and William eat with us?" Jean asked.

"I'd like that. I've been kind of lonely lately."

Jean gave Laurel a quick hug. "You should visit more often."

"I will. Thanks." She kissed her mother's cheek and headed for Jessie's. It was a clear day, and sunlight glistened brightly off the snow, making Laurel squint. She didn't mind. At this time of year there weren't enough daylight hours, even on clear days. And when clouds hung over the valley, it never seemed to get truly light but looked more like dusk.

In the sunlight her fears of the previous night seemed silly. She knew she shouldn't allow herself to be frightened so easily. Adam had been gone a month, and sooner or later she had to learn to depend on herself and less on others. What if something were to happen to him? She'd truly be on her own.

By the time she arrived at Jessie's, Laurel was looking forward to working on the book nearly as much as visiting her friend. They were close to completing the six-year project Jessie had promised her husband she'd finish. When they'd started, Laurel had thought it wouldn't take more than a year, maybe two, but it was much tougher than she'd expected. And now she worried they wouldn't finish before Jessie died.

She's getting on, Laurel thought. *She's failing a little every day. We've got to finish Steward's project.*

When Laurel pulled into the drive in front of the small cabin, smoke drifted lazily upward from the chimney. Jessie peeked out the front window and waved. Laurel returned the gesture and climbed out of the car. The door of the cabin opened before she reached the front steps.

"Good morning to you," Jessie said. "I was hoping you'd come by." She gave Laurel a warm hug. "Come in. Come in. It's freezing out."

Laurel stepped into the familiar, friendly home. It was disorderly as always. Crowded shelves and paintings cluttered the walls, throw rugs and well-worn furniture cluttered the front room, and scattered pots and pans and baked goods cluttered the kitchen. It felt just right and friendly to Laurel. Her tension slipped away.

Jessie hobbled into the kitchen. "Let me fix you a cup of hot cocoa."

"Mmm. Sounds good." Laurel removed her gloves. "Do you want to work today?" she asked, slipping off her coat and hanging it on a hook just inside the door.

"Oh my, yes. Of course."

Laurel followed Jessie into the kitchen and leaned against the counter. She watched the old woman, whose hands now shook slightly as she stirred the cocoa. Laurel knew better than to try to help her. Each year Jessie had grown more stubborn and more determined to do things for herself.

Jessie filled two cups with the rich hot chocolate. "Ah, there you are," she said, handing Laurel a cup and taking one for herself. "Now then, let's sit a minute and chat." She smiled and her eyes smiled too, nearly disappearing within deep wrinkles. "I want to know how you're faring."

Laurel settled herself on a settee opposite Jessie, who sat in her overstuffed chair. Jessie sipped her cocoa, then with her eyes bright she said, "We're nearly finished. It's hard to believe. I'd say maybe a couple more weeks of steady work and we'll be ready to send it off to the college.

They contacted me. They're waiting and are still very enthusiastic. They have a publisher all set up."

"I hope they like it."

"Well, of course they will. We did a fine job on it, and Steward would be proud. He did such thorough research, and I think we make a good team. I just wish he were here to see it completed." Jessie teared. "His *Alaskan Anthology,* finished." She dabbed her eyes with a handkerchief she kept folded inside her shirt cuff. "I'm getting sentimental in my old age. But I don't suppose it will be much longer before I join my Steward."

"Don't say that. I'll bet you're around for a good long while yet."

"Maybe. But I don't mind going, really. I'm ready." She paused. "I'm missing Steward more and more. I can hardly wait to see him."

Laurel understood. Every time she thought of Adam, an ache squeezed her chest, rising into her throat, and she would long to feel his arms, to hear his voice. "I think I understand, but I'll miss you so much. I can't imagine your being gone."

Jessie smiled. "It's good to be loved. And I thank you, but I'm sure you'll go on just fine without me. You have your own family to think about."

"Yes. I just wish Adam would come home." Laurel took a drink of cocoa, then cradled the cup in her hands. "Last night I had a visitor."

Jessie raised an eyebrow. "Oh?"

"I was just thinking of going to bed when I heard a ruckus out in the chicken coop. I went to investigate and found a fox along with two dead hens and a rooster nearly gone." She straightened slightly. "He won't be back. I shot him."

"I've lost a few hens to pesky critters myself over the years."

"You ever get scared?"

"Oh, sure. There are dangerous things in this world."

"I knew I had to go out there and take care of the chickens. I can't afford to lose them. But I was scared. And I was imagining all kinds of things. I feel silly now, but I wish Adam had been there. William and I need him."

Jessie nodded sympathetically. "Have you heard from him?"

"I received a letter a few days ago. He's in England, hoping to be sent on a mission. He said that very little is happening and he's waiting to get another assignment. He's stationed with a group of pilots but hasn't seen any real fighting. And he's sick of the food and promises that when he gets home he'll even eat rutabagas." She smiled. "I'll just be glad to get him home."

"It will be a fine day when all our young men come home."

"I just don't understand any of it. Why do wars have to happen?"

"There are lots of reasons for war, but I think the main one is man's need for power and domination and his desire for possessions. The big countries want to get bigger, the small countries want to get big, and they all want what someone else has."

"Why?"

"Man's sinful heart. Throughout time humans have battled for supremacy over one another, and I suppose it will continue to the end of time."

"It just makes me so mad. I think men like violence. In his letter, Adam sounded disappointed because he hasn't seen more fighting."

Jessie smiled softly, her oval eyes pained. "I'm sure it's not that Adam likes violence. He knows important things are happening in this war, and he wants to be one of the men recording them. The events of war must be documented. We can always hope that humans will look more closely at history and grasp the tragedy of war and think before they begin another one." Jessie paused. "And I'm sorry to say it does seem that humankind rather enjoys upheaval."

"I hate the men who started this war, and I hate that men want to fight." Laurel's words were vehement and heated, and until she'd spoken she hadn't realized the depth of her emotions.

"I'm not so sure anyone wants to fight," Jessie said gently. "I'm certain that for most it's a desire to do what's right that prompts them. They recognize that evil stalks and attacks the innocent and vulnerable, and someone has to come to the victims' aid. Where would we be if no one was willing to stand up to our enemies?"

"I know what you're saying, but it's still very confusing to me. And I miss Adam. I want him home."

"He'll be home. Don't you worry about that. Your Adam is one of those who cares about the ones being tread upon." She held Laurel's gaze. "He's doing the right thing. You and I need to pray for our brave fighting men, including the ones who write about it all so that people won't forget."

"I know you're right," Laurel said. "But I'm afraid for him. The Germans have been bombing London." Her mind wandered to her husband. Where was he? Was he safe? Was he involved in a battle somewhere? *Please come home to me,* her heart pleaded.

Chapter 12

ADAM STOOD OUTSIDE THE CONFERENCE ROOM AND WAITED FOR THE BRIEFING to end. He glanced at his watch—0500 he read, then yawned, thinking he could have used more sack time. He wished he were inside getting the story, but rules were rules—no newsmen allowed. He'd been away from his family eight months and still hadn't managed to get on top of a good story; to be part of a real mission. Once more, he thought in frustration, he'd have to wrangle the information out of one of the pilots or crew members. It usually wasn't difficult. A lot of the airmen were happy to tell Adam what they knew. For the most part, the men trusted him, and in many ways he'd become one of them. Still, if he didn't make a mission soon, he might as well go home.

The door swung open and men trailed out. "Hey, Chuck, how'd it go in there?" he asked, matching the veteran pilot's steps. "How about letting me tag along today?"

The pilot barely glanced at Adam.

"You have to get me on a mission. How can I report what's happening if I'm not there?"

Walking with a swagger, Chuck kept moving. "I don't *have* to do anything."

"Well, yeah, sure. You don't *have* to. I didn't mean that." Adam hated groveling.

Without looking at Adam, Chuck asked, "Why you want to go up so bad? You're not a flier. You're a reporter."

"Just give me a minute and I'll explain." Adam was tall but not long-legged enough, and he had to work to keep up.

Chuck stopped, folded his arms over his chest, and stared at Adam, one eyebrow raised and his mouth rotated slightly sideways. "All right. I'm listening."

This better be good, Adam thought, knowing it could be a defining moment. "What you guys do is important," he began, making sure to sound sincere. "People back in the States need to know that you put your necks on the line, and they need to know how. The story has to be told."

"You don't have to go up with us to tell it. Anyone can fill you in. Just ask. For crying out loud, we've got more stories than you can shake a stick at." He chuckled. "Heck, you already do ask. Some days I feel like part of an inquisition."

"I know you don't want something written that's not authentic, and if I'm not actually there, feeling and hearing the action, it's not going to be real. Anything less will feel artificial. If people are going to understand, they've got to get it firsthand."

The rest of the flight crew disappeared through a door leading to the mess hall. Chuck looked like he was thinking.

"To write about what you guys do with any kind of authenticity I have to feel the ride, the fear, the jubilation, and the thankfulness of the B-17's wheels touching down on that runway when the mission's completed. Otherwise, it's just not going to hit home with the readers," Adam continued.

Chuck rested a hand on Adam's shoulder. "I like you, Dunnavant. I don't want your wife and son to get a telegram stating, kindly, of course, how you died fulfilling your *duty* to your country."

Adam was getting annoyed. "What I do is important. And just like the rest of the men and women serving this country, I take risks. My wife understands that."

"You don't have to go up—you shouldn't."

"No. I should. To do this right I have to." Adam met the captain's gaze.

Chuck ran a hand over his face. "You're tougher than I thought." He blew out his breath. "I shouldn't do this. All right. We're heading into France this morning. There'll be flak, probably Jerrys. They've got some good pilots. We're liable to lose planes." He waited, giving Adam an opportunity to back out. "I'm flying the lead in this mission. You'll be in my plane."

"I'm ready." Adam kept his gaze on the big man's solemn, gray eyes.

Chuck slapped him on the shoulder. "All right, then, today's the day. Be on the airfield at 0700." Without another word, he strode off. "I hope you got flight training," he called over his shoulder.

"'Course I do," Adam said. He was stretching the truth. He'd had minimal instruction, just enough to get him out of a plane if it were going down.

Wearing a one-piece flight suit plus heavy gear, Adam walked on to the field early. He wondered how the airmen could do much of anything while wearing their insulated suits, flak jackets, and parachutes. They were cumbersome and heavy.

He double-checked his camera equipment, making sure everything was in good working order, then patted his jacket pocket with his pencil and writing pad. "Guess I'm ready. This is what I've been waiting for." He tried to show confidence, but his stomach felt queasy, and adrenaline overload was giving him the jitters.

Ground crews gassed up planes and checked and rechecked the aircraft for flight readiness. Fighter pilots were the first aircrew on the field. Their planes would serve as escorts to the bulky, slow-moving bombers, which were easy targets. Engines fired off one by one. The air reverberated, sounding like a monstrous beehive. Adam's heart rate climbed, and so did his anticipation.

With the fighter planes in the air, bomber crews dashed across the tarmac to waiting B-17s. Adam watched for Chuck. When he spotted him, he ran and joined him.

"You didn't change your mind, eh?" Chuck grinned.

"No way. I can't wait."

He puffed on a cigar. "All right then. You take your pictures and write your story, but stay out of the way. We've got a job to do."

"Yes, sir," Adam said, keeping pace with the pilot.

The air pulsed with the deep throb of B-17 engines. The heavy bombers were stacked and ready for takeoff. Adam sat on a bench along one wall, surprised at how crowded and loud it was inside. Even while on the ground, you had to strain to make yourself heard.

"What's he doing here?" asked John Lewis, a cocky engineer.

Dale Evanston, the navigator, glanced at Adam. "Captain said it was all right," he hollered.

Lewis glowered at Adam. "That's all we need—a self-important journalist on board."

"Is self-important the same as arrogant? I figure you'd know." Adam grinned.

"Roll up your flaps," Lewis sneered.

"All right, you two," said Dale. "We've got Jerrys to kill. This is no place for your adolescent squabbling."

"Right." Adam leaned against a bulkhead.

"You'll need oxygen once we get up there. The gear is over there." Dale nodded at a face mask attached to a toggle. "Not much oxygen at twenty-four thousand feet. There's a headset. You'll need it if you want to talk to any of us."

Adam nodded and put on the headset. *Better,* he thought. At least no one would have to yell.

The reality of what he was about to do set in. He rested a hand on his bouncing leg and pushed his foot flat against the floor to quiet it. Taking a deep breath, he prayed for peace and protection. Still, his stomach jumped. This was his first real combat experience.

Adam grabbed the mask and practiced putting it on and taking it off. He leaned back, resting against his parachute. The feel of it gave him a small sense of security. At least with a parachute, a person had a chance of making it if the plane was hit. The idea of jumping from a dying plane made his mouth go dry.

Dale checked maps laid out in front of him, then glanced at Adam. "You got it figured out?"

"No problem." Adam glanced at the crew.

One of the waist gunners said, "First time's always the hardest. After you've made a few runs, you get used to 'em—kinda." He offered Adam a sideways grin.

"I figured," Adam said, taking out his pad and pencil. He needed to record the surroundings—the sounds and smells, the duties of the crew, as well as his own intense feelings. He took several photographs of the inside of the bomber and wrote that it must be a little like being in the belly of a whale and being served up as a meal.

Adam's insides vibrated in tune with the thrum of the B-17. The bomber's engines surged, and the plane moved onto the runway. It rolled down the airstrip, made a tight turn, then headed back, picking up speed. Adam gripped the bench. Sweat ran into his eyes, and his heart hammered beneath his ribs. There was an upsurge in the engine's cadence. They moved faster. The plane vibrated so hard it felt as if it would shake apart. The engines roared.

Adam loved speed, and the thrill of flight swept away his uncertainties. A moment more and they would be in the air. He felt the wheels leave the ground, followed by a sense of buoyancy. It was brief, however. This was a B-17; it would not take to the air with ease. The huge plane gradually dragged skyward.

Adam's mind moved to Palmer, his wife, and his son. Laurel was probably working in the garden with William alongside, doing his best to help. It was the busy season, the time of harvest. She would have cabbages to cut and potatoes and carrots to dig. Adam could almost smell the starchy odor of spuds laid out in the root cellar. He hoped Laurel had found adequate help and felt a twinge of guilt at not being there. *This is war*, he told himself. *There are higher priorities. We'll have other seasons.*

The heavy plane dropped into an air pocket, bouncing Adam back to the present. He had a job, and for now it was here. He picked up his camera, and trying to stay out of the crew's way, took photographs. He flashed pictures of the gunner sitting in a bubble atop the aircraft and of Dale as he worked out figures and watched for landmarks. The waist-gunners kept watch on either side of the plane.

He started toward the cockpit.

"What do you think you're doing?" Lewis asked.

"Figured I'd better get some pictures of the pilot and copilot."

"Good luck getting those cleared through the censors." He chuckled. "You'd be smarter to stay clear of them altogether. They gotta concentrate."

"I'll stay out of their way."

"Go ahead," Dale said, "but remember, this is no game. When we reach France, we'll climb. You'll need to be in your seat, oxygen on."

"Gotcha."

Lewis glowered.

Adam removed his headset and made his way to the crowded cockpit. It was slightly quieter. "Captain, you mind if I take a few pictures?"

"No. Nothing's going on right now."

Adam snapped five photographs in quick succession, catching the men as they piloted the heavy aircraft. They kept their eyes on the instruments. Sunlight glimmered through the window. They were over the English Channel. What would they find in France?

Chuck glanced at Adam. "Make sure to get my good side." He grinned.

"I'll do that."

"And if you're going to write a story about this flight, make sure you spell my name right. It's Chuck Hoffman." He proceeded to spell it. "My wife and kids will get a kick out of seeing me in a newspaper or magazine."

"I'll get it right."

"Can you have a copy sent to my home?"

"I'll see what I can do." Adam gazed out the windows. Downy clouds occasionally obscured the scenery, but for the most part, he had a clear view. He maneuvered so he could get photographs of the sea passing beneath them as well as other planes. With that done, he let his camera hang loose and grabbed his writing tablet and pencil. He asked, "I know how big this bird is, but what's her top speed?"

"Two hundred eighty-seven miles per hour."

Adam gave a low whistle while he wrote in his notebook.

"And we can cruise at twenty-five thousand feet."

"Yeah, I heard—that's why the crew uses oxygen?"

"That's right. And you probably ought to go back and get yours on. We're climbing." The captain had to yell over the rumble of the four engines.

"How far we going today?"

"About 160 miles. No problem for this Heavy."

"You ever have any trouble with antiaircraft fire?"

"Oh, yeah. We can count on it."

"Don't worry though," said the copilot. "Chuck's the best. I've seen him fly one of these things without tail feathers."

"You mean the tail was missing?" Adam asked, wondering what had happened to the tail gunner.

"Yep. Part of it, anyway."

"I'm impressed." Adam smiled. "Where we heading?"

"Rouen, France."

"I've seen a lot of planes come back damaged or heard about the ones that didn't make it."

"Yeah, the Krauts are ready and waiting. They've got fighter planes and antiaircraft guns." Chuck nodded toward the window. "See that shoreline? That's France. And the Germans will do their best to make sure we don't see home again." He glanced at Adam. "You better get in the back and put on your oxygen."

Feeling the stir of fear in his belly, Adam retreated and donned his breathing equipment. It was getting cold and he was thankful for his flight suit and gloves.

Soon after Adam settled on the hard bench, an explosion fractured the air outside the B-17, rocking them wildly. Adam moved alongside a gunner so he could see out. Puffs of smoke and flashes of light erupted about them.

Fighter planes left formation and dove away toward the green patchwork below, pursuing enemy planes. Another blast alongside them splintered the skies, and the plane bumped and lurched. The crew impressed Adam. They calmly carried out their duties, clear-headed and steady. They knew what they were doing.

"I don't see any bogeys," one of the gunners said. "I don't see nothin'."

Adam figured he must look scared because Lewis offered a smile and reassuring nod. "We'll come out of this. Been here before."

"I figured," Adam said. His stomach tumbled, and a vision of Laurel receiving a telegram announcing his death flashed through his mind.

Making a broad turn, the plane headed for its first bomb run. "You're right there, Captain," Dale said.

They started down.

"We've got a bogey at ten o'clock!" The turret gunner swiveled his gun mount and fired. Magazines clattered, spitting shell casings.

Tracers skittered across the front. The plane bucked. A burst of red exploded just outside Adam's window. He double-checked his parachute to make sure it was strapped on securely.

Lewis cranked open the bomb bay doors. They headed down.

"More flak, Captain!" the copilot yelled.

"Oh, yeah! This is a rhubarb run for sure," Lewis hooted.

"Rhubarb?" Adam asked.

"We're running so low we can see the rhubarb," Lewis smirked.

They continued to track. Adam chanced a peek out the gunner's window. They were coming up on what looked like a railroad yard.

"We're hit! Captain, we're hit!" Adam heard as the plane bucked.

The B-17 held its course. Then the bombs were gone, and the plane nosed up. Below, bright bursts and billowing smoke rose. The plane hopped with each explosion. The men cheered.

"Another bogey at two o'clock!" one of the gunners hollered.

"We got no help!" another crewman yelled. "We need air cover!"

The plane rumbled and turned heavily toward the left. Adam's stomach somersaulted.

A blast shot away the gunner's tower, taking a man with it.

"That's it. We're in trouble now!" shouted Lewis.

A spray of fire cut across the ship's nose. The gunner's body jerked and slumped. The bomber shook and bucked, then pitched forward and began a steep descent.

"Time to hit the silk!" Dale called. "Everyone out!" He pushed open the door. Gripping the side rails, he stood against the wind.

Adam's mouth had gone dry, and he thought he was going to be sick. He glanced up at the place where the turret gunner had been. He was gone and so was the tower. The cockpit was splattered with blood. Chuck and the copilot were both dead.

Lewis leaped out the door and was sucked from sight.

Adam stared. He'd have to jump. Everything he'd been taught had gone out of his mind. He couldn't remember how to open the chute.

"Come on!" shouted Dale. "Time to go!"

The plane tipped.

"Now or never!" he yelled and grabbed Adam, shoving him toward the door. "You know what to do?"

Adam looked down at his parachute harness. He tapped his rip cord handle. "Get free of the plane and pull this?"

"That's it. And get rid of that camera. It's liable to knock you out cold," Dale shouted.

Adam pushed it inside his jacket. "No way! I'll need it!"

Dale shrugged and pushed him out.

Adam tumbled. His stomach rose into his throat. He was going to be sick. Wind whistling, he grabbed the ripcord and pulled. The chute rustled as it unfolded, then snapped open. Adam was jerked upward. Gulping air, he gripped the lines.

The roar of the plane drew his gaze. Trailing smoke, the B-17 rolled, then spun. It tumbled earthward, its downward passage protracted. Adam watched as it slammed into the ground and torched.

Remembering that he was falling into enemy territory, he tore his eyes from the spectacle and surveyed the landscape. He needed to get his bearings. Below lay a patchwork of farms, fields, and forest—no cities or towns. The only landmark was a river winding southward. How would he escape this country?

He spotted two drifting chutes and silently cheered. He wasn't alone. Trained airmen would know what to do, how to get help.

A burst of gunfire cut through the quiet. Horrified, Adam watched bullets tear through one man. His body jerked, then lay limp as he continued to descend. *That must be Lewis.* He looked up and saw Dale. Pulling on his lines, he tried to steer the chute away from the enemy fire. His efforts made no difference. *Lord, make me invisible,* Adam prayed.

Studying the countryside, he tried to decide which way he should head once he was on the ground, that is, if he was still alive when he got there. *The river. That's the only answer. People live along rivers. Maybe I can find help.*

Another burst of gunfire shattered the whoosh of the wind. Dale yelled. More shooting. He screamed, then slumped in the harness.

The ground rose up quickly. Adam prepared to land but drifted toward a grove of trees. *Please not that,* he thought, heading straight at a broad oak. He plunged through splintering limbs that cut and scratched as he dropped. Rather than falling all the way to the ground, he stopped abruptly, dangling a few feet above the earth. He was tangled in the limbs.

Sliding a knife out of his knapsack, he cut the lines and dropped to the ground. He couldn't leave the chute hanging on the limbs of the tree. It would be like leaving a signpost of his arrival. Glancing about in search of approaching German soldiers, he struggled to yank it free. He pulled harder. Finally the chute gave and he tumbled backward.

After stashing the damaged parachute in a hollow trunk, he turned and studied the French countryside. He stood in the midst of an oak and beech grove. Beyond lay what looked like an endless sea of rolling hills, dotted with trees, cattle, and sheep.

He needed to get as far away from the drop spot as possible, but where should he go? "Anywhere's better than here," he said, dragging his rifle out of his pack. He crouched beside an oak, pressed the gun against his shoulder, and peered through the sights. It gave him a sense of control, and he felt slightly better.

A twig popped. Adam dropped to his stomach, his automatic ready. He caught a glimpse of movement in the brush. Pressing into the ground, he rested his elbows on the grass and steadied his firearm. He worked to quiet his breathing.

Someone emerged from behind a tree. Adam touched the trigger.

"American? You American?" asked a skinny, dark-haired woman with a child strapped to her back.

"Yes," Adam said, rising and keeping the rifle on her.

The woman forced a smile. "Monsieur, maybe you help me and my Adin?" She patted the child. "Please."

"Help you? How?"

"You take us to American soldiers. They can help, yes?"

"No. I don't know where any soldiers are. Do you?"

She shook her head no, her brown eyes holding Adam's. "You came from the plane?"

"Yes."

Her eyes filled with moisture. "I hoped . . . maybe . . . there were American soldiers. I think maybe they are waiting for you." She sat and transferred her little boy into her arms. He remained quiet. Holding him against her chest, she rocked. "There is no hope for us."

Adam expected German soldiers to appear at any moment. He scanned the trees and the fields. "I have to get out of here. I've got to go. They're probably looking for me."

The woman continued to rock. She didn't look up.

What should I do? Adam wondered. It wasn't right to just leave her and the boy. He couldn't do anything for them. "Sorry I can't help you." Guilt settled over him like a weight. He checked his compass. He'd head northwest. Staying low, Adam started across the field to the nearest grove of trees.

"Wait. Monsieur, wait. Please wait." With the little boy in her arms, the woman ran after him. "I will go with you. You will help me. Yes?"

"No, I can't help you."

"But if I do not escape France, they will kill me and my son."

"Why? You're French, aren't you?"

"*Oui.* I am French." She stared at the ground and appeared to be thinking. When she looked at Adam, her dark eyes challenged him. "I am also a Jew."

Adam had heard that Jews were being exterminated, but he hadn't found any hard evidence to prove the rumors. He sat and propped his rifle between his knees. Scrubbing his face with his hands, he looked at her. *She knows French. That'll be a help.* "All right. You can come with me, but I don't know what I can do for you. I need to get out of France. Do you know your way around this country?"

"*Oui.*"

"Do you know anyone who would help an American?"

"I do not know. Maybe . . . I can find someone." She scanned the field and the forest. "Come. We go this way."

Adam stood and followed, wondering if he was doing the right thing.

Chapter 13

THE ONLY THING OVERRIDING ADAM'S HUNGER WAS HIS THIRST. HE WISHED Elisa had chosen to follow the river he'd seen from the air. Hopefully, they'd pass by a stream or river soon; he watched for one.

Already they'd been walking for hours. Elisa continued on without complaint, revealing no sign of fatigue. Her stoicism quieted Adam's own grievances. Even her young son did not complain. Adam wondered at his age. He was small, but the look in his eyes gave him the appearance of being older than a child. Part of the time Adin traveled in the pack on his mother's back, and at other times he walked. His legs looked more like sticks than limbs, but he managed to keep up.

Elisa led the way, trudging steadily northward on a dusty road. Adam remained alert to danger, but from time to time he studied his uncommon partner. Although obviously sturdy, she looked critically thin; her colorless, ankle-length dress nearly swallowed her. A belt cinched at the waist was the only thing providing a glimmer of the curves that had once been. Perfectly arched brows and a pallid forehead framed dark, serious eyes that reminded him of large, iridescent opals. Well-defined cheekbones angled softly toward full lips that held no sign of happiness.

A bell jangled in the distance. It hung from the neck of a brown-and-white milk cow that grabbed mouthfuls of grass, then chewed contentedly. She surveyed her domain, a broad green pasture that rose and reached out beyond a knoll. At one end a band of sheep grazed. Beyond a cross fence a farmer and a boy, whom Adam assumed to be his son, piled hay into the back of a wagon. The man lifted his hand in greeting. Elisa and Adam returned the gesture.

"Could we get something to drink or maybe eat here?" Adam asked. They'd seen few people, and those they had passed had either ignored them or eyed them with suspicion. This might be their only opportunity.

"Not here. Soon we will have water. I know a place. And I have a little food."

They moved on, and with the passing minutes Adam became more and more pessimistic about making it back to England. How would he ever be reunited with the allied forces? Although he was certain the fatally wounded bomber had been spotted, there would be no rescue. He would have to find his own way out—but how?

The roadway divided into two lanes, one continuing west and the other turning north. Elisa stopped. She seemed indecisive.

Adam waited for a few minutes, then asked, "So, which way?"

A cooling breeze played with Elisa's dark hair. She brushed it off her face. "This road leads to Le Havre on the coast. The other will take us north to Amiens." She paused. "I have friends near Amiens." Shaking her head, she continued, "But I do not wish to put them in danger." She looked at Adam.

The intensity of her dark brown eyes bore into him. It was unsettling.

"I do not know if they will help. They have children, three little ones." She paused. "If they were arrested . . . it would break my heart."

"Can we get help in Le Havre?"

"I know no one there. It is a large township. It sits along the coast, but the Germans are very vigilant. The channel is closely guarded. I do not know how we could cross." She was unable to hide her despair.

"*Maman*." Adin tugged on her skirt and said something to her in French.

Elisa spoke to him in gentle tones, then looked up at Adam. "He is hungry. Always hungry." Her eyes teared. "I have only bread." She scooped up the little boy and, cradling him against her chest, headed off the road into a grove of oak. Making sure they were well inside the copse, she sat and reached into a knapsack. She brought out a paper bag and retrieved a chunk of dark bread. Breaking off a portion from the softer insides, she handed it to her son. He pushed it into his mouth and, with his cheeks bulging, nuzzled close to his *maman* and chewed.

Huge dark eyes so much like his mother's stared at Adam. Elisa tore off another piece, picked off a spot of mold, and offered it to Adam.

He nearly refused, knowing he was taking from their meager supply, but his empty stomach ached. Accepting the offering, he said, "Thanks."

They ate the meager meal in silence, alert and listening for German soldiers. Adam kept his rifle in hand. The Browning automatic, known as a BAR by servicemen, gave him some comfort. This was a soldier's weapon of choice. It was powerful, accurate, and held twenty rounds in the magazine.

"Monsieur, why is it you Americans wait so long?" Elisa asked, ending the silence.

"Wait so long for what?"

She chewed and swallowed. "Your army has not come to help us. We wait and hope, but the Germans, they take over our towns, kill our people—and still the Americans do not come."

"What do you think those planes were all about? Those were U.S. bombers. They were sent to take out German targets. We can't just traipse in and take over," Adam said incredulously, unable to push down his defensiveness. "And we weren't at war. This wasn't *our* war."

She glared at Adam, her brown eyes black. "And so you cannot be troubled? Our children are dying, our husbands . . ." Her voice caught. ". . . are dying."

"We've been supplying arms to the allies," Adam said, knowing the United States could have done more, or at least done something sooner. "We're still fighting our way through Africa. We can't just step into a war. An army needs weaponry, planes, and ships. The Japanese nearly destroyed our navy. We're building planes, but it takes time."

"*Oui.* I know. I am sorry . . . I am grateful." She forced a smile, but the gesture only made the sorrow eating through her more palpable and more painful to watch.

Adam couldn't look at her. He placed his last bite of bread into his mouth. It was stale and slightly moldy, but it had quieted his hunger. Still, they would need more than old bread if they were going to make it to Britain.

As if reading his mind, Elisa said, "We will find more to eat. Maybe we can catch a rabbit? Or find eggs at a farm?"

"You mean steal eggs?" Adam teased.

Elisa did not see the humor in his remark. "I will do whatever I must."

Keeping his eyes on the road, Adam asked, "Why do you speak such good English?"

"My parents. They were educated and believed their children also should be. I also speak German. It may be of help."

"I hope we won't need it."

She glanced up the road.

"So, you know people in Amiens?"

"Yes."

"Do you think they will help us?"

"If they can. They know many people, maybe some in the resistance. But . . ." She shook her head. "It is very dangerous." Elisa rested a hand on her son's head. "He is all I have. I will do anything to protect him." Her expression tormented, she added, "If we are caught, we will be killed."

He'd heard the stories. There'd been accusations of atrocities committed against Jews, but they seemed inconceivable. He'd hoped they were exaggerations. "You've got to get out of the country."

"*Oui*. But how? I was hoping you would know something or someone."

"I don't. Believe me, I would do something if I did." Adam pushed to his feet. "Now, we've got to find water." He glanced at Adin. "I can carry him."

"He does not trust strangers." She looked at her son. "But he is getting heavy." She spoke to him in French. The little boy eyed Adam suspiciously but allowed himself to be handed over to the American. At first Adin studied Adam, holding his body stiffly away from him. Finally he settled his head against Adam's shoulder and returned to sleep.

"I have a son, William. He'll be five in December."

"Adin is almost three."

"Three?" Adam said, unable to contain his surprise. The child barely looked two. A fresh rush of sympathy hit him. What kind of deprivation had this woman and little boy withstood? "He's a beautiful child."

"He is." Elisa caressed Adin's cheek.

By late afternoon they came upon a small lake, and Elisa filled her flask, and all three drank their fill before moving on. The August sun basted the travelers, dust adding to the discomfort. With each step it puffed into the air, coating their lungs and settling in their eyes. Feeling vulnerable they continued, often traveling parallel to the road, making their way through fields and groves of trees.

"Tell me about your home," Elisa said, breaking a long silence.

"I live in Alaska. Do you know where that is?"

"Yes. I am educated, remember?" She managed a small smile. "Alaska is very far north on the American continent, and it is cold."

"Actually, it's only cold in the winter. Summers are mild, and we get a lot of sun." He gazed at an open field dotted with haystacks, which looked very much like a painting he'd seen once and admired. In the painting the stacks of hay had merely been splotches of yellow paint dropped on a canvas. "I live in a broad valley with lots of farms."

"So, it is like here?"

"Yes, but not so open. We have mountains and thick forests surrounding the valley. It's beautiful there."

Elisa scuffed the earth, and a dusty cloud lifted. "Here we have mountains, but they are far away. I have visited them. They are . . ." She sought the right word. "Formidable," she said with reverence.

"The Alps?"

"Yes. One day when the war is over, you must go to see them." She looked at Adam with a penetrating gaze. "You have a family?"

"Yes. My father and mother died when I was a baby, but I have a wife, Laurel, and a son, William. Plus, Laurel's family feels like my own."

"Why are you here?"

"Most American men are fighting, except for the old or the ones who are too sick. I'm not actually in the army or the air corp. I'm a journalist. My job is to write about the war and take photographs."

"Is that what you were doing when the plane was shot down?"

"Yep. I was just a passenger on a bombing run. All I was supposed to do was record history."

"I saw you and the others in the sky. I thought you would be killed."

"I thought so too," Adam said, sadly remembering the men who had died. "I don't know why I made it." He felt a shadow of confusion. It didn't seem right that he had lived and the others had died.

"You are not to blame," Elisa said gently. "You did not kill those men."

"I know," Adam said, feeling as if she'd climbed inside his mind. How had she known? "You mentioned a husband. What happened to him?"

Elisa's eyes turned darker. She kept her gaze on the ground in front of her and hurried her steps. "He is dead. All of my family is dead. Except Adin."

Stunned and wishing he hadn't asked, Adam started to apologize. "I'm sorry. I . . ."

"The *Milice* took them." Her tone was venomous. She glanced at him. "The Germans."

"You don't know they're dead for certain then."

"I know. They were taken to the camps." She glanced at Adin, who still slept on Adam's shoulder. "The gas and the ovens."

"The gas and ovens?"

"Yes." She gave Adam a quizzical look. "You Americans do not know?"

"I'm not informed about what our government knows or doesn't know. I've only heard rumors about prison camps."

"They are extermination camps." Elisa shook her head. "The world watches while people die. Jews or anyone who helps them are the Gestapo's targets. Some are arrested and tortured. It would be better to die." She turned hard, hateful eyes on Adam. "There . . . at the camps Jews are killed and burned in ovens."

The ground felt as if it dropped out from beneath Adam, and he stumbled. Nausea swept over him. Did the U.S. government know?

"Thousands, maybe more, of my people are dead." Her eyes became awash with tears. "Why did you Americans wait so long?" Before Adam could speak, she held up her hand. "No. Do not say. There is no answer." She moved ahead, putting an end to the conversation.

Late in the day, a grinding and screeching din echoed from beyond a rise. Rumbling accompanied the clamor. The ground trembled. Adam and Elisa stopped.

"What is it?" Adam asked in an anxious whisper.

Elisa didn't answer. Motionless, she listened. "Germans!" She scooped up Adin, who had been walking beside her, and ran to the edge of the road. There were no trees or brush—no place to hide! "Come!" she called, galloping toward the rise.

"Where are you going? They'll see us!" Adam called.

Just as a tank crested the hill, he dove off the road and lay flat. "They'll see us!" he hissed, looking about for a hiding place.

"This way!" Elisa called, dropping to the ground. Staying low, she crawled forward. Adin clung to her neck. She stopped abruptly and pushed him into the side of a bank. She followed him, disappearing into the earth.

"What in the world?" Adam asked, hustling after them. *There must be some kind of tunnel or culvert or something,* he thought.

Elisa peeked out of a drainpipe. "Come. Come. Quickly!"

Adam doubted it was wide enough to allow for his frame, but he had no choice, so he slid in, feet first. Lying on his belly, he pushed himself backward. By the time the tank rumbled above, he had managed to squeeze completely inside. Elisa and Adin hid behind him. Lying in the darkness, Adam prayed.

Adin whimpered and Elisa shushed him, then in a soft voice said something in French. The child quieted.

A pair of black boots marched past. Holding his breath, Adam pressed his face down in his arms, hoping he had moved far enough into the pipe so he lay hidden in deep shadows. His heart hammered against his ribs.

Another soldier passed, then more. The men were talking, sounding confident and in high spirits. Adam wished he understood the guttural language. Minutes felt like hours, but finally the soldiers and their war machines moved on, leaving the three outcasts in their dark burrow.

Adam climbed free and stretched tight muscles. "I wonder where they're heading."

"One of the soldiers said Paris. They are preparing for an attack on the Americans. Hitler says Germany will move on America."

"They wouldn't dare do that."

"The Germans dare. They do as they choose." She faced Adam, meeting his eyes. "They will not stop."

Adam felt a surge of apprehension. *No. They wouldn't attack, not on American soil.* Even as he considered the possibility, he remembered Japan. They'd done it. His thoughts went to his family. Alaska was vulnerable. What would happen to Laurel and William if the Japanese or Germans attacked there? *They're alone. I shouldn't have left them.*

Just before dark Elisa, Adin, and Adam risked sneaking into a barn close to the roadway. Black clouds had blotted out the sun and thunder rumbled. Rain was likely, and Adin was already weak. Even a simple illness could kill him. Exhausted, they dropped onto a pile of hay and burrowed in to fend off the cold night air.

Weary, Adam lay staring into the dusk, listening to the last whistles of birds settling in for the night, the whisper of the wind, and the first splashes of rain on the barn roof. The smell of hay and munching animals was comforting. It reminded Adam of home.

He studied Elisa and Adin in the fading light and felt a deepening kinship with them. Unable to explain the connection, he decided it must be a natural result of needing each other, a kind of solidarity. *Father, please let nothing harm them,* he prayed before sinking into a cavernous sleep.

The next morning Adam was prodded awake by something cold and wet. He opened his eyes and looked straight into the face of an inquisitive black dog. "Hello fel . . ." he started, then noticed a pair of boots and a shotgun directly behind the animal.

He sat upright. A large man who looked to be about thirty-five and wearing overalls stared at him. He was clean-shaven and wore a small cap.

The man said something in French.

"I don't understand," Adam said.

Elisa sat up. Brushing hay out of her hair, she spoke to the man in French, then told Adam, "He wants to know who we are. I told him we are just travelers who needed a place to sleep. I said our car broke down a couple of miles from here just before dark."

The farmer spoke again.

"He does not believe us," Elisa said, then responded to the man. Adam heard their names and the word American.

The man lowered his rifle and softened his stance.

"It is all right. He knows the truth."

The farmer held out his hand to Elisa and helped her to her feet. He said something, his tone pleasant. Adam stood.

"M. Arnaude Cervier wants to know if we would like some breakfast." Elisa smiled.

"Breakfast?" Adam asked in disbelief, his stomach gnawing on its own emptiness. "I can't think of anything better." He leveled a serious gaze on Elisa. "Did you tell him you're Jewish?"

"No. But he knows." She looked down at her son who clung to her legs and spoke to him.

The man smiled and leaned over to tousle Adin's hair. The boy huddled close to his mother. The farmer leveled serious eyes on Elisa and spoke in a somber tone.

"What did he say?" Adam asked.

"Monsieur Cervier wants to help. He and his wife have assisted others like us."

Silently Adam thanked God. It had felt as if they'd been abandoned, but the Lord had been watching over them.

For two weeks Adam and Elisa worked for the farmer and waited for the help he'd promised. Arnaude Cervier and his wife, Nadine, had hidden many Jews and managed to smuggle them out of the country with the help of others in the resistance. However, German security along the coastline had been tightened. They would have to wait.

Adam and Elisa waited uneasily . . . always watching for Germans. None came. The waiting was good for Adin. Having more food and a warm bed had brought the color back into his face. He was stronger and even smiled on occasion. Sometimes he chased after chickens or marveled at the eggs they laid. One morning while Adam was milking, Adin watched. Seizing the moment, Adam turned the teat and splashed milk on the youngster's face. Giggling, Adin tumbled backward.

Adam gathered him up in a hug. Remembering his own son, he felt an ache for his home and family. He had to find a way to get back home—soon.

Adam straightened and discovered Elisa watching them. Her arms folded over her chest, she wore a smile that touched her eyes. "You are good for him." The smile faded. "I have not seen him play like that since his father was arrested."

Adam set Adin on his feet. "When was that?"

"Eleven months ago."

"Eleven months? How have you made it?"

"I do what I must. We stay here and there, eat from the garbage pails and pig troughs. We sleep where it is dry." She studied her hands. "And now, God has smiled on us. We will have our freedom and maybe even go to America."

"I hope so, Elisa," Adam said, tenderness for the woman welling up. He felt a compulsion to hold her and tell her the world could be beautiful and that everything would turn out fine. He wanted to make things right for her and for Adin.

His eyes slid from her face to the subtle curves beneath her simple cotton dress. They lingered a moment, then returned to her face. Her freshly washed hair hung in thick waves over her shoulders, framing unblemished pale skin and deep brown eyes. There was something hauntingly beautiful about her. He knew he should look away, but she drew him.

All of a sudden his mind returned to Laurel. He could see her and the hurt she'd feel if she knew his thoughts. This was a betrayal.

"I better get this milk into the house," he said. "They'll be wondering if I'm making butter." He hefted the pail and walked to the door. Elisa remained in the doorway. Adam stopped. "I have to get the milk in," he said and brushed past her.

Chapter 14

"It is time to eat," called Nadine. "Come in."

Adam understood enough to know the gist of what she'd said. He finished sorting through the dirt and roots in his hands and dropped hard round potatoes into a bucket, then shoved a pitchfork into the earth. He left it standing like a sentry. "I'm starved."

"Me too," said Elisa, dusting off her hands.

Arnaude pushed a wheelbarrow piled with potatoes toward the root cellar and parked it beside the stairway.

Adam and Elisa headed for the house. Adin slipped around Nadine and ran to his mother. "*Maman*," he cried, his arms uplifted.

"*Bonjour*," Elisa said tenderly and scooped up the boy, speaking lovingly to him in French.

Adam followed Elisa and Adin into the house, wishing they were Laurel and William and that they were gathering together at home in Palmer. Standing alongside Elisa, he washed at the kitchen sink.

The children had found seats at the table, and the cottage smelled of freshly baked bread and cooking vegetables. It conjured up images of home.

"*Asseyez vous*," Nadine said, nodding toward a chair.

Adam now understood some of the language and gladly obeyed, sitting across from the Cervier girls. Their blue eyes smiling, they studied him, still curious about the American in their midst. "Smells good," Adam said.

Elisa sat beside Adam, and Arnaude settled his thickset body at the head of the table. He'd rolled his shirtsleeves up to the elbows and had scrubbed his arms. Taking his wife's hand, he bowed his head and prayed.

After the soup had been ladled out and bread passed around, Arnaude settled a serious gaze on Elisa and spoke soberly.

"What did he say?" Adam asked.

Elisa's dark eyes had turned hopeful. "He said some people will help us escape . . . next week."

"Where are we going?"

Elisa turned to Arnaude and repeated Adam's question.

Arnaude spoke.

"It is to be a secret," Elisa explained. "If we do not know, then we cannot say . . . no matter what might happen to us."

Adam nodded. It made sense. He looked at Arnaude. "*Merci.*"

With a bob of the head and a smile for Adam, Arnaude spooned soup into his mouth.

Adam felt hope growing. Maybe he would make it home. He dipped bread into his potage and took a bite. The blend of vegetables and beef stock had a sturdy, wholesome flavor. "This is good," he told Nadine. "You are a good cook."

Nadine started to say something when the sound of a vehicle back-firing carried in from outside. They heard the grinding of gears. Arnaude went to the window and peered out. "Milice!" he hissed. While sliding the table toward the center of the room, he fired orders in French.

Adam caught sight of a German truck turning into the drive. It would take them no more than a couple of minutes to make their way from the road.

Everyone knew what to do. Seven-year-old Abella cleared off the extra dishes, rinsed them and set them in the cupboard. Five-year-old Lynette and the youngest, Claire, each moved a chair out of the way, while Nadine grabbed another chair and threw back a rug lying beneath the table, exposing the wooden floor. She slid her fingers beneath a hidden groove and lifted a door.

Adam stared at a hollow in the floor. He'd never have seen the trap door.

Arnaude yelled something.

"Get in!" Elisa grabbed Adin and climbed into the small cavity. Adam clambered in beside her. The two lay side by side with Adin tucked between them.

Arnaude hastily scribbled something on a slip of paper and handed it to Adam. "He will help you. Let no one see it," he said in French, and Elisa quickly interpreted. He fixed his eyes on his guests for a moment, then put a finger to his mouth and lowered the door.

Fear and darkness encased the fugitives. Adam strained to see while listening to the sounds of the table and chairs being returned to their rightful places. Clinking of flatware against porcelain told him the family members had reseated themselves and were now doing their best to eat.

Adam could feel the tension in Elisa's body and the tremble of her limbs. Adin whimpered. Elisa spoke gently. The little boy turned still. Adam laid a hand on hers and squeezed; then barely breathing, he turned his eyes to floorboards only inches above his head. He was certain the thudding of his heart could be heard.

A rap on the front door boomed. Adam nearly jumped.

A chair scraped overhead, followed by casual steps moving across the floor. The door creaked on old hinges as it was opened. "*Bonjour,*" Arnaude said.

A sharp German command cut into his greeting. The rap of boots moved into the house. A long pause hung over family and intruders. Finally a man spoke gently and evenly in German.

Like a snake tasting the air before it strikes, Adam thought.

Arnaude answered in broken German and with a smattering of French.

The German spoke again, only more sharply.

Arnaude answered. Adam thought he'd said Juden but wasn't certain. Both men were speaking rapidly.

Demanding steps traveled across the room, followed by a staccato of harsh angry German.

Nadine's plaintive cry interrupted the intruder's discourse. A child's sob stabbed at Adam. What if it were William who was terrified?

More orders were given. Elisa gripped Adam's hand and tightened her hold on Adin. A mix of German and French was shouted back and forth, then anguished cries from Nadine. Then weeping.

Something crashed to the floor. What sounded like the table being moved sent prickles of fear through Adam. His pulse accelerated. He felt as if massive amounts of blood were flooding his veins and overwhelming him. If only he had his rifle. Why had he left it in the barn? If they were discovered, what would he do? He tried to work out a plan. There was no way he could attack the soldiers without being killed first. Would he go quietly? And to what? His execution? A prison camp? And what of Elisa and Adin? *Father, hide us. Keep this place secret.*

Someone stomped on the floor directly overhead. It held firm, with no hint of hollowness. Arnaude had done well. The hidden door remained tightly closed. Then they heard more shouts, breaking dishes, and the clatter of falling furniture and unnamed objects. Above the uproar, Arnaude's voice carried, calm and entreating. Elisa pressed her face against Adam's shoulder, and he felt wetness. She was crying.

Nadine's voice pleaded. The children cried.

Everything in Adam screamed for him to stop hiding and help. But to do so would mean death for Elisa and Adin. He couldn't do that to them. He squeezed his eyes closed and forced himself to remain still.

A sharp order was given and quiet enveloped the house. The command was repeated, and footsteps marched toward the front door, then moved outside and across the porch. No more protests were heard. Everything turned quiet.

Adam felt as if he and the house had been swallowed up in a pervasive silence. Now he knew what it was like to be buried alive. Sounding far away, an engine fired and drained the last of Adam's hope. *No! Not these good people!*

The vehicle moved away.

Only silence and the sound of his own breathing remained.

Adam, Elisa, and Adin remained, still and waiting. After a while Adam heard the rhythmic breaths of sleep. Adin had fallen asleep. *Good,* he thought, envious of the child's trust.

Several minutes passed. They remained silent and motionless. Finally Adam whispered, "They're gone. I don't think they're coming back."

"We wait a little more," Elisa said softly.

More time passed and still no sounds came from above. Finally Adam fumbled in the darkness for the latch, unhooked it, and pushed open the door just a few inches. A wedge of light cut into the darkness.

He peeked out. No one was there. He lifted it fully and stood, gazing at the room. The rug had been thrown back and the table moved. Chairs lay on their sides, shelves were stripped, their contents littering the floor. The front door stood open.

Adam glanced down at Elisa and Adin. "You wait," he said, climbing from the hideaway. Staying low, he crossed to the window and peered out. Unbelievably, the world looked normal. Chickens clucked and pecked at the ground, the cow stood in the corral lazily swishing her tail, and the wheelbarrow filled with potatoes remained where Arnaude had left it. Even the pitchfork Adam had jabbed into the ground stood.

With Adin cuddled against her, Elisa joined Adam. Her face was stricken. She'd seen this before. Her eyes rested on the wheelbarrow. "They took no food. They did not come for food."

Adam rested his hand on her shoulder.

She glanced at him, then turned her eyes to the yard. Her voice dripping with loathing, she spoke in French.

Adam righted two of the chairs, then dropped into one of them. Now what? The Cerviers were gone. They would most probably be killed. How would he, Elisa, and Adin escape the same fate?

Her face a mask of despair, Elisa's gaze took in the room, then rested on the cavity where they had hidden. "Why did they not see it?"

"I don't know. Arnaude is a good carpenter. He made it sturdy." Adam stared out the window, then said softly, "I think God answered my prayer."

Elisa nodded half-heartedly and rested her cheek against her son's dark hair. "I hope he hears the Cerviers' prayers also."

"They are good people," Adam said. He turned and looked at Elisa. "Now we need to figure out how to stay alive."

Elisa wiped at her nose. "Arnaude gave you a piece of paper?"

Adam reached into his pocket and unfolded the scrap. Two names were written on it. One he recognized as a town that lay near the coast, and the other was a person's name. He handed it to Elisa.

"He must have meant we are to go to Abbeville and meet someone named Jacques Billaud." Her eyes brightened. "He must be the one who will help us." She shredded the paper.

"How far is Abbeville from here?"

"Many days travel."

"I'll get my BAR," Adam said, as if using the name often used by servicemen would fuel his confidence. The Browning Automatic was a heavily built rifle, powerful and considered dependable. However, in these overwhelming circumstances, it was probably about as helpful as a popgun. One man, a woman, and a child against the Nazis had little hope of success. "While I'm out there, I'll fill the canteens." Adam started for the door.

Elisa nodded. "Arnaude and Nadine will not be back. We can take what we need."

"You really believe they have no chance?"

"No. And for this I am sorry." Elisa headed for the kitchen cabinet.

With a heavy sigh, Adam said, "I'll get some eggs too. If I stuff my pack with straw, that ought to protect them."

"Ah, yes. That is good."

Adam hesitated. He knew Elisa must be feeling the same sense of hopelessness he was feeling. "Everything will turn out all right," he said, trying to encourage her. "We'll find Jacques. We'll make it to England. I know it. God will take care of us."

Elisa faced him, anger and torment touching her eyes. "God? I have not seen him. I pray your belief will be enough."

Adam had no response. What could he say? God did seem far away.

Adam stopped to glance at the throbbing fireball in the sky. He mopped his face and neck. He wouldn't have expected this kind of heat in September. He gulped down a few mouthfuls of water and handed the flask to Elisa, who shared with Adin. The three continued on, careful to stay off the road whenever possible. The enemy might appear at any moment.

Evidence of the German occupation was everywhere. Empty bomb canisters, shell casings, German helmets, and food rations littered the way. More than once Elisa kicked at a piece of refuse, watching with satisfaction as it sailed away.

Although Adam had never experienced the same degree of persecution as Elisa and her son, he remembered the hurt and hatred he had felt growing up as an orphan. He and the other boys in the orphanage had never known when the overseer, Eli Hersch, might decide to parcel out his special punishment. Eli had taken pleasure in brutality.

Living in fear, never knowing when torture might come, had cut deeply. Adam understood the hopelessness that accompanies an agonizing situation that seems to have no end. He remembered hatred so deep that it engulfed him and how he'd clung to and nurtured it. That hatred had placed a wedge between himself and God. He prayed Elisa and Adin would not fall prey to the same snare.

Elisa slowed as they approached a village. Even the friendliest-looking person could turn out to be an enemy. On the outskirts people worked farms, and Elisa explained how, like the Cerviers, these people would not be allowed to keep what they grew but would be forced to hand over all but a small amount of their crops to the German army.

They walked into the hamlet. It was clear that the French and Germans had battled over this piece of ground. The town had been destroyed by shelling. Adam wondered how many French had died defending their homes.

He itched to photograph the damage but didn't dare expose his camera to probing eyes. Portions of stone walls stood like dead remains; they were all that remained of homes and businesses. Some buildings had two or three walls still standing while others were no more than piles of rubble. A few had windows and rooftops. A gust of wind sent grit into the air and into Adam's eyes and nose causing his eyes to water.

Adam stopped in front of a stairway that for all intents and purposes led nowhere. The stone steps stood alongside a wall, but the rest of the building had been blown away. It was a disturbing site and gave him an empty, horrified sensation in the pit of his stomach.

Gripping his rifle, he cautiously moved through town. No one remained, except for an occasional woman or child searching through debris. Thunder rumbled in the distance, and the air smelled of rain. Adam studied bulging black clouds moving across the farmland toward them. "We better find shelter."

Elisa resettled Adin on her hip. "It will feel good to get off my feet."

Adam nodded and offered Adin a smile.

The boy held out his arms to the American.

"Ah. He likes you," Elisa said, offering her son to Adam.

He draped his rifle over his shoulder and took the youngster, swinging him onto his shoulders. "A building back there looked pretty stable. At least it had part of a roof."

Moving back to the building, he picked his way through fallen rock, mortar, and glass that littered the street. When he reached the bombed-out structure, he set Adin on the ground, motioned for the boy to stay with his mother, and proceeded into the dark gaping shell. His skin prickled with tension.

A main room was cluttered with the usual assemblage of rock and mortar. He also spotted an overturned table and a broken chair. He peeked inside a small side room. It was empty. Moving back into the central area, he stopped in front of a crumbling doorway that led to a bombed-out room. A sign saying "toilette" hung over the entrance. "Hey, at least we have a lavatory," he called.

Elisa joined him. "Ah, yes. And it will stay fresh as a summer breeze, no?" She chuckled.

Adin was asleep before nightfall. With his stomach full of bread, cheese, and a raw egg, he'd snuggled into a blanket beside his mother. She kissed his forehead. "I wish I could tell Nadine how much I appreciate her gifts." Sorrow robbed her dark brown eyes of their richness. "It is evil . . . what the Germans have done. Even the little ones suffer." She smoothed Adin's hair. "This is not for him. He deserves a better life."

"He'll have it," Adam said with an assurance he didn't feel.

Elisa settled unbelieving eyes on him. "I have no identification papers. If we are stopped, Adin and I will be arrested and killed."

"We won't be discovered."

"I hope you are right. I hope this is not a foolish American dream." A cold wind blew through the vacant windows. She tucked the blanket more tightly around Adin. "And what is it your son is doing now?"

"I wish I knew," Adam said sadly. He was quiet, then said, "He's probably having breakfast." His voice faltered. He missed his family.

"And what is it that he does with his days?"

Adam had nearly forgotten Elisa was there. He focused on her and tried to think. "He loves to fish. The salmon run is over, but he'll still try for one. He and his uncle, Brian, will go. First he has chores though. We have a farm, and there's always a lot to be done." He smiled softly. "I wonder if they've had the fair yet. He loves the fair."

Adam picked up a stick and poked at the embers in the fire. "This time of year farmers show off their produce and livestock. We grow cabbages this big." To demonstrate the size, he held his hands out as if he were holding a basketball.

"Really? That is very large."

"They get big from the long hours of sunlight." Adam's mind wandered to Laurel. She probably had all the canning done for the winter, and the carrots, onions, and potatoes would be stored in the root cellar. Hopefully the smokehouse was also well stocked, with plenty of fish, canned salmon, and game.

She thinks I'm dead. An ache settled in the center of him. *Father, let her know I'm alive and that I'm coming home.*

"You seem far away, Monsieur," Elisa said.

The tenderness in Elisa's voice unsettled Adam. He needed tenderness. "I was thinking of home and how things would be there now."

"Tell me about it."

Adam closed his eyes and imagined it, then stared at the fire. "It's beautiful. The leaves on the trees have turned gold and red. The air is crisp and cool, and in the mornings ice is on puddles and frost covers the fields. The first snows are already in the mountains. Everyone's getting ready for winter."

"Ah, so you have a lot of snow in winter?"

"Yes. Everything turns white."

"But of course. We get snow here also. It is beautiful."

Lightning lit the sky and Elisa startled. Thunder followed. She gazed at the heavens. "When I was a child, storms frightened me." She hugged her knees. "It is still so. I am afraid. Only now I think it is the Germans who frighten me."

"What will you do after the war?" Adam asked, hoping to distract her.

"I do not know." Elisa rested her chin on her knees. "My family is gone, my friends . . . gone." She studied Adin. "We will begin again—in a new place." She settled dark eyes on Adam. "Is there a place in America for people like us?"

"America always has room for quality people. Maybe I can help. I'll talk to immigration after we're rescued."

"Is America as grand as everyone says?"

"It's grand, all right. But not perfect. There are good people and bad people, but we're free to live our lives as we want. A person can go as far as his or her dreams will take them. You can too. All it takes is desire and hard work." He nodded at Adin. "He will have every opportunity."

"We are Jewish. Are Jews welcome in America?"

Adam had heard stories of people who hated Jews. He chose his words carefully. "There is a place for you and Adin. That doesn't mean it will be easy. Some people dislike certain groups of people, but mostly Americans' arms are open to immigrants."

"I think I will go there." Sadness touched her. "It will not be the same as now. I will not have you." She rested a hand on Adam's arm.

The contact felt like a jolt of electricity. Adam looked at her hand. It was small, with slender fingers and broken nails. He wanted to cover it with his own.

"Your wife is very lucky."

Adam was silent. All of a sudden he didn't know what he felt, except that he cared deeply for this French woman.

"I think I love you," Elisa said softly. "I know it is wrong, but I cannot help how I feel. You are a . . . good man." She smiled. Leaning close, she brushed his hair off his forehead and caressed his cheek. "I am thankful we met."

Adam searched her eyes. Lovely and deep brown, they reminded him of the dark chocolates that came in fancy boxes. His feelings for Elisa were powerful. Was it possible that he loved her? Cupping her face in his hand, he leaned toward her and kissed her. It was not a kiss of passion but of tenderness and admiration. *Of course, I feel respect and fondness for her,* he told himself, trying to justify his behavior.

"You are the bravest woman I've ever known," he whispered. "I will never forget you."

Elisa covered his hand with hers. Tears escaped the corners of her eyes, running in narrow paths down her cheeks. "And I will love you forever."

That night they slept cradled together with Adin beside them. Adam knew it was improper. He had a wife and son waiting for him, but somehow sleeping separately in this hostile world seemed wrong. They were together in a battle to survive. In this, they were one.

Laurel would understand, Adam tried to tell himself, but he knew the hurt he would see in her eyes if she knew his feelings. He didn't love Laurel any less, and all he'd shared with Elisa was one kiss. But Adam understood that he was betraying his wife, and yet, he longed to pull Elisa closer. What if this moment was all the lifetime he had left?

Chapter 15

Luke pushed against the wrench and leaned into it. The bolt wouldn't budge. Sweat trickled into his eyes, and he wiped away the stinging dampness. *A cool breeze would feel good,* he thought. Eyeing the stubborn bolt, he hooked the wrench in tightly, gripped the bar again, and pushed. All of a sudden it broke free, and his knuckles ground into the hinge of the steel door. He cursed and pressed the injured hand between his knees. His fingers throbbed. He straightened and shook off the pain, then examined the scuffed knuckles. The skin was peeled back, and blood oozed. With another shake of the hand, he glared at the unyielding door. Now what?

A shipmate stepped through the hatch. He looked at Luke and smirked. "Having a good day, huh?"

"Yeah. Great." Luke grabbed a rag from his back pocket and wrapped it around his damaged hand, which still pulsated with pain. "I need some air," he said to the empty corridor.

He stored his tools and headed for the fantail, several levels up. By the time he climbed the last stairway, his sweat-soaked shirt clung to him. "It's hotter than blazes," he complained.

Stepping onto the deck, he leaned against a bulkhead and savored a breeze that cooled his damp skin. Huge propellers churned the water at the stern of the ship. Closing his eyes, he thought of Alaska. The first snows had probably already fallen, and the hunting season was in full swing. He imagined himself in the high country, his cheeks burning from the cold and his sights set on a mountain sheep. The ram would be resting on a craggy ledge, fall sunshine illuminating his heavy, white coat. He would hold huge curling horns aloft with pride.

Luke heard voices and opened his eyes just as someone shouldered past him. "Hey!" Luke yelled. "Watch it . . ." His eyes focused on the offender. "Barry? Barry from the *Nevada*?"

"Luke? Is that you?"

"Barry! For crying out loud, what are you doing here?"

Each man gripped the other's arm.

"I can't believe it's you!" Luke said. "How'd you end up on the *Wasp*?"

"Put in for it." Barry grinned. "I told you I'd be back."

"You look good."

"I feel good. Healed up just like the doc said, and here I am." He let loose of Luke. "I heard the ship's been in the Atlantic dodgin' U-boats."

"Yep. We've had a real ride, all right, but so far so good. We managed to sink a few along the way. Now we watch for Nip Zeros and Kamikazes." He pulled his wet shirt away from his body. "I'd rather be in the Atlantic. Me and the heat don't get along."

Glancing at another sailor, Barry hefted his sea bag to his shoulder. "This is Lance. He was showing me around."

"I'll take over for you," Luke said.

"Fine by me." Lance headed down the corridor.

"Thanks," Barry called after him, then turned to Luke. "Landing on this can is real interesting." He shook his head. "Whew. What an experience."

"Yeah. Planes come in pretty fast. A couple of days ago one of the flight crew fell overboard while signaling a plane down. Guess he wasn't paying attention."

"They fish him out?"

"Well, he didn't go far. He fell into a safety net. He was more embarrassed than anything." Barry's open, friendly face crinkled into a smile.

"Never thought I'd see you again," Luke said, suddenly choked up.

"Good to have you aboard, old friend."

"Figured you needed someone to look after you."

"I'm fine. It's you we got to worry about."

The two friends quieted and stared at the Pacific.

"Maybe we'll sail home together after the war's over," Luke said. "Hope it's soon. I'm a little tired of watching and waiting for torpedoes, knowing that sooner or later they're coming."

"I'm ready for a fight. Been on leave long enough. Heck, I figure if I was supposed to get it I would have kicked the bucket back at Pearl Harbor."

"You were pretty shot up, all right."

Barry shifted his eyes to the churning water. "Yeah." He looked at Luke. "You off duty?"

"No. Just came up for some air." He raised an eyebrow. "You'll see."

"I need to store my gear."

A horn brayed. Barry dropped his duffel bag. "What's going on?"

"Probably spotted a sub or Jap plane." Luke ran for the stairway. He took the steps two at a time, then hurried down a corridor. Barry followed. Both men fell easily into their assigned duties and checked doors and fire hoses as they made their way through the ship. Rewinding a hose, Luke said, "This sea is crawling with Japs. We're always on alert."

A bell sounded, signaling the all clear. "False alarm," Luke said flatly. "You get all pumped up and ready for battle, then nothin'." He shrugged. "Can't complain. I've seen plenty of action."

He moved down the passageway and Barry followed. "Doesn't stay quiet around here for too long. A week and a half ago a kamikaze was headed right at us. I figured we were done for. I started praying. God must have heard 'cause that Jap splashed into the sea right off the bow."

"I'd say God's watching over you, old buddy." Barry slapped Luke's back.

"I pray he keeps it up."

Barry and Luke sat in one of the safety nets off the flight deck. Sailors used them as hammocks. Time spent here was the best you could get on the ship. The steady breeze was refreshing, and the gentle sway of the nets was soothing. Luke gazed at a choppy sea. "Without escorts we'd be sitting ducks," he said, nodding at a destroyer lying off starboard.

"Those poor slobs probably have some rough days," Barry said as the accompanying ship dipped into a deep trough.

"Yep. When the seas get rough, the men strap into their bunks. Many a time I've been thankful I'm on a carrier."

"Heard there's a typhoon bearing down on us now. Guess we're all in for a bumpy ride," Barry said, apprehension touching his voice.

"Don't worry. The navy doesn't take its ships through foul weather unless there's no way around it."

The contingent of ships skirted the worst of the storm, but the seas were rough. The destroyers bounced through waves as they continued their vigil over the aircraft carrier. Even the *Wasp* did its share of rolling. Many men were sick. Queasy and a bit green, Luke worked his shift with a bucket beside him. The hours passed slowly.

Finally off duty, he headed for the galley in search of something to drink. After filling a cup with tea and a touch of sugar, he sat at a table, resting his head in his hands.

Leaning into the rising floor, Barry set a tray laden with a salami sandwich, a pile of potato salad, and two pieces of chocolate cake on the table across from Luke, then sat. Through a mouthful of sandwich, he said, "They sure feed you good here." He studied Luke. "How come you're not eating? You're not sick, are you?"

Luke eyed the sandwich. "I'll be just fine, but I'd appreciate it if you'd get that food out of my face." The smell of salami sent waves of nausea through him. He felt a cold sweat break out and fought a roiling stomach.

"Sorry." Barry took several large bites and finished off the sandwich. "That better?" He grinned.

Luke didn't answer, only shook his head. Leaning his elbows on the table, he held his cup in both hands and sipped.

"You ever heard of an aircraft carrier sinking?"

"In a storm? Nope. But there's always a first time." Luke wondered whether he would feel better if he put something in his stomach. "I heard of a carrier that had its flight deck beaten so bad by waves that it curled over the bow. Stayed afloat, though."

Barry let out a long, low whistle while catching his coffee mug sliding across the table as the ship rode a large wave. "I would've liked to seen that." He shoved the last of piece of cake in his mouth and stood, picking up the other. "I better get back to work." He headed out of the room, then stopped. "I figure this storm'll blow itself out and we'll be fine by tomorrow. See you at breakfast?"

"Hopefully," Luke said and watched as his friend swaggered out of the mess hall.

Barry was right. By the following day the ship's movement was barely discernable, and the skies were mostly clear. Barry was already halfway through his breakfast when Luke joined him.

With a cup of coffee and a plate of eggs and toast, Luke sat beside his friend. He took a swig of coffee. "I'm sweating already."

Barry nodded. "Yeah, me too."

"I'd like to be in Alaska about now. Get out of this heat," Luke said, taking a bite of eggs.

"Too cold for me. I'd like something a little more temperate." Barry studied Luke. "You were going to tell me about some of your adventures. Where you been?"

"Pretty much everywhere—Gibraltar, Scotland, England, the Mediterranean." He shrugged. "And soon the Solomon Islands."

"What kind of action have you seen besides the kamikaze?"

"We've faced off with the Germans, watched two fish from a U-boat slide past the bow. We've lost a few planes." He stopped eating and met Barry's eyes. "Why didn't you go home? You were shot up pretty bad."

"I was home. But after I rested up, I was ready to get back into it. Figured I couldn't just loaf around in Oregon." He grinned. "Seems to me, if God saves a man's life, that man ought to do something with it. So here I am."

"You got here just in time. We'll be crossing the equator tomorrow. There's an initiation for sailors who haven't been that far south. Pollywogs become shellbacks." Luke grinned. "Heard it's quite a party."

Barry raised an eyebrow. "Party? From what I've heard I'd say more like torture."

That night Luke couldn't sleep, so he made his way to the fantail. He sat on the deck and rested his back against a bulkhead. A moon the color of cream hung low in the sky. It looked as if someone had taken a bite out of it, but it was bright enough to cast a glow across a quiet sea.

He studied the water. Instead of seeing beauty, his mind manufactured subs lurking below the surface. The ship had played so many games of cat and mouse with German U-boats and Japanese subs that he couldn't think of anything else. He hated the furtive match. An all-out battle would be easier to take.

The Battle at Midway was how it ought to be. He wished he'd been there. *We gave it to them good. I'll get my turn,* he told himself. *Sooner or later I'll have my chance.*

The following morning, all sailors considered "pollywogs" were told to assemble on the flight deck. A sharp breeze cut across the bow, and a lot of nervous joking took place as the men waited. Luke was in no mood for fun. He didn't care about crossing the equator. He wanted to either fight this war or go home. Through the night his thoughts had been on his family and on Mattie. He wanted to get on with his life, but what he wanted had nothing to do with reality.

Festivities went into full swing. King Neptune's Court was assembled, and the "pollywogs" were pushed forward. The seaman playing the role of King Neptune held a homemade scepter and wore a poorly constructed crown made of cardboard and tinfoil. It was tipped sideways on his head and looked as if it might fall off at any moment. Beside King Neptune stood his queen. One of the men had plopped a mop upside down on his head and had donned an Hawaiian muumuu. He'd painted his lips and cheeks red. Another sailor played the royal baby. He made a grand entrance. Luke recognized the rotund man dressed in what looked like a diaper, but he didn't know his name. Momentarily Luke forgot his surly mood and chuckled. So did the others.

"No laughing," the king bellowed. "You have all been charged with crimes against the royal family." He proceeded to read a list of charges. All pollywogs were found guilty and required to pay for their crimes.

Luke's dark mood lifted. Along with trepidation over what the pollywogs' punishment might be, anticipation filled the air as the ceremony began.

Pollywogs were ordered to undress down to their skivvies. Then they were forced to crawl on hands and knees through garbage hauled out from the kitchen and spread over the deck. While they crawled, mates sprayed them with water so cold it felt like icy barbs against Luke's skin. He didn't know which was worse, the gunk under his hands and knees or the freezing water.

After this punishment the pollywogs were told they weren't repentant and that the royal barber waited for them. Luke's head was soaped down, and he was held securely while his head was shaved. He could feel the nicks left on his scalp.

Next he was shoved into a line making its way toward the royal baby, whose stomach had been smeared with something sticky and slimy. Pollywogs were forced to kiss the rotund belly. When it was Luke's turn, he kneeled in front of the pot-bellied man, grimaced and closed his eyes, then leaned forward to fulfill his duty. The royal baby grabbed his head and smeared his face into his grubby stomach.

Everyone laughed. Luke pulled free, wiping gunk from his face. He watched as Barry took his turn. His friend was having a good time. Wearing a broad smile, he threatened to punch the royal baby. In spite of the threat, he was treated like the others. After having his face pushed into the man's belly, he came up for air laughing.

The last obstacle was the royal dentist. Luke was plunked down into a chair and forced to open his mouth, and a vile-tasting liquid was squirted into the back of his throat. Gagging and spitting, he broke free. Someone offered him a bottle of something to drink, and he gulped down a mouthful, then realized it was liquor. He choked and sputtered as the fiery liquid burned its way down his throat and into his stomach. It did the job and rid him of the unpleasant taste. Luke turned to watch the others make their way through the penalties.

After the initiation the men received certificates stating they were now shellbacks and would never be lowly pollywogs again.

"Shellbacks," Barry said, throwing his arm over Luke's shoulders. "We did it. Next time it'll be our turn to initiate the pollywogs. Can't wait."

Luke's temporary elevation in mood faded. He knew fun was important. From time to time they needed to let loose, but he also knew that many of them would probably never make another trip over the equator or home. He looked at Barry. "Yep. Next time it's our turn."

"Hey, what's wrong, buddy?"

"Nothin'." He wiped a hand over his face. "Guess I'd just like to go home. 'Cept I don't exactly have a home. Not with Ray Townsend living there anyway."

Barry was quiet for a moment, then said, "Since I made it through Pearl Harbor, me and God have an agreement. I talk to him and he talks to me." He let out a breath. "I'm not the same anymore. Oh, I'm me, all right, just better . . . I think. Anyway, I've been learning a lot about living. One thing I think I'm starting to understand is that we can have enemies, but we can't hold on to our anger."

Wearing a sideways grin, Luke asked, "How do you go about doing that?"

"Not sure exactly. But I don't think God hates the Japs or the Germans . . . or even your stepfather."

Luke stared at his friend. "God hates evil. The Bible says so. It's clear. It says that God hates our enemies."

"Maybe so, but just 'cause evil exists doesn't mean we should go around hating and hating. It can eat a person up. I'll bet Ray Townsend could tell you a lot about that. Seems to me it was hate that set him off."

"It's not the same. I'm not like him."

Barry raised an eyebrow and leaned against a bulkhead. "After I got shot up, I was real mad. I hated the Japs. I'll be honest with you. I'm not crazy about them now, but I'm done with the bitterness. And you need to be too." He met Luke's eyes. "Especially what you feel about your stepfather. Eventually you got to make things right."

"He's not my stepfather. He's married to my mother, that's all."

Barry looked Luke in the eyes. "Bitterness has a hold on you, friend. You got to let go of it."

Luke knew he was right, but he also knew there was no way he could let it go. He hated Ray. He'd always hate the man. "I got to do what I got to do."

Barry didn't answer right away. Finally he said, "I got a friend back home. I ever tell you about Jennifer?"

"No. But I bet I know what she looks like—tall, blonde, and beautiful," Luke said, hoping to lighten the conversation.

Barry frowned.

"Sorry. Go ahead."

"Jennifer's a good friend. She helped me see how my hating Japs was wrong."

Luke couldn't believe what he was hearing. Didn't all Americans hate Japs? It was unnatural not to after Pearl Harbor.

"I mean I even hated American Japanese, and when I had the chance, I let them know how I felt. But after I started praying more and reading my Bible, well," he shrugged, "the hatred just kind of seeped away. I know Germans and Japanese are America's enemies, but this war isn't a personal thing. I don't know any of the enemy, not personally, I mean. I'm not fighting against men. I'm fighting tyranny."

"That's got nothing to do with how I feel about Ray Townsend, who, by the way, I know personally. He's the guy who killed my father and married my mother. I can't forgive him." Luke narrowed his eyes. "A person can't forgive just like that. It's not possible."

"It is."

Luke started to walk away. "You don't know what you're talking about. Your father wasn't murdered, and you haven't had your home and family stolen. This guy deserves to be hated."

"Maybe he does. But *you* don't deserve it. Hating's like a disease. It'll eat you up from the inside out, and you deserve better."

Luke yanked his cap out of a back pocket and pulled it down over his shaven head. "Ray Townsend deserves to die, and I pray to God he does," he said, then turned and walked away.

Chapter 16

EXHAUSTED, MATTIE STEPPED THROUGH THE GATES OF THE PORT OF Embarkation. Ten-hour days were draining. At first the job had sounded exciting. Working at the port meant being part of the world as she and other workers filled requests from ships coming and going. Soon reality replaced fantasy.

Mattie stood for hours pulling parts and packing orders. She'd yet to meet anyone from an exotic location; however, she had watched many sailors and soldiers depart. As ships pulled away with military men standing along railings, she always felt sad, wondering what horror they might be sailing into.

To make matters worse, her supervisor was cantankerous and always demanding more production, more perfection. No matter how hard the employees tried to please, it was never enough. Mattie found herself missing her work in Anchorage but quickly corrected her negative outlook. "At least I have a job," she told herself, "and a place to live, enough to eat, and friends. It's not so bad."

She walked, imagining herself putting up her feet and drinking a cup of tea. She hoped Meryl hadn't worked over and was preparing dinner. With a fair amount of coaching, Meryl had become a decent cook. Mattie plodded on.

Meryl had changed a great deal since first arriving in Seattle. She was still the gregarious, imposing woman Mattie had met on the steamer, but she was much less spoiled and less demanding. Meryl had found a position as a teller at a nearby bank and actually enjoyed working. She'd also reconciled with her parents, who'd had difficulty accepting their daughter's independence.

Beyond all the palpable changes in Meryl, one mattered the most—she had proven to be a good friend, loyal and caring. She liked having a good time, often dragging Mattie out to the clubs, but Mattie couldn't deny that she enjoyed the fun. Eager sailors and soldiers were always looking for dance partners. Meryl was a flirt, but she defended her teasing as her contribution to the war effort. "Those poor men deserve a little pleasure before being shipped out," she'd said more than once. "Besides, they know I'm just flirting," she added with an innocent smile.

Mattie turned the corner onto their block. Shouts carried from an alley running alongside her apartment building. Alarm prickling the hairs on her arms, she stopped and stared into the shadows. People were yelling and shaking their fists at someone. It was Jasmine.

What's going on? Mattie wondered, moving closer. Jasmine stood with her back pressed against a brick wall. Her eyes were wide, filled with fear and hurt . . . and something else—indignation. All of a sudden she straightened and threw back her shoulders. "Please, let me pass."

"You're not going anywhere, especially not into this building," a man Mattie knew as Sid Spencer yelled. His face was redder than usual, and his pudgy cheeks reminded her of partially withered balloons.

"Go back where you came from," someone shouted.

Jasmine ignored the comment and tried to push through. The crowd closed ranks.

Indignation growing, Mattie made her way to Jasmine's side. She glared at the crowd; some she recognized as neighbors. "What are you doing? Why are you mad at Jasmine?"

"Well . . . look at her," Sid said.

Mattie glanced at Jasmine. "And?" she asked, meeting Sid's angry eyes.

"You her friend?"

"Yes."

"You should choose your associates more wisely." His gaze slid to Jasmine, then back to Mattie. "Seems you both got the wrong color of skin." His lips shifted into a cruel smile.

Mattie couldn't believe what she was hearing. All the years of intolerance and bigotry she'd endured flared and boiled through her.

"Wrong color?" she asked indignantly, then repeated, "Wrong color?" If she were a male, she would have spit; instead she balled her fists and let loose an angry growl. "You get out of here! All of you! Now!" A few people had the decency to look away, but the crowd didn't budge.

"What is this?" Mattie heard Meryl say as she strode through the mob and stood with her friends. Her hazel eyes, sparked with gold and fury, swept over the people. "I never dreamed this could be possible! I thought we were neighbors and friends." She put an arm over both Mattie and Jasmine. "You two all right?"

"I'm perfectly fine," Jasmine said with a defiant look at the aggressors.

"Well, I'm not," Mattie said. "These people were attacking Jasmine, saying she shouldn't live here." Her voice quavered.

Meryl turned back to the intolerant crowd. "You should be ashamed of yourselves. If I were you, I wouldn't show my face in public." With that, she swung around, flinging wild curls off her shoulder and faced Mattie and Jasmine. Cheerfully, as if none of the ugliness had happened, she said, "I bought everything we need for lasagna. And I'm starving." She fingered the paper bag she carried that was bulging with groceries. A loaf of French bread protruded from the top. Eyeing the narrow-minded pack, she said, "Please, excuse us."

Sid puffed out his barrel chest and stepped in front of her. "Not until we're done with our business."

"As far as I'm concerned, you are done with *your business.*"

"She don't belong here," Sid growled, looking at Jasmine. "No col-oreds allowed. That's the rules."

"She has every right to live here," Meryl said haughtily.

"No more. We got a new manager, and he don't want no coloreds in the building."

Roseline Talbot hobbled up to the group. "What's all this ruckus, Sid?" She leveled pale blue eyes on the man. "Now, you just settle down. You know as well as any of us that Jasmine's never been any trouble. Why would you want her out?"

Sid seemed lost for words. He compressed puffy lips and his ruddy complexion deepened. "She'll only bring in more of her kind."

Mrs. Talbot looked at Jasmine. "How long have you lived here, dear?"

"Nearly three years."

"Hmm. Seems to me if you were going to bring in 'more of your kind' you would have done it by now." She smiled at Sid. "'Course that would be a good thing, since Jasmine here is such a good neighbor." Placing a hand on Jasmine's arm, she said, "Come along, dear."

Again Sid blocked the way. "Not so fast. She don't belong and you know it. Now, I ain't got nothin' against her personally, but you know if you let one in they'll all come in." He unsuccessfully tried to hold Mrs. Talbot's gaze. "You know what I mean," he added lamely.

Mattie stepped forward. "So tell me what terrible thing happens if they do?" He didn't answer right away, so Mattie repeated, "Tell me. What happens?"

The man eyed her. "The whole neighborhood goes to pot. Hoodlums move in, and pretty soon you've got drunks on the streets and you got to worry about being robbed . . . and worse."

Mattie looked over the crowd. "How can any of you believe that Jasmine is bad for our building just because of the color of her skin?" Mattie knew she was heading for trouble but couldn't hold back. "Jasmine works hard and never causes trouble. She's a fine person." She glanced at the Negro woman. "I'm glad she's my friend."

"Two peas in a pod . . ." Sid said.

Another man sidled up beside him. He turned pale blue eyes on Mattie. "You're nearly as dark as she is. You sure you ain't a Jap?"

Momentarily shocked, Mattie didn't know what to say. If the situation weren't so serious, she would have laughed.

Meryl stepped in. "What she is or isn't is none of your business. Now let us pass, or I'll be forced to call the police."

"So, she *is* a Jap. I knew it."

"No. She's not." Meryl glared at the man, and taking Mattie's hand, shouldered her way through. Jasmine and Mrs. Talbot followed in their wake.

"This isn't the end," the man threatened. "Not by a long shot."

Mrs. Talbot stopped and turned to face him. She peered at him, her watery eyes flashing with anger. "You'd best watch your step. The Lord doesn't take kindly to those who persecute his children. If you do any harm to any of these young ladies, he'll see to you." With that, she turned and walked away, sliding her arms into Jasmine's and Mattie's.

Once inside the front doors, Mrs. Talbot said, "Why don't you all come up to my room. I'll put on some tea." Everyone agreed, and Mrs. Talbot hobbled up the stairs, Meryl supporting her and Mattie and Jasmine following.

Mattie's mind replayed the incident over and over. She felt sick to her stomach. She'd never been part of such a volatile clash. It was disturbing and disappointing.

When they reached Mrs. Talbot's room, the old woman fumbled with her key but finally pushed it into the lock. After a moment of wrangling, she managed to open the door and smiled up at her companions. "This lock is nearly as cantankerous as that Sid." She chuckled. "Come in." She shuffled across the tiny apartment and opened a window. "Oh my, it's stifling in here."

Meryl sat in a well-stuffed chair with a large doily on the back and two matching doilies on the arms. She slipped off pumps and planted her feet on an ottoman. "I can't believe what just happened."

Jasmine settled on a sofa and stared at her hands. "I'm thinking of moving. My sister lives across town, and she said I can stay with her for a while."

"You can't give in to them," Meryl said. "You have to stand up to people like that."

Her bravado gone, Jasmine offered a defeated smile. "I appreciate that you care, but you don't understand. It's not as easy as you think."

"But—"

"Meryl, you *don't* understand," Mattie said, anger growing. *It was supposed to be different here,* she thought.

Meryl frowned. "I suppose you're right. But this kind of injustice needs to be stopped. It makes me so angry."

"It does need to stop," Jasmine said, "but I'm not the one to do it. Someday things will be better. But not today."

Mrs. Talbot carried a silver tray with delicate china cups and a teapot. She placed it on a coffee table. Her hands trembling, she filled the cups with golden liquid. Offering Jasmine a cup, she said, "This was a wedding gift to me and James. Of course, he didn't think all that much about it, but I've always loved it." She smiled and tucked a wisp of hair back away from her face.

"It's beautiful," Jasmine said. "Thank you."

After everyone was served, Mrs. Talbot sat on a straight-backed chair. "There now, that's better." She sipped her drink.

Quiet settled over the room. The women drank their tea as each retreated to their private thoughts.

Mattie set her cup in its saucer and looked at her friends. "I thought things were different here. I came to Seattle to get away from people like Sid and the others."

Mrs. Talbot offered Mattie a gentle smile. "There are people like that everywhere, dear. All we can do is be an example and help folks see that God created us all and loves us all."

With a sigh, Mattie reluctantly accepted that truth. However, she didn't much feel like loving people such as the ones they'd just stood up to. Jasmine, whose years of hurt etched her face, only nodded.

Jasmine moved a few days later. It was more battle than she was willing to take on. However, the anger and frustration of the tenants didn't go with her. It shifted—Mattie became the new target.

Hateful letters were left at her door and dropped in her mail slot. Several of the tenants refused to speak to her. Some threw malevolent looks and cruel remarks. Some even took aim at Meryl. One day while approaching the apartment building, Meryl was pelted with raw eggs from an unseen foe who also threw accusations—calling her a Jap lover.

"It makes me so angry," Meryl said. "How can people be so utterly dim-witted and cruel?" She measured out sugar for a batch of cookies and dumped it in a bowl.

"I thought we were going to conserve the sugar," Mattie said. "We don't get much."

"Yes, I know. But I've just got to have some sugar cookies. I've been craving them." She smiled. "When I was little and upset, Cook would make sugar cookies. They always helped." She cracked an egg and dropped it into the bowl, then tossed the shell into the sink. "All of this is very distressing," she said as she stirred. "I just don't understand."

Mattie leaned her elbows on the kitchen table. "Maybe we should move."

"No. Never."

"I'm afraid something awful is going to happen. I don't know why people think I'm Japanese."

"They're just looking for someone to take out their frustrations on. And your features are kind of oriental, plus you've got black hair and brown eyes. It makes you an easy target." She added flour to the mixture in the bowl. "I'm sure all this will pass. We just have to wait it out."

Steps sounded in the hallway, then an envelope was slipped underneath the door. Holding her body stiffly, Mattie stood, staring at it as if it were a snake ready to strike.

Meryl wiped her hands on her apron. "Seems to me people could have the decency to deliver mail in the standard fashion," she said matter-of-factly and walked briskly across the room. She jerked open the door and stepped into the hallway. After looking up and down the corridor, she walked back inside and closed the door soundly. "The nerve." She bent and picked up the envelope. Sliding a well-manicured fingernail under the fold, she scanned the contents. Her mouth formed a hard line, and her eyes narrowed. "Hmm. Some people are very small."

"What does it say?"

"Nothing important. I'll just throw it in the trash." She crossed to the kitchen sink.

"What did it say?"

"Nothing."

"Let me see." Mattie grabbed the letter. Her hand trembled as she read. This one was the worst. Her mouth went dry. After hurling grotesque threats, the author promised that Mattie would be turned over to the authorities and shipped to an internment camp.

"It's all just a bunch of nonsense," Meryl said. "No one will touch you, and you won't be sent away. If government agents do try to arrest you, all you have to do is show them your identification."

Mattie wanted to believe her, but fear strangled her confidence.

Meryl grabbed the letter, tore it in half, and threw it into the trash. "It's nothing but rubbish. Don't listen to a word of it."

Mattie bit a quivering lip and closed her eyes. Tears leaked onto her cheeks. "I left Alaska to get away from this." She wiped her eyes. "Now I'm hated for being something I'm not."

Meryl crossed the room and hugged Mattie. "Everything will be all right. They can't do anything to you. This all will pass."

"I wish that were true," Mattie sniffled.

Meryl gave her an extra squeeze and returned to her baking. She spooned batter onto a cookie sheet. "Why don't you just tell them you're native Alaskan?" She brushed a stray curl off her face.

"That won't help. They'll just hate me for being an Indian." Mattie stood and walked to the closet. "I'm going down to the drugstore to call my mother."

Meryl slid the cookies into the oven. "Wait until tomorrow. It's dark out. You shouldn't be wandering around at night, especially with things the way they are."

"I'm tired of hiding, and I need to call home." Mattie could feel the tears again. She longed for family. Since arriving in Seattle, this was the first time she was truly homesick.

"At least wait until this batch of cookies is done, and I'll go with you."

"No. I've got to face things on my own. I can't hide behind you."

"Mattie. Please."

Mattie headed for the door. "I'll be fine. There are plenty of street-lights along the way, and the store is only a block and a half away."

City lights shimmered in puddles, and cars sprinted past, spraying water onto the sidewalk and onto Mattie. She moved away from the street, walking quickly. Doing her best to look confident, she held her shoulders back and her chin up, but her eyes darted to every dark corner and behind each parked car. A cold wind tugged at her coat.

Buoyed by the lights of the drugstore, she relaxed slightly and stepped inside. Nodding at the man behind the counter, she walked to the phone booth, heels clicking on newly washed tiles. She dug in her change purse, took out a nickel, and dropped it into the telephone. It chimed as it fell into place.

Thankful she'd sent money home for telephone service, she waited. Mattie smiled, remembering how her grandmother had said the new contraption wasn't to be trusted, yet Atuska enjoyed the conversations with her granddaughter.

Mattie gave information to the operator, then waited for the call to be put through, watching customers come and go. She caught a glimpse of someone standing outside the window. The person wore a trench coat but quickly disappeared, and Mattie wasn't able to see a face. A shiver of fear moved through her. *Don't get yourself into a tizzy over a raincoat,* she told herself.

Hoping for a distraction, Mattie studied an elderly man bent over the counter. He puffed on a cigar between sips of coffee. He also wore a trench coat, as did many men.

The operator returned, instructing Mattie to add more money. She dropped more coins into the phone.

"Hello," Affia's voice echoed. She sounded far away.

"Mama, is that you?"

"Yes. It's me. Mattie? It's good to hear you. Are you all right?"

"Yes. I'm fine."

"Are you sure? You don't sound all right."

"I'm just a little homesick." Mattie cradled the phone as if that would bring her mother closer. "I miss you."

"We miss you too. I think about you every day. Will you be able to come for a visit soon?"

"No. I can't miss work. And I don't have money for the fare."

"Of course." There was a pause. "Are you happy?"

"Yes." Mattie wished she were telling the truth. She had been happy until a couple of weeks ago. "Seattle is a beautiful place," she said. "And I have good friends, especially Meryl. I wish you could meet her. You'd like her."

"Maybe you can bring her when you come for a visit."

"I hope so. I miss you and Grandma . . . and everyone. Please say hello for me."

"I will."

"How is Grandma?"

"Not so good. The cold is giving her trouble. It's getting harder for her to get around. The doctor said it's old age."

"I'm sorry she's not well, Mama. Tell her for me?"

"I will. She's already asleep for the night, but I'll tell her in the morning." She was silent a moment, then asked, "How is your job? Do you still like it?"

"Yes. I get to see people from all over the world, but I don't like watching the sailors and soldiers going off to war. It makes me think of Luke."

"Have you heard from him?"

"Yes. He's in the Pacific on a ship called the *Wasp*."

"We're praying for him." Affia's voice trailed off as if she had something more to say, then she was silent.

"Mama, is everything all right?"

She didn't answer.

"Mama?"

"I have bad news . . . about Adam. He's missing. He was writing about a bombing mission, and the plane was shot down . . . in France somewhere. The family hasn't received any word of his whereabouts."

Mattie felt the pang of grief. "How awful. How is Laurel?"

"Scared and sad. But she believes he'll come home."

A singsong voice instructed Mattie to add more coins. "I have to go, Mama. Please let Grandma know I love her, and tell Laurel and Jean too."

"I will. We love you."

The phone went dead. Mattie held it a moment, then hung up. Adam was probably dead. What would happen to Luke? She hated the war.

Her heart heavy, she headed back to the apartment building. News of Adam and her fear about Luke had replaced thoughts of her own troubles. She didn't remember to watch for danger.

A large man stepped from the shadows of an alley. He wore a trench coat and a broad-brimmed hat, which kept his face in shadow. Terror surged through Mattie. She tried to walk past him. He grabbed her.

"Let me go!" she screamed, struggling to free herself.

He tightened his hold and clapped a hand over her mouth, then pulled her against him. "Shut up!" he hissed.

His voice sounded gravelly and hushed. Mattie didn't recognize it.

He wrapped an arm around her neck and squeezed, cutting off her breath. "Japs don't belong here. You all deserve to die."

Mattie tried to speak but only managed a squeak.

"Shut up!" His breath was labored. "You're not wanted here. Leave, or you'll wish you had." He chuckled. "An internment camp or a grave is the only place Japs belong." He chuckled, and the laugh rattled in his throat.

Mattie tried to turn so she could see his face.

"You don't want to do that." He squeezed her neck harder. "Do as I say." He twisted her arm back more, sending a shooting pain into her shoulder, then unexpectedly shoved her to the ground and ran, disappearing around a corner.

Shaking with fear and rage, Mattie pushed to her feet. Life was supposed to be better here. Wasn't there any place that was safe?

Mattie stared at the spot she'd last seen the man, then shouted at the empty street. "I'm not leaving! I'm not!"

Chapter 17

DAYS PASSED AND WHOEVER WAYLAID MATTIE DIDN'T REAPPEAR. THE threatening notes and personal bullying decreased, and it seemed that people had lost interest.

Still, Mattie never went out without watching for the man who had attacked her. Occasionally she would see someone wearing a trench coat similar to the one her assailant had worn, and she'd wonder if it might be him. Finally she resolved she'd never know who had come at her out of the dark and decided it was time to put her fears behind her. Life needed to return to normal. Mattie did her best to go about daily activities as if nothing had ever happened.

On a Saturday morning, two weeks after the attack, Mattie and Meryl sat at the kitchen table drinking coffee, nibbling on buttered toast, and reading the morning newspaper. A knock reverberated at the door.

"Now, who could that be?" Meryl asked, sounding bored. Two more sharp raps sounded. She folded the paper and headed for the door. Before she reached it, the knocking resumed. "I'm coming," she said irritably, yanking open the door.

Two policemen, straight-backed and stiff, stood in the hallway. One was tall and looked to be in his early thirties. The other was short and much older. His stomach pressed against a blue shirt and drooped over his belt. "I'm Officer Hewitt, and this is Officer Decker." He nodded at his younger partner. "We're looking for a Mattie Lawson."

Meryl didn't reply.

"Is she here?" The officer peered through heavy glasses resting on a bulbous nose.

Mattie's heart raced in her chest. Why would the police want to talk to her?

Resting a hand on one hip, Meryl asked, "And may I know why you wish to speak to her?"

"We have some questions for Miss Lawson," Decker said.

"I'm Mattie Lawson." She joined Meryl at the door and pressed her hand against her stomach, hoping to quiet its flip-flopping.

Both men eyed her closely. "You'll need to come with us," Officer Hewitt said.

"Go with you where? Why?"

"We need you to come to the station and answer some questions."

"But I haven't done anything," Mattie said, panic mounting.

"We'll wait while you dress," Hewitt said resolutely, then rocked back on his heels.

Unable to believe what was happening, Mattie stared at the men. "Can't you tell me what this is about?"

His voice prickly, Officer Decker said, "All that will be answered at the station. And we don't have all day."

She had no choice. "I'll come with you; just give me a few minutes." Mattie retreated to her room, and with shaking hands, removed her bathrobe and pajamas, then dressed quickly.

"Mattie," Meryl said, rapping softly on her door. "Can I come in?"

"Yes."

Meryl walked into the room, dressed and coiffed. "I'm going with you. Those two aren't going to cart off my best friend, especially when we don't even know why."

Mattie felt like hugging Meryl. "What's happening?" she asked, her voice quaking. "Why would they want me? Do you think this has anything to do with the threats I've been getting about being Japanese?"

"Maybe." She studied her friend. "You don't really look Japanese. Either way, we'll get this straightened out." She hugged Mattie. "Try not to worry. I'm sure it's all just a misunderstanding."

Pulling a brush through her hair, Mattie stopped and gazed at herself in the mirror. Could she be mistaken for someone of Japanese ancestry? No, she decided, then reluctantly returned to the front room and the waiting police officers.

Meryl laid a protective arm around Mattie's shoulders. "Why does she have to go with you? Can't you ask your questions here?"

"Standard procedure, ma'am." Officer Hewitt pushed up his glasses. "We've had reports that she's Japanese, and we can't take chances. All Japanese citizens have been moved to relocation camps, and for good reason. We've got to be careful about spies. They've been found all along the coast." He shifted his gaze to Mattie. "Why didn't you register?"

"I'm not Japanese."

Both officers scrutinized Mattie. Hewitt seemed to be in charge. "You look like a Jap."

"She does not," Meryl said. "Don't you know what a Japanese person looks like?"

"I'm *Alaska* native. That's why my hair and eyes are dark."

"Your eyes look kind of slanted to me."

"I'm not Japanese!"

"That's not for me to decide, missy."

Mattie's panic grew. "Please. I promise not to go anywhere. Let me stay here until this mistake is cleared up."

Both men smiled, seeming amused. "Just stay, huh? And we're supposed to believe you'll be here when we come back?" Officer Decker smirked.

"Yes. I have nowhere to go."

"Enough," officer Hewitt said, taking her arm. "Come with us." He led her into the corridor and steered her toward the stairs.

Meryl closed the door and locked it, then followed. "I'm coming with you."

"You're not allowed in the squad car," Decker said. "You'll have to find your own way to the station."

"I'll be there just as soon as I can," Meryl promised Mattie. "Please don't lose hope."

Mattie managed a tremulous smile before being maneuvered down the stairs and through the front doors. Officer Hewitt pushed her into the back seat of the car, closed the door, and took his place behind the wheel. Meryl remained on the sidewalk and watched as they pulled away.

"This is a terrible mistake. I'm not Japanese. I'm from Alaska." Fighting tears, she added, "Please, you have to believe me."

"We don't have to believe nothin'," Hewitt said. "Our job is to protect this city and this country, and any Jap roaming around free is a danger to the United States. There's a war going on. Remember?"

Knowing she would get nowhere with these men, Mattie sat back. She breathed slowly, hoping to quiet her nerves, and stared out the window. What was she going to do? *Father, how could you let this happen?* Mattie wanted to crawl inside herself, except even there she would find no solace. She hated who she was. Now she'd be forced to defend her identity, one she'd done her best to conceal. It was hard to imagine that she'd be forced to use her heritage as a provision for release.

After arriving at the police station, Mattie was photographed and fingerprinted. She felt like a criminal. No one spoke to her, except to give instructions. After all the procedures were completed, she was seated in front of a desk where a police officer sat at a typewriter, punching the keys with his index fingers. He ignored her.

When he stopped typing, he didn't look at her right away. Instead, he removed a pack of smokes from his pocket and thumped out a single cigarette. After tapping it on the corner of his desk, he lit it and took a long drag. Smoke swirled around him as he settled droopy eyes on Mattie. "So, what's your story? How did they miss you when the rest of the Japs were collared?"

"Miss me?"

"Yeah." His eyes sparked with interest. "Were you hiding? What were you up to?"

"Nothing. I'm not Japanese. I'm an Alaska native. My family lives in Alaska. You can call my mother. She'll tell you."

The policeman leaned toward Mattie, peering at her. "Well, I got to say, you don't look like a Jap." He pulled open a drawer, lifted out a folded form, and slid it across the desk. "Fill this out." He handed her a pencil.

After answering pages of questions, Mattie was locked in a cell that smelled of stale urine and unwashed bodies. She was sure the bedding was infested with insects, so she sat on a bench, arms folded over her chest and rested her head against the wall. She couldn't remember ever feeling more humiliated. *God, this is so unfair. I don't understand. How could you let this happen?*

She heard a door open and close, then footsteps.

"Mattie? Oh, Mattie. How awful," Meryl said, stepping up to the bars. "How could they do this to you?"

She moved from the bench to the iron barricade. "They still think I'm Japanese. I answered all their questions—pages of them. They said they would check it out, but I don't really know what they're doing. I'm afraid they're going to send me to one of those camps."

"I'm sure they can't do that. Try not to worry. I contacted my parents, and my father said he would speak to his attorney right away. We'll have this straightened out in no time." She wrapped her hand around Mattie's.

"I hope so." Pressing her lips together and squeezing her eyes closed, she tried to hold back the tears. "Tell your father thank you."

"I will." Meryl forced a smile. "I brought you a magazine and a candy bar, but they wouldn't let me bring them in."

"That's all right. I don't feel like candy or reading. I can't think. My mind just goes round and round. I wish Luke was here."

Mattie spent that day and night in jail. The following morning Jasmine came to visit. "I heard you were here. I'm so sorry. I'm sure they'll figure this out. I feel like it's my fault. If you hadn't stood up for me, no one would have bothered you."

"It's not your fault. It's just stupid people."

Jasmine smiled. Her teeth looked very white against her black skin.

"How do you do it?" Mattie asked.

"Do what?"

"How do you live with the . . . injustice? I'm so mad!" Then more quietly she added, "And ashamed. I want to be anyone other than who I am."

Jasmine smiled kindly. "Now that just won't do. You can't hate what God created."

Mattie frowned. "I wish he had made us all the same."

"The world would be pretty boring, don't you think?" Jasmine crossed her arms. "I just don't listen to the voices, especially the ones inside my head that say I'm not as good as everyone else. God knew what he was doing when he made me. I'm special just the way I am."

"I wish I could believe that. All my life I've felt inferior to other people, and someone has always been around who made sure to tell me I was. Kids teased, parents wouldn't allow me to play with their children—"

"I know, but you can't listen to that. It's not you or me they're mocking, but who they think we are."

"I know, but it doesn't help." Mattie looked at Jasmine. "When I came here, I thought I could be somebody, not an . . . outsider."

"Do you think that just because you move people won't see the color of your skin? No matter where you go, you'll be there. You can't leave yourself behind."

"But I want to. That's what I'm saying."

Jasmine's dark eyes flamed, and she lifted her head slightly. "You should be proud of who you are. How can you walk on this earth as a representative for God if you're ashamed of his work?"

"What do you mean, 'his work'?"

"Well, he created you, didn't he?"

Mattie knew Jasmine spoke the truth, but she couldn't grasp a sense of who she was. Most of her life she'd only known self-loathing. "It's not so easy to just change my mind."

"Of course, it isn't, but God will help you to see, if you let him."

"I can't be like you. I wish I could but—"

"God's not asking you to be like me," she snapped, sounding almost angry. "You must embrace who *you* are." She looked down at herself. "Do you think all the wishing in the world could make me something other than a Negro?"

"No."

"So, what am I going to do about it? I've got to accept it. There's no other way. And then I live my life the best I can, not being ashamed and not hiding. You've got to think about what it is God wants you to do while you're here on this earth, and your heritage is part of that." She gripped the bars. "Mattie, you've learned a lot here in Seattle, but what have you taught Seattle about you? About your people?"

Mattie was taken aback. It had never occurred to her to help anyone understand her heritage. She'd spent most of her energy trying to conceal her background. The click of shoes on the tile floors carried through the cellblock.

A police officer stepped up and unlocked the door, then swung it open. "You're free to go, Miss Lawson."

"I am?" Mattie asked, stepping out. "So you know I'm not Japanese?"

"I don't know nothin'. Just that I'm supposed to release you." He didn't smile. "Go through that door and turn right. They have your possessions at the desk."

Stunned, Mattie sputtered, "But what can I do to make sure this doesn't happen again?"

The officer shrugged.

"What if I had some kind of special identification?"

He walked away, acting as if she'd said nothing.

Mattie had no way of knowing that someone else wouldn't turn her in. She would have to live with the worry. Now, eager to be free, she hurried out. After collecting her belongings, she pushed through the station doors and stepped into the fresh air. The sun was shining and felt warm. It was wonderful to be free. It was hard to believe she'd spent less than twenty-four hours locked up. It had seemed much longer.

Linking arms, Jasmine escorted her down the steps. Mattie glanced at her friend and wished she could be like her. Maybe in time, but she doubted she'd ever have that kind of strength. She did feel stronger though. Trying to think confidently, Mattie took long strides as she headed for the bus stop.

Jasmine waited with her. "Remember what I said."

"I won't forget," Mattie said, determined to at least give it some thought.

"I'll be thinking about you. Please come and visit me and my sister."

"I will," Mattie promised just as her bus rumbled to a stop. With a quick hug, she said, "You take care of yourself. Thank you for being such a good friend." She stepped onto the bus, found a seat, and waved at Jasmine as the bus pulled away. *Lord, help me to be more like her,* she prayed, but felt little hope of ever reaching a place where she could happily accept who she was. The scars left by those without eyes to see the truth were deep and her self-loathing and bitterness deeper.

Chapter 18

His stomach rumbling with hunger, Luke walked into the mess hall and headed for the chow line. He'd nearly missed lunch. Only a handful of sailors were still dishing up. Luke grabbed a plate, dropped a spoonful of mashed potatoes on it, and drizzled lumpy gravy over them. He added two slices of ham and a spoon of cooked corn. After grabbing a glass of milk, he headed for a table.

"Hey, Luke, over here," Barry called.

Luke headed toward his buddy. Setting his tray on the table, he sat across from him. Barry's plate was empty. "It's about time I got some chow," Luke said. "Feels like I've got a hole in my gut." He took a bite of potatoes. Talking around the food in his mouth, he asked, "So, why are you still here? I thought you came up more than an hour ago."

"I did, but I got commandeered along the way. One of the guys was working on a hatch that wouldn't seal and needed some help." He drained the last of a glass of water. "He just needed someone who knew what to do. Works good now."

Luke nodded and kept eating.

Barry glanced at his watch. "It's 1440. Why you so late?"

"With so many Nips prowling around, the brass is nervous. I had orders to check all the hoses . . . again. And I had to do it before I went off duty."

Barry rested his arms on the table and leaned forward. "To tell you the truth, I'm feeling kind of jumpy myself. We're like sitting ducks out here."

"I doubt we got anything to worry about. We have good cover. Eleven planes just came in, and they're set to launch another batch."

Barry eyed the dessert rack. "I'm so edgy I'm not even hungry." He settled a serious look on Luke. "I think somethin's up. We're in for it. I can feel it. Wouldn't be surprised if we faced off with the Japs, maybe even have a full-scale battle. You know, like at Midway."

"It's about time. The Japs have been pushin' and pushin'. I'd like to put 'em in their place. If we're gonna win this war, we've got to be more aggressive."

"We've hit 'em pretty good."

"Maybe." Luke took a big drink of milk. "But they've been hitting right back. Them slant eyes have taken the East Indies, Sumatra, Burma, Borneo, Java, and a bunch of places I can't pronounce. And now they're working their way through the Solomon Islands."

"Why do you think we're here?" Barry leaned back and clasped his hands behind his head. "We'll stop 'em." He eyed the desserts again. "Maybe I *am* hungry." He stood and headed for the stand. After choosing a large piece of chocolate cake, he strolled back to the table and sat. "I'm not about to let anyone take away my little pleasures." He cut into it with his fork and pushed a bite into his mouth.

Luke grinned. "Didn't think a little thing like a war could keep you from your chocolate."

Barry chewed with satisfaction. "You got that right."

"I hope you're right about us winning this thing," Luke said, taking a bite of ham. "The Japs are cocky. They think they can beat us." He cut off another piece of ham and swiped it through his gravy. "The kamikaze pilots are the worst. They gotta be crazy—crashing their planes into a ship and killing themselves." He pushed the meat into his mouth. "You wouldn't think they'd do something like that unless they were sure the sacrifice was worth it. They must believe they're gonna win the war."

"I heard they're drugged. They don't even know what they're doing." He forked another bite of cake into his mouth. "The Japanese have been putting out a lot of propaganda. I think they're nervous. 'Course, that's not necessarily good. Sometimes a nervous enemy is more dangerous."

Resting his arms on either side of his cake plate, Barry leaned forward. "We've been pounding them, especially in the Marshall Islands.

And don't forget Wake Island. We hit 'em really hard there." He shook his head slowly. "I got to say, I'd like to have seen their faces when our bombers came in over the cities on mainland Japan."

"That was months ago." Luke pushed his nearly empty plate aside. "And after making those bombing runs, our planes didn't even have enough fuel to make it back to base. They crashed in China. I don't call that winning."

The carrier made a shift toward starboard, and Luke grabbed the table. "What?"

Two explosions in quick succession followed, rocking the ship and throwing Luke and Barry to the floor. It felt as if the *Wasp* had been lifted out of the water. Another blast rattled from up forward. The ship convulsed.

Luke grabbed hold of the table and dragged himself from the floor. Another thunderous roar ripped through the carrier, and he scrambled to maintain his footing. "I think the forward magazines blew!"

A siren wailed. Barry staggered to his feet and headed for the door. Luke followed. The ship listed.

As the two men made their way through the companionways, more explosions shook the vessel. Sailors scrambled to duty stations. When Luke and Barry stepped onto the upper deck, they entered a living nightmare. The stink of oil and gasoline was heavy. Airplane parts, ammo, and men's bodies littered the deck. The forward antiaircraft guns had been ripped apart and scattered. A cloud of smoke hung over the carnage. Fires seemed to be burning everywhere.

Dodging bullets from exploding guns and burning planes, Luke headed for the bow. Officers and crew calmly but quickly carried out their duties. Men manned the guns, put out small fires, helped the injured, and hauled bombs away from flames. Burning planes were too hot to approach. One at a time they blew up with their payloads.

"We need to get water on those!" Luke yelled, running forward. He nearly stopped when he saw the damage to the bow. It was beyond comprehension—a large portion of the forward deck was missing, and blackened bodies lay in grotesque positions, mouths in indistinguishable faces were drawn back in shriveled grins. One man lay with his arms bent at the elbows, his hands seemingly protecting his face;

another lay outstretched, his arms at his sides. He stared through burned-out sockets.

Luke choked back nausea and kept moving, staying low.

Barry was at his side. "Don't worry about them. They're not feeling anything now." He rested a hand on Luke's back. "We'll make it."

Luke managed a nod, then yanked a hose free. He turned the nozzle. No water. He closed it off and turned it again. Still no water. Throwing it aside, he headed for the next hose. Barry followed. The two men ripped it away from a bulkhead, but it was the same—no water.

"The lines must be busted," Luke shouted, ducking as exploding bombs and ammo sent shrapnel and bullets zinging across the deck. A piece of burning matter fell on him. He grabbed at it, burning his hands. Gritting his teeth against the pain, he tossed the material aside. His hands felt as if they were still on fire. He steeled himself against what he might see and looked down. His fingers were blistered and red, but the burns didn't look serious.

What should he do now? What could he do? How did you fight a fire without water? And even if they could find water, the blaze was out of control. The flames were consuming the carrier.

Was it time to give up and abandon ship? Something in Luke wouldn't allow the thought. He headed aft. Most of the damage seemed to be in the bow; maybe the hoses in the stern were undamaged. Ignoring the pain in his hands, he grabbed one and turned it on. It worked.

He immediately unfurled the lines. "Get water on those fires," he hollered, connecting hoses and dragging them toward the bow. Other men got the idea and began to hose the flames, but the fire was out of control. The crew might as well have been using eyedroppers to hose it down.

More explosives went up, and the fires burned through more of the ship. Heat singed Luke's eyebrows and scorched his face. He knew he was blistered.

The ship slowed and turned astern. The flow of air decreased. The maneuver was meant to slow the fires. Maybe they had a chance. Moments later a series of blasts squelched all hope. Luke lost his grip on the hose, and it broke free. Water spiraled wildly. The explosions had come from the forward part of the hanger. *It had to be bombs,* he decided.

The smell of gasoline intensified, and heat seemed to be coming from everywhere. Luke thought this must be what it felt like to be in an oven. He began to fear that he and everyone else would be roasted alive. They were in real trouble. A firefighter's clothes torched. He screamed, ran for the railing, and hurled himself over the side.

The smell of charred flesh in his nostrils, Luke watched in horror. *God, help us,* he prayed, then turned and did what he knew to do. He captured the wayward hose, pointed it at ammo threatened by flames, and cooled the heating artillery.

Barry grabbed him. "We got to get out of here. It's gonna go. The whole ship—all of it."

"Where do we go?" Luke asked, keeping the water flowing.

"Off the ship. There's nothing else we can do. We're cooked."

"We haven't gotten the order to abandon ship. I'm not leaving."

"We gotta go."

Luke shook his head and moved the water toward a burning plane. "Not until the captain gives the order," he hollered.

"All right. All right," Barry shouted, grabbing hold of the hose behind Luke. "I'm not leaving you. If we don't make it, it's your fault."

Stunned, Luke looked at his friend.

Barry grinned. "Just teasing." He turned his attention on the hose.

A few minutes later the order came: Abandon ship.

Luke couldn't believe it was happening. He'd never envisioned himself bailing out. He watched as boats and rafts were lowered. Men climbed down rope ladders; others, unable to hang on to hot cables, leaped into the sea. The injured were lowered down and helped into rescue crafts.

"It's time," Barry said.

"All right. I'm coming," Luke said, keeping the water on the flames. Finally he dropped the hose and followed Barry.

The two headed aft along with the others. The evacuation was orderly and calm—too calm Luke thought, wondering if it was hopelessness that brought quiet. They'd lost their ship to the enemy. An intense bitterness filled him.

A scream cut through his thoughts. Luke turned and watched a sailor, his shirt aflame, running erratically. "Stop!" he shouted, sprinting for the man. As he ran, he searched for something to smother the flames. He couldn't find anything.

Luke hurtled himself at the sailor and threw him to the deck. He could feel fire burning through his shirt as he forced the hysterical man to roll. Luke slapped at the last stubborn flames.

The sailor lay panting and shaking, his eyes closed. Luke leaned on one arm, trying to catch his breath. "You nearly killed us both," he said lightheartedly. Offering a hand, he added, "Come on, we've got to get off this tub."

"Thanks," the sailor said, allowing Luke to pull him to his feet.

"You'll be fine," Luke told him, hoping he sounded convincing. It looked like the man had some bad burns. He glanced over the rail. Adrenaline pulsed through him. A slick of burning oil covered the ocean.

What sounded like thunder rumbled up from below. There was nothing Luke could do to avoid the blast. He was thrown through the air. The next thing he knew he was hanging from a beam and struggling to breathe. His shirt had twisted with his dog tags and had caught on the timber. Nearly strangling, he sucked in hot air.

Glancing below, he saw a burning ocean. If he pulled himself free, he'd drop and be burned alive. "Help! Someone help!" he tried to call out, but the shirt was so tight around his neck that he could barely make a sound. He caught a sailor's eye, and the man hurried to the rail. The shirt ripped, and Luke dropped slightly. All at once it shredded, breaking the chain that held his dog tags and ripping the shirt from his body. He plunged downward toward the burning sea.

Reaching out blindly, he sought a handhold. Nothing. The next moment he felt heat and took a deep gulp of air before plunging through the flames and beneath the surface. Pushing upward with his arms, he forced himself to stay below the waterline. He opened his eyes. They stung intensely and his skin throbbed. Above, on the surface, all he could see were flames. Fire was everywhere. His lungs screamed for oxygen. *I can't die like this! Not like this—cooked in a sea of oil!*

Desperate, he sought an opening free of flames and thought he spotted one. It was several yards away. He'd never make it. Pulling with his arms and kicking as hard as he could, he swam toward the haven. His lungs felt as if they would burst. He had to breathe—NOW!

Luke broke through the surface and gulped heated oxygen saturated with oil fumes. He choked and coughed. His throat and lungs felt like fire. He swam in a circle, seeking a way out. He was trapped. At any moment the flames would engulf him.

"Help!" he called, his voice a gravelly whisper. "Help!"

He had no chance. His life would end at Guadalcanal. He turned hurting eyes toward the ship. It sat low in front, enveloped by flames and smoke. Soon it would sink.

Mattie's face hung in his mind. He'd never hold her again, never call her his wife. This is what she'd feared. "I'm sorry, Mattie," he whispered.

Treading water, his thoughts turned to his family—to Susie, Brian, Laurel, and his mother. He even thought of Ray—who didn't seem so evil at this moment. Luke had never mended the relationship. Now it was too late.

Flames creeped across the surface of the water toward him. He tried to swim away but had no place to go. Fire and oil were everywhere. He searched for a raft and made another feeble plea for help. Paddling in a circle, he sought a way out. Fire burned his face, and he dunked beneath the waves to cool his blistered skin.

There was no escape.

Chapter 19

LUKE IS GONE, MATTIE THOUGHT, AWAKING FROM A FITFUL SLEEP. SHE ADJUSTED a small pillow she'd placed against the train window. Resettling her cheek against it, she watched a white world slide past. The hours and miles since leaving Seattle had not eased her grief. She'd hoped that docking in Seward would bring comfort, that being on Alaskan soil might bring a reprieve from the anguish that gnawed at her insides, but she experienced no reprieve. Alaska may have been home, but changing locations did not relieve her suffering.

I should have married him. Tears burned her eyes. *Oh, Luke, I'm so sorry. I loved you. I did. I do.* She sniffled and wiped away what seemed like endless tears. *I made a terrible mistake. Now it's too late.*

She grabbed a handkerchief she'd tucked inside her sleeve and dabbed at her eyes and nose. Not marrying Luke hadn't helped at all. In fact, Mattie was sure it made her sorrow more profound.

She studied a grove of ice-encased trees. Limbs, twisted and tangled, looked like hideous groping creatures—distorted and aching like Mattie's heart. She leaned her face against the cold glass. Life hurt too much. She didn't want to live.

Like a tortured slave, Mattie's anguish remained, seeming to deepen with each passing mile. She thought she knew now what the term "weeping and gnashing of teeth" meant. Nothing existed except the heartache. Like a caged animal, Mattie prowled the car, searching for an escape from her grief. She could not break free of it. Finally she returned to her seat.

Mama, I need you. She envisioned home. It couldn't be far now. Things would be better there. Mattie turned her eyes to the mountains, expecting to find the sense of wonder they'd always brought. Nothing. She felt nothing.

The train slowed, and Mattie watched Palmer move past. It had grown, become a real town. Of course, compared to Seattle it was little more than a hamlet, but for now that was fine with Mattie. She didn't need the restlessness of the city.

Mattie thought about Meryl, who had been so worried about Mattie that she'd wanted to accompany her. It hadn't seemed right to drag Meryl from her life while she sorted out her own. Mattie had insisted she would be fine. Now she wished Meryl were here, helping her to forget.

The train lurched to a stop. Mattie stood, retrieved her bags off the rack above her, and moved down the aisle. She wondered who would meet her. A visit home should have been a joyous occasion. *If only this were just a visit like any other. Maybe if I pretend, it will seem so.*

Stepping off the train, she glanced about. A man about the same height and weight as Luke and dressed in a navy uniform stood with his back to her. Mattie's heart fluttered. *He's alive!* The sailor turned. Mattie held her breath. It was someone else. Her emotions tumbled, and the ache inside her swelled.

"Mattie," someone called.

She turned and saw Celeste striding toward her. *Celeste?* Mattie hadn't expected her. They hadn't been especially close.

Her blue eyes vibrant as ever, Celeste grabbed Mattie in a bear hug. "How wonderful to see you! We've missed you!"

"I've missed you too," Mattie managed to say. She spotted Laurel and dropped her bags.

"Mattie!" Laurel said and hurried to her friend, catching her in her arms. "I'm so glad you're here." They clung to each other.

Mattie felt Laurel's strength and became stronger.

Finally they stepped back and looked at one another. "You look good for a city girl," Laurel teased.

"I liked the city," Mattie said and managed a smile.

Laurel's eyes turned serious. "It's good to have you home." Wiping away a tear, she said, "We've missed you."

Celeste picked up the bags. "Your mother and grandmother are beside themselves. They're so excited. They've been preparing all week."

"I can't wait to see them."

"They would have come, but it's hard for your grandmother to get out so we volunteered to escort you." Laurel threw an arm around Mattie's shoulders. She gave her a tight squeeze. "Oh, it's so good to have you here."

"It feels good to be here," Mattie said, meaning it. She glanced around and was reminded of the many good times she'd had here. It was strange she'd forgotten them.

Laurel's expression was serious. "I know it's hard to believe that something good is going to happen, but don't give up hope. He might be alive."

"I pray so."

"I think he is," Celeste said.

"His ship went down, and he's missing. Where could he be?" Mattie asked, unable to believe.

After a cumbersome pause, Laurel said, "We must keep praying. I have a feeling. I don't think he's gone."

"What about Adam? Is he all right?"

Laurel's expression turned stoic. "We haven't heard anything."

"I'm so sorry." Mattie rested a hand on Laurel's arm. "I wish this war would end."

"Me too." Laurel patted Mattie's hand. "God is in control. Adam and Luke are in his care."

Mattie looked at Celeste. "What about Robert?"

"I just got a letter from him. He's fighting in Africa, but there are rumors that his division is being sent to Italy soon. Maybe the war will be over before then," she said, making an effort to sound cheerful. She looped her arm through Mattie's. "We better get you home."

The three women climbed into Laurel's pickup and headed out of town. Mattie studied the heavy snow on the mountains and the white fields. "Looks like winter's early."

"It's been cold, and as you can see, the snows have come." Laurel gripped the steering wheel as they bounced over a mound.

"In October, anything can happen," Celeste said. "It could warm up and we might have an Indian Summer."

"It's been colder than usual in Seattle. 'Course, they get more rain than anything else." Laurel watched the icy road slide beneath the front of the truck. "Have you had news about the war in the Aleutians?"

"Oh, yes. It's awful," Celeste said. "The Japanese have occupied Kiska, Attu, and Unalaska. The government managed to evacuate a lot of people, but some were taken prisoner. It's frightening. We've been practicing drills just in case."

"I prayed for you all the time you were on the ship," Laurel said. "It doesn't seem safe to be traveling in the Pacific."

"I was a little scared," Mattie admitted, "but we took the Inside Passage and it's supposed to be safe." She wiped fog from the window. "Why do there have to be wars anyway?"

"I don't know," Laurel said. "We all wish it would be over." She glanced at Mattie. "I believe Adam and Luke are alive."

"How can you know?"

"I just feel it. If they were gone, I'd know. I have to believe." Her eyes glistened. "William talks about his father all the time." She smiled. "He's made him into a real war hero."

Silence settled over the cab.

Celeste ended the quiet. "So, Mattie, are you going to stay for good?"

"I don't know. Maybe, I really do like Seattle."

"What's it like?"

"Big and beautiful. The city sits right on a large bay called Puget Sound, and it's much warmer there though it does rain a lot. The city has lots of tall buildings, clubs where you can listen to bands and dance, and lots of movie houses. Outside the city the countryside is real pretty, with forests, lots of mountain ranges and a big mountain called Mount Rainier. It's beautiful, but nothing like McKinley."

"Are the people different?" Celeste asked.

"Different, how?"

"Well, I know you wanted to live in a place where people treated you better."

"Most of the people didn't seem to even notice that I was native. Some did, but it was better than here." Looking at Laurel, she added, "You were right, though. I couldn't run away from my heritage."

A crease furrowed Laurel's brow. "I'm sorry. I wish it had been better for you."

"It wasn't bad there. I liked it, very much."

Laurel offered a small smile. "Well, we're glad to have you back home."

"Their loss, our gain." Celeste smiled.

"Thanks."

Laurel turned the pickup into Mattie's drive and stopped. The dilapidated cabin didn't look as bad as Mattie had remembered. It was tiny and run-down but appeared tidy and hospitable. The front door opened immediately, and her mother stepped out. Her grandmother followed, her hands folded over her chest. Their eyes filled with love and expectation, the two women hurried toward the truck, Atuska shuffling.

Mattie's spirits climbed. Opening the door, she said, "Thanks for picking me up. I'll see you." She climbed out, grabbed her bags out of the back, and set them on the ground just in time to step into a much-needed embrace. "Oh, Mama," Mattie hugged her mother tightly. "I missed you."

Her grandmother rested a hand on her granddaughter's back, and Mattie turned to the old woman, enfolding her in her arms. Atuska's soft cheek rested against Mattie's. She could feel the wetness of her grandmother's tears. "It's so good to be home."

Her grandmother took a step back and gazed at her. The old woman's eyes shimmered, nearly disappearing in the folds of her skin. "It is right that you are here. I am thanking God for bringing you back to us."

"Me too," Mattie said, realizing that the pain she'd carried with her all the way from Seattle had eased. She began to believe she had hope for happiness again.

Affia circled an arm around her daughter's waist and hugged her as they walked. "I knew you would come back."

"Mama, I don't know for sure that I'm going to stay."

"You'll stay," her grandmother said, wearing a playful smile. Her eyes rounded into half moons. "I know my Mattie. She could not leave for good."

"We'll see," Mattie said, wondering if she was ready to completely surrender.

∿

Luke carefully shifted from one hip to the other. The more hours he spent in bed, the more his body ached. His face throbbed, and he gently pressed on the bandages swathing them. He'd been burned and wondered how bad the scarring would be. The doctor had assured him the burns weren't deep and would heal. At least when he got home he wouldn't shock his family; he just wished he knew where home was and who his family was. And even more, he wished he knew who *he* was.

Holding up his hand, he studied it. He had neither a wedding ring nor a mark where one might have been. Who and where was his family? He concentrated, trying to remember. Nothing.

No one knew to whom he belonged. He'd been fished out of the ocean when the *Wasp* sank, but he had no dog tags or other ID on him. He lay unconscious for days, and no one came forward to identify him. Of course, it was difficult to identify someone whose face was hidden by bandages. He wondered if anyone in the military hospital would know him once the bandages came off. Unfortunately for Luke, most of the survivors from the ship had already been sent home or reassigned. Some had been sent to other hospitals. If only he could remember.

Days passed, and Luke's dressings were removed. Although his skin looked red and sore, the scarring was minimal.

No one knew him. He'd asked every conscious patient in the hospital. People were beginning to think he'd lost his mind. Maybe he had. Why couldn't he even remember his own name? With each passing day Luke felt more lost, as if he'd been set afloat in some great ocean—alone.

The doctor told him the amnesia would resolve itself in its own way and its own time. Luke wanted an answer now. His body had regained its health, his scars were healing, and he'd soon be shipped back to the States. If he didn't remember by then, he hoped that being in his own country would help.

The trouble was, even the idea of returning to the States was unsettling to him. He didn't know anyone there. Where would he go? Who would he contact? At least here he knew the doctors and nurses and was comfortable with his surroundings. It felt like a safe harbor.

"So, how're you doing today?" the company chaplain asked, sitting in a chair beside Luke's bed. He smiled, his eyes warm.

"OK, I guess."

"You remember anything?"

"Nothing. It's discouraging. How long will it take?"

"Can't say, son. Our brains are mysterious things. Only God knows."

"What if I never remember, and my life is gone forever?"

"That's very unlikely. But if it were to happen, you'd begin again and build a new life."

Luke shook his head. "I don't want a new life. I want *my* life."

"I know, I know." The reverend stood. "It will happen in God's time. He knows you, where you came from, and where you're going. He'll see to it that you get where he wants you to be."

"I believe you, but I don't know why. I can't remember. Do I know God?"

The chaplain smiled, his blue eyes crinkling. "Sounds to me like you do." He took Luke's hand. "Let's pray together. That all right with you?"

"Sure."

The chaplain closed his eyes.

Luke closed his, thinking, *God, please tell me who I am.*

"Dear Father in heaven," the chaplain began. "We thank you for being a loving father to us, a father who never takes his eyes off his children. You know our sitting down and our rising up. You understand our thoughts. You know our paths and our lying down. You know all our ways." He paused, as if contemplating the power of an all-seeing God. "Father, although this young man feels alone, he's not. Help him to know and understand that you are with him. And, Father, you know the right time for him to remember. While he waits, fill him with your peace.

"Father, I also pray for those who love and miss him. His family doesn't know what has become of him. Their sorrow must be great. Comfort them. Assure them he is well, and give them peace as they wait."

The chaplain paused. "Lord, I pray also for all the young men and women who are fighting in this war. Keep your hand of love and protection upon each one. Carry them through the battles safely, and when it is all finished, carry them home.

"I pray for your intervention in this war. It is ugly and vile. Our enemy, Satan, is gloating, but not forever. You are the destroyer of evil. Help each of us to love and to forgive our enemies. I pray that all humankind will know your love. Amen."

Luke felt a stab of hatred for the Japanese. It was a familiar sensation, and he tried to hang onto it, hoping it might reveal a piece of his lost memory. The feeling quickly evaporated, and once more, he felt cut off. Luke looked at the chaplain. "I hope your prayer works. I don't know how long I can take not knowing who I am."

The chaplain stood. "God hears us, and he will answer. It may not be in the way we want or the time we want, but he'll do what is best."

"Why did you pray for our enemies? They're the ones who put me in here."

"They're part of God's creation too. The men and women fighting on the other side also have families, people who care. They matter to God. And he tells us to love our enemies."

Luke knew he'd heard the words before. He peered into his mind and tried to remember, but he couldn't. Still, he knew the words were significant. Maybe reading the Bible would help. He looked at the chaplain. "Do you have a Bible I could borrow?"

"Sure. I'll bring one over later today."

"Figure I ought to read up on God so I can know if I want to believe in him or not."

The minister smiled. "Sounds like a good idea." He moved on to the next bed.

Luke clung to the peace he felt while in the chaplain's presence. He didn't feel quite so alone. *God, if you're real, help me. Please.*

Chapter 20

ADAM, ELISA, AND ADIN STOOD ON A RISE OVERLOOKING THE TOWN OF Abbeville, which lay in a valley with the Somme River flowing through. Adam imagined that on a bright day it probably looked inviting. Today, however, a drizzle soaked the landscape and draped the town in a murky haze.

The three travelers were drenched and cold to the core. Poor Adin shivered and snuggled against Adam's chest, but he could do little to help the boy. Adam's skin was goose-fleshed and cold. He eyed a nearby farmhouse. Smoke trailed into the sky from a stone chimney, and lights glowed within. He imagined himself and his comrades inside, sitting before the hearth and eating a bowl of hot soup with warm bread.

He gazed at Adin in his arms and tried to protect him with his soaking coat. The boy whimpered softly. "We've got to get out of this weather. If we don't, Adin's going to end up sick."

"*Oui*. Yes. I know, but we must also find Jacque Billaud. He is the one who will help us."

Adam gazed at Abbeville, a field of rooftops and chimneys. How would they find one man among so many? "I know we've got to find him, but first we need to get dry and warm. What good is this Jacque if we're dead?" He met Elisa's dark eyes. "Shelter first."

"*Oui*." Elisa caressed her son's forehead, kissed his cold skin, then looked back toward the city. "There. We will stay there." She pointed at a small, stone church just inside the city, a kilometer or so west of where they stood.

"All right," Adam said and started walking. Elisa stayed beside

178

Adam. He laid an arm protectively over her shoulders. "How do you plan on finding this Jacques Billaud?"

"I will search. Someone will know of him."

"You're Jewish."

"*Oui,*" she stated flatly.

"Won't people know that?"

"Maybe, yes, but this is for me to do." She eyed Adam. "Your French is not so good." She smiled.

"You have a point." Adam stared at the city. It could take weeks, maybe more to find this Jacques. And what if they didn't find him? How could they get out of the country? German patrols persistently sought any who would escape their tyranny. If they were discovered . . . Adam's hopes dipped. *Father, help us. This is impossible without you. You know where this Jacque Billaud is. Lead us to him.* His empty stomach grumbled. *And, Lord, please help us find something to eat.*

"I have been thinking of a plan," Elisa said. "You must wait with Adin. I will go into the town, the saloons. Is that the right word? Saloon?"

"If you mean a bar, yeah, saloon will do."

Confusion touched Elisa's face. "I will go in those places, and maybe someone will know this man. Is it not so?"

"Yes, it is so." Adam gave Elisa a squeeze. He admired her courage and tenacity. He let her loose. "You might find him in a bar, but if he doesn't frequent those kinds of places, you'll come up empty . . ."

"I will find him."

"And what about the Germans?"

"You say God will protect. I shall much appreciate your prayers."

Adin whimpered and said something to his mother.

"He is hungry," Elisa said, heading toward a bridge. She stopped at the shore and stepped beneath the overpass. Adam followed with Adin. Elisa swung her pack off and dug into it.

"At least it's not raining under here." A sharp breeze swept over them, and Adam shivered. "It's not warm either."

Spitting out a string of French, Elisa swung her pack away from her. "Nothing. I have nothing for him!" Tears filled her eyes, and she wiped at them furiously. "What am I to do?" She sat and pulled her knees against her chest, wrapped her arms around her legs, and stared at the river.

Cradling Adin, Adam sat beside her. The boy climbed into his mother's arms, and she caressed his wet hair and kissed his head. She returned to staring at the river, her eyes wide and bleak.

Adam removed his coat and draped it over her and the boy. "We'll find something. Don't worry."

"It is much easier for you. This is not your child."

"I understand and care . . . a lot."

Elisa looked at him but said nothing.

Adam wished he could stop her pain, but he couldn't do anything to help her. His mind wandered to Abbeville. "Maybe we can find something in town. A restaurant would have food."

"Ah, yes. The waiters will smile and ask if we would like a cognac to go with our white fish in cream sauce. Of course, we will say *oui*," she continued sarcastically. "Then while we wait for our meal, they will bring us tender asparagus drizzled with melted cheese . . ."

He laughed. "Stop. My stomach is cramping at the thought."

Elisa smiled. "I wish it could be true, but . . ." She pulled her sweater pocket inside out. "We have no money."

"Restaurants throw away food all the time."

Elisa's eyes widened. "Ah, yes. The garbage?"

"Yes."

"Why is it that I did not think of this sooner?"

"The stuff on top should be fresh." The idea of reaching into a trash bin to eat turned Adam's stomach, but he was hungry enough to try it. "Come on. Let's go find lunch."

Elisa stood. "Maybe we can look for Jacques also?"

"Sure."

They stepped out from beneath their temporary shelter, and the rain stopped. Sunshine splintered between clouds. Moisture trickled from blades of grass, and mists rose from puddles. Adam balanced Adin on his shoulders, and Elisa walked beside him as they entered the city. Narrow cobblestone streets ambled between brick buildings. The last of the rain dribbled off steeply pitched roofs. Adam thought he caught the aroma of cooking onions, and his mouth watered.

The city seemed alive. An occasional car negotiated the winding streets. People were busy. Some swept away debris from their porches, while others cleared rain gutters or hurried toward some unknown destination. Adam and Elisa were careful not to make eye contact.

Elisa sniffed the air. "Ah, yes, something smells very good."

Adam smiled. "I'd say there's a restaurant close by. Come on, this way." He took Elisa's hand, glanced up the street, then led her across. They moved past the church they'd seen from a distance. Its arched, stained-glass windows gleamed in the sunlight. A statue of the Virgin Mother stood as guardian in a grassy corner in front. "Maybe we can come back here after we get something to eat," Adam said, adding a silent prayer for mercy and direction.

He stopped. "I think the smells are coming from there." Adam pointed at a café. The building had a row of narrow windows across the front. As they passed, he tried not to stare at the people seated inside enjoying a meal.

"Oh, how I wish we could go in," Elisa said.

"We'll eat." With Adin on his shoulders, Adam strode on. "This way." He circled around to the back of the building. A door leading into the restaurant was closed, and a trash bin stood a few feet from it. Doing his best to think positively about its contents, Adam handed Adin to Elisa and walked to the container. Gingerly he lifted the lid. The smell of rotting food assaulted him, but he showed no revulsion and peeked inside.

"I figure whatever's on top ought to be pretty fresh." He lifted out a chunk of cabbage with some sort of casserole slopped over it, then smelled it. "I think this is all right." He handed it to Elisa, then returned to foraging. He picked up a large piece of meat. It seemed fine. He hung on to it and returned for a scrap of fish, which disintegrated in his hand and fell back into the refuse. He noticed a chunk of bread and grabbed it. Unable to stand the stink any longer, he slammed the lid back down. "That ought to see us through for now." Smiling, he turned to face Elisa and Adin. "Let's go."

Elisa tore off a piece of the bread and gave it to Adin. He chewed contentedly as they made their way back to the church. She stopped at the end of a stone walkway in front of the stone building. With a quick glance about, she ran up to the large double doors in front.

Adam yanked on a heavy wooden handle. The door didn't budge. "It's locked." He followed the steps down, then walked to a grassy patch around the corner of the church.

Trees and brush grew against the block wall. The greenery had been allowed to grow wild, creating a tunnel of sorts. Beneath the natural hollow, the ground was dry and the sheltered were protected from the wind. Adam retraced his steps and called quietly, "Come on. In here."

Elisa and Adin joined him, and Adam studied the food they'd found. "Looks like a feast."

Elisa tasted the casserole. Her eyes opened wide, and she smiled. "It is. Here, Adin, you try." She gave her son a bite, and he chewed happily, then scooped up a handful.

"You should have some," Elisa told Adam. "Please."

Adam took a portion. It tasted rich and buttery. He tore off a bite of the meat. It tasted like lamb and was very good. "Try this." He offered Elisa a portion of the meat.

For a few minutes they ate in silence, satiating their hunger. Elisa licked her fingers, then rested her back against the wall. "Good, very good. I think we should visit that restaurant again," she said with a smile. She closed her eyes and pulled Adin close. "Ah, if only the church were open. It would be much warmer inside for Adin. And I think German soldiers do not like churches."

"We might be safer in someone's barn outside of town."

"*Oui*, but to find Jacques we must stay here." She pushed to her feet. "I will go and search. You stay with Adin."

The boy said something to his mother. She answered in French.

"What is it?"

"He wonders where I am going. I tell him he must stay with you."

Adam looked at the boy. Dark eyes stared out of a gaunt face. Adam wished he spoke French. That way he could search for help, and Adin could wait, secure with his mother. He offered the youngster a smile. *He should be playing games, singing songs, and laughing, not struggling to live and hiding from German soldiers.* Sorrow pierced him.

"I must go now," Elisa said. "Maybe your God will help us," she added. She was silent a moment. "For this I am sorry."

"For what? You didn't do anything."

"Ah, maybe not, but this is my country and here you are." She grasped his hand. "Please be safe. I thank you for your help." She pressed his hand to her cheek. "I love you."

Adam's heart ached. If only he could make the world beautiful for her. "We'll be here when you get back. I promise."

Her dark eyes mournful, she squeezed his hand. "I will be back . . . soon." She blinked back tears. "If the soldiers come, you must pray to God. I believe he hears you." Hastily Elisa bent and kissed Adam, then turned and walked away.

Adam moved to the front of the building and watched her until she disappeared around a corner. A passer-by eyed him curiously. Adam nodded, doing his best to look nonchalant. When he was certain no one could see him, he returned to the refuge.

He lifted Adin, then sat with his back resting against the rock wall. The boy nuzzled close and was soon asleep. With a smile, Adam caressed the boy's dark hair and thought of his own son and . . . Laurel. The stark realization of his betrayal hit him. *Father, help me to be loyal and still be what Elisa needs me to be,* he prayed. *And as she searches for Jacques, keep your hand upon her. Protect her from the enemy.*

With the emptiness in his stomach eased, his eyes felt heavy. He thought of Elisa. Did he love her? Were his feelings only admiration and a sense of unity brought about because of mutual need?

He looked down at the boy. His lashes looked black against his ashen skin. Adam wondered if he'd live. At home, William was strong and vigorous. *Thank God he lives far from here.* Adam felt the emptiness of separation. How many months had it been since he'd seen his son and Laurel? He didn't even know anymore. *Laurel probably thinks I'm dead. Everyone does. Maybe I am; it just hasn't happened yet.*

If he made it back, what would he tell Laurel about Elisa? *Nothing,* he decided. *It would hurt her too much. No one has to know.* Even as he tried to convince himself that there was nothing between himself and Elisa, he couldn't deny the powerful and intoxicating feelings he had for her. *I won't give in to them. I've already done and said more than I should. We are comrades because of circumstances.* "That's all it is. All it can be," he said, remembering the love in Elisa's eyes and his own response. If they made it out of France, how would he put her behind him?

"Adam," Elisa's voice cut into his dream. "Adam. Wake up. I think I found him!"

Dragging himself awake, Adam focused on Elisa's face. "What?"

Elisa smiled brightly. "I found him."

"Just like that?" He pushed himself upright.

She sat. "But of course. As you have said, God is powerful, and I think I believe that is true. I have the address of a Jacques Billaud. It must be him." She glanced at Adin. "I pray for his sake." She stood. "Come. We must go. Many soldiers are in the streets, and soon it will be dark. We cannot be on the streets after curfew."

Adam could hear the fear in her voice. He caught hold of her hand. "Don't be afraid. I'm sure he's the one, and we'll be out of here in no time."

Elisa kneeled beside Adam. "And when we are saved, what happens to us?"

Adam hadn't wanted to face this inevitability, not yet. "I have a wife and a son, and I love them. I can't love you, Elisa."

She held his eyes. "I know. And for this I am sorry."

Darkness came too quickly. The streets emptied. Adam knew the danger was growing. If they were caught out after curfew, they had no explanation, no papers.

Staying in the shadows, the refugees made their way across town. Finally they stood before a scarred, wooden door. Elisa double-checked the address. "This is it," she whispered.

"What if you have the wrong address?"

Elisa took a deep breath. "I will pretend we are lost and we will go on." She faced the door and knocked. A minute later it opened and a teenaged boy peered out. "*Bonjour*," Elisa said, then asked for Jacques Billaud. A young man with intense blue eyes came to the door. He spoke to Elisa. The blue in his eyes deepened, and he stiffened. He started to close the door. Elisa pushed her foot between the door and the frame. "You are Jacques Billaud, are you not?" She said more, but all Adam understood was the pleading in her voice.

The man pushed, but Elisa did not move her foot. He shot a command at her. She didn't budge.

Adam knew that if he intervened it might make things worse, but he had to take a chance. "I am an American," he said. "We need your help." The man studied him, a look of understanding crossing his face. "My plane was shot down," Adam continued.

Jacques eyed him suspiciously. "You are American?"

"Yes. You speak English?"

"Some." He was noncommittal. "Why have you come to my house?"

"Arnaude Cervier gave us your name. He said you would help us."

"And how is it that you know Arnaude?"

"We were traveling, and we slept in his barn. He helped us."

Jacques thought a moment. "And how are Arnaude and his wife? Too bad they have no children."

"They have two . . . girls," Elisa said. "*Milice,* they come and take the whole family. That is when he gave us your name."

Jacques paled and looked stricken. "Come in."

After a change of clothing and a warm meal, Adam and Elisa sat at a table with Jacques while Adin slept. Jacques filled some glasses with wine. He sipped his and looked at his guests. "How did you meet?"

"I saw his plane coming down and his parachute," Elisa said. "I decide I must help him."

Adam smiled at Elisa, and she brightened. "Without her I would have been captured a long time ago."

Jacques frowned. "I have a plan, but it is very dangerous. You will go by boat even though the Germans have mined the coastline."

"When can we leave?" Adam asked.

"It is not so simple. The Germans inspect the boats. The man who will help us knows the waters, but there are many mines."

"We have no choice." Adam looked at Elisa. "I can go alone. Elisa and Adin can stay until the occupation is over."

Jacques looked at Elisa. "You are Jew, no?"

"*Oui.*"

Turning to Adam, he said, "She must go. If she is found . . ." He seemed unable to finish. Abruptly he said, "They cannot stay."

"So, the Germans *are* killing women and children." Adam felt sick.

"*Oui*," Jacques said. "When they look upon the little ones, they see only future Jews. Hitler has ordered all Jews to be killed. There is no mercy." He finished the last of his wine and set the glass on the table. "You will go together."

Two days later Adam, Elisa, and Adin were smuggled aboard a fishing boat and hidden in the hold. Amid the overpowering stench of fish, they huddled beneath a tarp.

Nauseated by the odor and the closeness, they waited. Hours passed, but the boat remained at the dock. *Something's gone wrong*, Adam thought. When he heard the sound of German orders, he heard the whisper of death. His heart hammered beneath his ribs, and he could barely breathe.

Elisa gripped his arm. Adin whimpered. Lifting him, Adam held the child tightly against his chest, muffling the sound. Footfalls sounded overhead. Adin quieted, and the three refugees held absolutely still. A mix of French and German rained down from above, then more footsteps, then a barrage of orders followed by the staccato tread of boots. Finally it was silent.

Elisa let out her breath. "They've gone. We're safe." She took Adin and cradled him. "We are safe."

Shortly after that the boat moved and felt as if it were gliding. The sound of waves washing against the sides of the craft told Adam they were moving away from France and toward freedom. Soon the small vessel rocked in the swell.

Someone opened the hatch, and light flooded the hold. A ladder was dropped. "It is time to come up," a man's robust voice called. "We're moving into the channel."

Grateful to be free of the fetid hold, Adam steadied the ladder while Elisa climbed up. With Adin slung over his shoulder, Adam followed her. A sharp, cold breeze greeted him. He breathed deeply. Fresh air smelled wonderful.

The engines were fired, and the tiny ship headed toward England. Adam knew a sense of freedom and hope he'd never experienced before. He was going home.

With Adin balanced on a hip, Elisa stared at the lights on the shoreline. "I shall not see my home again," she said sadly. "I pray for my family—if they are living."

Adam rested a hand on her shoulder. "A good life is waiting for you and Adin. One day you'll be happy again."

"I am hoping so." She turned and looked at him. "But I cannot be completely happy. There will be no you and me in this new life."

Adam couldn't refute her. He loved Laurel and William, and he could never walk away from them.

Elisa forced a smile. "Ah, but it is life, and for that I am grateful."

Adam left her there and went to the bow of the vessel where he joined two crewmen watching for mines. Using a light, they slowly scanned the waves.

One of the men shouted and pointed, and the boat quickly changed course. Adam thought he'd seen a shadow in the water. His stomach tightened. They weren't home yet.

They moved on, twice more barely avoiding disaster. Finally they motored into deeper waters. The hum of engines grew louder, and they picked up speed. The wind turned cold, and rain splashed the boat and its passengers.

Morning cast a soft light on the English shoreline as the fishing vessel chugged into a small harbor. Elisa stood beside Adam with Adin between them. "We will begin our new life, and it will be a good one. I have promised Adin." Her chin trembled. "Maybe we'll see each other again if I come to America."

"Maybe," Adam said, but they both knew it would never happen. "I won't forget you." He wanted to hold her, but he knew it was time to return to the real world, to put fantasies behind him. A deep ache burrowing inside, he searched Elisa's dark eyes. "You saved my life. I won't forget."

"And you saved mine." Her eyes brimming, Elisa turned toward the approaching pier.

Chapter 21

UNABLE TO KEEP FROM SMILING, LAUREL GRIPPED THE STEERING WHEEL AS she bumped down her mother's driveway. Braking, she turned off the engine and threw the truck into first gear. "Mama," she said, hurrying toward the back porch. "Mama!"

Jean stepped onto the porch, wearing a troubled expression. "What is it?"

Laurel flew into her mother's arms. "It's Adam! He's alive! They found him!"

Jean embraced her daughter. "Praise God!"

Stepping back, Laurel wiped away tears. "He's safe and on his way home! I've been laughing and crying all the way here." She clasped her mother's hands. "I thought he was alive, but I was afraid . . ." She couldn't hold back the tears and returned to her mother's arms. "I've been so afraid."

When Laurel's weeping turned to sniffles, Jean held her daughter away from her and smiled. "Come inside. Mattie's here."

Mattie stood beside the table, her expression unreadable. "I heard your wonderful news," she said. "I'm happy for you."

Laurel remembered Luke. He was still missing. She walked to Mattie and took her friend's hands. "We'll hear from Luke too."

Mattie managed a smile and hugged Laurel. "I keep praying and hoping I'll get word. Maybe soon, huh?"

Jean closed the door and said confidently, "That son of mine isn't one to give up. He'll be home." She crossed to the stove. "Laurel, how about some coffee or tea?"

"No, thank you. I've got things to do. Adam's on his way. He'll be here this week!"

"We'll have a celebration. I'll fix a supper he won't soon forget," Jean said. "Is that all right?"

"Yes, of course. He'd like that. I can't wait for him to see William. He's grown so much." Laurel walked to the kitchen window and looked out. "I'm glad the cold weather didn't stay. I hope the warm temperatures hold."

~

Adam watched the countryside slip by as the train neared Palmer. He'd expected cold and snow, but the ground was bare and the temperature relatively warm, almost balmy for Alaska. He glanced at his watch. Thirty minutes more.

He thought of Laurel, and his heart hurried. He couldn't wait to hold her. He wondered what William was like. It had been nearly a year since he'd set off, thinking he could change the world. The only thing that had changed was him. He couldn't identify exactly what was different, but he knew his time in Europe had stolen something from him.

Just that morning, when he'd stood in front of the mirror, he'd been able to see the physical changes—he looked tired and thin. But there was something more—on the inside. He was different. Laurel would notice. His mind wandered to his wife and he couldn't keep from smiling. He imagined her standing in sunlight, her auburn hair shimmering, hazel eyes clear and intelligent. His love for her welled up, then guilt quickly followed. How could he have betrayed her?

Adam's mind then returned to France and Elisa. Conflicted, his heart warmed and cringed all at the same time. He cared deeply for her, but what he'd done was wrong. Guilt and shame engulfed him. He hadn't really loved Elisa. He'd admired her and needed her, but he'd not loved her. There'd never been anyone for him except Laurel. He'd let them both down.

He'd allowed his feelings of isolation and anxiety to rule him. Elisa—vibrant and brave—had drawn him like a magnet. He squeezed his right hand into a fist and gripped it with his left. *Lord, I'm sorry. Forgive me.*

How could he put what had happened behind him? *Laurel will know. She'll see it.* Adam closed his eyes. *Father, help me forget. I don't want to hurt her.* A quiet voice spoke to him. "It was your decision, and now it is yours to make right."

Adam knew he would have to face up to what he'd done. He'd have to tell Laurel. But how?

He tried to justify his actions. *It wasn't that much. We didn't really do anything.* His heart knew the truth and wouldn't release him from his shame.

The train slowed as it pulled into Palmer Station. Adam gazed out the window, searching for his family. He saw Jean first. She stood with Ray and the children on the platform. Then his eyes found Laurel. All thoughts flew from his mind except that he loved and needed her. She spotted him, and her face brightened, reminding Adam of a daisy in the morning sun. Laurel waved and ran alongside his window.

Love surged through Adam. "Laurel," he called, then grabbed his bag and moved out of his seat and down the aisle to the exit. The train was still moving when he descended the steps and stood on the departure landing. Unable to wait, he tossed his bag to the ground and jumped, then ran to Laurel.

Catching her into his arms, he said over and over, "Laurel. Laurel." They clung to each other. Adam buried his face in her hair. She smelled of lavender and soap. "Oh, I missed you. I missed you."

Holding her face in his hands, he looked at her. "I thought I'd never see you again. I love you." Oblivious to onlookers, Adam kissed her.

Someone patted his pant leg. "Adam," came a small voice.

He looked down at a smiling Susie.

"I missed you too."

Adam smiled and scooped her into a big hug. "I missed you." Next he turned to Brian. "My word. You're nearly a man. How old are you?"

"Almost fourteen. I had a birthday just before you left."

Adam gently gripped his shoulder. "You've become quite a young man."

"I just turned eight," Susie said. "Mama says I'm small for my age but that I'll grow later."

"I'm sure you will." Keeping his arm around Laurel, Adam looked for William.

The boy stood with his grandmother, gripping her hand and watching the reunion. He had an air of reserve about him. Maybe it was distrust.

Adam turned to his son. "William? Can that be you? You've grown so tall." He walked toward the youngster. Laurel followed. Adam kneeled in front of William and placed his hands on the boy's shoulders. "Why, I'd say you're the spitting image of your grandpa."

William straightened and threw back his shoulders, his gray blue eyes filled with delight. "Yep. I sure am. And I like farming too." He smiled. "I'm almost five."

"I swear, you've grown a foot."

"William, give your daddy a hug," Laurel said softly.

William obediently put his arms around his father's neck. Adam hefted him into his arms and stood with an exaggerated groan. "You're so big I can barely lift you."

"Mama said I'll be a strapping young man one day and I'll help you on the farm." As if he'd finally recognized the man who held him, William threw his arms around his father's neck and hugged him tightly. "I'm glad you're home, Daddy."

Jean hugged Adam and William together. "It's so good to have you home."

Ray grasped Adam's hand in a firm grip. "Good to have you back, son. We were real worried for a while there."

"I was too . . . for a while," Adam quipped, his worries momentarily forgotten. Still holding William, he circled his free arm around Laurel and sucked in a lungful of air. "It's great to be back."

～

Laurel hummed "Don't Sit Under the Apple Tree" as she turned a piece of sizzling bacon. Adam had returned, and life was good again. However, a sense that something wasn't right nagged at the back of her mind. He seemed different. They weren't the same as they had been before he'd left. Laurel tried to quiet her concerns with sensible speeches about how a person couldn't go untouched by war, and she told herself that in time Adam would be himself again. Still, she knew it was something more.

She speared another piece of bacon and turned it. *He acts as if he's hiding something,* she thought, then told herself, *It must have been awful over there. I don't blame him for not wanting to talk about it.*

"Morning," Adam said, striding into the kitchen. He planted a kiss on the back of Laurel's neck and cuddled her against him. "You smell good. Better than that bacon."

Laurel turned and smiled up at him, gazing into his deep blue eyes. She pushed back the strand of hair that always found its way onto his forehead. "I'd darn well better." She hugged him around the neck.

"Where's William?"

"Outside playing."

"Already?"

"It's nearly nine o'clock. You slept late."

Adam ran a hand through his hair. "It'll take time to adjust to being home."

"You said you came by ship from England?" Laurel asked.

"Uh-huh."

She carried a plate of eggs to the table. "How did you get from France to England?"

A shadow settled over Adam's face. "Uh, by fishing boat."

Laurel set the bacon on the table beside the eggs. "I hope you're hungry." She took toast out of the oven, placed it on the table, then grabbed two plates and silverware and laid them out. "Every time I think of you leaping out of that plane I get the shivers. I can't imagine. How did you do it?"

Adam filled the two cups on the table with coffee. "You do what you have to." He returned the pot to the stove and offered a half smile. "I have to admit, though, it scared the tar out of me. I'd never imagined myself parachuting. And to make matters worse, Krauts were shooting at us while we floated down." The blue in his eyes darkened. "Only two other men even made it out, but they were shot and killed before they hit the ground."

"Oh, Adam, how awful." Laurel rested a hand on his cheek. "I'm so thankful you're here."

"Me too," Adam said, hugging her.

"I just can't imagine how you made it across France all the way to England without being captured."

Adam released her and sat. He picked up a slice of bacon and took a bite, then placed two pieces of toast on his plate. "The farmers were helpful," he said, not looking at Laurel.

"It's good to know people are helping our soldiers over there."

"Yeah, I don't know how I would have made it otherwise. One family hid me and arranged to have someone get me out of the country. They were good folks."

"Did they speak English?"

"Yeah, some." He took another bite of bacon.

Laurel sat across from him. "Seems strange that French farmers would speak English. Do they teach it in the schools?"

"Yeah. I guess." Adam slid two eggs onto his plate. "I'd just like to put it all behind me." His tone was brusque. "All right?" he added more gently.

Laurel felt hurt and shut out. "I just wondered how you managed to get home. I prayed all the time you were missing."

"I knew you'd be praying. And God was watching out for me." Adam bit into his toast. "Let's talk about something else."

All that week Adam avoided discussions about his time overseas. Laurel was certain something was troubling him. He spent more and more time alone, working or fishing, and he'd shut her out. She was frightened for them. Something had wedged itself between them. Worried, Laurel decided to talk to Ray.

When she drove into the driveway, Ray was out by the woodshed splitting wood. He was so intent on his work that he didn't notice her. She stepped out of the car and walked to the shed where she stood and watched him.

When Ray turned to grab a chunk of wood, he saw her. "Well, howdy. How long you been here?"

"Long enough to know you're working too hard for an old man." She grinned.

"Old man? Why don't we make a wager—"

"No. No. I'm sure I'd lose that bet. I know you're not old, just maturing." She smiled. "The way you were swinging that ax, I figure you're still pretty young."

Ray glanced at the double-edged maul and leaned it against the stump he'd been using for splitting. Taking a handkerchief from his back pocket, he wiped sweat from his face, then scanned the sky. Like cotton candy, wisps of white stretched across a pale blue canopy. "It's downright cold. Figure winter's not far off."

"It'll be here soon."

"It's nice having Robert home, even if it's just for a little while. Celeste is as happy as I've ever seen her. I suspect those two will marry soon. I doubt they'll wait until the war's over." His eyes sparkled.

"They're in love." Laurel knew she needed to get beyond the banter but didn't know where to begin. She glanced at the house. "Mama working today?"

"Yep." Ray studied Laurel. "So, what's on your mind? You don't usually come out this way just to keep me company."

"Actually, I need to talk to you about Adam."

"I could use a break." He nodded at a stack of uncut logs. "Have a seat."

Laurel sat, then studied her hands, still unable to figure out just where to begin. Taking a deep breath, she looked at Ray. "Over the past year or so, you and I have become friends, and I trust your judgment."

Ray settled on a round of sawed spruce. "Trouble at home?"

"Why would you think that?"

"I've got eyes. I can see Adam's not himself."

"So you noticed it too."

"I figure he's been through a lot. War changes men. You'll get him back, but it's liable to take time."

"You think so?"

"I do." He leaned forward and rested his arms on his thighs. "Adam's made of good stuff. He'll be all right."

Laurel wasn't satisfied. "We seem far apart. He keeps to himself and won't talk about what happened over there." The next words were hard to say aloud; she'd barely had the courage to think them. "I think he's hiding something from me. I was hoping you could talk to him."

Ray didn't answer right away. "I could do that, but I doubt it'll do any good." He rubbed the palms of his hands together. "I'll see what I can do."

"Thank you. I appreciate it."

"Is he going to be around this afternoon?"

"I'm not sure. He's supposed to be writing. The paper's been after him for a story, but he just sits in front of his typewriter doing nothing, then goes outside and walks around the property and on up the road." Laurel intertwined her fingers. "Something's wrong. I know it."

Ray stood, his large frame towering over Laurel. "Maybe I'll just wander over that way later today."

"Thank you." Laurel pushed to her feet. Her relief was replaced by a fear of what Ray might discover. She hoped it wasn't anything too horrible.

~

"Howdy," Ray said, joining Adam at the paddock fence.

"What brings you out this way?" Adam asked.

"I was hoping to get my hands on that little boy of yours. Haven't seen him much lately. I get to missing him."

"Yeah, I know what you mean. He's a real go-getter." Adam returned to staring at his Belgian, whose nose was buried in a stanchion filled with hay. "William's taking a nap. He'll be up soon."

"I'll just wait around then."

Adam breathed deeply and leaned against the fence. "I swear, nothing smells like the Matanuska in fall. Best air on the planet." He studied a naked tree. Gold and yellow leaves carpeted the ground beneath it.

"Yep. It's real nice this time of year. Before you came we had some snow. Almost looked like winter was here." Ray leaned on the fence and studied the Belgian. "That's a fine horse you've got. He's a little big for a packhorse though. You plan on doing any hunting this fall?"

"I was thinking I might, then I figured I'd write about it." Adam eyed Ray. "'Course, I don't know a lot about hunting. I could use a guide and teacher. Maybe a packhorse." Adam grinned.

"I'd be pleased to take you out. The company would be good." Ray was quiet for a long while. "Heard you haven't been able to do much writing lately."

"Laurel been talking to you?"

"She's worried."

"She's got no reason. I'm fine. It'll take a little while to get back into the swing of writing, but it'll come."

"Yeah, I figured. It's tough when a man comes home from war." He cleared his throat. "Sometimes it helps to talk things out with another man."

Adam studied Ray. "What did Laurel say? She send you here to talk to me?"

"Not exactly." Ray stuck his hands into his jean pockets. "I told her I'd come 'round for a visit—see if there was something I could help with."

"Nothing's wrong." Adam turned and stared at the house. "I really don't want to talk about the war. It was ugly over there, and I'd rather forget the whole thing."

"Sure. I understand." Ray braced his foot on the fence. "'Course, I thought you were sent over to write about the war. Seems you're having some trouble doing that. If you're going to get it down on paper, you've got to think about it. I s'pect talking about it might help. Figure the paper won't be none too happy with you if you don't send them a story."

"Yeah." Adam's mind boiled with memories. He'd hoped it would all just go away—Elisa and his guilt. But it seemed like the more time he spent trying to forget, the worse he felt. He knew things weren't right between him and Laurel, but he didn't know how to fix them. How could he talk about any of it without telling her what happened?

He looked at Ray and took a deep breath. "I did have some trouble over there, and I guess I need to talk about it."

Ray waited.

"I met a woman who helped me. Her name was Elisa. I probably wouldn't have survived without her." He paused. "She was Jewish and had a little boy named Adin. We spent a lot of time together traveling. She helped get me out of the country. Elisa's a brave woman."

"Sounds special," Ray said.

Adam nodded.

"And?"

Adam picked up a stone and tossed it up the driveway. "We became close. I started caring about her and her son . . . more than I should."

"You saying you were unfaithful to Laurel?" Ray asked, his tone cool.

"No . . . not exactly." Adam glanced at Ray. "We traveled together, all the way to London. We depended on each other." He let out his breath. "When you're in that kind of situation, a bond develops." He stopped and looked at Ray. "Elisa told me she loved me." He could barely bring himself to say the words out loud. "For a while I wondered if I loved her, but nothing happened. Not really."

"What does 'not really' mean?"

Adam picked up a piece of hay, broke it in half, then tossed it. "I kissed her, but that's all. Then I told her it was a mistake, I loved my wife and son, and there was no future for us." Even as Adam lay out his defense, he knew he had no excuses.

Ray rested an arm on the fence, then settled an uncompromising gaze on Adam. "I understand how it could happen, but that doesn't excuse it." He was silent a moment, then said solemnly, "You've got to tell Laurel."

"I can't."

"If you don't, the secret's going to fester and set between you two and eventually destroy your love." He shook his head. "Look at what's happening already. You can't hide it. You've got to tell her, son. You have to."

Chapter 22

ADAM KNEW RAY WAS RIGHT, BUT THAT DIDN'T DRIVE AWAY THE DEMONS OF fear as he stepped into the house. Laurel was on her hands and knees scrubbing the kitchen floor with a wire brush. He watched her. Hair falling into her face, she scoured vigorously, then dipped the brush into a pail of soapy water.

She glanced over her shoulder. "Adam." Laurel sat back on her heels. "I didn't know you were home." She blew back wisps of hair and wiped her forehead with the back of her hand. "What a job. I don't know how we manage to carry in so much of the outside." She gazed at his feet and smiled. "Well, I suppose maybe I do. Look at the mud on your boots."

Adam lifted a foot. Black muck clung to the sole. "Oh, yeah. Sorry. I guess I ought to be more careful." He exited and scraped the bottom of his boots on the edge of the porch, then returned. "I'll make sure to wipe the mud off from now on."

Laurel returned to scrubbing, moving the brush in broad circles over the wooden floor. Adam admired the way her slender body moved in a rhythm, and he liked that she'd taken to wearing denim overalls some of the time. They suited her.

She stopped and looked at him. "Do you need something?"

"No. Uh, well . . ." He had no reason to delay any longer. "I . . . I was wondering if we could talk."

"Is something wrong?"

Adam didn't answer.

"Adam? What is it?" Laurel dropped the brush into the bucket and stood. "Adam?"

Adam took a deep breath. His body felt tight. What would he say? How could he tell her about Elisa? "Can we sit?"

Laurel crossed to the table and sat.

Adam did the same, sitting across from her. He rested his arms on the table and clasped his hands. He stared at them, then straightened the tablecloth and smoothed a wrinkle.

Laurel waited.

Finally he looked at her. The hazel eyes he loved were trusting and filled with concern. *Concern for me,* he thought, shrinking back and telling himself she didn't have to know.

She placed a hand over his. "Adam?"

He gazed at her hand. The nails were neatly trimmed, the fingers long and slender. *She doesn't deserve this.* He forced himself to look at her. "I have to tell you something."

"What is it?" Laurel gently squeezed his hand. "Is it about the war?"

Her uncompromising support only made Adam feel worse. He abruptly pulled his hand free and walked to the kitchen window.

"You can tell me anything. Please. Maybe I can help."

"No. You can't help." Adam turned and faced her. "And stop being so nice. I don't deserve it."

Laurel's expression registered surprise. She straightened her back and folded her hands on the table in front of her.

"What I have to say is about the war and it isn't." Adam leaned against the counter and folded his arms over his chest. "It was awful over there. Not just for me and the other Americans and the Brits, but for the French too. They've lost their country, their homes. The Germans invaded and conquered," he said derisively. "German soldiers are everywhere. No one's safe, especially not the Jews. If they're caught, they're thrown into extermination camps and killed . . . even the women and children."

Laurel gasped.

Adam knew he was laying down reasons for his behavior when he had no excuses. "Anyway, never mind that. After my plane went down, I managed to make it to the ground without getting shot." He hesitated. "I met a woman and her little boy. Her name is Elisa, and her son's name is Adin. She wanted to help, and she needed help. She and Adin were hiding from the Germans. They're Jews. Adin's only three." Adam's heart softened at the thought of the boy. "He's small—never had enough to eat. He's got big brown eyes and a sweet personality. Every time I looked at him I thought of William." Adam knew he was avoiding the heart of what he had to say.

Laurel offered him a gentle smile and started to speak.

"No. Let me finish." Talking about it had brought everything back, only more clearly. The people, the place, the fear felt close. "Elisa spoke English, and she helped me. She knew her way through France."

Adam returned to the table and sat. "Actually, Elisa and I helped each other. She was hiding and looking for a way out of the country. Her husband had already been captured and was probably dead. If the Germans found her and Adin, they would kill them. I had a rifle, plus I think Elisa saw Americans as the ones who would save her people. She felt bound to me."

"Are Elisa and Adin all right? Did they make it out?"

Adam nodded and wondered whether he should say anything more. She wouldn't know what had really happened if he left things as they were, but all he had to do was look into Laurel's trusting eyes and know she deserved the truth. He reached out and grasped her hand. "I love you. You know that."

"Of course," Laurel said, her tone tight.

Adam kissed her hand. "Elisa and I spent a lot of time together. In fact, we ended up working for a farmer who helped us and gave us the name of the man, Jacques Billaud, who got us out." Arnaude's face and jovial personality filled his mind. He and his family were certainly dead by now. He felt sick. "Before we could connect with Jacques, German soldiers arrested the farmer and his family."

Laurel turned pale. "What happened to them?"

"They were suspected of hiding Jews and were probably executed."

Tears filled Laurel's eyes.

"Elisa and I hid with Adin until the soldiers left. After that we were on our own, but we still had to find a way out of France." He shook his head. "Elisa and I got close . . . really close." He let the sentence hang.

Understanding dawned on Laurel's face. The color drained from her face and her jaw squared. "How close, Adam?"

Adam compressed his lips as if he could prevent the truth from being told. "She told me she loved me."

Laurel's finger's rubbed the surface of the table. "And what did you feel?"

Adam met her eyes. "For a while I thought I might love her, but I didn't, not really." He hurried on. "Nothing happened . . . I did kiss her . . . once, but I never stopped loving you. I always loved you, always thought of you."

For an explosive moment, Laurel said nothing. Her face was expressionless. Finally she blurted, "So, while you were kissing her, you were thinking of me?" She pressed her palms together in her lap and stared at the floor. Then she stood, walked to the wash bucket, seized the brush, and returned to scrubbing.

Adam watched her for a long while, then said, "Laurel, please. Say something." He crossed to her and kneeled in front of her. She scrubbed around him. "Please. Say something."

All of a sudden, Laurel sat back on her heals, allowing the brush to rest in her lap. She stared straight ahead, took a gulping breath, then finally looked at him. Her eyes brimmed with tears. "What do you want me to say?"

Adam was silent for a moment. He couldn't look at her. "That you forgive me. That you love me."

Laurel leaned on the brush, grinding it into the floor. "I never believed you could do such a thing." She met his eyes. "Why?"

"I don't know. I was lonely, afraid—"

"And I wasn't? Do you know what it was like? I waited. Day after day, wondering if you were alive. I was alone and afraid too." She pushed to her feet and threw the brush at the pail. It bounced off the side and dropped to the floor. "You went off to write about the war. Instead you . . . instead . . . Were there others?"

"No. Of course not."

"I remember how you were before . . . when I first met you. You were always after some woman! I thought you had changed!" She headed for the door. "I can't stay in this house! When William wakes up, take him to my mother's." She yanked open the door, then whirled around and glared at Adam. "I never want to see you again!"

Her emotions boiling, Laurel ran to the truck. She felt as if her heart had been ripped out. Sobs came in deep gulps. She started the engine, and pushing hard on the gas pedal, spun the tires as she backed up and headed out of the driveway. She caught a brief glimpse of Adam standing on the porch.

How could he? How could he? "I hate you!" She sobbed. "I love you." She quickly pushed through the gears and sped down the bumpy road.

Without making a conscious decision, she drove to Celeste's. She would understand. She would help. "Please, God, help me. I can't bear this." She wept, barely able to see through her tears.

Filled with pain and fury, Laurel skidded to a stop, then stepped out, slammed the door closed and stormed to Celeste's front door. She rapped hard, then walked in without waiting for an answer.

When Laurel stepped in, Celeste was getting up from a chair. "What's wrong? Laurel?" She walked to her friend. "Something's wrong."

Laurel couldn't hold her anguish in. She pitched into Celeste's arms and cried.

"What's happened? Is it William? Please. Tell me."

"No. It's not William," Laurel said, straightening and dabbing at her nose. "It's Adam. He . . . he was unfaithful." Fresh tears filled her eyes and spilled onto her cheeks.

"Are you sure? He would never—"

"He did. He told me himself. When he was in France, he met a woman." More tears swamped her. "I can't believe it. I never thought . . ."

Celeste grabbed a clean handkerchief from a pile of folded clothing. "Here. Now sit on the sofa, and I'll make us both a cup of tea."

Laurel let the story spill out, then sat sniffling into the handkerchief. "What should I do?"

"You don't know?"

Laurel shook her head no.

"You'll be angry for a while, then you'll forgive him and go on with your lives. That's what you'll do. You couldn't possibly consider a divorce."

Laurel's thought processes hadn't gone that far. The word *divorce* sounded like a shotgun going off in her head. "But how can I forgive him?"

"What else can you do?" Celeste sat beside Laurel. "You have to consider the circumstances. Being in a war isn't like everyday life. I can't even imagine how awful it must be. And Adam wasn't exactly unfaithful. He just cared about that woman and her little boy. He was in a country far from his home, and he needed a friend."

"That's what you'd call her—a friend?"

"Well, maybe not exactly a friend, but mostly that's all they were. He didn't love her, and he told you he loves you. Right?"

"Yes. But he said he thought that *maybe* he loved her."

"And he said he never stopped loving you. Laurel, everything will be all right." Celeste smiled.

Laurel shook her head. "Things can never be the same."

"Not right away, but one day they will be. Do you think that loving someone and being married to someone is always perfect and unspoiled? Love involves people, and people aren't perfect."

"Yes, but—"

"You have to forgive him."

"I don't know how."

Celeste thought a moment. "You start with prayer. God will help you. Be thankful Adam is safe. What if he was still missing, like Luke? Just thank the Lord he's alive and here." She glanced at the window. "I wish Robert didn't have to go back. Just be thankful Adam doesn't have to return."

Laurel knew Celeste was right, but she felt so betrayed. How could she forget?

"Adam didn't do anything, not really. He got a little attached to a woman and kissed her in the midst of horrible circumstances. He loves you. That hasn't changed. Go to him. Love him. I know you two can work it out."

Laurel took a deep shuddering breath. "I don't think I can." She chewed a nail. "I'm not ready yet. I don't want to forgive him. He doesn't deserve it."

"Don't let the sun go down on your anger. That's what the Bible says."

Laurel couldn't believe Celeste was being so glib about this. "I don't think that verse was about infidelity," she nearly yelled.

"Maybe not, but what else are you going to do?"

"I told him I never wanted to see him again."

Celeste smiled. "I don't think he believed that. Do you?"

Laurel shrugged. "I don't know. I thought I meant it at the time."

"Get! Go on, get!" someone shouted from outside.

"Who's that?"

"Robert," Celeste said. "What's going on?" She walked to the door and peered out. "Robert? Is everything all right?"

"You've got a moose in your garden."

"No! I've still got carrots and potatoes in the ground." Celeste rushed out and ran to the garden patch.

A cow moose stood, munching carrot tops. She appeared perfectly content and unafraid.

"Go on! Git!" Celeste waved her arms in the air. The beast didn't move. Celeste ran to the shed and grabbed a pitchfork, then headed into the garden.

"Be careful. You never know what one of those animals will do," Robert warned. "Maybe you ought to just leave her be. She'll go on her way."

"I will not! She'll ruin the last of my garden." Holding the pitchfork out in front of her, Celeste moved toward the huge animal. "Leave! Now! These vegetables are mine!" She lunged at the beast, who simply flinched and took a single step backward.

Laurel grabbed a broom off the back porch and joined Celeste. She waved it in the air while Celeste hollered and poked at the animal.

With two antagonists to face, the moose thought better of staying and moved along. Just as Robert returned with a rifle, she sauntered through the muddy patch, her feet sinking and making a sucking sound with each step. The three friends followed, continuing to shout and brandish their weapons.

The moose wasn't moving fast enough for Celeste, so she ran at her. The animal loped into nearby brush and disappeared. Her pitchfork raised in triumph, Celeste hooted. Distracted, she stumbled, and her feet slipped out from under her. She pitched backwards with a squeal. Stunned, she sat motionless and silent, then laughter spilled out. Unable to quiet her giggles, she explained, "All this for a few carrots and potatoes. My root cellar's full. I don't even need them."

Robert chuckled. "You've always had to have your way."

"Is that so?" Celeste asked, grabbing a handful of mud and flinging it at him. It splattered against the side of his shirt.

"Ah, so that's how it is." Robert headed for Celeste.

She scrambled to her feet. "I didn't mean it. It was an accident." Giggling, she ran, but Robert lunged and grabbed her, swinging her around. Finally he pinned her against him and kissed her. "When are you going to marry me?"

"When the time is right," Celeste shot at him.

Laurel knew Celeste loved Robert and would marry him if only he'd be more reasonable about his expectations for a wife. He planned on having a lot of children, and she wasn't sure she wanted any. Robert believed a wife should stay home and take care of the house and family. Celeste wanted to fly a bush plane.

Laurel hoped they could work out their differences. They loved each other. It would be wrong if they missed out on sharing their lives. Her sadness deepening, she wondered what would become of her and Adam. Her heart heavy, she turned to leave.

Adam stood a few yards away, his pain-filled eyes on her. He stepped toward her. "I took William to your mother's. She said he could spend the night. Would you come home?"

Laurel studied him. He looked miserable.

"Please, Laurel. I love you. I'll always love you."

He'd always been good to her. How could she think of living without him? "All right," she said. "We'll talk."

Laurel headed toward the truck, and Adam walked beside her. Both were careful not to touch the other.

"I'm so sorry. I never wanted to hurt you."

"I know," Laurel said, realizing she'd already forgiven him.

Chapter 23

LUKE UNWRAPPED A CHOCOLATE BAR AND PUSHED THROUGH THE DOOR leading from the canteen. He wandered toward the barracks, wondering what he would do with his day, his life. His physical injuries had healed; even the scars from his burns were fading. His mental state was the problem. He still couldn't remember who he was or where he came from. After weeks of working with a psychiatric doctor, his mind remained locked. He only had whispers from the past—an occasional flash of face or location, nothing more.

He took a bite of his candy and chewed. It tasted rich and sweet. Then he looked at the bar. "I like chocolate." He puzzled over how he could know menial things and not remember what mattered most, such as his name.

He walked past the barracks and headed for the bay. A nurse with long black hair and brown eyes walked toward him. She reminded him of someone. Maybe he knew her. She offered a friendly smile as they passed but gave no indication that they might be friends. *Maybe I know someone who looks like her,* he thought, his frustration intensifying. He needed to know who he was. A frightening thought pressed down on him. *What if I never remember?*

Luke stopped at a fence that separated the base from the harbor. The Long Beach port was dotted with private sailing crafts vying for space with navy ships. Sails fluttered in the breeze. Luke could hear the snap of canvas. Heading for the open sea, a destroyer cut through the blue waters. Luke wished he were on it. He wanted to do something other than lollygag around the base wondering where he belonged.

Either I go back to fighting or I go home, he thought, gloom enveloping him. If only he knew where home was. Leaning against the fence, he gazed at the ship, trying to make out the men on deck. Maybe he knew one of them.

A breeze nearly snatched his cap from his head. He pulled it down snugly.

It was December. *Shouldn't the wind be cold? And shouldn't everything be covered with ice and snow?* he thought.

He struggled to follow the thought. He must have lived where winters were harsh.

An image of snow-covered mountains flashed into his mind. He worked to retain the mental picture. The mountains were imposing and rugged, with heavy layers of snow. As quickly as it had come, the picture disappeared. He closed his eyes, hoping to recapture it, but it remained illusive.

Depression settled over Luke. He needed to talk to someone. He had to do something. He headed for the chaplain's office.

Lieutenant John Atwood sat behind his desk, his face in a book. He straightened and looked at Luke. "Well, Luke. Good to see you." Using the back of his index finger, he pushed heavy-rimmed glasses back in place. Light blue eyes settled on Luke. "Come on in." He closed the book.

Luke stepped into the tidy office. A desk and chair sat in front of an open window, a wooden file stood to one side, and a large bookcase crowded with books—theological aids and a number of novels—covered the opposite wall. Otherwise, the room was empty. The reverend loved books and often loaned them to Luke, who was a slow reader. He'd struggled through *Of Mice and Men* and *The Grapes of Wrath,* both by John Stienbeck. The stories had been moving. He glanced at the shelf and thought that maybe he would borrow another.

The chaplain joined him. "You're welcome to take one when you go."

"Thanks, but I don't know which one."

The stocky, friendly man crossed to the bookcase. He ran a stubby finger over bindings. "Let me see. Which would be good for you?" He stopped, pulled one from the shelf, studied it a moment, and then handed it to Luke. "*Our Town* should do the trick. It might jar something for you."

"Thanks," Luke said, accepting the book. He opened to the first page and read a few lines. "Looks interesting." He snapped the book shut. "I was wondering if we could talk. I've got some questions."

The lieutenant glanced at his watch. "Sure. Have a seat." He stepped around his desk and sat, then leaned on heavy arms on the desk, clasping his hands. "So, how has it been going for you?"

"All right, I guess." Luke leaned back in his chair but a moment later sat forward and rested his arms on his thighs. Finally he straightened and folded his arms over his chest. "Actually, I'm frustrated. Pieces are coming back, but I can't remember where any of it comes from or who the people are that I see. I'm beginning to think I'll never put it together, and I can't stay here forever. Sooner or later I've got to go—somewhere, either to fight the war or . . . or I don't know where. I'd say home, except I don't know where that is."

The chaplain didn't speak. He studied his hands, then finally said calmly, "You can't rush these things. You have to proceed with caution. The human mind is a tricky thing and needs to be handled delicately. I'd say if you're getting glimpses of people and places, then eventually it will all unfold—you'll remember. It could continue the way it has, one little piece at a time, or you might be flooded with memories all at once." Setting his eyes on Luke, he added, "I know it's hard, but be patient."

"You don't know what it's like. I feel like I'm stuck on a raft somewhere in the middle of the ocean, and I have no way to get my bearings. Which way do I go to find land?"

"I'd say that's a good picture of where you are right now. I know it's tough, but you've got a lot to be thankful for. You could have gone down with your ship. A lot of men did. Your injuries mended well, including your burns. I can barely see the scars. And from what the doctor says, what's left will heal." He settled serious eyes on Luke. "It could be a lot worse."

The chaplain spoke with a slight Southern drawl, which always made him sound as if he were calm. The constant serenity was usually quieting, but today it irked Luke. He wanted this man to feel what he was feeling.

He blew out a breath. "All right. You're right." He pushed out of his chair and walked to the window. "It's not easy to wait for a life, especially when it's the one you've already lived." He caught a glimpse of the nurse he'd seen earlier. Again he had the sensation of knowing her. He forced his eyes back to the lieutenant. "Either way, I need to move ahead, do something with my life. Even if I never remember who I am or where I come from, I can't stay here. I want to get back into the fighting, to help beat down the Japs."

The chaplain removed his glasses. He pressed his fingers against his forehead as if he were soothing a headache. "I understand, but it's not that simple." He replaced his glasses. "I tell you what. Why don't we start meeting a couple of times a week? Maybe we can sort out some of the images you're getting and pin them down. Then you might remember more."

"Sounds good. Can we start today?"

The lieutenant chuckled. "Sure." He pulled out a piece of writing paper and a pen from his drawer. "Why don't you start by telling me what you've been seeing."

The next couple of weeks Luke met with the chaplain two times each week and gradually regained more of his memory. He saw faces of people he knew. He also saw images of a countryside and of towns. However, he still couldn't recall names, including his own. In the end he was no further ahead than when he'd started, and his frustration deepened.

One afternoon he sat on a stool peeling potatoes outside the mess hall. "There are always potatoes to peel," he grumbled.

A lanky sailor wearing his dress blues walked past and said casually, "Looks like you'll be peeling all night." He eyed a box piled with potatoes.

His voice sounded familiar. Luke studied his face, then asked, "Do I know you?"

"I don't think so. Should you?" He raised his eyebrows in question.

"Nah. I was just wondering." Embarrassed, Luke focused on the potato in his hands.

"See you around," the man said and strode away.

Luke glared at the potato. He cut out a dark spot, then turned it over searching for other spots. A sense of familiarity crept over him. The potato felt comfortable in his hand, and he thought he could smell the aroma of damp earth. He knew about potatoes. Why?

Staring at the scarred vegetable, he could see a farm and tilled earth. The image was fuzzy, but gradually textures meshed and became clear. Then he envisioned a house surrounded by farmland. *It's my home! I remember!* His mind moved on to a man driving a tractor and cutting perfect furrows into dark soil. Luke concentrated on the figure. He needed to see the man's face. When he did, he knew he'd recognize him. As if a camera were being brought into focus, the face became clear. "Dad," he whispered. "Dad." At the same time, pain scored his heart. His father was dead, and he knew how he'd died.

Gripping the potato, he prayed, "Lord, help me remember more. Please, all of it."

Then it happened—his mother, sisters, brothers, Mattie, everyone—he remembered them all, and he knew he was Luke Hasper. He dropped the potato, ran into the kitchen, and yelled, "I'm Luke Hasper! I'm Luke Hasper!"

Striding up to the kitchen supervisor, he said, "I've got to go. I need to talk to someone. May I be relieved of duty, sir? Please, sir."

The man grinned. "So, you're Luke Hasper, huh. Well, glad to know you." He laughed, slapping Luke on the back. "Sure. Go ahead." He glanced around the kitchen. "I'm sure I can get one of these blockheads to peel a few potatoes."

Luke ran out of the building and headed for the chaplain's office. He moved past the secretary without waiting to be acknowledged, rapped on the door, and opened it.

John Atwood looked up, surprise on his face. He started to speak, but Luke cut him off.

"I'm Luke Hasper! Luke Hasper! My family lives in Alaska! And I've got friends there too. Palmer's my home, and that's where I belong!"

A broad smile creased the minister's face. "Well, it's nice to know you, Luke Hasper." He stood and shook Luke's hand. "Do you remember everything?"

"Yep. I think so. My family moved from Wisconsin to Alaska where we have a farm. My little brother, Justin, and my father are dead," he said quietly. Then in an acrid tone, he added, "A man named Ray Townsend killed him." He could feel the bitterness.

"He killed your brother?"

"No. My father." He remembered the wedding between his mother and Ray, and resentment burned deep.

"Sounds like you've remembered all the important stuff."

"Yeah. Even that my father was murdered."

"Murdered?"

Luke nodded. "Uh-huh." He sucked in a breath. "And then the man who murdered him married my mother."

Lieutenant Atwood's face went gray. "Luke, why don't you sit down."

Toxins of hate spread through Luke as he poured out the story. To him it felt fresh, as if it had just happened.

When he finished, the chaplain sat silent for a long moment. When he spoke, he chose his words carefully. "That's a lot for you to absorb all at once. You sure you're all right?"

Luke squared his jaw. "Yeah. Fine."

The chaplain rubbed his palms together. "It'll take time for you to sort all this out. I think it would be good if you continued to see me. I'd like to help."

"I don't see why, sir. I'm fine and ready to go back to sea."

The chaplain smiled. "I know you think you're ready, but you need time."

"No. I'm fine. I'll have my gear packed and ready to go if you'll just say the word. I need to get back out there."

The lieutenant stood and walked to the window. He watched a company of men trot past, then turned and looked at Luke. "I hear a lot of bitterness in your words, and I understand why it's there." He rocked back on his heels. "From what you've told me, though, it sounds like your father made the decision about his life. Ray Townsend didn't kill him. The bear did."

Luke folded his arms over his chest. He'd heard this before.

"All you've been through with your family isn't easy to deal with. I understand that. But I've seen lots of different kinds of hatred and reasons for it in my day, especially since the war began. They all lead to the same place . . ." He leaned on the desk and met Luke's eyes. "Hate's a killer to the one who carries it."

Luke could feel the fire of his hate, and with all that had happened, he figured he had a right to hang onto it. Besides, he didn't know how to extinguish it and wasn't certain he wanted to. He remembered his mother's pleas for him to forgive. He hadn't been able to. He pictured Ray Townsend sitting on his father's tractor, and he clenched his teeth. "Sir, I don't know how to let it go."

"It's not easy, son. But it's possible." He sat and leaned back in his chair. "You might want to start by grieving. Have you ever allowed yourself to mourn your father's death?"

"I don't know. Never thought about it much. I think I just got mad and stayed that way."

John glanced at his watch. "I have an appointment. Can you come by tomorrow at this same time? We'll talk some more."

"Yeah. Sure." Luke stood and walked to the door. "Thank you for the help."

His steps heavy, Luke headed for the barracks. He'd remembered who he was, but he also knew that Justin and his father were dead and that Ray and his mother were married. He also knew Mattie didn't love him. A pain rose up from deep inside and radiated through him. Maybe it would have been better if he hadn't remembered.

He dropped onto his rack, lay back, and rested his head on folded arms. His thoughts turned to Mattie. *She probably thinks I'm dead. What if she married someone else?* He closed his eyes and immersed himself in the memory of her. He missed her, the longtime friendship they'd shared, and their mutual love. He knew she'd loved him once.

His mind flashed to Alex, Mattie's brother. He was dead, and it was his fault. Luke could see the grinding ice and water sweeping away his friend. He'd been the one who had insisted they go out on the ice that day. Alex shouldn't have died.

The similarity between what had happened between himself and Alex and what had occurred between his father and Ray hit him. He felt the weight of guilt drop onto his chest. He couldn't breathe.

"Alex was my friend. I didn't want him to die," he whispered.

A voice in his mind said, "And Ray didn't want your father to die either."

Luke rolled onto his side. A confusion of memories and questions tumbled through his mind. Maybe he was just as bad as Ray Townsend. *No. I didn't hate Alex. I didn't want him to die. Ray hated my father, and when he died, it was exactly what Ray wanted.*

The parable from Matthew 18 about the unmerciful servant floated to his consciousness. The master had forgiven his servant's debt; then that same servant was unable to forgive a man who owed him money and he'd had the man thrown into prison.

The last two verses of the parable sent a shock of fear through Luke. *And his master was angry and delivered him to the torturers until he should pay all that was due to him. So, my heavenly Father also will do to you if each of you from his heart does not forgive his brother his trespasses.*

Luke saw himself in that man; but even so, when he thought of Ray, all he felt was rage. How could he rid himself of it? Maybe grieving his father's death would be a place to start. The pain that had been lodged in his heart for so many years was firmly rooted. He concentrated on it, and this time when it swelled he didn't push it down but allowed the tears he'd held in check for so long to flow.

Chapter 24

MATTIE SWEPT DIRT INTO A DUSTPAN, THEN DUMPED IT IN THE TRASH. SHE gazed out the window. Winter had transformed the valley into a fantasy world of white. Tree limbs were encased in heavy frost, their trunks mounded with snow, and bushes had been transformed into crystal plumes. She'd seen this many times, but it still caught her imagination and filled her with wonder.

Mattie placed the broom and dustpan in a closet and quietly closed the door. Her grandmother was sleeping. It was her habit to nap mid-morning and rest her ancient body. Sometimes she seemed closer to death than life. She slept now, her mouth puckered into a smile, frail arms folded over her stomach and her legs, like skinny posts, folded at the ankles.

She'll be gone soon, Mattie thought sadly, unable to imagine life without the tenacious old woman. How could someone be here one moment and the next, gone forever? *She'll be happy to go. She wants to be with the ones who have already departed.*

Her mind moved to Meryl and the letter she'd received from her. Meryl had told her she was holding off getting a roommate so her best friend would have a place to stay when she returned. In many ways Mattie craved Seattle, but since arriving home the world had seemed peaceful in contrast to the big city. In a small way the pervading tranquillity had penetrated her soul. Seattle offered her opportunities and more freedom than she had here, but she didn't want to leave just yet. She had only so much time left with her grandmother, and Mattie feared if she moved on now she would soon return for a funeral. However, studying the old woman, she thought, *I have to say good-bye sometime.*

Mattie crossed to Atuska and pulled the coverlet that had sagged to the floor up over her shoulders. Atuska moaned softly and rolled onto her side. Mattie smiled, remembering how her grandmother had tried to reassure her about Luke. She'd been so certain he was well, in spite of the fact that he was still listed as missing. Where was he? *Probably at the bottom of the ocean,* she thought, anguish squeezing her insides. *I wish I'd married him.*

The sound of an engine and the crunch of tires carried in from outside. Mattie went to the window. It was Jean Townsend. *Odd,* Mattie thought. *She's usually working at this time.* Had she heard from Luke? Or had she heard about him? Fear dredged through Mattie.

Mattie could read nothing by looking at Jean who was huddled against the wind, her face hidden by a hood. She seemed in a hurry, and a moment later a knock sounded at the door. Mattie's feet were fixed to the floor. Jean rapped again.

"Is someone here?" Atuska asked, her voice raspy and groggy. She pushed up on one elbow.

"It's Mrs. Townsend," Mattie said, moving to the door. *Please, let him be alive,* she prayed and opened the door.

Jean smiled; in fact, she was beaming. *It's not bad news,* Mattie thought, relief washing through her.

"I'm so glad you're here. I thought I saw someone at the window." Jean paused. "I have news." She pulled a folded telegram out of her coat pocket. "He's safe."

Mattie felt as if the wind had been knocked out of her. For a moment she couldn't breathe. Finally she asked, "He is?" A flood of joy flowed through her, and she added, "I was so afraid."

"He's coming home!" Jean announced, sweeping Mattie into her arms.

"When will he be here?"

Jean glanced at the telegram. "I don't know. It doesn't say."

Mattie turned to her grandmother. "Did you hear? Luke's alive! And he's coming home!"

Atuska was sitting up. She smiled. "I knew it. I knew his spirit was still earthbound."

Mattie looked at Jean. "Where has he been?"

"I don't know about before, but now he's in California."

"I have to talk to him," Mattie said. "I have so much to say. Do you know where in California?"

"At the Long Beach Naval Base."

Atuska hobbled to the door and circled an arm around Mattie's waist. "God has answered our prayers."

"Yes," Mattie said, hugging the old woman. "But I have to go. I have to talk to him. Now. To tell him how I feel. He doesn't know." She put on coat and gloves. "Do you think I can call him at the base?" she asked Jean.

"I don't know. Maybe."

"I have to try."

"Of course you must, but be careful," her grandmother said. "The roads are icy."

"I will," Mattie said, stepping onto the porch. She stopped suddenly. "I forgot. Mama took the truck."

"I'll take you," Jean offered. "I'd like to talk to him too."

The car bounced over a snowbound road, occasionally bumping to the side where the snow was deep. The tires would spin, then grab and push them back onto the packed grooves. Her heart pounding in anticipation, Mattie wished Jean could drive faster. She was going to talk to him! "I pray I'll get to speak to him," she said.

Jean reached out and patted Mattie's gloved hand. "I'm sure you'll be able to. Just have the operator connect you with the base. They'll get him for you."

Mattie thought over what she would say. First she had to tell him she loved him. And then . . . a pang of fear pulsed through her. What if he didn't love her anymore?

Finally Palmer emerged from the white landscape. Jean stopped at the mercantile, and before she could shut off the engine, Mattie was out of the car and hurrying toward the store.

Celeste was bent over the counter and writing in a ledger. She looked up at Mattie. "Hi." She brushed back golden curls. "How are you? Your mother was in earlier and she—"

"I'm fine," Mattie said breathlessly. "I need to use the telephone."

"Is something wrong?" Shadows of concern touched Celeste's sky blue eyes.

"No. Everything's right," Jean said, stepping inside and closing the door. "Luke's alive."

"He is? How wonderful!"

"We need to call him," Jean explained.

"Well, of course. This is such great news!" Celeste danced around the counter and hugged both Jean and Mattie. "I'm so happy for you."

Mattie moved to the telephone mounted on the wall.

The operator made the connection, and Mattie added coins, then waited. She tapped a nail against the shiny, black telephone. "Just a moment please," the operator said. Mattie straightened, her heart picking up its pace. "They're putting me through," she said.

"Long Beach Naval Station," a woman's voice crackled.

"I . . . I was wondering if I could speak to a Luke Hasper, please," Mattie said. "He's stationed there."

"Can you tell me his rank and serial number?"

"Uh, I don't know any of that."

"I need to know more than just his name, ma'am."

"I don't know anything else, just that he's there." Mattie was beginning to feel frightened that she wouldn't be allowed to talk to him.

"I'm sorry. It's impossible for me to connect you."

"You don't understand. We thought he was dead, and we got this telegram saying he's alive and that he's stationed there."

There was a long pause, then the woman said a little more sympathetically, "I'll see what I can do. Please hold."

Mattie leaned against the wall.

"What's happening?" Celeste asked.

"I think they're looking for him. Anyway, I hope so." Minutes passed. Jean busied herself searching shelves; Celeste stood at Mattie's side. An operator interrupted and told her to add more coins. Mattie did.

Finally the woman returned. "I'm sorry, ma'am, but I'm unable to locate Luke Hasper. I'll make sure to get a message to him. Do you have a number where you can be reached?"

"No. Our phone was disconnected," she said, knowing the woman didn't care a whit about her personal life. "I'm using the one at our local store."

"That will do."

Mattie gave the woman the number. "Could you have him call me at 2:00 P.M. tomorrow? Tell him I'll be here. Tell him I'll be waiting."

"Yes, ma'am. And could I have your name, please?"

"Mattie. Mattie Lawson."

"I'll relay the message." The line went dead.

Mattie stared at the receiver, then hung up. Dejected, she leaned against the wall and slowly let out her breath. "He'll call tomorrow. The woman said they have to find him."

Jean nodded. "Well, tomorrow isn't that far away." She gave Mattie a one-armed hug. "It's a lot better than never."

"I know. I was just hoping." She could feel tears of disappointment burning the backs of her eyes. "I wish mama hadn't disconnected the telephone. Grandmother never liked it." She shrugged. "When I came home it didn't seem necessary."

Jean laid an arm over Mattie's shoulders. "It'll be fine." She walked to the counter and laid several items on it. "I need to pay for these." She sorted through the purchases.

"Sure." Celeste returned to her place behind the counter and totaled the goods.

After paying for the items, Jean headed for the car. Snow drifted from a gray sky, and the air felt colder. She set the groceries on the back seat and climbed inside. "It's freezing."

Mattie slid onto the passenger seat. "I'm such a mix of happy and sad all at once. I know I should just be glad that he's alive, but I really wanted to talk to him." She looked at the snow accumulating on the front window. "I'll scrape it," she offered.

"No, I'll do it." Jean opened her door, but before stepping out, she said, "I wanted to talk to him too."

She scraped snow and ice from the windshield, then returned to the front seat. "Brrr. It's getting colder." She started the engine, put the car into gear, and backed around.

Celeste appeared on the store steps, hollering and waving her arms.

"Wait," Mattie said. She rolled down the window.

"He's on the phone! Luke! He's on the phone!"

"Oh, my Lord," Mattie said, excitement pulsing through her. She bailed out of the car and ran inside the store. Her hands shaking, she picked up the receiver and put it to her ear. "Luke?"

"Yes. Is that you, Mattie?"

Eyes filling and overwhelmed with emotion, Mattie barely managed to say, "It's wonderful to hear your voice. I thought I'd never . . ." She was unable to finish.

"Me too. I feel the same way."

"Are you all right?"

"Yes. I'm fine," Luke said.

"Where have you been?"

"When the *Wasp* sank, I was injured and admitted to a field hospital. I couldn't remember anything, not even my own name. For the last four months I haven't known who I was or who anyone else was, for that matter. I completely lost my memory, but I've got it back now."

Mattie tightened her grip on the phone. "Luke, I have to tell you how I feel."

"I love you, Mattie. I'll never stop loving you."

"I love you too."

"I knew it!" Luke chuckled. "While I was on the ship, I thought about you. When I was thrown into the water, I thought about you. And ever since I got my memory back I've been thinking of you." He paused. "Mattie, please marry me. Will you marry me?"

"Yes. Yes, I will." Mattie cried and laughed all at once.

Jean's eyes brimmed.

"I can't wait to see you. How long until you come home?"

"A couple of weeks. They have to process my papers, then I'm on my way. I'll fly into the base at Anchorage." Luke was quiet for a moment. "I can't wait to see you, Mattie, to hold you. Will you meet me at the air base?"

"I'll be there."

"We'll have a wonderful life together. There's good land in the valley. We can have our own farm, and we can raise our family in a place we both love."

Mattie was taken off guard. She'd figured that if Luke was found alive they would go back to Seattle. He'd seemed to like it there.

"Can I talk to him?" Jean asked.

"Oh. Yes. Of course." Mattie clutched the phone. "Luke, I have to go. Your mother's here, and she wants to talk to you."

"OK. I'll write and tell you the whole story. I love you so much."

"I love you."

Mattie cleared away the lunch dishes, her spirits still high. Luke would be coming home, and they'd be married. She was keyed up and needed to get out and walk. "After we get these finished, I think I'll go for a walk," she told her mother.

"I'll do them. You go." She smiled. "I know you have a lot to think about."

"Thank you. I do." Anxious to get moving, Mattie hurried to the bedroom she shared with her grandmother and pulled on warm clothing. She pushed her feet into fur-lined boots and headed for the door. "I won't go far," she said before stepping outside.

Frigid air greeted her, stinging her cheeks. She pulled her hood more tightly around her face and stepped off the porch. She moved away from the house, snow crunching beneath her boots. *Luke's coming home!* she thought, feeling more alive than she had in months. "And I'm going to be his wife." She lengthened her strides and headed for the road.

Snow sifted from the clouds, and the world was quiet and muted. A car approached and slowly moved past. Her neighbor, Mr. Johnson, sat behind the wheel, wearing a scowl. He kept his eyes forward, careful not to look at Mattie. He never looked at her. Although he lived simply and in a cabin no better than hers, he'd always made it clear that natives were a lower class. Just seeing him made her feel demeaned.

Her happiness diluted, she stepped back on the roadway and watched the car move away, then finally with determination, she turned and continued her walk. "He's not going to ruin my day." She followed a path leading to the river. The broad, frozen Matanuska was segmented into sections of smooth ice intermingled with rough snow-covered ridges. It wasn't a good place for skating.

Each breath carried cold, biting air into her lungs, but she continued, thinking of Luke and their wedding. It would be simple, with only close friends and relatives. She thought of a few people she'd like to be there, then her mind returned to Luke's plans to live in the valley. *After I tell him how I feel, I'm sure he'll move.*

Mattie faced the river and considered the kind of life she wanted for herself and the children she and Luke would have one day. *They're not going to live like I did. They'll have a better life. No one will even know they're Indian.*

With a white husband, Mattie was certain most people wouldn't think a thing about her heritage as long as she didn't live in Alaska. She could put her past behind her and build a new life. Of course, she had experienced the incident in Seattle. After much thought, she'd decided it had been a fluke and nothing to worry about.

Muffled noises, like those of a heavy animal moving through snow, carried from across the river along with snarls and sharp yaps. She scanned the opposite bank. A pack of wolves had surrounded a moose. Mattie instinctively took a step back and crouched, although she needn't have worried about being spotted. The pack was intent on bringing down the bull and hadn't noticed her.

Its sides heaving, the moose turned back and forth, facing its enemy. It pawed the snow and lunged, threatening with its heavy antlers. A wolf sprang toward the big animal, but the moose scooped him up with his horns and tossed him. The wolf let out a sharp yelp. Another pack member darted in, biting the animal's hindquarters. Then a cohort attacked from the other side.

The moose fought valiantly but was clearly weakening. In the end Mattie knew the wolves would prevail.

Saddened and revolted, she watched, wishing the moose would beat them back. He battled, then stumbled and dropped to his front hocks. Seizing the opportunity, the wolves surged in. One large gray clamped its jaws around the underside of the bull's neck. Another sank its teeth into the loins. The bull was dragged down.

Mattie turned away, unable to witness the end. She followed the trail the way she'd come, knowing she must leave this valley. She would not surrender to the human predators who wanted to drag her down.

Chapter 25

SCRUBBING AT A TWO-DAY STUBBLE, LUKE GAZED AT COOK INLET BELOW. It had been a long flight, but he was too keyed up to feel tired. He'd flown out of Southern California on a military transport, then landed in Bremerton, where passengers and goods were unloaded and mainte-nance work was done on the plane. Luke had napped on a cot tucked away in a side room. Several hours later he boarded again and the plane took off. Finally, he was almost home.

He imagined the reunion. Everyone would be waiting at the base in Anchorage. There'd be hugs and tears, kisses for Mattie, and a wedding . . . soon. Waiting was agony.

His eyes moved northwest to Mount Susitna. The lounging peak slumbered beneath a winter sun, its white slopes luminous. To the east and inland stood Mount McKinley, a distinct contrast. It did not lan-guish but towered above an imposing mountain range, the brilliant white of its rugged peaks and slopes shouting its supremacy. Luke soaked in its strength.

The plane passed over Fire Island, and he remembered the weekend he and his family had picnicked there. When he'd nearly died after being trapped in the sand, it had been Ray Townsend who refused to give up on him. Because of Ray's dogged determination, Luke had survived. Gratitude stirred within him; but as always, when Luke thought of Ray, he remembered his father and how he had died, and bitterness returned. *He probably helped me just so he could look good in my mother's eyes,* he told himself.

How would he and Ray manage to stay in the same house? He could barely tolerate the man's presence, even for a few minutes. He kneaded the back of his neck. His last visit home the loathing he harbored had been powerful and consuming. *A lot has happened since then. Maybe things will be better this time.*

Luke's eyes moved to shore and to Anchorage. Anticipation and pleasure replaced his dark thoughts. He was home. He and Mattie would share a life in this wild, unpredictable, and magnificent place. When he'd discovered she'd moved home, he felt great relief. Now everything would be perfect.

Anchorage passed below as the plane approached Fort Richardson. The town had swelled into a small city. *A growing population means more people needing produce,* Luke thought. Being a valley farmer might actually be profitable.

The plane descended and turned north, flying parallel to the Chugach Range, which rose up like a giant citadel at the edge of the broad plateau where Anchorage sat. The plane descended, and thickets of naked trees interspersed with groves of evergreens became distinguishable. Luke's anticipation grew.

A winding frozen river, its banks lined with trees and bushes, meandered west into the mountains. Against his will, Luke's mind traveled backward to the breakup that had killed Alex. He wished his old friend was still alive and waiting to greet him at the airbase.

The transport slowed and rolled slightly as the engines backed off. The landing gear lowered with a clunk. The craft tilted, the right wing dipping toward the ground as it swung around to make its approach. Mattie had said she'd meet him. Luke gazed at the earth below, his heart pumping hard. Was she down there?

Roadways could become unmanageable when the weather turned bad. She might not have made it. He'd heard of a recent heavy snowfall.

The plane's descent sharpened, then leveled as it sailed above the landing strip. The engines seemed to hesitate as they skimmed the runway. The wheels touched. The craft raced through a white world. Finally the plane slowed and bounced, then rolled smoothly past buildings and equipment. Luke was home.

He shrugged into his coat, hefted his duffel bag, and made his way to the departure ramp. He stepped into the welcomed cold. His eyes watered as he made his way down the ramp, searching the faces of those waiting. When he stepped onto the tarmac, he spotted Mattie. She waved, looking as if she were lit from inside. Her brown eyes and smile radiated joy. She pushed through the crowd.

Luke ran to her.

Without thought to spectators, the two threw themselves into each other's arms, then clung to each other. Reluctant to release her, Luke moved back just enough to take Mattie's face in his hands and stare into her warm, passionate eyes. He had no words to express his emotions. He kissed her, long and steady.

Her arms went around his neck.

They parted, but only for a moment. Luke whispered, "Oh, Mattie, I love you."

Her mouth was so close to his ear that he could feel the tickle of her breath as she said, "I love you. I'll never let you go again."

"You two gonna do that all day?" Brian asked.

Luke looked at his younger brother and grinned. "I'd like to." He gripped Brian's arm and pulled him into a hug. "Good to see you." He held the young man away from him. "You're all grown up. How tall are you now?"

"Last time I measured, five feet seven inches. Doc says I'll probably make six feet. I've been driving some too."

Luke caught only a glimpse of the young boy he'd once known and felt a pang of sadness at having missed so much of Brian's growing up. "Driving eh? I guess you're a man then."

Nine-year-old Susie held back. Blonde curls fell over her shoulders. "Welcome home, Luke."

He hugged her. "You've grown up too, Sis." He studied her. "You're a beauty. I'll have to keep an eye out for the fellas."

Blushing, Susie said, "Oh, Luke. I don't care about that kind of stuff."

"Won't be long before you do," he said with a grin.

He turned to his mother. She was thinner than the last time he'd seen her, and she looked weary. "Mom."

Her eyes teary, she wrapped her arms around her son. "I've been missing you, young man. It's good to have you home."

"Good to be here." Luke glanced around, thankful he didn't find Ray

Townsend. He hefted his duffel bag onto his shoulder. "Let's get home. I can't wait to see the place."

The house was pretty much the way Luke remembered it. There was a small addition and a shed Ray had built to store his hunting and trapping gear. Luke managed to get through the welcome from Ray, but the greeting was tense. He kept reminding himself that the time had come to forgive, to put everything in the past, and to begin living in the present.

He'd allowed himself to grieve his father's death as the chaplain had advised him, and he'd spent hours praying and asking for a heart of forgiveness. He'd even tried to see Ray Townsend through God's eyes, but he could still feel the anger and sense of betrayal. Maybe he wasn't able to forgive. "Just stay in the Word," John Atwood had said. "God will walk you through it. You'll see." Luke wanted to believe him, but it wasn't easy when nothing seemed changed. Maybe he was just being impatient.

That evening Mattie, Adam, Laurel, and William joined the family for dinner. When they'd all gathered around the kitchen table, it hit Luke that he was actually home. It felt so good that his face hurt from smiling.

His mother hummed as she prepared and set out the meal. When everyone was seated, she looked at Luke. Eyes shimmering, she said, "I can hardly believe you're here."

Everything seemed perfect. Then Ray sat at the head of the table with Jean at his right, just the way his father used to do. The bitterness started to rise. Ray didn't belong there. Then when Ray led the prayer, Luke's ire increased. Disappointment intertwined with his bitterness. Things weren't as he had imagined. Life here would never feel right.

"So, are you going to be sent back to duty or stay put?" Ray asked.

Luke took a slice of bread and buttered it. "I figured I'd stay put for a while. The army doesn't want me back out in the field. Guess the amnesia I had makes me unreliable." His tone was prickly. He set down his knife and took a bite of the bread. "Good, Mom. Just like always."

"Thank you."

"So, what are your plans?" Ray asked.

Luke didn't want an inquisition. He just wanted to eat and enjoy his family. With a heavy sigh, he placed his elbows on the table, looked at Ray, and pushed his tongue into his cheek. He wanted to tell the man it was none of his business, but rather than hurt his mother, he said, "Don't know for sure." He turned to Mattie who sat beside him. "I do know there's gonna be a wedding though. Me and Mattie are going to set up a home and raise vegetables and kids."

Mattie blushed.

"I thought you wanted to go back to Seattle, Mattie," Susie said.

"You don't want to live here?" Luke asked.

She set her fork on her plate, then took a drink of water. "I was thinking that maybe we could move to Seattle. Can we talk about it? Later?"

"I thought you'd come back for good." Luke felt a flutter of fear. "I thought you were happy here."

"I haven't been unhappy exactly, but you know how I feel about living here."

"No. I guess I don't."

"Luke, let's talk about it later," Mattie said. Obviously she didn't want to discuss something so important in front of everyone.

Others at the table tried to busy themselves with the meal.

"Sure. Sorry. I guess I've been in the army so long I forgot my manners." He pushed his fork into a pile of mashed potatoes, but his appetite was gone. Would this be the end of him and Mattie?

"So, when is the wedding?" Laurel asked.

Luke didn't answer right away. "We talked about getting hitched right away, but I want my shipmate, Barry, to be my best man. He can't get here for a few weeks."

Mattie smiled. "And my friend Meryl needs to arrange for time off from work." She glanced at Luke. "If the reverend can do it, we were hoping to get married in about three weeks."

Maybe it'll be all right, Luke thought and lifted Mattie's hand and kissed it.

"How can you possibly put together a wedding in that little time?" Jean asked.

"We want it very simple," Mattie said. "Just our closest friends and family. No big fuss."

"Well, I guess we can try." Jean didn't sound convinced.

Adam speared a piece of roasted moose. "I was hoping I could write a story about your war experiences, Luke."

"Sure. I'll tell you what I can remember."

"I was thinking your amnesia would give me a good angle for the story. Having you back is pretty much a miracle. While you were trying to figure out who you were, we were mourning, thinking you were dead."

"It's a miracle for me, that's for sure. When I was in the water with burning oil all around me, I thought I was a goner."

"Now you're here to stay, right?" Brian asked, glancing from Luke to Mattie.

"I don't know. Maybe. That was my plan."

Mattie kept her eyes on her plate.

"We can have a reception here at the house." Ray captured Jean's hand in his. "Would you mind having it here? Seems right, you two getting hitched at home."

The term *at home* hit a nerve in Luke. It wasn't Ray's home. Pictures of him and his father working on the place reeled through his mind. In the beginning they'd come every day, clearing away the wilderness, tilling the earth, and laying timber for the house. Luke could almost smell the aroma of freshly sawed lumber, see the strength in his father's hands while he held a form in place and drove home a nail. This was not Ray's home.

"Luke? Luke?" Jean repeated.

"Uh, what? Did you say something?"

"I was just wondering if having a reception here would be all right with you?" Anxiety lined Jean's face.

Luke glanced at Mattie. "I was thinking we could do it at the church. If that's all right?"

"The church is fine," Mattie said.

"What about our house?" Laurel offered.

Mattie smiled. "I'd like that."

"Sure—your place then." Luke felt as if he were being swept away in a bore tide of emotions. He needed to get out. Maybe some fresh air would help.

~

After saying a blessing over Luke and Mattie, the minister said, "I pronounce you husband and wife." He offered Luke a fatherly smile. "You may kiss your bride."

His blue eyes ardent, Luke gently took Mattie's face in his hands and kissed her. "I love you."

"I love you," Mattie said, a wave of passion and love cutting off her breath. The two clasped hands and turned to face their guests.

Meryl hugged Mattie. "You are the most beautiful bride I've ever seen," she gushed.

Mattie smiled and swallowed past the lump in her throat. She was certain there had never been a time in her life when she'd felt happier.

Luke lifted Mattie's hand and kissed it, then held it against his chest. "So, Mrs. Hasper . . ." He grinned. "I can't believe it. You're my wife."

"As it should be," Mattie said, remembering how close she'd come to losing him. "I'll never let you go."

They walked down the aisle and into the foyer where guests greeted them. A meal at Adam and Laurel's, rather than a party, had been planned. It seemed more intimate, an intertwining of families.

Luke leaned down and kissed Mattie, then said, "I'm starved, and I hear a feast is waiting."

"I'm always up for a good meal," Barry said, wearing a broad smile. He linked arms with Meryl. "You ready?"

"Absolutely." Throwing back her tangle of curls, she said, "I've always thought it a sign of good health when a man has a hearty appetite."

"Let's go, then," Luke said, keeping a tight hold on Mattie's hand. He led her out to the car, and after helping her in, ran around to the driver's side and slid in beside her. Immediately, as if he couldn't bear to be parted for even a moment, he pulled her close and kissed her, then settled behind the steering wheel with Mattie snuggled close.

Friends and family stood around a table laden with food at Laurel and Adam's home. "I think a blessing is in order," Adam said. He let his gaze fall on Luke and Mattie, who stood together, arms intertwined.

"What a day this has been. Our family grows." He looked at Affia and Atuska, then Ray and Jean. "It amazes me as I watch others join this family and become part of it. I'm one of those adopted." He paused. "We may not be connected by blood, yet in a mysterious and miraculous way we've become part of each other."

His gaze settled on Luke and Mattie. "Not so long ago we all feared Luke was gone, lost to us forever." He stopped, blinked away tears, and cleared his throat. "Now, here you are. And you're setting out with your new bride to begin an incredible adventure."

"OK, OK," Brian said. "We got it. You're not writing a book."

Quiet laughter broke out.

"That's all I had to say anyway." He took Laurel's hand. "Let's pray."

Everyone bowed their heads, and Adam began, "Father, in heaven, it's an honor to be here with this extraordinary family on this special day. Luke and Mattie have been dear to all of us for many years, and it's a true blessing to see them find each other." He paused. "We thank you for bringing Luke back to us. You're a good and gracious God. We pray that Mattie and Luke will have a long and happy life together. We look forward to being part of their joys, and we promise to be there to share in their sorrows.

"Father, we thank you for this wonderful food and ask that you would bless the hands of those who worked so hard to prepare it. Amen."

Amens were said all around, then Luke raised his hand. "I have something I want to say." He looked at his bride. "Mattie, thank you for sticking with me. We've been friends long enough; I figure you know me just about as well as anyone." He grinned. "And you married me anyway." There was soft laughter and applause. Luke added, more seriously, "I love you. I always will." He looked at Barry. "I also want to thank my buddy, Barry, who traveled all this way to share this day with me. You're a good friend."

Barry's face reddened, and he nodded. "What do you say we eat?"

A roar of approval went up, and Jean said, "It's buffet style. Everyone serve yourselves."

Brian and William were the first in line; the others moved in behind them.

Jean crossed to Luke. "Before you and Mattie set out on your own, I want you to know how much I love you. Ray and I both do. If you and Mattie ever need anything—"

"I know, Mom. Thanks."

Jean took Mattie's hand. "You've been family to me for a long time now, but today you became my daughter. I love you, dear." She kissed Mattie's cheek and hugged her.

"I love you, too, Mrs. Townsend."

"Maybe you ought to start calling me Jean." She smiled gently.

"Jean, then."

Sitting a little too close to Barry on the sofa, Meryl took a bite of salad and looked at Mattie. "Where are you going for your honeymoon?"

"A nearby inn."

Meryl frowned. "That's too bad. Seems you ought to go some place special and romantic."

"We don't need anything out of the ordinary for it to be special," Luke said, his eyes teasing. He hugged Mattie.

Meryl glanced at Barry, then turned her gaze to the window. "I guess you might say this place is romantic. To tell you the truth, I've never seen anything quite like it. I remember reading a book years ago, when I was very young, that described a land of mounds and mounds of snow and everything covered in ice crystals. I used to dream of visiting a place like that. And . . . well, here I am. Actually, this farm reminds me of one of those little glass globes with the scenes in them. You know, the kind you shake and snow swirls around?"

"I love those," Susie said.

Barry set his empty plate on the coffee table and casually draped an arm around Meryl's shoulders. "This is a great place. I'd almost consider moving here, but I don't think my family would like it. My mother and grandmother would definitely be unhappy if I moved so far from home."

"It suits us," Luke said. "I've managed to save up a little and figure if all goes well, we'll be building a house on our own piece of land come spring. Hope you'll make a trip back for a visit, maybe bring your family. You never know, they might like it and decide to stay."

"I doubt that. My family's been part of Oregon too long. It's in their blood—mine too."

Meryl leaned against Barry's arm. "Oregon." The word tripped from her mouth like a song. "I've never been there, but I've heard it's beautiful."

"It's got a little bit of everything—forests, farms, and mountains, and if you don't mind a few hours drive, you can even sink your feet into the sand at an ocean beach."

"Sounds almost perfect."

"Come and visit. You're always welcome at our place."

"I just might do that. Is there shopping nearby?" she asked, raising an eyebrow.

"Some. Not what you're used to, though, I'm sure. People don't usually come to Oregon for the shopping."

Meryl settled her eyes on Mattie. "Well, I suppose now that I've lost my roommate I should visit some new locations. Oregon's just as good a place to start as any."

Mattie knew Meryl; it wouldn't be long before she headed off to Salem. She and Barry had hit it off right away. Maybe something would come of it. She hoped so. She liked them both.

The little apartment in Seattle would be empty. Mattie wondered if there was any chance of convincing Luke to move. They still hadn't discussed where they should live, but it seemed clear he was set on Palmer. She studied her husband. He was full of dreams, dreams she didn't share. She would probably never see Seattle again.

Chapter 26

MATTIE STIRRED A TONIC INTO A CUP OF HOT TEA.

"Whatcha doing?" Luke asked, coming up behind her and peering over her shoulder.

"Making a remedy for my grandmother." Mattie glanced at Atuska, who was in her usual place on the sofa. "She's hurting a lot today," she said quietly.

"What is that stuff?"

She screwed a lid back on one of the jars and set it on a shelf with an assortment of other healing agents. "I added a mixture of willow bark and cow parsnip to her tea. It eases the pain."

"I'm impressed at how much you know."

"It's nothing." Mattie turned and faced Luke. "My mother and grandmother have been teaching me about remedies since I was a little girl. There are lots of natural medicines. You don't have to go to the doctor for everything."

Luke kissed her. "You're amazing." He studied the assortment of jars on the shelf. "How do you remember what's what and when to use it?"

"It takes practice, and I've had many years to learn." She lifted a jar and turned it around so Luke could see its label. "Plus, everything's marked." She grinned.

Luke pulled Mattie close. "I think it's wonderful the way you take care of your grandmother. She's lucky to have you."

"I'm lucky to have her. She's always been good to me." Mattie's eyes rested on the old woman. "I wish no one had to die. I don't know what I'll do when she's gone."

"I know. It still hurts when I think about my father." He stroked

Mattie's back and kissed her, then with a playful smile said, "I'm glad you have a good heart. One day I'll be old and need you to nurse me."

"And what about me?"

"Well, you'll have our daughter to look after you. She'll know all about these concoctions, just like you."

Mattie felt a twinge of unease. She hadn't planned on teaching her children the old ways. She intended to live somewhere else, where they wouldn't need to know. She glanced at her grandmother. Now that she was fading, Mattie had to admit to feeling pulled by all the old woman had taught her about the land and her ancestors. Somehow it seemed dishonorable not to hand down what she'd learned. If her grandmother knew of her plans, she would be hurt. Atuska had always treasured the old ways and had considered it her obligation to pass them on. Now, Mattie was considering cutting off that link.

She turned and gave the drink another quick stir, then set the spoon on the drain board. Carrying it into the front room, she kneeled beside the sofa. "Here, Grandmother. This will help."

Atuska blinked and struggled to focus on her granddaughter. Pushing herself upright, she took the cup and sipped. "Thank you. You're a good granddaughter." She smiled, her eyes looking like upside-down smiles. She took another drink. "This will make my aching bones forget how they feel for a while." Returning the glass to the table, she rested her hand on Mattie's arm. "You're good to me." Her expression turned sad. "I think I will miss you most of all."

"Please don't talk like that." Mattie pulled the woman's shawl around her shoulders. "You aren't going anywhere for a while."

"Oh, yes I will go . . . when it is my time. Sometimes I think I can hear the voice of my mother calling to me when I sleep, and it is still. I like it. I remember when I was a little girl and needed my mommy. She was always there." Her lips compressed, then turned softly upward. "Many wait for me, and it is my wish to go." She rested a withered hand on Mattie's cheek. "When it is time, I will leave here. Eternity waits . . . for every person."

Mattie knew her grandmother was right, but she didn't want to think about it. While her grandmother was rejoicing in heaven, she would still be here, missing her.

Atuska plumped a pillow and settled against it. Her face was wistful. "Sometimes I think of the place where I grew up and wish I could go there just once more. It was beautiful."

"Where was that?" Luke asked, sitting on a chair beside the sofa.

Her brown eyes soft, Atuska looked at him. "The Aleutians, on a small island not far from Unalaska. It was a good place to be a child." A look of whimsy settled on her face. "My mother and I used to pick berries. They were so delicious. And when my father and brothers would return with a kill, we would have a celebration. What fun we had." She looked at Mattie. "I wish you could see how it was. We would have such a wonderful party."

She returned to her memories. "We all brought food and sometimes gifts, and we would feast and dance. The men told stories." Her eyes sparkled. "When I was small, many of the tales frightened me. The storytellers were very good." She continued to drink her tea. "My favorite thing was the blanket toss." She chuckled. "I was very good. I didn't weigh very much, so the people would throw me up and I would sail so high I could see all the way to the other end of the village, sometimes even beyond to where the waves splashed against the rocks." She closed her eyes. "How I would like to go there again."

"I wish I could take you, but there's a war," Mattie said. "The Japanese captured the islands, and it's too dangerous to go there."

Atuska looked at her granddaughter. "I know, but it is still fun to think of it." Finishing her tonic, she returned the cup to Mattie, then closed her eyes. Soon her breathing became heavy, her body relaxed. She was asleep.

Mattie returned to the kitchen and set the cup in the washbasin. Luke joined her. He leaned against the drain board. "I bet she has some really good stories."

"She does. Ask her and she will tell you some—maybe even more than you want to hear." She gazed at the old woman. "I wish I could take her to her home."

"Maybe you can when the war ends."

"I don't think that will be soon enough." Mattie took Luke's hand in hers, pressed it against his chest, and rested her cheek on his wool shirt. His heart thumped steady and strong. "I hate the war."

Luke banked the fire in the small barrel stove in the corner of the cabin. In truth, their little house wasn't a cabin. It was a modified shed that sat only yards from Mattie's mother's house. For now it was comfortable enough, but Luke planned on building a proper home as soon as finances allowed.

He climbed into bed beside Mattie and cuddled close. "You're cold," she said.

"I know. It's freezing in here. I'd build a bigger fire, but I'm afraid it will get too hot and catch the house on fire." Luke pulled her close. "We'll have a better place soon. I promise." He kissed the back of her neck.

Mattie didn't reply. She stared at the wall where the soft light of the moon illuminated rough timber.

"Is something wrong? You were quiet all through supper."

"I've been thinking . . . about you and Ray. I wish you could patch up your differences. Your mother told me they would like us to stay with them, and I think it would be better than living here."

"Why is everyone so concerned about me and Ray? I don't know if I can change. I don't even know if I want to."

"You can. I thought you wanted to."

"Mattie, it's not that easy," Luke said, softening his tone. "Anyway, I figure we'll get our differences ironed out eventually—just not yet." He nuzzled her neck. "I found a piece of land. I think it'll work for us."

Mattie stiffened. She didn't want to talk about land. She wanted to move away.

"It's a good patch of ground, and not far out of town. You could walk into Palmer if you had a mind to, which would be good once we have kids. That way you could get them to and from school without much fuss. You could even take them to the doctor's if they got sick. And I thought it would be good if—"

"Luke, I'm tired. I want to go to sleep." Mattie burrowed into her pillow.

"Oh. I just thought we could talk about it for a few minutes, but if you're tired . . ." He rolled over abruptly and turned down the lantern. A moment later he sat up and fluffed his pillow, then dropped back down, his back to Mattie.

She knew he was hurt, but she didn't have the energy to talk about how their lives would be. Luke always envisioned a farm here in the valley, and she wanted out, anywhere on the outside. She stared into the semidarkness, listening to the pop of wood in the stove.

"Mattie," Luke said softly, "you awake?"

"Uh-huh."

Luke was silent a moment, then asked, "You don't want to stay, do you?"

Mattie didn't answer immediately. What was there to talk about? If they stayed, she'd be unhappy; if they left, he'd be unhappy. No way was right for them.

"Mattie?"

"No. I don't want to stay," she said softly.

"Why not? Both of our families are here. We have friends. It's right for us."

Mattie rolled over and faced Luke. She lifted his hand and kissed a fingertip. "You're a good man, Luke, and I love you. But this is something you don't seem to be able to understand. I don't know why. Even before I moved to Seattle I told you how I felt, that I wanted to leave. But you always act as if we should stay and that it's good for both of us. It's not."

"You've barely mentioned leaving since I got back. How can I know how you feel?" He sat up. "When you moved here from Seattle, you didn't come because of me. Why did you return?"

"I thought you were dead, and I needed my family."

Luke was quiet. "I'd figured you'd gotten over all that Indian stuff."

"Indian stuff?" Instantly angry, Mattie pressed her lips together. She knew better than to speak immediately. "When you say 'Indian stuff,' it sounds like you think I'm being silly, like what I feel is ridiculous."

"I don't think that. I just thought you were better, that's all."

Mattie sat up and hugged her knees. "I'm not. Nothing has really changed. And it's not *Indian stuff*, it's my life—the way people look at me, the things they say and don't say . . . the humiliation. I don't want my children to go through what I have."

"You think that just because we move away from Alaska you and any children we might have won't face troubles, that people won't be cruel?

I'm not an Indian. I don't have one ounce of Indian blood, but I've had my share of people's poison." His voice was angry.

"It's not the same." Mattie's mind returned to parties she couldn't attend, children who wouldn't play with her or taunted her, and adults who would rather cross the street than walk past her. She squeezed her eyes shut and pressed her forehead against her knees. The wounds inside still festered. She doubted they would ever heal.

She looked at Luke. "Of all people, I thought you would understand. You're supposed to love me." She blinked back tears. "I can't even count the number of times people have snubbed me or humiliated me because of what they saw when they looked at me." She punched the mattress with her feet. "I won't let that happen to my children."

"Mattie, it isn't going to be like that. I won't let it."

"You can't stop it. No one can. You can't change the way people think and feel. There are always going to be people who hate me or our children because of our Indian blood."

"Things are different now—better." Luke pressed his hand against her back. "We'll have a good life here. You'll see."

Mattie closed her eyes. A hollow ache swelled in her chest. *Why can't he understand?* She shook her head. "I wish you were right, but you're not." She threw back the blankets and dropped her feet over the side of the bed.

"What are you doing?"

"I'm going for a walk."

"In the middle of the night?"

"Yes. In the middle of the night."

"Mattie, it's freezing out there. It's not safe for you to go out."

"I've lived here all my life. I know what I can and cannot do. I'll be fine." She sat on a stool and pulled on a pair of pants and warm boots. Then she grabbed her parka, pulled it over her nightclothes, and shoved her hands into gloves. "I'll be back soon."

"At least let me go with you."

"No. I need to be alone."

"Mattie, be reasonable. Come back to bed."

Without another word, Mattie opened the door. Icy air flowed inside. She ignored the cold and stepped into the enchanted world of a winter night. Moon glow lay down shadows at the feet of the trees, giving the forest a mysterious air. Mattie had a sense of the unworldly and nearly retreated, but when she imagined Luke's response, she decided to keep going and headed toward the river.

It hadn't snowed for the last few days, so it was easy to follow a trail, which had already been laid down. The frozen ground crunched and squeaked beneath her feet. Frigid air burned her lungs with each breath. Mattie pulled her hood closed around her face.

When she reached the river, she stood and gazed at the area of cleared ice with mounds of piled snow along its edges. She and Luke had skated here just a few hours earlier. It had seemed a friendly place then. Now it looked lonely and unreal. She shuddered.

Her thoughts returned to the days when she and Alex and the Haspers had all skated here. She could still hear the laughter and the challenges to race. She smiled. Her mind then wandered to other childhood memories. It was here that she had made other friends too. She and Alex had worked hard to clear the ice. It had been his birthday, and children from school had joined him here. They'd been nice and even included his little sister in their play. After skating they'd built a snow house, then sat and talked about childish things—the puppy one boy hoped to get, the test they'd had that day, and the new teacher who was arriving the following day. Her mother had brought them hot chocolate, and they drank it together. It had been a good day.

Mattie still felt the warmth of her childhood. Alex had been a good brother. He'd often included her and never acted as if he was better than her just because she was "the little sister." The empty place he'd left inside her when he died was still there. She knew it would always exist. Oh, how she missed him. *Why did he have to die?*

A wolf's howl cut through the still night air. Mattie straightened and listened. Another cry carried over the dark world, and then quiet took hold once more.

Other memories flooded in. She'd had many good days at the river. Her mother had taught her how to swim, right here in this very spot. Here she and Alex had often fished together. She remembered how patient he'd been when he showed her how to bait the line and cast. When she pulled in her first fish, he'd been as proud as if he'd caught it himself.

She'd also spent many hours picking berries. Usually she went with Atuska, who gathered plants for her remedies. After returning to the house, her grandmother would prepare the berries. She dried some and canned others, and she would always patiently show Mattie how to dry and store the plants for the medicines.

Suddenly Mattie felt a sharp and unexpected connection with this place. Did she really want to leave, to forget? Would her children miss something extraordinary if she and Luke moved away? They'd never hear the sound of a wolf's cry in the night, or see the dance of the Northern Lights, or feel the thrill of flying across the snow on a sled towed by an eager dog team. Maybe living here was more a gift than a curse.

Chapter 27

MATTIE LINGERED. SHE'D CAUGHT A GLIMPSE OF WHO SHE WAS AND WANTED to know more. She scooped up a handful of snow, pressed it into a ball, and threw it at a nearby tree. It splattered as it hit the trunk, leaving a splotch of white. She felt a swell of pleasure. Maybe she did belong here.

A long, lonely howl of a wolf traveled across the river. The mournful tune reached a high pitch, then slid downward. It was answered by another wail not far away. The calls sounded wretched and lonely.

Mattie wasn't frightened. She'd heard the wolves many times. Their voices gave her a sense of reminiscence. They belonged here.

Another melancholy cry echoed over the harsh landscape, this one closer than the first. Mattie glanced back the way she'd come. She was a fair distance from the house, more isolated than she'd realized.

I should go back, she thought, but didn't feel ready to leave. Instead, she laid her head back and stared at the night sky. The moon's light illuminated the dark canopy, while stars glimmered dimly, enfolded in a misty gauze. Then a heavy cloud drifted over the moon, and the countryside was plunged into darkness. A cold draft of air moved over the earth. It was time to go.

Unable to see well, Mattie started back, her mind still full of questions. What would her life be like if she and Luke stayed in the valley? Had people's attitudes changed enough to offer a peaceful life to native Alaskans? She knew it was impossible to change everyone's mindset, but maybe enough transformation had taken place to make life more hospitable. Since leaving Seattle, no one had caused her trouble.

In some ways her childhood in Alaska had been magical. She had loved so much of it. Maybe Luke *could* be a shield against people's intolerance, and he was right about hardships being everywhere. No one could escape the ups and downs of living. Life had its sorrows.

A wolf called, then another and another. They were close. Mattie hurried her steps. Wolves rarely attacked humans, but it would be wise to avoid a confrontation. Placing her feet carefully, she hurried home, wishing the moon would reappear. The light would make it easier and faster to find her way.

Another lament from a nearby wolf raised the hairs on her neck. It sounded like it was between her and the house. She stopped to listen, searching for the lights of home.

She saw a shadow shift in the trees and her heart hurried. If the wolves were between her and the house, she could be in trouble. What was the best way to go? She gazed into the dark night. *Father, help me,* she prayed.

As if in answer, the clouds drifted, and again the bright orb lit the world. A wolf stood no more than ten yards away, its mouth open and tongue lolling. Its tail lay still and quiet. His nonaggressive stance gave Mattie a modicum of peace. However, her confidence quickly evaporated when she spotted others pacing among the trees.

She could see the cabin now, but if these wolves were hungry and after a meal, it was too far away. She couldn't run. That would only set off their instinct to chase and kill. She'd never make it. Could she frighten them by yelling? Hostility might ignite aggression. She decided her best course was to remain calm and act unafraid. Keeping an eye on the animals, she kept moving.

Using a soothing tone, she chatted amiably. "It's a nice evening for a walk, and I'm sure you wouldn't find me interesting at all, so you'd better just go your way and let me go mine." To her left, she heard a menacing growl. Her eyes darted to the shadows. A wolf watched her, his tail raised and teeth barred. The cabin seemed far away.

"Don't get tough with me," she said. "You'll find me a better warrior than you think. I'm small but ferocious." She picked up a stubby limb and kept moving. "You'd better keep your distance."

She could see six or seven wolves padding in the shadows among the trees. They were closing in. Pushing down panic, Mattie tried to remember everything she knew about wolves. *They aren't really dangerous to humans. They are not aggressive toward people,* she told herself.

The snow gave as she stepped into a hole and nearly fell. Quickly regaining her footing, she fought the desire to stop and press her back against a tree and brandish her weapon. Terrifying stories of wolf attacks tumbled through her mind. *Those were just stories. There's no truth to them.* She resumed talking. "Now, wolves, you don't really want to eat me. I'm not good tasting at all."

One of the animals veered in close, tail raised, hackles up, and snarling. "Get back!" she yelled in her biggest voice. "Stay back!" The wolf stopped. He stared at her. She glanced at the limb she held. It wasn't heavy enough. Mattie scanned the area for something sturdier. Spotting a short, heavy branch, she moved toward it. Keeping her eyes on the circling wolves, she slowly bent and grabbed hold of the thick limb, dropping the other. Extending it toward the nearest wolf, she said, "Stay back, or you'll feel this across the side of your head."

The animal stared and growled, then took a step toward Mattie. She couldn't believe this was happening. She'd never known anyone who'd actually been attacked before. *They must be very hungry.* The picture of the dying moose she'd seen filled her mind, and she shuddered.

Mattie searched for a tree to climb. A cottonwood was only a few steps away, its lowest branches within reach. Getting out of the animals' reach quickly wouldn't be easy. If the pack was intent on attacking, they would be on her the moment she tried to escape. Another wolf moved in, its head down and teeth bared. She had no choice. She took a step toward the tree. The wolf followed.

A rifle blast exploded. Mattie flinched. A second shot resounded.

Luke shouted. "Go on! Get! Get out of here!"

The wolves retreated into the darkness. Continuing to holler at them, Luke followed, galloping through thigh-high snow.

Letting out her breath, Mattie lowered her weapon. Her legs felt weak and she trembled.

Firing two more shots, Luke turned and trudged back to Mattie. "You all right?"

"Yes. Just scared. If you hadn't shown up . . ." She couldn't bring herself to finish the statement.

"I told you not to come out here." Luke sounded angry.

Mattie didn't want to fight. "I know. Let's go back inside."

"You could have been killed," he yelled.

"Yes, I know." She glanced in the direction the pack had headed. "I've lived here all my life and never had a problem with wolves. Why should I expect it now?" She looked at the club she'd been gripping and dropped it. "We don't know if they would have hurt me. Maybe they were just curious."

"Curious, my foot. They meant to have you as a midnight snack." His bluster wavered and he hugged her. "I'm just thankful you're all right."

Mattie's arms went around him.

"I'm sorry I yelled. I was scared." He loosened his embrace. "Let's go."

The door to her mother's cabin opened, and Affia stepped onto the porch. Holding up a lantern, she peered into the darkness. "What's going on? I heard shots. Is everything all right?"

"Yes. Everything's fine," Mattie said. "There were some wolves . . . Luke scared them off."

"Wolves? So close?"

"They followed me from down river."

"What are you doing out at this time of night?"

"Walking. Everything's fine, Mama. Go to bed."

"You're sure?"

"Yes."

"All right. Good night." The door closed with some hesitation.

Mattie and Luke headed for their small cabin. A smattering of snow fell. Mattie sighed. "More snow."

"You sound unhappy about it."

"It just makes more work." She pouted. "We'll have to tromp it down around the cache and the wood pile, and—"

"Mattie, I don't want to talk about the weather. We need to talk about what happened tonight. You could have been killed. This isn't Seattle. It's Alaska."

A heavy weariness fell over Mattie. She didn't want to talk about anything. She just wanted to sleep.

"What if they attacked you?"

"They didn't," Mattie said shortly. "Can't we talk about it tomorrow?"

"No. We'll talk about it now."

Mattie knew that tone. She could not avoid a discussion. She knocked off snow from her boots and opened the cabin door. "All right. We'll talk."

The small room felt hot after being outdoors. Mattie sat on the edge of the bed. "You're right. This isn't Seattle."

"What's that supposed to mean?"

Mattie said nothing.

"You're the one who's lived here all your life. You know how it can be. I don't want you hurt."

Mattie didn't look at Luke.

"Listen to me." Luke gripped her arms and pulled her to her feet. "I mean it, Mattie. Think next time."

Mattie was the one angry now. "If we lived in Seattle, I wouldn't have been out walking in the middle of the night. And you wouldn't have to worry about me being attacked by wolves or anything else."

"So we're back to that." Luke stripped off his coat. "What is it about Seattle? It's just a city where it rains a lot, a place full of strangers who don't care about each other."

"You don't know what it's like. I was accepted there."

"You call being ridiculed and thrown in jail being accepted?"

"That's not how it was. Before all that, everything was fine. They just made a mistake."

"Some mistake. You think you were more accepted there than you are here?"

"We've talked about this before." Mattie was quiet. What had happened to the tranquility she'd felt along the river, the tender memories of her childhood? They no longer seemed real. "I don't want to live here," she said matter-of-factly. "I don't think I can be happy here. Everything was different in Seattle." She rested her hands against Luke's chest. "I really think we could be content there. Please, think about it."

With a sigh, Luke sat on the edge of the bed and pulled off a boot. "I can't think about it. I know you believe it would be better, but it wouldn't be right for us." He hooked his thumb into the other boot and pulled. It dropped to the floor. "I'm the head of our home now," he said gently. "I'm responsible for making the right choices for us, and the right choice is here."

"How is it that *you* know what's right for *us*? I thought we were both part of this marriage."

"We are, but . . . Well, I just know I'm right about this."

Mattie sat down hard on a straight-backed chair. "And what if you're wrong?"

"Then I'm wrong, and I'll face the consequences."

"I thought you cared how I feel."

"I do, and that's one of the reasons we have to stay here. It's right for you." Luke leaned forward and rested his arms on his thighs. "Mattie, it's time to put your past behind you and start living for today. Thinking about past hurts just makes things worse."

"You're the one to talk about past hurts." Before he could respond, she said, "I'm sorry. I didn't mean that."

He stood and crossed to her. "You're right. I do need to work on some things, but this isn't about me." He caressed her hair. "You can't run away from your troubles or from who you are." He kissed the top of her head. "I love who you are, and being native is part of you and part of what I love about you."

Mattie couldn't stay mad. She leaned against him. "What you say sounds sensible, but I've tried, and I can't do it." She straightened. "Every time I think about the children we want to have and about their growing up here I get scared. I don't want them to go through what I did."

The song of a wolf resonated in the distance. She glanced at the window. "And it *can* be dangerous here."

"It's dangerous anywhere. Look what happened in Seattle when they thought you were Japanese. Around here a person just has to use his head a little more." He stripped off wool pants and draped them over the end of the bed. "Let's go to bed. It's late."

"We have to think this out carefully. I want to have a part in this decision. What we decide is going to affect our entire lives."

"No matter what we do, we won't have a perfect life. We will always have troubles."

"I know. I don't expect it to be perfect." Mattie walked to the window and stared out. "I think about you and Ray and how much it hurts you to see him living in your house." She turned to Luke. "If you lived somewhere else, you wouldn't have to face that all the time."

"That part I wouldn't mind, but . . . like you said, I've got to face it. Just like you, running away won't really help. I'm going to have to sort out my feelings."

"I'm not running away." She climbed into bed.

Luke stared at the ceiling. "That's right, because I'm not going to let you."

Lying on her back, Mattie folded her arms under her head. "Well, maybe I am, but moving would make life better for both of us." She snuggled against Luke. "Won't you please at least think about it?"

"I'll think on it, but—"

"No buts. Just think . . . and pray."

"All right." Luke rolled to his side and pulled Mattie close. He kissed her on the tip of the nose. "Those wolves missed out on a real treat."

"Luke! That's not funny."

"I'm just talking about how sweet you taste." He kissed her again, only this time with passion.

Mattie knew they wouldn't leave Alaska.

Chapter 28

ADAM DIDN'T MUCH FEEL LIKE A PARTY WHEN HE STEPPED INTO THE TOWNSEND kitchen. William hurried past his father and galloped toward the front room. Adam helped Laurel with her coat and hung it on a hook beside the door. The aroma of roasting meat pervaded the house. "Smells good," Adam said, trying to be sociable.

"Hello there," Jean said as William ran through the kitchen. She grabbed him, and resting her palms on his cheeks, kissed him. "How good to see you."

Adam's thoughts were with Elisa and Adin. He hadn't been able to shake thoughts of them all day—most days since he'd returned home. What had become of them? Had they actually escaped France? Were they safe? He'd heard reports of heavy bombing in London.

He stripped off his gloves and pushed them into his coat pockets. Adam's thoughts remained in London. The woman at the British immigration office had eyed Elisa suspiciously, and after discovering she was a Jew, had treated her with contempt.

I should have made sure they were safely settled somewhere before leaving the country. What if that clerk rejected their papers? What if Elisa and Adin had been sent back to France?

"Good to see you, Adam," Jean said, taking his hands and giving them a squeeze. "My, you're freezing. How about something hot to warm you up?"

"Sounds good. You have coffee?" He shrugged out of his coat.

"I do," Jean said, crossing to the stove.

"It's a cold one tonight. Looks like another storm, which is the last thing I wanted." Adam hung his parka beside Laurel's. "This time of year I'd like to be done with winter."

William disappeared into the front room, and a few moments later his steps were heard climbing the stairs.

"He always goes straight for Brian's room," Laurel said. "He just loves his uncle."

Susie leaned on the table and smiled at Adam. Sounding very much like her mother, she said, "You don't have to feel bad about February weather. It means spring is just around the corner. I figure by the time February gets here, we're nearly there."

"True, but we can still expect some powerful storms to blow through," Mattie said, stepping in from the front room. She hugged Laurel.

"You look wonderful," Laurel said. "Marriage agrees with you. Obviously my brother is taking good care of you."

"Very good." Mattie's eyes sparkled, and she whispered, "I love him more and more every day."

Luke sauntered into the kitchen, draped his arms around Mattie's shoulders, and kissed her neck. "Now that's what I like to hear."

Searching for a way to become part of the banter, Adam asked, "So, Luke, you been keeping busy?"

"Sure. 'Course with Mattie I don't have to work so hard. She does a lot. I've been thinking, though, that I ought to teach her checkers. I need a partner to keep me sharp." He grinned. "Up until just a minute ago, my little brother was beating the pants off me."

Jean handed Adam a cup of coffee. "Luke, what a thing to say."

Adam breathed in the aroma of the hot drink and sipped. "Good as always." He glanced about. "Where's Ray?"

"Should be here any time. He's just gotten himself a team of dogs."

"Really? He gonna race them?"

"Of course." Jean folded her arms over her chest.

The sound of a truck accompanied by the ruckus of barking dogs carried in from outside.

"That must be him," Brian said, hurrying to the back door. "We're gonna have our own sled team!" He grabbed a coat and hurried to meet Ray.

The entire family trudged outside to get a look at the team. The dogs were appraised, Ray was complimented on his choice of animals, then everyone moved back indoors.

Once seated at the table, Adam asked, "So, you going to race them in the Iditarod?"

"Oh, no. I'm not ready for anything like that, but I figure I'll enter some of the smaller races. I've got to get used to the dogs, and they have to get used to me. They look good, though, don't you think?"

"Well, I don't know much about sled dogs, but they seem strong and healthy."

"Yeah, I can hardly wait to take them out. I've got a good sled too."

"Ray told me I can work with him," Brian said, looking puffed up over the idea.

"Sounds like fun," Laurel said. "Adam, have you ever thought about doing something like that?"

He leaned back in his chair. "No. It's not for me. Don't you remember the last time I tried that? Luke and I were lucky to be alive after that ride."

After the meal, Ray pushed back from the table. "That was delicious. Thank you, Jean." He stood and strolled into the front room. Adam followed. Luke had to be shooed out while the women cleared the table and washed up the dishes.

Pipe smoke drifted into the kitchen. Laurel set the last plate in the dish drainer. "Men. Why is it that they have to have a smoke after a meal? It stinks up the place."

"I like the smell," Mattie said. "My father used to smoke a pipe. It reminds me of him. I kind of wish Luke would smoke one."

Laurel wrinkled up her nose. "Well, I think it's one of those male things. It can't possibly taste good."

Adam appeared in the doorway. "Have you ever tried it?" he asked, wearing a half smile. "It's not bad. I once knew a woman who smoked cigars."

"Really?" Jean said. "I don't understand that kind of thing." She removed her apron and hung it up, then lay a hand gently on Adam's cheek. "And how are you doing? You seem a little quiet tonight."

"I'm fine," he lied, knowing she could see the truth. "All right. I'm kind of all right."

"Things take time to work themselves out. I'm sure the world will look brighter to you soon." She shook her head. "I can't begin to understand what you went through over there. All those poor people. I thank my Lord that we're here safe and sound."

A blast of wind whistled around the house and puffed snow underneath the kitchen window. Jean hurried to it and pushed down hard to close it. "This thing is always getting stuck." With an extra hard shove, it finally thudded closed. "I'll have to have Ray fix it."

"Mama, do you want to serve dessert now?" Laurel asked.

"Yes." She crossed to the oven and lifted two pies from the warming shelf. "I made a blackberry and an apple."

After everyone had their dessert and drinks in hand, the family gathered in the front room to listen to Burns and Allen on the radio. Mattie and Luke sat close together on the sofa with Susie beside them. Ray lounged in an overstuffed chair, his legs thrust out in front of him. He concentrated on his pie. Greedily consuming two pieces, Brian seemed comfortable enough on the floor. Sitting beside him, William raced to eat as much dessert as he could before his mother put a stop to his gluttony. Adam sat on a straight-backed chair, looking slightly detached. Laurel was beside him, on the floor.

Jean walked to the radio and turned up the sound. "It always seems to fade this time of night," she said, returning to sit on the arm of Ray's chair.

Gracie gave a dim-witted reply to George Burns, and everyone laughed.

"She's so funny," Susie said.

"Yeah, silly like you," Brian quipped.

"I am not."

Jean gave Brian "the look," and he quickly turned his attention to scraping the last morsels of pie off his plate.

When the show ended, Mattie asked, "Where is Celeste? I thought she was going to be here?"

"She was, but she's not feeling well," Ray said.

"Anything serious?" Adam asked.

"No. Just the sniffles."

Jean refilled cups.

"Ray, can you tell us one of your hunting stories?" Brian asked.

"You've heard them all."

"I haven't," Laurel said.

"I don't think I've heard any." Mattie squeezed Luke's hand. "Neither has Luke."

He made no comment.

"I'd like to hear one," Adam said.

Ray lit his pipe, took a puff, and leaned back in his chair. "Well, did I ever tell you about my run-in with the wolves when I was down on the Copper River?"

"Nope," Brian said, leaning forward and resting his arms on folded legs.

He thought a moment. "That musta been nearly twenty-five years ago. Back when I was a young man." He looked at Luke. "I was probably about your age."

Luke remained stone-faced.

Ray continued. "It was about this time of year, and I was out checking a trapline. Late February and early March wolves tend to get cantankerous, what with mating season and hunger driving them."

"I thought wolves didn't attack people," Adam said.

Ray took two quick puffs of his pipe. "Generally you don't have to worry about them, but you never can tell for sure. I've heard a lot of stories about people being chased up a tree or into a cabin. And of course some folks never come out the woods, and no one knows what became of 'em. I s'pect wolves could be the culprit in some cases."

"They're dangerous all right," Luke said. "Mattie had a run-in just a couple of nights ago."

Laurel pressed a hand to her throat. "You did? What happened?"

"I went for a late walk. They were talking to each other, but I didn't think I had anything to worry about. Never had any trouble before. I don't know if they would have hurt me or not."

"They were lickin' their chops," Luke cut in. "I had to run 'em off. They were all around her, looking mean and hungry."

"Oh, Mattie," Jean said, worry in her voice.

"I hope I never run into any," Brian said. "What happened to you, Ray?"

"Well, like I said, I'd been following a trapline and was heading back to camp when I spotted a couple of wolves. They were tailing me. I didn't think much about it, figuring they weren't any real threat. Not long after that I caught sight of three more, and they seemed real interested in me. It was then that I thought they might give me trouble." He sucked on the pipe and let smoke escape from the side of his mouth. "I figured a few shots from my rifle would scare 'em off. So, I lifted my rifle and . . ." he paused for dramatic effect. "When I went to fire it, nothing happened. It was jammed."

Susie's eyes were big and round. "Oh no! What did you do?"

"I tried again. Still nothin'. So I kept moving. Things stayed peaceful for a while. They just dogged me. I'd nearly made it back to camp when one of them critters ran at me. I hollered, but he kept coming."

Ray leaned back in his chair and let his eyes trail the faces. Clearly he was enjoying telling the tale. "Before I knew it, he was on me, so I did the only thing I could."

"What?" Susie asked.

"I used that rifle like a club and hit him over the head hard. He went right down. Out cold." He chuckled.

"What about the rest of the pack?" Brian asked.

"Oh, they kept their distance . . . for a while anyway. I knew they'd come after me, so I started looking for a tree to climb. Before I could find one, another of those brutes took after me. I used my gun again, but this time it cracked when it hit. Got him over the head, though, which pushed him back. Almost right away another one was on me. Only weapon I had was my skinning knife."

"Were you scared?" Susie asked breathlessly.

"You bet. I was in a real fix. I still had at least four of those devils to take care of."

"Ray," Jean said softly, "maybe it would be better if the children didn't hear any more."

"They have to know what's out there. One day they'll be facing this world on their own."

Jean pressed her lips together and folded her hands in her lap.

Ray forged on. "I spotted this scraggly old cottonwood. Figured if I could climb up high enough, I'd be safe, so I kind of edged toward it. Didn't want to run. You never run from animals like that. It'll set 'em off for sure. They like the chase."

Ray's pipe had gone out, so he relit it. "By this time those wolves were getting closer and closer, sometimes jumping at me snappin' and growlin'. When I was about five feet from the tree, I knew they wouldn't wait long. If I didn't hurry, they'd get me. I decided to make a run for it. Now remember, I was real close; otherwise, I never would've run."

The room was silent, all eyes on Ray.

"Well, I lit out as fast as I could, and I lunged for that tree just in the nick of time. One of them beasts caught hold of my pant leg and nearly yanked off my britches."

Everyone laughed, including Luke.

"I ended up perched in that tree for a whole day and night before those wolves finally gave up on my comin' down."

"Did you see them again?" Brian asked.

"Nope, but I sure kept an eye out. Ever since then I don't trust wolves. Got to watch 'em."

"Adam, that sounds like a good story for the paper," Laurel said.

"Absolutely. I'll have to get with you, Ray. And you too, Mattie." He pushed to his feet. "It's getting late. We ought to go."

"Get your coat, William," Laurel said.

William stood and moseyed toward the back porch.

After saying their farewells, Adam, Laurel, and William headed home. A storm lay down fresh snow and whipped up the old, making it hard to see. Gripping the steering wheel, Adam peered through partially frosted glass. Snow hurtled through the lights and splattered the window.

"Maybe we should go back," Laurel said, glancing at William asleep in the back seat.

"We'll be fine," he said in a flat tone, revealing his miserable mood.

Laurel stared at the road. "Adam, I thought you were going to write about what you saw in France and England. I think you should."

Adam tightened his grip on the steering wheel. "I'll write about it when I'm ready." He hadn't meant to be so sharp, but he didn't want to be pushed. "You don't understand how it is."

"Tell me then."

Every time Adam tried to get the story down on paper, the events and people felt as if they were with him. He experienced it all over again—the plane crash, the deaths, the arrest of the farmer and his family, his feelings toward Elisa. She and Adin were gone, and he didn't know where. He should have done more for them. And he was reminded of the men who had died. It made no sense that he'd lived.

"Adam! Watch out!"

A moose stood in the car lights, snow swirling around it. Adam wrenched the wheel to the right. The car slid, then spun. They stopped with a thud, slamming against a snow bank.

Momentarily dazed, Adam stared at his hands still gripping the wheel. "Laurel, you all right? William?"

"Yes, I'm fine."

Adam swung around to check his son.

Lying on the seat, William pushed himself upright. "What happened?"

Adam sucked in a steadying breath and blew it out slowly. "A moose was in the road. I had to swerve to miss it. We're all right."

With a child's trust, William nodded, closed his eyes, and returned to his slumber.

"I'm sorry. I wasn't paying attention. Seems I have a penchant for doing the wrong thing these days."

"You couldn't have known about that moose. No one can see in this kind of weather." Laurel grabbed his hand. "This wasn't your fault, and I don't know what else you think you've done."

Months of fighting to maintain a brave front dissolved. "The men shouldn't have died."

"What men?"

"The crew on that plane. They faced battles every week, sometimes every day. They risked their lives to fight for people who couldn't defend themselves. I was just along for the ride. I'm nothing." He shook his head. "It should have been me, not them."

"Adam, that decision wasn't up to you."

He stared at Laurel.

"No one understands why some die while others live. You were doing what you'd been asked, what you knew how to do." She squeezed his hand. "I'm proud of you."

"And what about Elisa? I still think about her." Hurt touched Laurel's eyes, and Adam quickly explained. "Not that way, but I do worry about her."

Laurel studied the storm outside her window. "Of course you do. You cared about her and Adin. That's a good thing."

"Don't make me out to be better than I am. I was motivated by more than just wanting to help."

Laurel remained silent for a long while, then said, "You have to forget. Leave it behind. Those people are part of your past—part of our past."

"I feel like I let them down, everyone. I wasn't here for you and William, and I didn't do enough for them. I should have waited until I knew they were safe."

"What more could you have done?"

Adam's mind returned to the woman at the immigration office. "The clerk at immigration hated Elisa. I could see it. She might have sent them back. What if she did?" He shook his head. "I should have stayed, but all I could think about was getting home."

"You did your best. Elisa and Adin are not your responsibility. They were part of your life for a time. They're in God's hands. It's his will that will be done." She paused. "The last time I checked, you weren't him."

Her words hit Adam hard. He'd been overestimating his own importance, trusting God less, himself more. Plus, he hadn't been Elisa and Adin's savior; they'd been his.

"Adam, don't shortchange God. He's more powerful than you or me or anyone on the earth . . . or in heaven. He knows exactly the right thing to do. And even if that woman didn't like Elisa and Adin, she still had to follow the law. You said she was a clerk. It's not up to her to decide where they were sent."

She leaned against Adam's shoulder. "You've done nothing wrong . . . except not writing the story. That's what God asked you to do." She took his face in her hands. "He didn't ask you to fight in a war. He asked you to tell others about it. And I think it's time you did."

Adam felt a release of tension. Laurel was right. He had to trust that Elisa and Adin were exactly where God wanted them. And he needed to do what God had asked of him—to write. He'd forgotten.

"All right. I'll start tomorrow. I do have a lot to say. And I have photographs people ought to see."

Chapter 29

LUKE KNEELED IN THE SNOW AND SKINNED OUT A MINK. HOWEVER, HIS MIND wasn't on that mink; it was on Mattie. She'd still been sleeping when he'd left that morning, and he remembered how her hair had spread out over her pillow in black ribbons. He couldn't keep from caressing it, nor could he resist kissing her soft, gentle smile. They'd been married two months, but he'd still hadn't gotten over the flush of newness.

His mind returned to the previous evening. Again Mattie had tried to convince him to let go of his resentment and patch things up with Ray. It was something he knew he had to do eventually, but not yet. He wasn't ready.

He had to admit that Ray had been more than fair to him and had reached out in many ways. Luke was the one who had refused to change course; and no matter how deep he looked, Luke just couldn't forgive Ray. He understood that God had called his children to show mercy; he just couldn't seem to dredge up any. *Is it right to* pretend *to forgive?* he asked himself. *Isn't that just as faithless as hating someone?* What if his heart never changed?

He plunged his knife into the snow to clean it, then wiped it on his pants leg and pushed it into a sheath hooked to his belt. He sighed. It was time to mend the rift no matter how distasteful it felt.

He smoothed the snow and repositioned the trap. Opening the jaws, he reset the spring and baited it with a piece of rotted salmon, then carefully scattered snow over the trap and line. "That ought to do it." He stood.

Lifting the pelt, Luke ran a hand over the thick brown fur. "If the cold weather holds, I ought to do well at the winter carnival." He added the skin to the others already hanging from his belt. It had been a good season, but he still wouldn't have enough money to get himself and Mattie into their own place. Jobs had been scarce. It would be a long while before he'd be able to get a farm up and running.

Securing his snowshoes, he moved on toward the next trap. *When I'm finished, I'll go and see Ray,* he told himself. Luke pictured the meeting and tried to think of what he should say. He took a deep breath, the cold searing his lungs. The idea of capitulating to Ray made him cringe. If only he could find another way. Maybe if he were simply more courteous, change would evolve. *It might,* he thought, but he knew that even if it did no real healing would take place. They needed to talk, and he needed to forgive.

Through the years hurts had come his way, and he'd been able to let go of them. He was capable of forgiving, but this one had taken root and festered. He just couldn't seem to shake it.

Just having peace in the family is enough. Maybe I don't actually have to forgive. The idea had barely been traced in his mind when the spirit of God made it clear he wanted more. He wanted love. "I can't do that yet." He stopped walking, and clenching one hand in the other, said, "Father, you'll have to make me willing then. Even if it's just to make me willing to be made willing."

He gazed at the snow-encrusted world and thought of his father. They'd checked traplines together many times. When he was out here, he always felt his father's presence. But it wasn't the same. *Maybe one day I'll have a son who'll join me.* He liked the idea and hoped it wouldn't be long before he and Mattie could start a family.

She was home now, sewing and cooking and waiting for him. When he returned home, he knew she would greet him with a kiss and kind words. The tiny house would be warm, the aroma of dinner in the air. He hurried his steps, wanting to return to that safe haven. Maybe he wouldn't see Ray today. "No. I've got to go." He continued on to the next trap, following a path through the forest.

A dreary ceiling of clouds lay over the valley, and daylight looked more like dusk, making the forest seem dreary. Naked trees stood like ice-encrusted skeletons. The evergreens were more picturesque, with white pillows cradled in their boughs.

Luke kept moving, frozen snow squeaking beneath the slats of his snowshoes. His mind continued to puzzle over what to say to Ray. *I'm sorry. No. That's not right. I'm not sorry, exactly.* Luke didn't believe he'd actually done anything wrong. He'd caused his mother heartache, but if Ray hadn't done what he did, he wouldn't have had anything to get angry about. He'd accused Ray of some awful things. Did he still believe what he'd said?

Luke thought back over the events that led to his father's death—the taunts and trickery of Ray Townsend; the loss of crop sales instigated by Ray Townsend; outright threats made by Ray Townsend; and finally, the bear hunt and his father's death. Ray had been behind it all, and more. His father was dead because of Ray. Luke felt the flame of hurt and hatred flare.

His mind moved to his father. He'd chosen to stand and protect Ray. No one forced him. *That's how he was,* Luke thought with a mixture of pride and sorrow. *He always thought of other people. I wish he hadn't on that day.*

He forced his mind back to the problem. What could he say to Ray that would mend their relationship? That he wanted to start over? He didn't. Or that he thought Ray was a good man and deserved to be treated with respect? Luke wasn't convinced of that. He had to admit that Ray was different than he'd been when the colonists had first come to the valley, but whether or not he was a good man remained to be seen. Luke was still not certain Ray wasn't using his mother and others to serve his own purposes, and he continued to be suspicious of Ray's motivation for the help he offered after his father's death. It had gained him a wife and a farm.

Luke had thought and thought but was no closer to knowing what to do. He still wasn't sure he ought to say *anything.* The only real motivation he had to put things right was that the trouble between himself and Ray Townsend hurt his mother. Every time the family gathered, the strain between the two affected everyone. Now Mattie insisted he do something. *But what?*

Luke stopped. A bull moose stood in the path. It yanked a frozen branch from a tree and munched, then swung its huge head around and stared balefully at the intruder. Luke knew a cranky moose could be dangerous. He stopped and studied the animal. He hated to go around it. That meant tromping through deep snow, which, of course, was why the moose was in the middle of the trail. He didn't want to contend with the snow anymore than Luke did.

Still chewing, the bull leveled a distrustful gaze at Luke. A piece of the branch fell to the ground. The animal continued to stare. He lowered his head and blasted air out of his nostrils.

"Oh, brother. He's going to be stubborn," Luke said.

Now what? These animals hated to give ground and they were bigger than anything else using the trails this time of year. Luke would have to go around unless he wanted a confrontation. He studied him a moment longer and finally decided to give bullying a try. Maybe he could scare him off. He raised his arms over his head and waved, shouting, "Hah. Go on! Get on out of here!"

Instead of retreating, the moose moved toward Luke. After a few steps he stopped.

Luke moved back. "Well, that didn't work." Time to go around. He tromped through drifted snow, giving little attention to the animal.

Then he heard a grunt and the sound of heavy footfalls. Turning, he saw the moose heading straight at him. Snowshoes feeling like clumsy weights, he tromped toward a nearby spruce and glanced over his shoulder. The moose was still coming. Adrenaline shot through him. He was charging! Only a few steps more to the tree. The snowshoes felt like shackles.

Luke could hear the animal's breath and the crunch of snow. It was close. He grabbed for the lowest branch and missed. He had no time left. He'd have to duck behind the tree, but he wasn't fast enough. The bull dropped a heavy hoof on one snowshoe. Luke pitched forward, wrenching his foot free. He fell face first into the snow, then quickly rolled to his back. The beast had momentarily lost interest in Luke and took out his anger on the snowshoe, stomping it into pieces.

Just as the bull refocused and charged, Luke pushed to his feet. He fumbled for his handgun and fired twice, hitting the crazed animal in the chest. The moose stumbled forward and dropped. He was so close that Luke could have touched him. Crimson, steaming blood stained the forest's white floor.

Luke kept his gun on the bull and stepped toward it, but there was no need for caution. The animal was dead. Luke reholstered the firearm. "That'll be one to tell the grandkids."

He brushed snow from a log and sat staring at the animal. It was a big bull and would feed him and Mattie and her family for weeks. *Blessings come unexpectedly,* he thought, already formulating the story he'd tell his family.

He pushed to his feet. He had no time to waste. It would be dark soon. "I'll have to dress him out, then go back for the sled and haul him home," he said, pulling his knife out of its sheath. He bent over the animal and cut the jugular to bleed him out. After that, he removed the scent glands and proceeded to gut him.

With the beast skinned, gutted, and quartered, Luke stood. His arms and hands were bloodstained. With the back of one hand he brushed sweat from his forehead, leaving a smear of blood. Then he washed his hands in the snow.

He'd have to get Adam to help him haul the beast out. It looked as if the snow would start again anytime. Bad weather only meant more trouble and time getting the meat back to the house.

He strung up the quarters and headed home. He wouldn't have time to talk to Ray today. The powwow would have to wait for another time.

～

Mattie settled herself on a cushioned chair across from her grandmother. Taking one of Luke's shirts out of a basket, she examined a torn pocket that flopped over. She turned the shirt so it faced Atuska. "Now, how did he do this?"

"It is something men do," her mother said from the kitchen as she pressed her palms into risen bread dough.

Atuska looked up from her embroidery. "Men mutilate things." She clicked her tongue. "I can't count the hours I have spent repairing my family's clothes. Your grandfather was one of the worst. Every time he went hunting or fishing I would have more work." Sadness touched her eyes. "I should not complain. I wish he were here so I could sew for him."

The old woman peered at a piece of linen she'd been embroidering. Her hands trembled as she struggled to push the needle through just the right spot. "Oh," she said, dropping it into her lap. "I get so mad! I want to do what I used to, but my hands and my eyes won't work together anymore." She removed her glasses and rubbed her eyes. "I am old and useless. I can't even embroider a pillow cover."

Affia walked into the front room and leaned over her mother. Lifting the embroidery, she said, "It's still beautiful. Your eyes may not see so well, but your hands haven't forgotten what to do. You just can't see how wonderful it is." She smiled warmly. "Would you like a cup of chia?"

Atuska resettled her glasses on her nose. "Yes. Thank you."

Mattie pressed the wool shirt to her face. "This smells like Luke. It's strange that each person has his or her own smell."

"Not so strange," Atuska said. "We are each separate and unique, even our smells."

Mattie set to work repairing the shirt. The fire in the barrel stove popped and crackled. The house was warm and smelled of rising bread. It was a good day and a good time to tell her family the news that she was carrying a child.

Her grandmother returned to her sewing. She peered intently at the piece of linen, then pushed the needle through and pulled it out from underneath. She stopped and studied it. "Oh, dear. That's not right."

"Maybe we can get you new glasses," Affia said.

"No. We need more important things. I'm fine. When the sun shines and brightens the room, I can see much better." She glanced out the window. "If only the snow would stop, then I could see." She held up her work. In spite of her shaking hands and failing eyes, her intricate artistry had interlocked with the linen. She set it on her lap and rested the back of her head against the sofa.

"No one can create the beauty of the otter and sea lion like you." Affia returned to the kitchen. "Would you like a ginger cookie with your chia?"

"Yes. That sounds good." She took a cookie, dipped it into her tea, and took a bite. "My mother would have liked these." Ancient eyes rested on Mattie. "When I was a little girl, we did not have cookies. We had our barook and sometimes berries." Her eyes lit up. "And my favorite—Eskimo ice cream."

Mattie knew all about Eskimo ice cream. She'd never much liked the mix of seal oil and berries though. Grateful for cookies instead of dried fish and animal fat, Mattie took a cookie. "I like Mama's cookies."

"It's hard for you to understand, but when I was young I had a good life, better than today." She leaned forward. "The people in the village worked and lived together; we were a family. It was not like it is now. We shared the fun and the work. And how wonderful it was when the men returned with a whale. Everyone in the village gathered and helped pull it ashore; then the men would butcher it and the women worked side by side to cut the meat and preserve it."

She smiled and her face crinkled into a map of fine lines. "We would have a feast, then late at night we would enjoy music and dancing, and storytelling." She sat back, resting against the sofa cushions. "I wish you could have known what it was like. If you knew, you would not be so anxious to go away."

"I know a lot," Mattie said. "And I don't think you have to worry about me going anywhere. Luke isn't leaving this valley."

"Good." Affia smiled and bit into a cookie. She looked at her mother. "And I did what was right. I taught my children about the old ways."

"Yes, but it is not the same as living it," Atuska said. "It is sad that Mattie's children will not know what it means to live in and be part of a village—the bond between people, the love and trust."

Knowing her grandmother would be offended if she knew Mattie was grateful her child wouldn't grow up in a village, she only nodded and took a bite of her cookie and a sip of tea. "I know you loved growing up as you did," she said, glancing from her mother to her grandmother, "but there is a wonderful world outside of this place. I hope my children will get to see that world too." She looked at her grandmother. "You cherish your past and that's good, but we have a future. I want to see other places." Glumly she added, "Luke wants to stay put."

"Staying put is good, better than you know." The old woman stared into her cup. "Now it seems that everyone is doing as they please. People are going here and there, and they're too busy to care about each other."

She looked at Mattie, her gaze intense. "How can you be happy without being connected to someone or something?"

"I am connected. I have you and Mama and Luke and God. I don't need to know my dead ancestors or the way they lived."

Atuska shook her head sadly. "You do not know what you are saying."

Affia placed a loaf of bread in the oven to bake. "Mattie, I don't think your grandmother is saying it's wrong to look forward. But it is upsetting that you have no respect for your ancestors, or where you came from. Those people are your beginning."

There was nothing Mattie could say in response.

Atuska set her empty cup on a table beside the sofa and picked up her sewing. "I wish you had known how it was. You would be happier."

"Grandmother, I honor and respect you, and I know you are wise, but I think you are wrong about my being happy. When I lived in Seattle, I was very happy. I'm not the kind of person who needs to think on or dream about where I came from."

Affia put a mixing bowl in the sink. "Maybe it's time to talk about something else."

"We're just different," Mattie continued, ignoring her mother's warning. "But that's all right. I know you love the life you once knew, and hopefully I'll love the life I have. And I'll teach my children to think about their future and help them find joy in the world and be successful."

The brown in Atuska's eyes had lost its luster. "You do not understand that being who we are is enough. The world is not a bad place, and having adventures is good, but knowing who you are deep inside is what matters most."

"I understand." Mattie didn't want to talk about this anymore. It was time to reveal her secret. She rested her hand on her abdomen. Looking from her mother to her grandmother, she tried to think of the best way to say it. Finally she simply blurted out, "I'm going to have a baby."

"A baby?" Affia asked, then as understanding dawned, her eyes brightened and her mouth turned up in a smile. "A baby! How wonderful! I'm going to be a grandmother!" She hugged Mattie.

Atuska smiled. "Life continues." She set her embroidery in her lap. "Now it is even more important that you know about your beginnings. This child will want to know. I have taught you since you were a girl."

Mattie felt annoyed but said nothing.

"Such a blessing. All children are a joy." Affia took Mattie's hands. "When will it be here?"

"I think in the fall."

"Does Luke know?"

"No, not yet. But I know he'll be happy."

"Oh, how I would love to travel home, to take my great-grandchild to see the place of her beginnings," Atuska said. "She would love it."

"Grandmother, you called the baby a her. It could be a boy."

"No, it is a girl." She smiled knowingly, then said, "It would be good to see the islands again and the people. I wonder if anyone I know still lives there." Her eyes turned sad. "Annie was my closest friend. When we were girls, we would pick flowers and sometimes watch the men practice their hunting skills." She smiled and her eyes danced. "It was not right for the women to know such things, so we felt very wicked." Delight touched her face. "We also climbed the rocks and collected eggs for our mothers. And we promised each other that we would not grow up and move away, but, of course, we did."

As her grandmother shared, Mattie could hear the joy and longing in the old woman's voice. It pulled at Mattie. There must be a way to take her there. "Maybe when the war is over, we can go and visit," she said.

"Oh, how I wish," Atuska said. "But I don't think I will live to see the end of this war."

It was then that Mattie decided that as soon as the islands were free of Japanese control, she would take her grandmother home. Although she felt no connection with the place, it was important to Atuska. That's all that mattered.

"We will go one day, Grandmother. We will find a way."

Chapter 30

MATTIE PULLED ON A LIGHT SWEATER AND TRIED TO BUTTON IT OVER HER swollen stomach. It was too snug, so she fastened only the top button, then tenderly ran a hand over her abdomen. Her little one would be here soon.

She'd heard of a pilot who, it was said, would take anyone anywhere. He had a reputation for being fearless. With the Aleutian Islands now back under the control of the United States government, she'd decided it was time to take her grandmother for a visit home. Atuska's health had rebounded with the warmer weather, and now was the time to do it.

Mattie had been saving for months. If only she had enough money to pay the fare . . .

She closed the door to the tiny cabin and walked the few yards to her mother's house. Atuska was bottling herbs, and her mother stood at the kitchen sink, washing dishes.

Mattie dropped a kiss on her grandmother's cheek, then her mother's. "I'm going into town. Do you need anything?"

"I don't think so." Affia dipped a bowl into rinse water and set it on the drain board. "Mama, you need anything?" she asked Atuska.

"No. I'm just fine."

"I thought I heard Luke leave early this morning," Affia said.

"He's working out at the lumber camp today."

She eyed Mattie's stomach. "I wish you'd wait for a ride. It's not wise to walk so far in your condition. You're due soon."

"The doctor said that walking is good for me."

"What are you doing in town?"

"I need to get a few things at the store, and if Celeste is working, I thought I'd stay and visit." Mattie wasn't being completely untruthful. She did plan to go to the store, but she also intended on speaking to the pilot she'd heard about. Her mother would disapprove, but there was no need to raise anyone's hackles without cause. She'd wait to tell her when she knew for certain the pilot would take them.

"Don't walk too fast," Atuska said.

"I won't," she promised and headed for the door.

Mattie walked toward a shack sitting alongside a grassy airfield. She'd been told that's where she'd find Craig Wilson, the pilot. Gathering her courage, she stepped into what was supposed to be an office. It was mostly empty with only a single, very dirty window in front. Sunlight fought to filter through the filth that had accumulated on the glass. Enough found its way inside to illuminate a layer of dust on a wooden desk strewn with papers. A man sitting behind it leaned back in a chair, his feet propped on the only cleared spot in the center of the desk. His face was hidden behind a newspaper. He glanced over the top of the weekly. His eyes settled on Mattie, then without a word, he returned to reading.

Feeling out of place, she closed the door and walked stiffly to the desk. Resting her hand against the small of her back, she shifted her weight, hoping to find relief from the aching that had settled there. The man didn't look up. Mattie stared at the paper. Finally she cleared her throat. Certain he was ignoring her because she was native, she became angry.

The man acted as if he hadn't heard her.

"I was told that a pilot, Craig Wilson, works out of this office." She fought to keep her tone civil. "Is it true that he'll fly anywhere?"

The man peered over the paper and lifted his heavy brows. A runaway hair sprang up from the front of his head; another drooped toward his left eye. Mattie would have bet that's the way it was when he'd climbed out of bed that morning. "Where you thinking of going, missy?"

Missy? Mattie fumed, suppressing a retort. Now was not the time. As calmly as she could manage, she said, "The Aleutians."

He lowered the paper. "Only a knucklehead would head out that-a-way. We managed to chase them Japs out, but that doesn't mean the war is over. No telling when they might decide to move back in."

"I'm sure there's no threat of that. They've already seen what the United States Army will do to them if they try."

The man eyed her suspiciously. "There aren't any guarantees." He dropped his feet and leaned on the desk. "Why would you be interested in flying out over the Aleutians? A young thing like you—makes no sense." He let his eyes rest on her abdomen.

"It doesn't have to make sense," Mattie snapped, feeling her resolve unravel. Trying to gather her patience, she said, "Please, can you tell me where I can find Craig Wilson?"

"Someone looking for me?" Mattie turned to see a short, stocky man with red hair and blond eyelashes walk into the room. He flipped the door closed, then with quick, short strides, approached Mattie. He threw the man with the newspaper a look of displeasure, then turned hazel eyes on Mattie and extended his right hand. "Craig Wilson." His grip was solid. "You are?"

"Mattie Hasper." She decided immediately that she liked Craig Wilson. He had the look of someone who would tackle most anything; plus his face was open and honest. She felt comfortable coming right to the point. "I was told you'd be willing to take me to the Aleutians."

He raised an eyebrow. "I don't know about that. It's still pretty much off limits. Hasn't been that long since we took back the islands. I doubt the United States Army would welcome tourists." He smiled. "You have a good reason for going there?"

"Yes. For my grandmother. She's old now and will probably die soon. She grew up on an island near Unalaska and is longing to see it before she dies."

Craig rubbed a clean-shaven chin. "Sounds like a good reason, but I can't fly out just yet. Still don't know how safe it is."

"I know, but my grandmother has been sick and she's been feeling a little better just lately. I'm afraid that she won't be able to go if we wait. I have money."

"Money or not, it's a risk."

"I was told you weren't afraid of anything, and that you traveled anywhere your plane would take you. Please. I'll pay you whatever you want." She met his eyes.

"A hundred bucks?"

Mattie tried not to look surprised. A hundred dollars was impossible. She continued to stare at him. "I know that's not your regular price."

A smile appeared. "Just testing you." He took a deep breath. "All right. I'll take you." He eyed her stomach. "When's the baby due?"

"Oh, not for weeks."

The man at the desk folded the paper and set it down. "Not a good idea, Craig. If I were you—"

"You're not me." Craig turned to Mattie. "We have to go tomorrow; otherwise, you'll have to wait another week. I've got trips scheduled. Tomorrow's my only free day."

"We'll be here." She pulled out a change purse from her pocket and opened it.

"Put that away. If we get back in one piece, I'll let you know how much you owe me then." He offered her a sideways grin. "I have a feeling the United States government isn't going to be too happy with us. This might be worth it, just to give 'em a hard time."

"Thank you, Mr. Wilson." Mattie turned and walked away, then stopped and looked back. "What time?"

"Daybreak. It's a long trip. Don't be late."

"No, sir. I won't," Mattie answered. Now all she had to do was convince her grandmother and Luke that it was a good idea.

Luke and Mattie had dinner with her mother and grandmother that evening as they did most nights. During the dinner preparations Mattie thought over what she would say and waited for just the right moment to share her plan. It never came. Even during the meal she never seemed to have an opportunity.

The dishes were nearly finished, and she still hadn't said a thing. Setting the last plate in the dishdrainer, she took a deep breath. It was now or never. "Grandma, I have something I want to talk to you about," she said, drying her hands on a towel and walking to the table where her grandmother sat sipping a cup of tea. "I have a gift for you."

Atuska's eyes sparkled. "A gift?" Her voice trembled slightly. "What could you have for an old woman like me?"

Luke set aside the newspaper he'd been reading and looked at his wife.

"It's something I've been wanting to do for a long time. I've been saving up."

Affia, who stood at the kitchen sink, turned to listen.

With a glance at her mother, Mattie plunged ahead. "For a long time now you've been saying you want to see your home. Right?"

Atuska nodded.

"Well, I've arranged for it to happen."

"How could you do that?"

"I hired a bush pilot."

"You hired a bush pilot?" Luke asked incredulously.

"Yes. He said he can take us tomorrow."

"Tomorrow? How do you know he's any good?" Luke asked.

"He was recommended by people I trust. You've heard of him. Craig Wilson."

Atuska reached out and took Mattie's hand in her gnarled one. "It is a kind thing you want to do, but I cannot go flying all the way out there."

"Why not? People do it all the time."

"No. You can't take her out there," Affia said. "Her health isn't good."

"Mama, it'll be safe. Mr. Wilson's a good pilot." She turned to her grandmother. "It's what you said you wanted."

"Mattie, no. I won't have her out there on a tiny plane," Affia said.

Atuska straightened her spine. "Daughter, when did you become the one who decides for me?" With a stubborn set to her eyes, she studied Affia, then turned back to Mattie. "I will go." A smile lit her face. "I will see my home."

"Who's going to fly with her?" Affia asked.

"Me," Mattie said.

"What?" Luke stood and walked into the kitchen. "What about the baby?"

"It's not due for another three weeks."

"And what if something goes wrong?" He shook his head. "I don't like this."

"Nothing will go wrong, and I want to go. I've never been there," Mattie said, realizing she really did want to see the place where her grandmother was born. "Please, Luke."

He blew out a long breath. "All right, but I'm going with you."

The next morning Mattie, her grandmother, and Luke arrived at the airfield. They were early. The sun hadn't yet touched the top of the mountains. Craig Wilson was inspecting his plane. Mattie walked up to him. "Good morning. We're ready."

He looked at the cluster of people. "I don't remember your saying there was going to be a crowd," he quipped.

"Is it too many?" Mattie asked, looking at the small plane.

"No. This is a four-seater. She'll do fine. I was just teasing." He winked, then opened the door of the plane. "Climb on in."

It took a little effort for Atuska to clamber in, but Luke and Craig helped, and finally the old woman was settled in a tiny seat. "It's very crowded in here." Her eyes sparkled with excitement. "How wonderful. I'm going to take my first plane trip."

Mattie sat beside her and took her hand. "I'm nervous. Are you?"

"Oh, no. Just happy." She smiled broadly.

Luke sat in the seat beside Craig, then glanced at the passengers in the back. "When I was on the base, I went up a couple of times. You'll love it."

The engine started, and the craft vibrated. Mattie kept a hold of her grandmother's hand as they taxied out to the grass strip called a runway. Bouncing, the plane moved into position. They headed down the runway, quickly picking up speed. The plane lifted, and Mattie felt a sudden sensation of lightness. They climbed smoothly, and the airport fell away below them. Mattie's stomach remained on the ground, and she closed her eyes for a moment. Her grandmother let out a small, "Oh."

The mountains looked tall and broad. Mattie was suddenly afraid they might fly right into them. "What about the mountains? They look awfully tall."

"Don't worry. We're not flying over them." He banked the plane. "We'll go south and travel out over Cook Inlet."

Mattie stared at the ground. Everything looked very different from the sky. The fields and forests reminded her of a patchwork quilt made of greens and golds, and the Matanuska River looked like a broad silver ribbon, its broken channels like tattered strips of trim. The valley seemed small and crowded between mountains.

Craig headed the plane southwest toward the inlet and the long arm of islands that reached into the Pacific. Occasionally he pointed out sites, seeming to enjoy the trip as much as his passengers.

Atuska was quiet, but her eyes were alight with wonder as she took in the world below.

"Your granddaughter tells me you're from the Aleutians," Craig said to her.

"Yes. I grew up in a small village near Unalaska. It was a good place with good people." She smiled, continuing to keep her eyes on the sites.

"Grandma, if you loved it so much, why did you leave?"

"I had to. Your grandfather had to go . . . to find work. I thought we would go back though."

"If you had known, would you still have left?"

She answered immediately. "Yes. There was no other way." Her eyes turned soft. "And we were happy. The valley is a good place."

Emerald green islands passed below them. Craig dropped to a lower elevation so the travelers could see more clearly. Cliffs hedged in an island, cutting sharply into velvet green fields. The island looked as if it were floating in a blue sea.

A soft smile had settled on Atuska's lips. Mattie knew it had been right to come. Any amount of money was worth it.

They had to make two stops to refuel, but each only added to the adventure. Mattie liked takeoffs the most. It was an exhilarating sensation to move so quickly over the ground and then lift into the air.

"That's Unalaska down there," Craig said. "We'll have to stop to refuel, then head home."

"We're landing in Unalaska?" Atuska asked.

"Yes."

"How wonderful. When I was a child, we used to travel there by boat. My father would always buy us a peppermint stick. Oh, how wonderful that tasted. And once he traded furs for a music box for my mother. It was beautiful."

The engine of the plane cut out and sputtered. Mattie's stomach dropped. "Is something wrong?"

Craig didn't answer. He was working with the controls. More sputtering.

"What's wrong?" Luke asked.

"Don't know for sure. Probably nothing too serious. I'll just set it down and take a look." Craig grinned. "Don't worry. Something always needs attention in these old crates. We'll be fine. Either way, I'll fix whatever's wrong, and we'll be on our way."

When the wheels touched the runway, Mattie's tightened muscles relaxed, and she let out a sigh of relief. The pilot might have had complete confidence in his plane, but she didn't. They'd circled the landing field, and the engine had run rougher and rougher. She'd started to worry it would cut out completely.

Men dressed in uniforms and wearing stern expressions strode toward the plane. Craig climbed out and explained his reasons for being there, then stood silently while given a stern reprimand. He offered a curt apology, and then he and his passengers were offered a meal.

Craig walked beside Mattie as they headed for the mess hall. "You owe me for this."

"You're not really in trouble, are you?"

"If you mean, am I going to lose my right to fly? No. But I don't like getting chewed out anymore than anyone else." He offered her a sideways grin.

"It's for a good cause. My grandmother's loving this." Mattie smiled. "Thank you for bringing us."

"Hey, I like adventures." He headed for a hanger. "I'll have this thing fixed and back in the air in no time."

"You're not going to eat?"

"Later."

Mattie, Luke, and Atuska were sitting at a table eating sandwiches when Craig walked in and sat down. "Bad news." He rested his arms on the table. "It's going to take longer to fix the plane than I thought."

"But you'll be able to fix it, right?" Luke asked.

"Oh yeah, but we're not leaving today. If we're lucky, tomorrow."

"Can I contact my mother?" Mattie asked.

"Yes. They have phones. The commander's not happy though. He made that clear. But he said they'd put us up for the night."

"What's an extra day or two?" Luke said nonchalantly. "I don't mind. It's kind of interesting here."

Mattie said nothing, but she'd been hoping they'd be able to return home. She'd been having abdominal cramps and would have felt more secure if she were home. *They're probably nothing,* she tried to reassure herself.

Mattie didn't say anything about the pains, however. She went to bed, hoping the cramps were simply prelabor. She'd been told that many women had them weeks before their babies were born. However, these didn't stop. Instead, they intensified. Finally she couldn't lie on her bunk any longer. She needed to tell someone.

Throwing back the blankets, she sat up, then waited while another cramp wrapped itself around her abdomen. She breathed slowly and waited for it to pass, then crossed to Luke's bunk. "Luke. Wake up."

Mumbling something unintelligible, he rolled to his side.

"Luke," Mattie said more loudly.

"What? Is something wrong?"

"I don't know, but I think I'm going to have the baby."

He catapulted upright. "What? Now? But you can't. It's not due for three weeks."

"I know. But maybe the baby doesn't know that."

"OK. Everything's fine." He swung his legs over the side of the bed. "I'll get someone. There must be a doctor here." He stood and gently pressed Mattie down onto his bunk. "You stay put." He pulled on his pants and a shirt and disappeared out the door.

Close to tears, Mattie asked, "Lord, why now? I don't want to have my baby out here on this piece of rock."

The door swung open, and Luke returned with a man Mattie guessed must be the doctor. "You all right?" Luke asked.

"Yes, but I'm still having pain."

"How often are the contractions coming?" the doctor asked, holding her wrist and taking her pulse.

"I don't know. I think every couple of minutes."

Luke looked at the doctor. "You know anything about delivering babies?"

"When I trained I learned about everything, including that, but nowadays I mostly treat soldiers. You know, cuts and scrapes, a flu bug now and then." He smiled at Mattie. "But I figure that between the two of us we'll manage just fine. Babies are born every day. They pretty much know what they have to do."

The doctor's words were meant to calm Mattie, but they only made her more anxious. Even if the baby knew what to do, she didn't.

Hours passed, and the labor intensified. Atuska and Luke took turns sitting with Mattie. Word spread throughout the base, and men congregated in the hallway outside her room. A birth was something extraordinary, especially in this place.

Exhausted and frightened, Mattie prayed the baby would come soon. Labor was more difficult than she'd expected. She began to doubt she could make it through. Finally it was time to push. Atuska sat with her. She held Mattie's hand and crooned in an ancient tongue. Luke paced. Mattie wished he'd leave. His nervousness only made her more tense.

Atuska looked at the young man. "It is time to get the doctor," she said evenly. "You go and bring him here."

"Right. I'll be right back," he said and hurried out the door.

Atuska sponged Mattie's forehead. "Soon your little one will be here." She looked weary but poised. She smiled. "Children are a blessing from God."

Mattie tried to concentrate on the baby and how wonderful it would be to hold it. Another contraction built. She bore down. The pain felt as if it would break her in two. With a deep groan she gripped her grandmother's hand. "I can't do this anymore. Please, Grandmother. Isn't there something you can do? Help me."

The doctor walked in. "I hear we're about ready to have a baby."

"I think it is time," Atuska said.

The doctor examined Mattie. "You're nearly there." He grinned. "We've got men lined up in the hall. They're taking bets on what time this baby arrives."

Mattie didn't care about the men or their bets. All she could think of was getting the baby out. Another wave of pain swept over her. She pushed, struggling to expel the child. "Ohhh," she moaned.

The doctor said, "Push, Mattie. It's almost here."

Luke held her hand.

"One more big push will do it," the doctor said.

Gritting her teeth and letting a shriek loose, she bore down, and her little girl entered the world.

A small cry escaped her daughter's lips. Joy flowed through Mattie. "Let me see her. Please."

The doctor cut the umbilical cord and handed the child to her mother. She cradled her baby girl against her breast. The infant had dark hair and a round puckered face. She blinked oval eyes and pressed a fist to her mouth, sucking hard.

Mattie marveled at this child. Only moments before she'd lived in an unseen world.

Her grandmother gently ran a crooked finger over the child's forehead. "She looks just like your mother did. So beautiful."

Love, like none she'd ever felt, flooded Mattie. She caressed the little girl's golden cheek and smoothed her thatch of dark hair.

"She's beautiful," Luke said.

Mattie studied her daughter. She looked native, and Mattie loved every corner of her. In a flash of understanding, she glimpsed God's love for his children, his creation. She was God's creation, even the parts that were Indian.

Mattie kissed her baby girl's cheek. This child was the next link in her family's line, a family created by God, and just as this child was precious and cherished, so was she.

Through tears, she looked at her grandmother. "I know now what you meant about loving who we are. I'm not ashamed or angry anymore. I know that when God created me . . . that what he made was good."

Atuska cradled the child's head. "Yes. Very good."

Chapter 31

ATUSKA LOOKED SMALL BENEATH THE PILE OF BLANKETS. DESPITE HER GRAVE condition, her withered face looked peaceful.

Heavy-hearted, Mattie stepped into the stuffy bedroom. It was happening. Her grandmother was dying. "I brought you some broth." She set a tray with soup on the nightstand beside Atuska's bed, then helped prop up the old woman on pillows. She could feel the bones beneath her cotton nightdress.

"Maybe I'll have some later," Atuska said, her voice unsteady.

"Please try to eat some. Just a little."

She nodded and allowed Mattie to spoon hot broth into her mouth. After only a few sips, she weakly lifted a hand. "No more." Lying back against the pillows, she closed her eyes.

Returning the bowl to the tray, Mattie sat in a chair beside the bed. She gazed at her grandmother, taking in every feature. Her face looked shrunken, the skin parchmentlike. Her chest rose and fell, a rasping squeak accompanying each breath. *Lord, does she have to die now?* Mattie couldn't hold back her tears. She lifted her grandmother's hand and caressed its cool, shiny skin. *Life won't be the same without you.* She sniffled. Little Mara would not know her great-grandmother.

Atuska opened her eyes. "It's not a time for weeping. It is time for me to go ahead. And it is good—I miss many people, and now I will see them again."

Nodding, Mattie wiped away her tears. "It's just that . . . I . . . I don't want you to go. I need you. Especially now, since I've just discovered who I am. And Mara will need you."

277

"Your mother will be here. She knows and understands." Atuska coughed, then struggled to regain her breath. "How is Mara?"

"She's good. Always hungry. Mama said she looks like your mother."

"Yes. And my mother is honored that her great-great-grandchild is named after her." She coughed, then asked, "Can I see her?"

"I'll get her." Mattie stood and started to go, then stopped. "I think she smiled at me this morning."

"I'm not surprised. I knew from the beginning that she was smart." Atuska reached for Mattie's hand and clutched it with surprising strength. "Will you teach her about our people?"

"I will. I promise."

"Good." Atuska relaxed her hold and closed her eyes. "I have been waiting . . . for you . . . to know who you are." She blinked and looked at Mattie. "I am filled with joy."

"If only I'd known sooner." She willed away new tears. "We could have shared so much."

"We shared a life." She took a gasping breath. "Soon you and Luke . . . will have your own home. Remember . . . he needs you," she wheezed. "You have led the way and now . . . you . . . can help him."

"Help him what?"

Her grandmother didn't answer. Her eyes were closed, and her breaths became no more than panting whispers.

A chill wind blew, but Mattie barely noticed as she laid a bouquet of flowers on her grandmother's grave. Everyone except Luke had gone on ahead to the Townsends'. He stood back, allowing Mattie room to say a private farewell.

With a hollowness in her chest, she stared at the freshly mounded earth. She knew her grandmother wasn't there. She was having a grand reunion. *I'm sure you're at a potlatch greater than any you knew here.* Mattie smiled, imagining her grandmother's joy and how she would be dancing and singing. She nearly giggled as she imagined her grandmother being flung skyward in the blanket toss. *She's happy. That's what matters.*

Brushing away tears, she said, "I'll carry our history with me. I won't forget. And your great-grandchildren will know you and our ancestors."

She sniffled into her handkerchief. "I'll tell them. I promise." She kneeled and rested a hand on the new grave. "I'll miss you."

Mattie stood and walked to Luke, who held the baby. When she reached them, she burrowed into his free shoulder. "It hurts so much. I don't know how I'll ever get used to her being gone."

"I know." Luke held her. Snowflakes drifted from the gray sky, then caught by the wind, swirled around the small family.

Mattie stared up into the white eddy. "It's early for snow. Grandma loved winter. If she knew, she'd be happy."

Holding Mattie's hand and cuddling Mara in his other arm, Luke said, "We better get up to the house. I wish I'd brought the truck."

"It's all right. I'd like to walk." She took the baby and set her in a sling inside her coat.

Luke studied the little girl. "I love to look at her. I never get tired of it."

Mara whimpered and nuzzled her mother. Mattie could feel her milk come in. "I'll feed her on the way. By the time we get to the house, her tummy will be full and she'll be happy."

"I wish my dad had lived to see her. He would have made a great grandfather."

"I know. I wish it too." She took Luke's hand, and with Mara suckling contentedly, they walked toward the house.

When they reached the driveway, Luke stopped. "I still can't get used to this place being called the Townsends'. It ought to be the Haspers'." His tone was harsh.

"I've been thinking on something my grandmother said just before she died."

"What?"

"She looked at me and said, 'You have led the way and can help him.' She was talking about you. Do you know what it could mean?"

"What were you talking about before that?"

"She said you needed me."

Luke kept his eyes straight ahead. "Huh. That's strange." Glancing at Mattie, he smiled. "'Course, she's right. I do need you."

Mattie nodded. She thought she understood what her grandmother had meant. Did she dare bring it up now? Snugging her gloves, she glanced at Luke. "I think I know what she wanted to say."

"Well, spit it out."

She took a breath. "There are things in life we don't understand, things we can't change but have to accept. Like my heritage. I used to hate it, then God opened my eyes." She glanced at the baby. "Now I understand, and I'm glad of who I am. And I'm ready to face the people who hate me without hating back."

"Let me guess. You want me to make peace with Ray?"

"It's time, Luke."

He shook his head. "I can't. I've thought about it a lot, believe me. He doesn't deserve it. He took my father's life and my home. And I don't trust him." He looked at Mattie. "I want to do the right thing, but . . . I'm not sure that giving in to him is the way."

"Luke, the house wasn't yours."

"My father would have wanted me to have it. If he'd known . . ." He chewed on the inside of his cheek. "Anyway, now I don't have a house."

"One day we'll have a home."

"I don't know how we'll ever come up with enough money."

"Something will work out. We could homestead."

"It's a hard way to go." He glanced at her. "Do you really want to do that?"

"It would be all right. But I'm happy now just as we are. We don't have to decide or do anything right away."

"I want us to be out of that tiny cabin before winter sets in. It's not a fit place, not for a baby." He looked at Mara. "I want her to have a decent life." He blew out a breath. "Sometimes I feel like I'm still that teenager who moved here seven years ago—excited about the future and at the same time scared to death of it."

Mattie smiled at him warmly. "Sometimes I still see that boy. You were so intense and so eager. You wanted to experience all of Alaska at once." She took his hand. "I remember when Alex brought you home with him that first time. I thought you were the most handsome boy I'd ever met." She paused. "I still do; only you're a man now."

She leaned against him. "Sometimes you still get that dark look in your eyes, and I'm afraid for you." She stared at the roadway. "If you can't forgive Ray, the anger will get bigger and bigger, and it'll hurt you in ways you cannot understand. I know. I hated people I didn't even know."

"I'm going to treat him decently. It's just that sometimes the past gets the better of me. And if I talked to him about it, I wouldn't know what to say. I don't want to lie. I'm still mad, and I'm not about to pretend I'm not. You know the Bible verse about gnashing teeth—sometimes I feel like that, and I wonder if I'll ever be able to let go of this."

"Of course you will. God lives in you, and he makes everything possible."

"It's not so easy, Mattie. Other things, stupid things, drag on me too."

"Like what?"

"Well, sometimes I feel like a failure. Everyone around me is content and happy. You're even feeling good about being you. Adam's settled and content. Robert and Celeste aren't even married, but he's got his own place just waiting until he gets back from the war. Nothing's happening for me, us." He grasped her hand. "I feel like something in me is missing. Otherwise, I'd be able to just forgive and get on with living."

"Do you think it has anything to do with Ray?"

Luke shrugged.

They started down the driveway, and Jean stepped onto the porch. "I was about to send a search party," she quipped. "Come on in." She peeked at the baby as Mattie passed.

"Mattie, there you are," said Celeste and hugged her. "I'm really sorry about your grandmother."

"Thank you." Mattie gazed around the crowded room. It was packed with friends. In the last few years her grandmother hadn't gotten out much, but the people of Palmer hadn't forgotten her. Many had visited her, often bringing something she might need. *How could I have thought the people here were unkind?*

The kitchen table was laden with food, and the guests were mingling. Affia joined Mattie and Jean. "It was kind of you to have the reception here," she said. "I know it was a lot of work. Thank you."

"I wanted to help." Jean circled an arm around Mattie and the baby. "I was glad to do it." She gazed down at the infant. "You are a beautiful child."

"Grandma says . . . said she looks like Mama."

"She does, and like you too."

Her eyes tender, Jessie joined them. She took Affia's hand. "If you need anything, anything at all, you call me. I'm not far." Her eyes misted. "It always hurts to lose someone we love." She paused, then held out a book. "This is for you." Affia accepted the gift. "It's the book Laurel and I have been working on all these years."

"You finished it? How wonderful!" She ran a hand over the dark blue binding.

"Your mother always wanted the outside to know her Alaska."

"Thank you. It's a beautiful book." Affia turned it over, then thumbed through several pages. It contained photographs and pictures of Jessie's paintings. "It's wonderful! Thank you." She offered it to Mattie.

Taking the book, Mattie examined it. So much of what her grandmother loved and believed in lay within the pages. "It's a wonderful thing you've done. I'll need several copies for my children and their children." She hugged Jessie and then Laurel, who'd just joined the cluster of women.

"Some of your grandmother's stories are in it," Laurel said.

"They are?"

"Yes," Jessie said. "She told them to my husband many years ago. You will also see a couple of pictures of her and yourself when you were just a baby."

"Me?"

Jessie gently took the book, opened it, and turned to a page with a photograph. "Here's one." Pointing at a picture of a round-faced native girl, she said, "That's you."

A mix of joy and sorrow pulsed through Mattie as she looked at the picture of her mother with a child in her arms. A tiny native woman, her grandmother, stood beside them. She and her grandmother had shared many days. Their time together had been a gift.

Luke and Mattie were the only guests still remaining when Ray said, "We'd like you to stay a while so we can talk to you about something."

"Sure." Luke cast a questioning glance at Mattie. They sat at the kitchen table while Jean went to fill cups with coffee.

"You need to get off your feet," Ray told her, taking the cups and the coffeepot. "You sit. I'll take care of this."

"Yes, sir," she said with a smile and took a chair beside Luke. Gazing at Mattie, she said, "You look tired, dear."

"I am, but I know I'm not as tired as my mother. I'm glad her sister's here. It will be good for her to have company."

Ray set coffee in front of Luke and Mattie, then poured a cup for himself and one for Jean. He set the coffeepot on the stove and returned to the table with the drinks. Lowering himself into a chair, he let out a long, slow breath. "It's been quite a day." He sipped his coffee, glanced at Jean, then looked at Mattie and Luke. "We asked you to stay for a reason."

Luke kept his eyes on the big man.

"We've been thinking about the living arrangements over at your mother's, Mattie. You must be real crowded with the baby."

"The cabin is small, but we've been fine. We can't move into the house. With the baby plus Luke and me, it would be too cramped. It only has two small bedrooms."

Luke's expression had become wary, and he tapped the floor with his foot. Mattie clasped his hand, hoping to steady him.

"Well, what we were thinking," Ray continued, "is that we've got more room here than we need, and we'd count it a privilege if you two and the baby would move in with us." His eyes settled on Luke. "I could use some help, what with hunting season just starting. I've got several trips lined up and won't be here much for a while, and if all the signs prove right, we'll have a good year for trapping. I'll probably need some help on that too. I figured we could split the proceeds."

"I don't know," Luke said.

"I was also thinking I could use a hand with the dogs. Brian's a big help, but I remember how good you and Alex were that one year, and I figured that having you around would be good. If you have a mind to, you could work with them, do some training."

"I don't know that much."

"You know more than you think. I've seen you with them."

Jean reached across to Mattie. "Your mother told us that her sister's planning to stay on for a while. That means there isn't possibly enough room for you to move into the house. I'd like to have another woman here with me. I'd like to have a woman's company, and Brian and Susie would love to have you here too."

Mattie liked the idea of living in a larger house, and she'd always loved Jean. She looked at her husband. "Luke?"

"I'll have to think on it," he said, pushing away from the table. "Thank you, Ray, for thinking of us." He grabbed Mattie's coat. "We better get going. It's nearly dark, and we've got quite a walk."

"I'll drive you," Ray offered.

"No. That's fine. The weather's good, and I'd like to walk." Luke pulled his hat down over his ears, then leaned over the table and kissed his mother. "We'll let you know what we decide," he said and hurried out of the house as if a dog were nipping at his heals.

Mattie tucked the baby into a sling inside her coat, and offering Jean a small smile, followed Luke.

Luke and Mattie were silent for a long while, the only sound the crunch of frozen earth and dry leaves. The cry of an eagle fractured the stillness. Mattie liked the idea of living on the farm. She hoped Luke did too.

Finally she asked him, "What do you think we should do?"

Luke didn't answer right away. With a sigh, he said, "I'd hoped that by this time we'd have our own place."

"It will happen. We just need to be patient."

"I know that living with my mother would be more comfortable. We're pretty cramped in that little cabin." He glanced at Mattie. "What do you want?"

"I love the farm. I always have. I know it won't be easy for you and Ray, but it seems he wants things to be better between you two. Otherwise he wouldn't have asked."

"I don't know if I could live in the same house with him."

"Maybe this is a way to make peace between you."

"By watching him run my father's farm and his house . . . and being with my mother? I don't know."

"He said he'll be gone a lot."

"You want to do it, don't you."

"Yes. It would be nice."

Luke stopped at a frozen puddle and slid across. Taking Mattie's hand, he pulled her toward him. "All right. We'll do it. I figure you've got a lot of wisdom in that head of yours." He kissed her gloved hand, then looked at her with serious eyes. "But it's just until we get our own place."

Chapter 32

Luke turned off the road and into his driveway. The house looked much like it always had; and in spite of the fact that it wasn't his, it felt like home.

Mattie and I will have our own place some day, he told himself. He just didn't know how he'd make it happen. Work was hard to come by in the valley, and though Luke could get a job in Anchorage, he and Mattie both hated the idea of moving away from Palmer. This was home. He itched to get his hands into soil of his own, to till even rows, to plant and grow vegetables, and to raise strong, healthy livestock.

He stopped the car, and Brian ran out of the barn. He was shouting and waving his arms. His pulse escalating, Luke opened the truck door. "What's wrong?"

"The new Guernsey's trying to calve, but she's havin' trouble. Ray's not here. Can you help?"

"Sure." Luke strode toward the barn, Brian beside him. "How long she been laboring?"

"I think since this morning."

Luke stepped through the barn door and into gloom. The odor of hay and manure was familiar, offering a sense of comfort. He headed toward a light at the back of the barn.

His mother stood in a stall beside the Guernsey, stroking the cow's neck and speaking softly to her. She glanced at Luke. "I'm so glad you're back. I was getting worried and wasn't sure what to do."

Mattie stood at the stall gate, the baby in her arms. Susie leaned against her.

Luke smiled at them both, then turned his attention to the cow. "Brian said she started this morning."

"Close as I can figure. I came out to check her first thing. She was restless, you know how they are—lying down, then standing up, over and over." Her brows knit with concern, she continued, "Since this is her first, we don't know how she'll do."

Luke lit another lantern. "Why is Ray gone? He should be here." He hung the light on a hook just inside the stall door.

"He had a hunting party to take out. He had to go."

Luke moved across the stall. The laboring bovine followed him with soulful eyes. He swung open the top half of a Dutch door. Sunlight poured into the enclosure. "That's better." He turned and faced his mother. "Seems to me, if a man's going to run a farm, he ought to be around when a cow's about to drop its first calf. Dad never would have left."

"Luke, please. Not now."

The cow bawled forlornly. "Hey there," Luke said, approaching cautiously. She stomped a back foot and swished her tail, then turned and faced the corner of the pen. "Everything's all right. You're doin' fine." He gently ran a hand along her neck and across her withers, then rested it on her abdomen. A few moments later he felt the muscles tighten. The Guernsey pushed, trying to expel her calf. Blasting air from her nostrils, she let out a sick bawl. Luke caressed her side. "We'll have your baby out soon." The contraction passed. The cow lay down, pushing through another, then stood. She lay down again and stood again. Another spasm gripped her. She pushed, but no calf appeared.

"She's been doing that all morning. I'm really worried. We can't afford to lose her."

"I'd better take a look and see what's going on." Keeping his hand on her, Luke walked to the cow's rear end. When he lifted the tail, he could see blood and water but no calf. With the next contraction a small hoof appeared but quickly disappeared again. Something was wrong. *Probably a leg's bent back,* he thought. He'd have to get it straightened if the calf and cow were going to live. The calf might already be gone. Luke grabbed a rope, hooked it to the cow's halter, and tied her to a corner post. Then he rolled up his sleeves, and resting a shoulder against her hind end, he felt for the calf. The muscles tightened, pressing his arm against her pelvis. Closing his eyes against the pain, he waited for the contraction to pass, then continued his search. He found one front leg, followed it back to the body, and felt for the other. Sure enough, it was bent underneath the calf. He'd have to pull it forward.

Glancing at his mother, he said, "I'm gonna need help."

"I'll do it," Brian said. "I'm not a kid anymore."

"Well, you're right about that."

"Is she gonna die?" Susie asked.

"No, she's not going to die," Jean said. "Luke knows what to do."

Luke met his mother's eyes, then looked at Mattie and Susie. He felt the weight of responsibility mingled with resentment. Ray should be here. The cow and calf were his. This was his farm. "I'll need a short length of rope," Luke said.

"I'll get it." Susie ran toward the front of the barn and reappeared a few moments later with a rope. She handed it to Luke.

"Thanks." Luke tied a slipknot in both ends. "Mom and Brian, I want you to hold her steady. Talk to her and keep her calm."

"Can I help hold her too?" Susie asked.

"No. You're not big enough. There's no telling what she'll do, and I don't want you getting hurt. Stay there with Mattie."

The blue in Susie's eyes muted. She was hurt.

"We could use your prayers," Luke added. "Would you keep praying?"

She nodded and offered a small smile.

"I'm gonna have to snag that back leg and pull it forward." He glanced at Brian. "I might need your help when it comes time to pull out the calf." Luke reached in with the rope. The cow bellowed and buffeted Jean and Brian.

Inside her up to his shoulder, Luke searched for the leg that was bent under. When he found it, he struggled to slip the loop over the hoof. A contraction came down on his arm. "That's a strong one," he said with a groan. "If I can just get this leg forward." His arm ached. The loop came off before he could tighten it. Trying again, he guided it over the calf's foot and pulled gently. It caught, then held. "Got it."

"Hold her steady," he said, pulling gently to reposition the leg forward. When he had it, he secured the second loop over the other hoof. "On the next contraction I'm gonna pull." He looked at his mother and Brian. "Take care she doesn't knock you by swinging her head."

"We're fine," Jean said, gripping the halter tightly.

"Hey, Brian, can you pull while I work with the calf?"

"Sure." He grabbed the rope.

The cow bellowed and stomped her back leg, jerking her head up and backward. "You all right?"

"Yep," said Jean.

"OK now Brian, keep steady pressure," Luke said as he guided the calf's head into the pelvis. He waited for the next contraction. When it came, he grabbed the rope. "I got it now. Help Mama." He hauled on the calf. "All right. We've almost got him." Two hoofs emerged, then spindly legs, and finally the calf's pink nose, then a white face. Seeming to know her baby was nearly there, the Guernsey pushed harder. Luke let her do the final work.

All of a sudden the calf came out, dropping to the hay-covered floor along with a gush of blood and water. It lay still and quiet, encased in a translucent bubble. Luke quickly freed its feet, wiped mucous from its face, and cleared its mouth.

"Is it alive?" Jean asked.

He didn't answer but rubbed the calf hard all over. "Come on there. Open your eyes. The world's waitin' for you." Its nostrils flared, and the calf let out a tiny bawl. Wearing a smile, Luke stood. "Looks like she's going to be all right." He untied the Guernsey so she could sniff her baby. She immediately started licking.

Luke walked across the stall, dropped to the hay-covered floor, and rested his back against the wall. "We did it." He smiled. "We've got ourselves a new little heifer."

Jean sat beside Luke. "You did a fine job."

Susie peeked through the gate. "Can I come in and see it?"

"Yes. Come in," Jean said.

She crossed to her mother and stood beside her, eyes fixed on cow and calf. "She's not very big."

"She won't stay small for long," Luke said. "She'll grow fast."

"Why is the mama cow licking her?"

"She wants her new baby clean, just like Mattie makes sure Mara's clean," Luke explained.

"Mara gets baths."

Luke leaned his arms across bent knees. "Well, this is a cow bath." He grinned.

The family stayed for a long while, watching mother and baby get acquainted. Finally the calf stuck its front legs straight out in front and tottered to its feet. Legs straight and stiff, it stood, shaking and teetering. Then taking hesitant steps, it walked toward its mother, then fell. She didn't move for a few moments, sides heaving, then with a great effort pushed herself upright again. She worked to maintain her balance, then wobbled toward her mother, nuzzling her. The Guernsey sniffed her baby and resumed licking it, nearly knocking the calf off its feet again. Finally the young heifer found its way to her mother's udder and tasted her first meal.

"She looks hungry," Susie said.

"Most calves have little trouble figuring out where the feed is," Luke said.

Susie's brows knit in puzzlement. "How come a baby cow can stand up and walk so soon, and people can't?"

"Good question." Luke picked up a piece of straw and broke it in half. "I guess it's because they need to. Otherwise, how could they eat?" He stood and looked down at his bloodied clothes. "I'm a mess. I need a bath."

"Are you going to have a calf bath?" Susie teased, her blue eyes alight.

"Hot water and soap sounds better." Luke ran a hand over the Guernsey's back. "Well, you've got yourselves a fine calf." He glanced at his mother. "You going to keep her or sell her?"

"I don't know yet."

"I'd be interested in buying her if I had a place of my own." His eyes settled on Mattie. "Sure wish we could figure out a way," he said wistfully.

Jean stood. "Something will work out." Her eyes sparkled, and she added, "You need to have faith."

"I don't see why we can't buy the calf now," Mattie said. "We could keep it here." She looked at Jean. "If you want to sell it, that is."

"I'll ask Ray."

Luke leaned against the barn wall. "It's hard to be patient. I don't know how we'll ever come up with the money to get our own place."

"What about homesteading? We talked about it," Mattie said.

"Even that takes money, and I'm not going to have my family living in a tent."

"Ray's been keeping an eye out for farms coming up for sale," Jean said.

"He can't take care of his own place, let alone help me find one." Luke shoved his hands into his pants pockets. "Well, I got to get cleaned up." He headed for the house.

Ray returned the following day, a large ram and a chunk of cash to show for his efforts. He was whistling while he unloaded his gear.

Feeling cranky, Luke walked into the barn. "You seen the new calf yet?"

"Nope, but I'm fixin' to just as soon as I get this sheep hung up. I did real well this week. Everyone in the party bagged a ram, and they paid well. I could use a hand."

"I'm kind of busy. You ask Brian?"

"He's in town. S'pect he'll be back soon, but I'd like to get this animal up and out of harm's way."

"All right. Just wanted to give that Guernsey a handful of grain first." He shuffled toward the stall. The cow licked up grain from his hand, and then Luke patted her face and scratched between her ears.

Ray leaned on the gate. "Heard she had a hard time of it and you pulled the two of 'em through."

"You nearly ended up losing the cow and calf. I did what I had to. Too bad you didn't."

"I did what I had to, but I'm sorry this fell on your shoulders." He ran a hand over the cow's soft nose. "I checked her before I left and figured I had time to take care of business and get back before she came fresh."

Luke swung around and glared at Ray. "You knew better than to leave. All you think about is hunting. If you're not careful, this farm will fail. Then where will my mother and my brother and sister be? Not to mention all my father's hard work."

"It's not going to fail." Ray scratched the place between the Guernsey's ears. "I know I'm no farmer, but I'll make sure the place holds its own. I had to go out. Those men were countin' on me, and I was countin' on their money." He plucked a piece of straw from a stack and stuck it in his mouth. He was silent for a long while, then looking at Luke, said, "I'm going to enter the dogsled race set for late November."

Keeping his eyes on the Guernsey, Luke said, "You should do well. The dogs are in good condition."

"You know, ol' Frank Reed wanted to test out his dogs in this race, but he's got a bad case of gout. Can't work the dogs and doesn't figure he'll be fit even by then. He's lookin' for someone to run his team for him. I mentioned your name."

"Oh?" Luke couldn't shut off his adventurous spirit, and he liked the idea of competing against Ray. In an offhanded way he asked, "Why November? Snow's not usually set by then."

"Yeah, I know, but the folks who decided on this one don't want to wait. They said we're supposed to have heavy snows early. It'll test the teams' mettle." The straw in Ray's mouth bounced as he chewed. "Prize money is being offered. Every racer puts into the pot, and the winner takes all. Would be a real help to you and Mattie, what with the new baby and all. Might even help with your house savings."

"Why do you care? If you want us out of the house, we'll be gone."

"That's not it. Just figured you'd be interested." Ray threw down the piece of straw and headed for the truck. "Guess it was a bad idea."

Over the next few days Luke thought about racing and was intrigued. The prize money would help, and it would feel good to beat Ray; but after deciding to get along with Ray, he wondered if it would be a good idea. It might add fuel to bitter fire. Even as he considered the rift between them, it felt smaller than it had.

It's just a race, he thought. He needed to decide soon before someone else stepped in to drive Frank's team. He decided to talk to Adam.

"So, you're asking my opinion?" Adam asked, leaning on his ax handle. "I don't see any reason why you shouldn't race. You think you're good enough?"

"Sure. I've got as good a chance to win as anyone else. I exercise Ray's dogs and do some of the training." He paused. "He's got a good team. I'd like to beat them."

"Just them?"

"No. Everyone racing." A crooked smiled spread across his face. "I have to admit that it would feel good to beat Ray."

A frown creased Adam's forehead. He planted his ax in a stump. "Let's walk."

The two men started down the road. Adam pulled his coat closed. "Cold." He gazed at distant mountains already layered with snow. "If the weather stays cold and we get some good snows, you might have a decent race."

"Maybe."

"So, do you want to know what I think about all this?"

"All what?" Luke asked, knowing he was referring to Ray.

"You and I both know it's time for you to settle things with Ray. You've got to let go of all the hostility you're carrying around. To tell you the truth, Luke, I don't understand. It's been years, and the whole thing was an accident in the first place. And in the second place, Ray Townsend has proven he's a man of integrity. He helped you and your family from the very beginning, and since he married your mother, he's been good to her and to the rest of the family. He's a decent man and doesn't deserve your ire. You just won't give him a chance, and it's time you did."

"You don't know what I feel. I've been thinking about setting things straight. There's no rule that says every person has to like every other person."

"No, but God says we're supposed to love our enemies." Adam's expression was stern. "I'm glad you're thinking about it. I'd say Ray's been more than patient with you, and it's time for you to act like a man."

Luke hadn't expected a sharp reprimand. His first impulse was to walk off. He didn't need this, but the bit about acting like a man needled him, so he stayed. He grabbed a handful of snow and packed it into a ball, then heaved it at a fence post. It splattered. "I know something has to happen. I just don't know exactly how to do it."

"Take a step, just one step, and let God help." Adam paused. "You know what happened with me and Laurel . . ."

"You guys seem fine now."

"We are, but not because of anything we did exactly but more what we allowed God to do in us."

Luke nodded slowly, wishing he knew how to let God inside.

Neither spoke for a long moment. Adam gazed out over the white fields. "You know, Luke, if you like Ray, you're not betraying your father. He gave up his life for Ray." Adam laid a hand on Luke's shoulder. "Good things are never easy. I know your father would want you to let go of all the hatred you've got bundled up inside and to get along with Ray. In fact, he'd be real happy if you loved him."

"Not so sure I can do that."

"In your own power, no. You have to let God work. Let him in. Allow him to change you. Let yourself be willing to be made willing if that's where you have to begin."

"Willing to be made willing, huh?" Luke smiled to himself. He'd already prayed that very thing, but nothing had happened. "I'll think on it."

"Don't wait too long. You never know how much time you have to make things right."

Chapter 33

PREDICTIONS WERE RIGHT. HEAVY SNOWS HAD COME TO THE VALLEY. LUKE and Ray were primed for the run to Susitna Station and back. The race promised to be tough. Temperatures had warmed and would make for a rough go.

"The snow's not looking good," Luke told Frank, chucking pieces of dried, frozen fish into a bucket.

"Won't bother my team none. They seen worse. They're ready." He lifted one of his crutches and gazed at his bad foot. "Wish I could go. It ought to be a hoot." He chuckled. "But you'll come through for me. You're good with the dogs. From what I can see, they trust you. Ol' Butch'll see you through for sure. He's a first-rate lead dog." He squinted into the sunlit yard and gazed at yapping dogs, each tethered to a small house. "Yep, wish I was goin' along."

"I'll do my best for you," Luke said.

"Just leave the tough stuff to Butch. He'll know what to do. Never let me down yet." He smiled at Luke. "I'd like to see you give that ol' Townsend a run for his money."

"I aim to." Luke hefted the bucket. "Well, better get this feed to them." Doubts needling him, Luke headed for the dogs. *I know what I'm doing,* he told himself, throwing a hunk of fish to Butch, who pounced on it. Then he moved on to the next dog. It would be a long, hard race. He'd never done anything like it before. With soft snow and thawing waterways, it would also be dangerous.

He tossed out the last portion of fish and headed back to the house. *I fought in the war. Got wounded twice and made it through. Figure I can handle this.*

On the morning of the race, temperatures hovered just above thirty degrees. Gray skies reached low, and the town looked as if a wool blanket had been thrown over it. Spirits were high, though, as twelve teams lined up to begin. Mushers stood four abreast in three rows. Dogs barked and whined. Many, anxious to be on their way, lunged against their harnesses. Some snapped and growled. Butch stood quietly, focused. He knew his job and kept to it.

Ray and Luke were both in the front row. Ray was driving the second team, and Luke was outside on the opposite side of the street. One team separated the two. He glanced at Ray who, with a sparkle in his eye, saluted him.

Luke didn't know how to respond, so he simply nodded and turned his attention to his dogs. He took a deep breath, hoping to relieve the tension bundled in his gut. *This is just for fun. Relax.* In spite of his words, the race felt important. It was a chance to show what he was made of. Although he'd been in battle and had been wounded, Luke felt as if Ray still saw him as a boy. This was his opportunity to show what kind of man he was. For reasons he didn't understand, it was important.

Frank hobbled to Luke. "I expect you'll take care of my dogs."

"I will."

"They're important to me. I want to win, but mostly I want you and those dogs back in one piece." He studied the team. "They'll do right by ya'. Trust 'em. They know what to do." Unable to disguise his own hunger to race, he clapped Luke on the back. "Good luck to you."

"Thanks."

Jean and Susie stood talking quietly with Ray. Jean caught Luke's eye and smiled and waved. He returned the gesture.

Standing at the side of the road, Mattie held up Mara and waved the little girl's hand at her daddy, then joined Luke. A fox ruff nearly concealed the baby's face. Luke pushed back the fur fringe and nuzzled the pudgy face. Her dark brown eyes laughed and her little puckered mouth smiled. Paternal love spilling over, he kissed her.

"We'll be waiting for you at the Little Susitna Roadhouse," Mattie said. "I'll be praying."

"Thanks. I'll be thinking of you two." He glanced at Butch who stood quietly, his eyes on the road in front of him. "He's ready."

"Be careful. No race is worth your life. And remember, I love you."

Luke kissed her. "I love you too. And I'll be careful."

Brian walked up and shook Luke's hand. "Have a good run."

"I'll do my best."

The postmaster, who was acting as the race official, walked to the end of the street. He raised a handgun in the air. The dogs knew it was time, and their anticipation carried through the reins and into Luke's hands. His anxiety fell away, leaving only keen enthusiasm. He looked at the dogs and the official, then gave Ray a glance. It felt as if time had slowed.

With the blast of the gun, the teams exploded. Drivers hollered, "Mush!" With a dissonant blast of barking, the dogs broke into a run. They pulled hard, working to break free of the pack and into the lead. Dogs, sleds, and drivers sprinted through the town, while families and fans cheered them on.

His blood pulsing, Luke felt as if he were flying. He lay out the whip, letting it snake above his line of dogs with a fierce crack. It was a moment like none other. Barking dogs, cheering friends, the slice of runners, and biting wind thrilled him. He ran behind the sled. His weight would only slow down the dogs, and it was important to get into a good position.

As they left town, Ray was in the lead with Luke three sleds behind him. Luke wasn't discouraged. They had a lot of miles to cover, and anything could happen.

Ray lifted his whip and strung it out above his team. "Mush!" He pulled away. The word around town was that his lead dog was the best they'd seen in years. The solid black-and-silver husky knew his job and did it well. He was known to be jealous and wouldn't easily give away a lead.

Luke knew the dog. He was good, and so was the rest of the team, but not better than his. "You may not want to give up your place, but you will," he said. Continuing to run behind the sled, he yelled, "Mush!" Luke knew he had an advantage over Ray. He was younger and lighter. His weight would be less of a drain on the dogs, and his stamina would win out.

Light snow began to fall, but the temperature remained warm. Luke wished it would drop. The sled moved faster and more easily over frozen

ground. Wet snow stuck to the blades, bogging down the sleds and making the dogs work harder, which meant Luke would have to run more.

Sucking in cold air, he stepped onto the rails. He'd have to pace himself. With some satisfaction, he noticed Ray was also riding. In spite of
the conditions, the dogs were running well. All he needed to do was to
keep Ray in sight. His time would come.

Hours passed, and Luke's exhilaration faded. Determination drove
him now. His back and legs ached with fatigue, his body craved rest, and
his face burned from the wind and stinging snow. He'd passed two other
teams. Now only one team separated him from Ray, and he was closing
the distance.

The trail cut into deep snow, and the mushers moved through
rounded hillsides dotted with evergreens. The hills rolled to distant cliffs
and rugged mountains, whose ridges were smoothed by ponderous
snowfall.

The tranquility lulled Luke toward sleep. He dared not rest. He concentrated on his dogs, the cold, and the dangers that lay ahead. He'd
have to watch for overflow. Water would sometimes lie between the ice
and snow of frozen lakes or rivers. A musher couldn't get wet. It could
mean death. He'd also have to keep an eye out for soft ice. Some streams
moved rapidly and didn't freeze, especially when temperatures were
warm. The closer he got to Susitna Station, the more water he'd have to
negotiate. The area was made up of a myriad of lakes, ponds, and
streams.

He watched the dogs' gait. The ice and snow could damage their
pads, sometimes so badly that they'd be unable to pull and would
become part of the cargo instead. He couldn't afford to lose any. Plus,
these were Frank's dogs. He loved them, and Luke didn't dare return any
damaged due to carelessness.

Ray abruptly stopped his team. Luke and the other musher moved
past him. "You all right?" Luke hollered.

"Yep. Just givin' the dogs a rest and a drink." He saluted as Luke
moved by.

I probably ought to rest my team too, Luke thought. *Since Ray's
stopped, I'll have time.*

The other team moved out of sight, and Luke pulled off the trail. Bracing his hands on his knees, he gulped in air. Then he glanced down the trail but saw no one. Luke hauled out a bottle of water and gulped down several mouthfuls. At least the warm temperatures had kept him from having to melt snow.

When Luke returned to his position on the sled and yelled, "Mush," he saw no sign of Ray. The snow had stopped. The clouds had thinned, lying in a blue sky like misty pools. Icy wind cut into his face. The temperature was dropping.

Luke pulled his hood closed and imagined how it would be when he pulled into Palmer ahead of Ray Townsend. His family would cheer for and hug him. A sense of triumph filled him.

Dusk moved over the empty, white world, and Luke wondered how far it was to the roadhouse. He started to look for lights. Darkness closed in, and he slowed his pace, waiting for the rising moon to light the blackness. He allowed the dogs their lead. They would follow the path. Cold closed in with an icy grip. Luke felt it creep down his neck and into his body. He was getting too cold. He stopped and rewrapped the heavy scarf around his face and tightened his parka. When he began again, only his eyes were exposed.

After what felt like hours, lights finally appeared in the blackness. Luke hollered his delight and relief. He'd nearly decided to make camp out in the open. However, the idea of hot food and a warm bed waiting for him kept him moving.

As he slid into the tiny settlement, Mattie greeted him. "You're the second one in!" She threw her arms around Luke even before the sled completely stopped. "We have a tent set up. Your mother's been keeping it warm, and we've got some stew."

Luke was almost tempted to follow her, but he needed to take care of the dogs. "Which tent?"

"That one," Mattie said, pointing at one of several.

"Tell Brian I need a hand."

Brian fed and watered the dogs while Luke checked and doctored paws. The dogs were finally settled, and Luke gratefully headed for the tent. When he stepped inside, the warmth felt almost hot. "Hi," he said to his mother while Mattie folded him in her arms and kissed him. Weary, he sat on a cot and rubbed his face.

Jean stood in front of him with a bowl of hot stew. "Try this. It'll warm you up."

"Thanks." He took the offering.

"Do you know how far back Ray is?" she asked.

"Not far. He should come in any time." He'd heard a tinge of fear in his mother's voice and was reminded that he hadn't given Ray a thought the last several miles. Guilt settled over him. Another team jangled into the makeshift tent city. "That's probably him."

Jean peeked outside. "It is," she said, a lilt in her voice. She moved outside.

Luke remained where he was and tried to eat. Now that he was warm and resting, he could barely stay awake. Mattie huddled beside him. The baby slept in a fur-lined box. "It's harder than I thought, and today was the easiest day. 'Course, the snow's heavy and wet. The runners don't move through it so good. Feels like the temperature's dropping though." He took a bite of stew. "I've got Hatcher Pass in front of me."

"You'll make it," Mattie said. "I know you."

Luke hoped she was right. Even the thought of not finishing sent a wave of humiliation over him. No. He wouldn't let that happen. He handed her the last of his stew. "I've got to sleep. Wake me in three hours."

The moment Luke's head rested on the mattress, sleep enveloped him. When Mattie woke him three hours later, he felt drugged. The sound of a team moving out of town gave him a surge, and he came awake. He had to get moving.

It was Ray who'd left ahead of Luke. *He must not have slept,* Luke decided, then remembered hearing something about Brian taking care of his dogs. He'd grabbed a quick meal and a couple of hours of sleep, and was off. Luke had seen him function on less. Beating him wouldn't be easy, even with their age difference. He felt a sort of pride as he thought of the man's unyielding determination and stamina. Ray was tough.

Luke yelled for his dogs to mush and used the whip, careful not to actually strike any of them. He and the dogs would have to work harder if they were going to win.

It took a couple of hours to close the gap between himself and Ray, but Luke had him in sight and was gaining on him. The trail was narrow, and it would be difficult to pass. Still, Luke pushed the dogs.

As they edged closer, Butch was careful to keep the team and sled clear of the other team. He kept his eyes on the trail, only glancing at the other dogs who strained to pick up the pace and maintain their lead. Some barked and snarled as Luke's team came up even. They ran side by side for several minutes, neither able to gain the advantage. Luke kept his eyes straight ahead, unwilling to be distracted even for a moment. Finally Butch, straining on the harness, pulled ahead.

Only then did Luke nod at Ray, unable to conceal a smile. Ray looked unruffled and again saluted. Luke wished he'd stop doing that. It was annoying.

Another team was still in the lead. Now he'd have to concentrate on overtaking them. He worked hard to open up the distance between himself and Ray as he approached a narrow canyon. Sheer ice-encrusted rock walls shot up on both sides. He gazed at the top of the ridge several hundred feet above. Heavy snow sat on top, curling over the lip. Luke hoped the warmer weather hadn't softened the shelf enough to send it crashing down. No matter, he couldn't do anything about it.

Mountains, their rugged ridges smoothed by heavy snow, loomed. The trail rose in front of him, then curved around a wide bend. Luke glanced behind him and could see Ray emerging from the canyon with another man not far behind. "Mush," he called to the dogs who padded forward, their tails wagging and tongues lolling.

He knew about Hatcher Pass. It was long and steep, rising about three thousand feet. It was the toughest part of the race. He could feel the drop in temperature as they climbed. Icy fingers found their way inside his parka. The cold intensified, and Luke felt as if he'd opened up his coat.

When darkness again draped the landscape, giant pines became shadowy sentinels. It was difficult to see, and the temperature plummeted. Should he stop? He dared not, or he would be caught. Setting his jaw against the challenge, he kept on.

At least the road had been cleared. The Independence Mine saw to that. Exhausted, the cold burning his lungs, he rode. The dogs showed the strain. He prayed they could hold out until they made the town of Willow, where he'd planned to stop.

Luke imagined home. A fire and a hot meal would await him. His mother or Mattie would be baking. He could almost smell the aroma of fresh bread. Why was he out here, in the dark, in the cold . . . alone? He couldn't think of a good reason. Still, he kept going. He had no choice.

Gradually the ground leveled, and the dogs and sled moved more easily. Luke ran. All of a sudden the trail dipped and moved downhill. He barely had time to grab hold of the handles and jump on before the dogs and sled began a speedy descent.

Below him, bathed in moonlight, lay a valley of rounded white hills and shadowy valleys. Willow was close. He could rest soon.

As he came out of the pass, Luke heard dogs behind him—their panting, the jangle of harnesses, and the swooshing of runners. He barely had time to glance behind him before Ray slid past.

"Watch out for deep snows. They're wet and will slow you down," he called, then saluted . . . again.

Believing he'd had a good lead, Luke had been lulled into complacency. He gritted his teeth as he considered the older man's joy at overtaking him. *I'll show him,* he thought, rolling out his whip and calling to the dogs. They moved faster and faster until they were moving too fast. Luke saw Ray disappear around a tight bend and put out a foot to slow down. He wouldn't make it!

"Whoa," he called. The curve hurtled toward him! Butch led the string of dogs around . . . the sled followed and tipped. Luke leaned against it. The sled righted and they slid through.

Letting out his breath, he relaxed his shoulders slightly and allowed the dogs to choose their own pace. The wind had picked up, and he could see clouds scudding across the moon. A storm was moving in, which wasn't good for mushers.

Chapter 34

THE SETTLEMENT OF WILLOW WASN'T MUCH MORE THAN A WIDE PLACE IN the road, but to Luke it looked like heaven. The wind had whipped up, and snow was falling at a slant. Ice encrusted his upper lip and chin, and his eyes burned. He was worn out, and his legs and back ached. His hands felt as if they were permanently fixed to the sled. All he could think of was getting inside and getting warm.

Ray waved as Luke and his team approached. "We've got a place to stay for a few hours. Food and a bed are waiting for the both of us."

"Where?"

Ray pointed at a small cabin tucked into a pine grove. "See you after you get your dogs bedded down." He turned and strode toward the small house.

Luke and Ray sat at a table laden with bacon and eggs, biscuits and gravy, and plenty of coffee. Luke's stomach felt hollow. "I figure I'm hungry as a wolf," he said, shoveling in a giant bite of eggs.

A middle-aged woman Luke knew only as Josephine said, "Well, you eat right up. I've got plenty."

He nodded and cut into the biscuits. When he finished off his first cup of coffee he still felt chilled and asked for another. Looking too small and skinny even to manage the large coffeepot, Josephine clapped a hot pad over the top and refilled his cup.

"This is mighty good," Ray said. "Thanks much, ma'am."

"You're very welcome. I'm always glad to help out."

Wind rattled the windows and rafters. Josephine peered outside. "That storm's really pickin' up. It just came out of nowhere." She eyed her two guests. "Hope it lets up soon. Otherwise, you'll likely end up stuck here."

"We'll be moving on." Ray leaned on the table and looked intently at Luke. "The snow's pretty soft between here and Little Susitna Station. Even with the storm, it's not as cold as it ought to be. You watch yourself out there. Sometimes it's hard to spot soft ice, especially along the Little Susitna. It flows pretty fast in some spots, and this heavy snow is liable to cover up dangerous ice, or no ice."

"I've been around long enough to know what I'm doing," Luke said defensively.

Ray shrugged. "I won't worry then." He pushed away from the table. "That was real good, ma'am. Thanks for your hospitality." He stood. "You said we could catch a few winks?"

"Go right up those stairs and turn right." Josephine offered a friendly smile. "You'll find two beds in there."

"Could you wake me in two hours?"

"I sure will."

Luke followed, leaving the same instructions. His body craved sleep, but he wasn't about to let Ray lead out.

Feeling surprisingly refreshed, Luke fitted the last dog in the harness and threaded the reins to the back of the sled. The storm had quieted. He and the dogs were ready to move out.

Ray got away first, but Luke managed to keep him in sight. Another team was still in the lead, so Luke pushed his dogs hard. They were approaching the halfway point. Soon he wouldn't have enough time or space to close the distance. *What really matters is that I beat Ray,* he told himself, flailing the whip.

The country he moved through was different from what he'd seen so far. Spindly spruce and birch stood in open fields. Deep, mounded snow concealed thickets of underbrush, small ponds, and lakes. Luke felt vulnerable. This wasn't the kind of countryside he was used to. He'd seen patches of soft ice, so he was especially vigilant. He wondered if he could find a way around the myriad of lakes and ponds. Maybe he should skirt the area?

A fox darting back and forth in an open field caught his attention. It was trying to catch a sprinting rabbit. He zigzagged, then pounced, but came up empty. His pointed ears forward and tail twitching, he dashed, then pounced again. The rabbit evaded him. Luke chuckled.

When he looked forward again, Ray was gone. Where was he? "Mush!" Luke called, searching the landscape. He spotted a place where sled tracks cut off and headed down an embankment, then disappeared into the forest. It had to be Ray.

Luke called out, "Gee," and the dogs turned. Dodging trees and bouncing over mounds, he looked for his stepfather. Ray had spent many hours in this area and knew it well. Luke was sure that following him would cut his time. Still, he had to catch him before he could overtake the lead musher.

Ray must have opened up his lead, because no matter how hard Luke pushed, he couldn't close the gap between them. The going was rough, and Luke was breathless. His legs ached and felt like lead. Maybe he'd made a mistake. It was too late to go back to the main trail. He'd lose too much time.

Finally he saw Ray several hundred yards ahead sprinting through a forest of scrub pine and birch and across open patches of frozen water. *He's good.* Luke couldn't help but be impressed. Ray had taken this route because he was skilled in this type of terrain. "He's got more stamina than I gave him credit for. He's really something."

Gritting his teeth against his own pain and exhaustion, Luke pushed on. Why did he feel he had to beat Ray? What was he trying to prove? Why did any of this matter?

His thoughts wound back over the years. Even before his father's death, he'd hated Ray. But it wasn't until he'd shown up at their farm to tell them Will Hasper was dead that the emotions had deepened into an odious loathing. Luke could feel the ugly force of the moment, and a shudder went through him. *But why did my father give his life?*

The dogs, sled, forest, and ice-covered lakes seemed to fade away. All he knew was the voice of God. "Will Hasper knew where his destiny lay—he had eternity with me waiting for him. Ray had no hope."

Luke nearly stopped. He'd never considered what it would have meant to Ray if he'd died that day. His father's sacrifice had offered Ray Townsend a future. Was his father's choice also God's choice? And if

God had decided that it was Ray who should live and not his father, then whom should he hate? God?

Luke was confused. He thought back to the Ray Townsend he'd first known. He'd been a man warped by bitterness and consumed by anger. Luke's mind reeled forward to the confrontation he and Ray had in the barn. Luke had threatened him with a pitchfork. He'd even drawn blood. Yet Ray had refused to fight him. He'd no longer seemed to be angry and bitter. Luke's mind moved to the present. Ray, the man who now loved and cared for his mother and his brother and sister, was nothing like the man Luke had known in the beginning.

Was it possible that his father had known about the Ray Townsend who existed inside and understood that the shell of the man was a distortion? A sick feeling moved through Luke. If so, Luke had sided against God. He was the one who'd been wrong. All these years, it had been him.

Ray disappeared over a ridge. Luke stopped at the crest and watched as the man moved across a frozen riverbed. A loud creak and pop echoed. Ray's team stopped. His lead dog crouched, then suddenly dropped and disappeared along with two others. Ray hauled on the sled and pulled it backwards. The ice cracked, and another dog disappeared. Whining and yelping, the canines paddled and struggled to escape the icy river. Tangled in the harness, they fought to extricate themselves. The more they thrashed the more tangled they became.

"Dear God," Luke said. Ray needed his help. He hollered, "Mush!" Leaning forward, he swirled his whip over the team's back and headed down the embankment.

Ray had given up on trying to pull the sled and the dogs free. Now he walked gingerly toward the place where the team had fallen in. When he got close, he dropped to his stomach and dragged himself across the ice. He hauled on the harness, managing to free one dog and cutting another loose with his knife. After a good shake, the animals loped back to shore and rolled in the snow.

When he reached the lead dog, the ice splintered and Ray dropped into the frigid water. Standing in the icy river up to his chest, he grabbed one dog and tossed him clear, then grabbed the other and pitched him on the ice before struggling to pull himself free. The ice broke again and again, holding him prisoner.

"Ray! Hold on!" Luke yelled. He stopped the team and ran to the frozen waterway. Grabbing a broken limb, he stepped onto the ice, jamming the branch down in front of him as he walked.

"Get out of here!" Ray yelled. "You'll fall in. Get back!"

Luke ignored him. He punched the ice again and broke through. Then he moved around the spot, testing the thickness. Each time he stepped closer to Ray, the limb pushed through. Finally he moved downstream and tried again. The ice held. He took a tentative step, tested it again, then took another step. While Ray clung to the ice, Luke moved closer.

Shivering uncontrollably, face white, Ray sank below the water. "Ray!" Luke screamed. "Ray!" He didn't want him to die. The possibility created an aching chasm inside. "I want you to live!" he shouted. "You have to live!"

Gasping, Ray reappeared.

"I'm coming. Hang on." Luke dropped to his stomach and crawled forward, holding out the branch. He wasn't close enough. He pushed forward. Finally it was within Ray's reach. "Grab hold!" Ray stared at the end of the branch, seeming confused. "Grab hold!"

He reached for the lifeline but couldn't hang on. He tried again. This time he got a good handhold and slapped at the water with his legs, trying to climb free. Each time he managed to get his body onto the ice, he broke through.

"Don't struggle," Luke said. "Just hang on, and I'll pull you." Ray did as he was told. When he seemed to have a good grip, Luke clambered onto his knees and hauled on the branch, praying it wouldn't break and that the ice would hold them both.

When Ray was partially out of the water, a long drawn-out creak followed by a splintering groan echoed from beneath the ice. Luke stopped. The ice held. Taking a deep breath, he pulled. Finally Ray was completely free of the water. Moving slowly and cautiously, Luke dragged him to the bank.

Shivering so hard it looked as if he were having seizures, Ray tried to stand; but his knees crumpled, and he fell.

"We've got to get you dry," Luke said, pushing a shoulder under Ray's arm and helping him to his feet. He guided him to a level spot, then ran to his sled and removed a fur blanket.

His lips blue against a white face, Ray struggled to get his coat off, but his hands were shaking too hard.

"I'll do it," Luke said, unbuttoning the parka and stripping it off. Ray dropped and lay shivering in the snow. "I'm gonna need some help," Luke said, but Ray acted as if he didn't hear. "Come on. We've got to get your body warm. Get up. Now!"

Ray was beyond hearing and didn't respond. Luke stripped off the rest of his stepfather's clothes, wrapped him in the blanket, then removed his own outer clothing and huddled inside with him, vigorously rubbing Ray's arms and back. His skin was so cold it stunned Luke. He didn't know how the man could survive. But he wasn't about to give up and continued rubbing him down, then held Ray against him, offering his own body's warmth. The shivering eased, and Luke asked, "You any better?"

Ray nodded. "Yeah. I think so."

"OK. Stay put. I'll start a fire."

Luke climbed out from under the blanket and walked to the sled to get the tinder. He made a small pile out of dry paper and wood chips, then with trembling hands lit a match and held it to the mound. A puff of smoke, then a tiny flame appeared. "I got it." He glanced at Ray who lay bundled in the blanket, his eyes closed. "I'll have you warm in no time." Luke added bits of wood and blew on the small fire. It grew, and he laid more wood on it. When the fire was strong and crackling, he returned to the lump beneath the blanket.

"Ray?" He didn't answer. A knife of fear cut into Luke. What if he died? *Not now.* "Ray," he said louder.

The big man blinked, then opened his eyes.

"Come on. I've got the fire going."

Ray nodded and struggled to his feet. He dropped to one knee. Luke bent, maneuvered a shoulder under him, and helped him rise. The two moved slowly toward the fire. After settling Ray, Luke filled a coffeepot with snow and set it in hot coals. "I'll see to the dogs."

The water hadn't penetrated the thick undercoats of the team. They lay in the snow, seemingly content. Luke tethered all the dogs, then doled out dried salmon to each one. By the time he'd finished, the snow in the pot had melted. He added coffee grounds, then sat close to the fire, holding bare hands out to the flames. "Feels good." He glanced at Ray, who was still huddled beneath the blanket. "How you feeling?"

"Better, thanks to you. That was good thinking." He shook his head. "And it was also stupid. You took a big risk." He looked at Luke. "I should have known better, especially after a heavy snowfall. I could have killed us both."

"You didn't. And the dogs are fine. We'll be on our way again in the morning." He eyed the sled, which was tipped half in and half out of the water. "I don't know about your sled though," he said, gathering up branches and constructing a makeshift drying rack.

"We'll pull it free, but not right now."

Luke draped Ray's clothing over the rack. "They should be dry before morning." He glanced at Ray. "You think you could eat something?"

"You bet. I'm starved."

"That's a good sign," Luke said, heartened.

Ray stood and looked at the blanket draped around him. "I've got another set of dry clothes in my pack." He looked out at the sled stuck in the ice. "'Course, it's a little tough getting to it."

"I've got some." He grabbed long underwear and tossed them to Ray. "They're not going to fit, but they should do until your clothes dry."

"Thanks."

Luke retrieved biscuits and dried beef from his pack. Ray had managed to get the bottom half of the underwear on. They were skin tight and rode up to his midcalf. Luke laughed. "Guess I'd better do some more growing." He handed Ray a couple of biscuits and a piece of dried meat, then poured them each a cup of black coffee. The two men sat quietly and ate, staring at the flames.

Night closed in, and blackness wrapped itself around the mismatched pair. A wolf howled in the distance, and the dogs lifted their heads to listen, then returned their noses to the inner layers of their fur coats. Stars in a black sky winked, and a glow from the moon below the tree line promised to brighten the darkness.

Luke knew this was the time God had set apart for him and Ray. It was time to settle years of bitterness, but first he needed to know how and why his father had died. He ate a piece of dried beef, washed it down with coffee, and dredged up his courage. "I figure you know how I've felt about you all these years."

"Yep. No misunderstanding that." Ray sipped his coffee and stared at leaping flames.

"I never understood why you hated my father so much."

"I didn't hate just him. I hated nearly everyone. Most of all, I hated God. Couldn't forgive him for takin' my Ellie from me. I figured he had no cause to do such a thing. Then I blamed myself." He studied his biscuit. "I still don't understand, but I figure he'll explain it to me when I meet up with him." He glanced at Luke. "Anyway, to answer your question, your father was just a target for my fury."

"Why him?"

"He was everything I wanted to be and couldn't be." He picked up a stick and poked the embers. "You have a right to be proud of your father. He was a decent man. I wish I'd known him as friend. He had all the usual good qualities—hardworking, smart, honest, and trustworthy. But he was also one of those rare people who knew who he was and why he'd been put on this earth." Ray slowly shook his head. "Back then, I just didn't get it. I was plain jealous. And since he was an outsider, I figured I had good reason to hate him."

Luke met Ray's eyes. He could trust him to speak plainly and truthfully. "Why didn't my father run from that bear? He didn't owe you anything. Did you beg him to stay?"

"Nope. I told him to leave . . . I wish he had." Ray looked at the night sky. "That's what I mean. Your father wasn't like other men. He cared about someone like me—someone who'd belittled and slandered him and done just about everything possible to bring him down."

Letting out a long breath, he lowered his eyes. "I didn't understand it then, but I think I do now. It wasn't that I deserved anything good from him, it's just that he wanted to give it." He smiled softly. "Kind of like God." He focused tear-filled eyes on Luke. "I swear, I want to do everything in my power to be like him."

A crooked smile emerged. "Your mother keeps reminding me I have to be like me, not him. I guess I agree, but your father was the kind of fella who believed in living what he believed. I'll always be grateful to him—not just for saving my life, but for showing me what it means to be like Christ. I aim to try too. I'm just not as good at it."

You're doing a pretty good job, Luke thought, but wasn't ready to say anything.

Ray stared at the flickering flames, then turned his gaze on Luke. "I want you to know I fought my feelings when I realized I loved your mother. I figured it was wrong. I didn't deserve someone like her, especially not Will's wife. I felt like I was betraying him . . . Sometimes I still do," he said softly.

Luke could feel the years of bitterness wash away like a tide sweeping out the dirty foam from a beach. He felt better, cleaner.

"You know, you're like your father. You came out on that ice to get me, not thinking about yourself. I owe you." Then he saluted . . . again.

"Why do you keep saluting me?"

"Respect. I respect you, Luke."

"Oh," Luke said, feeling small that the gesture had irritated him. "Thank you. And you don't owe me." Luke knew he was the one who had taken rather than given. "When I saw you out there, I knew you had to live. I didn't want you to die." He pushed his booted feet closer to the flames. "My life would be emptier without you . . . I didn't know it until that moment." He looked at Ray. "I don't hate you anymore. I'm free from it . . . at last." He smiled. "Sorry it took me so long to see the truth."

"Your father would be proud of you."

Neither man spoke for several minutes.

Ray broke the silence. "Your mother and I have been doing some talking lately, and we have made a decision." He settled serious eyes on Luke. "We've just been waiting for the right time to tell you. I figure this is it."

Ray stood. "Celeste and Robert are getting married . . . finally. He'll be home for a few weeks, and until the war is over Celeste will live with his mother." His eyes sparkled. "My cabin's going to be empty soon . . ."

Before Ray could finish, Luke interrupted. "Thanks, but no. It's a nice gesture, but Mattie and I couldn't take your cabin."

A crooked smile appeared on Ray's face. "You didn't let me finish."

Luke shut his mouth.

Taking a deep breath, Ray continued. "We, your mother and I, were thinking that since I'm no farmer and you are, well, that you should have the farm. We can live in the cabin."

Luke stared at Ray. He thought he must have misheard.

Ray laughed. "I don't think I've ever seen a more stunned look in all my life." He sat close to the fire.

"I don't know what to say."

"Say yes. It belongs to you. It was your father's, and now it should be yours. He'd want you to have it."

Luke couldn't answer.

Ray smiled. "You and Mattie and the baby can have a real good start there, and the Haspers will continue to farm in the valley."

Luke still didn't reply. He was afraid that if he did he'd blubber.

"Well, what do you say?"

Pressing down his emotions, Luke sputtered, "Yes. Yes. We'll take it!" He grasped Ray's hand and said more quietly, "We'll take it."

Luke understood that God's blessing had been waiting. It had been his own sin that had kept it from him. He shook Ray's hand. "Thank you. You're a good man. My father would've liked you. I'm proud you're my family."

Silence settled over the two men.

Ray stretched. "Well, I guess we won't win that prize money. It's a cryin' shame."

"Nope. Guess not." Luke grinned. "I'd say we won something a whole lot better."

Dear Reader

When I started this project I could not have imagined that as I finished, the news would be filled with images of the attacks of September 11th. Our country mourned, but people gathered strength from God and drew close to one another.

President Bush's words "A Day in Infamy" took me back to another time, another president, another day. Those events are presented in this book, which seems beyond coincidence.

We are at war today as we were then. We've lost our innocence, yet we are stronger, more resolved, and ready to stand up to the enemy. We do not stand alone, however. He who is in us is greater than he who is in the world.

We do not need to be afraid. God has not forgotten us. He waits for us to bring our heavy hearts to Him where He will restore broken spirits and make forgiveness possible.

America has been in this place before, and sadly, war sometimes cannot be avoided. There are causes worth giving our lives, such as freedom and providing a future for our children and grandchildren. We can be assured God will not send us out alone.

As we fight this war, let it not be one of the heart. Do not cling to anger, which breeds hatred and bitterness. I pray we will not lose sight of our God and Father who first loved us. May we seek His will and His way.

Especially in these troubling times, may God bless you and fill you with peace and joy.

You may reach Bonnie at:
Bonnie Leon
P. O. Box 774
Glide, OR 97443
E-mail: Leon@rosenet.net